THE NOBLE SLAVES

broadview editions
series editor: Martin R. Boyne

THE NOBLE SLAVES

Penelope Aubin

edited by Carol Stewart

broadview editions

BROADVIEW PRESS – www.broadviewpress.com
Peterborough, Ontario, Canada

Founded in 1985, Broadview Press remains a wholly independent publishing house. Broadview's focus is on academic publishing; our titles are accessible to university and college students as well as scholars and general readers. With over 800 titles in print, Broadview has become a leading international publisher in the humanities, with world-wide distribution. Broadview is committed to environmentally responsible publishing and fair business practices.

Library and Archives Canada Cataloguing in Publication

Title: The noble slaves / Penelope Aubin ; edited by Carol Stewart.
Names: Aubin, Penelope, approximately 1679-approximately 1738, author. | Stewart, Carol (Carol Ann), editor.
Series: Broadview editions.
Description: Series statement: Broadview editions | Includes bibliographical references.
Identifiers: Canadiana (print) 20230489060 | Canadiana (ebook) 20230489079 | ISBN 9781554816231 (softcover) | ISBN 9781770488915 (PDF) | ISBN 9781460408230 (EPUB)
Subjects: LCGFT: Novels.
Classification: LCC PR3316.A68 N63 2023 | DDC 823/.5—dc23

Broadview Editions
The Broadview Editions series is an effort to represent the ever-evolving canon of texts in the disciplines of literary studies, history, philosophy, and political theory. A distinguishing feature of the series is the inclusion of primary source documents contemporaneous with the work.

Advisory editor for this volume: Norah Franklin

Broadview Press handles its own distribution in North America:
PO Box 1243, Peterborough, Ontario K9J 7H5, Canada
555 Riverwalk Parkway, Tonawanda, NY 14150, USA
Tel: (705) 743-8990; Fax: (705) 743-8353
email: customerservice@broadviewpress.com

For all territories outside of North America, distribution is handled by Eurospan Group.

Broadview Press acknowledges the financial support of the Government of Canada for our publishing activities.

Canada

Typesetting and assembly: True to Type, Claremont, Canada
Cover Design: Lisa Brawn

PRINTED IN CANADA

Contents

Acknowledgements

I would like to thank Ian Campbell Ross for his advice on the preparation of this edition. Any mistakes within are my own.

Introduction

Finding herself shipwrecked on an island in the Gulf of Mexico, Teresa, one of two heroines in Penelope Aubin's *The Noble Slaves* (1722), decides that rather than complaining about her lot she will live free from temptation in the wilds. Declaring that "the Woods shall be my Oratory" (p. 45), here meaning a place for private prayer, she commits herself to solitary worship heard only by God. Via the novel itself, however, Teresa's thoughts and words do find an audience, just as the author intended; and while many of Aubin's virtuous characters, female and male, retreat from the world, their author very definitely did not. Three poems by Aubin appeared in print between 1707 and 1709, and she went on to become a significant literary presence in the 1720s. In that decade she published seven of her own novels, four translations of French novels, and an edition of Thomas Mannington Gibbs's (c. 1696–1720) translation of Marin le Roy, sieur de Gomberville's *La Doctrine des moeurs, tirée de la philosophie des stoïques* (1646) as *The Doctrine of Morality ... According to the Stoick Philosophy* (1721). Between 1721 and 1722, Aubin's output rivalled that of Daniel Defoe (1660–1731) (McBurney 252). From the advertisements that survive, we know that after she ceased to publish fiction, Aubin was still finding an audience when she set up her self-styled "Lady's Oratory" at York Buildings in London between 1729 and 1730: "oratory" here meaning a place for public speaking. She set out to oppose and indeed mock the teachings of the controversial and eccentric Dissenting minister John "Orator" Henley (1692–1756) and also mounted coded attacks on the administration of Sir Robert Walpole (1676–1745). According to one commentator, Aubin rivalled Henley for the town's applause ("Stonecastle" 1: 184). Her play *The Merry Masqueraders; or, The Humorous Cuckold* was performed at the Little Theatre in Haymarket in 1730, with the author appearing on stage to deliver the epilogue.

All but one of Aubin's novels reached at least a second edition, and the extent of her readership may be judged by the fact that an Aubin novel or translation can be found in numerous catalogues of books for sale in the eighteenth century.[1] Edward Harley, second

---

1 See, for example, catalogues of books for sale by Woodman (1732); Thomas Payne (1758 and 1786); Thomas Evans (1771); L. Davis and C. Reymers (1768); and Lockyer Davis (1783).

Earl of Oxford (1689–1741) and son of the politician Robert Harley (1661–1724), owned a copy of *The Noble Slaves* (*Catalogus* 5: 320). After her death, Aubin's works found a place in Lownd's, Minerva's, and Earle's circulating libraries. *The Noble Slaves* was reprinted in London, Dublin, and Belfast and appeared in a posthumous anthology, *A Collection of Entertaining Histories and Novels, By Mrs. Penelope Aubin*, in 1739. The novel was included, alongside Samuel Richardson's *Pamela* (1740) and *Clarissa* (1748–49), in a 1758 catalogue of "the most esteemed and useful English books, proper to form a select library." Happily, most of these books could be bought from the shop belonging to John Whiston and Benjamin White, compilers of the catalogue. A 1768 Belfast edition of her *Life and Surprizing Adventures of the Lady Lucy* (1726) was promoted as being by "Mrs. Aubin, Authoress of The Noble Slaves." The novel appeared in a three-volume *Collection of Novels, Selected and Revised by Mrs. Griffith* (1777)—the editor being playwright and author Elizabeth Griffith (1727–93)—where it was praised for "the rich vein of Religion and Virtue which transfuses itself throughout the whole of the narrative" (3: 46). Five American editions appeared between 1797 and 1814 (Bannet 47).[1] Aubin's voice was heard throughout the eighteenth century. Despite Aubin's popularity in her own time, until very recently only her first novel, *The Strange Adventures of the Count de Vinevil and His Family* (1721), has been in print.[2] The "rich vein of Religion and Virtue" that brought Aubin esteem in her own time has contributed to her neglect in ours. Samara Anne Cahill identifies Penelope Aubin as one of those "victim[s] of the obscurity reserved for women writers with a reputation for pious didactic fiction" (Cahill 86). Others include Jane Barker (1652–1732) and Elizabeth Singer Rowe (1674–1737). Feminist scholarship of the 1970s and after found it easier to recognize the achievements of those women writers of the seventeenth and eighteenth centuries who appeared to challenge constructions of gender and sexuality, while more conservative figures got a less sympathetic hearing or were simply ignored. Earlier twentieth-century commentators who took notice of Aubin

---

1   Not everyone was convinced of her worth, though. Clara Reeve dismissed "Mrs St. Aubin' [sic] as a mediocrity" (2: 132).

2   Penelope Aubin, *The Strange Adventures of the Count de Vinevil and his Family*, in *Popular Fiction by Women 1660–1730: An Anthology*, edited by Paula R. Backscheider and John J. Richetti, Oxford UP, 1996, pp. 113–51. In addition to this edition of *The Noble Slaves*, Broadview recently published a volume containing two novellas by Aubin, *The Life of Madam de Beaumount* and *The Life of Charlotta Du Pont*.

concurred with the assessment of Griffiths. Aubin's fictions are "[u]nusual in their high moral tone," according to W.H. McBurney (260); "pious polemic" is John J. Richetti's pithy description (211).

Aubin certainly wanted her novels to be seen as morally worthy. The frequent reminders in her work of the existence of divine Providence can be read as a marker of religious belief, though such reminders could also work to make literary entertainment acceptable to Puritans in the seventeenth century and beyond. Her prefaces lay out her reforming purpose and guide a reading of her novels as didactic in intent, as do her interjections in the narrative. She establishes her credentials in the Preface to *The Strange Adventures of the Count de Vinevil and His Family* and sets herself against the prevailing decline in standards:

> Since serious things are in a manner altogether neglected by what we call the gay and fashionable part of mankind, and religious treatises grow moldy on the booksellers' shelves in the back shops ... the few that honor virtue and wish well to our nation ought to study to reclaim our giddy youth; and since reprehensions fail, try to win them to virtue, by methods where delight and instruction may go together. (114)

Aubin is also at pains to draw a distinction between herself and her more scandalous contemporaries. In the Preface to *The Life of Charlotta Du Pont, an English Lady* (1723), Aubin primly distances herself from "other female Authors my Contemporaries, whose Lives and Writings have, I fear, too great a resemblance" and notes that she has ignored her bookseller's advice to write in a style "careless and loose" as the modern age seems to prefer. Female desire is readily acknowledged in the work of Aphra Behn (1640–89), Delarivier Manley (c. 1663/70–1724), and Eliza Haywood (c. 1693–1756)—though seldom leading to a happy conclusion—while Aubin's women are resolutely, even militantly, chaste.[1] In *The Noble Slaves*, Teresa and Emilia, the novel's chief female protagonists, are repeatedly taken captive by lustful Arabic men. Not tempted by their Muslim captor, "one of the most beautiful and accomplish'd Men of his Nation," Emilia repels his advances in a decisive fashion by stabbing him with a dagger. Even more strikingly, the enslaved girl Maria, taken to the bed of the Persian emperor in *The Noble Slaves*, tears out her own eyeballs and throws them at him rather than witness the shame of

---

1 Readers should note that certain plot details are revealed in this and subsequent paragraphs.

her own rape. Where there is religious ambiguity there is seldom a happy ending. In one of the interpolated tales Clarinda allows the Count de Chateau-Roial, himself an ordained priest, to free her from enforced claustration so that they may elope together. Later he becomes sick and dies, and Clarinda returns, this time voluntarily, to a convent.

The framing narrative in *The Noble Slaves* takes the form of a series of shipwrecks, periods of captivity, escapes, and the eventual reunion of two married couples. Out in a pleasure boat in the Gulf of Mexico, Teresa, the only child of Don Sancho de Avilla, is washed ashore on the coast of a desolate island. Soon she discovers Emilia, a French gentlewoman, and her husband, the Count de Hautville, who have also been swept ashore after a shipwreck. Don Lopez, Teresa's suitor and soon-to-be husband, is also washed up on the island in the following chapter. They all sail together for Spain, but the ship is seized by Barbary pirates in the Straits of Gibraltar. The men are taken captive to be sold for ransom, while the women are carried off to the Algerian governor's harem. Emilia stabs the governor, and they escape. Seraja, a widow converted from Islam to Christianity, takes them in, and they survive by sewing and selling their work in the market. Don Lopez and the Count de Hautville escape from captivity thanks to the intervention of Eleonora, a one-time mistress of the governor. Hearing that their husbands are free, Teresa and Emilia venture out to look for them but are captured by a Muslim prince. Ximene, his jealous wife, provides a poison for them to take, but she and the prince mistakenly drink it themselves and die. Another Muslim lord takes Emilia and Teresa to his palace, but they escape by climbing down a curtain tied to the roof. They are given food and shelter by Andrea Zantonio, a Venetian who was himself washed ashore on the North African coast while searching for his beloved Eleonora—the same Eleonora who aided the escape of Don Lopez and the Count de Hautville. Afraid of being recaptured, the husbands return to Spain where, after further delays, they are eventually reunited with their wives, who return by way of Venice. Six months later Teresa is abducted again, this time by a Spanish nobleman. She breaks her leg trying to escape from captivity but is ultimately rescued by Don Lopez, who kills her abductor.

Despite Aubin's claim to avoid "those loose Writings which debauch the Mind" in a work that will offer the reader virtuous models to imitate, *The Noble Slaves* is, as even a brief outline suggests, not lacking in sexual incident, violence, transgression, and adventure, all introduced at giddying speed. So much so that Chris Mounsey, arguing against the longstanding consensus about Aubin's reputation for piety, contends that her moral posturing is merely a fig leaf to disguise her real intent, which is to divert rather than to "reclaim the giddy youth" and sell novels (Mounsey 55–75). The very first commentary on Aubin's fiction made a similar charge. In No. 58 of his journal *Le Pour et le Contre* (1734), French author and cleric the Abbé Prévost (1697–1763) characterized Madame Aubin as the London-born daughter of an émigré French officer driven to publication by financial need. According to Prévost, the author was an ugly woman who turned to public preaching in the late 1720s when her novels no longer enjoyed success.

While the evidence about Aubin's financial circumstances is still unclear, we now know that Prévost's account of her parentage was false. Pioneering biographical research by Debbie Welham has shown that Aubin was in fact the illegitimate daughter of baronet Sir Richard Temple (1634–97) and his mistress Anne Charleton, making her the half-sister of Richard Temple, first Viscount Cobham (1675–1749), and granddaughter of Walter Charleton (1620–1707), physician to Charles I (r. 1625–49), Charles II (r. 1660–85), and James II (r. 1685–88) (Welham, "Particular Case" 67–69). Aubin was her married name, as Elizabeth Griffith had in fact noted in her *Collection* in 1777. In 1696 Penelope married Abraham Aubin (d. 1740), the eldest son of a merchant family from Jersey. Penelope and Abraham married without parental consent, and a clandestine marriage was certainly not a good beginning: it cost Penelope *née* Charleton her marriage portion of £1000. Sir Richard, according to a deposition made by Anne Charleton, at first vowed not to give his daughter a farthing. The couple seem to have believed that Penelope's mother kept for herself bequests made to Penelope in Sir Richard Temple's will and went to the court of chancery to try to prove it, without success. Abraham Aubin was initially disowned by his mother for marrying without her consent, though the couple later went to Jersey, where Penelope was required to begin working in the Aubin family business as a condition of Sir Richard's future financial support. His death in 1697, with no provision made for his daughter, meant that such support never materialized. In the first decade of the eighteenth century, Abraham Aubin was away from home serving as an army officer, stationed in Spain and Portugal during the War of the Spanish Succession (Baer 55).

At this time Penelope Aubin was clearly active in business matters that could have brought in some income. In 1702 she advised Thomas Fairfax, fifth Baron Fairfax of Cameron (1657–1710), and Richard Savage, fourth Earl Rivers (c. 1654–1712), in the matter of a salvaging—meaning treasure-hunting—expedition in the Caribbean where she might have been a potential investor, and in 1708 she declined an invitation from George Douglas, thirteenth earl of Morton (1662–1738) and Charles Egerton (1654–1717), MP for Brackley, to take part in a controversial scheme, headed by suspected pirate John Breholt, to repatriate British pirates who had settled on the island of Madagascar. It was thought that the immense store of treasure supposedly held there by the pirates would be returned to the nation and help to offset the National Debt. Egerton offered Aubin a share in the venture if she would help to organize a petition by the pirates' wives for their husbands' pardon. Although her deposition to the Board of Trade suggests that she had never met Breholt, she told Egerton she had a low opinion of the shipmaster and advised him not to involve himself in the project. Aubin's deposition advised against the venture (see Appendix C2, pp. 195–97), and it never took place.

At the same time, she was already venturing into print in politically inflected poetry: there is little to suggest that financial need was the driving force behind these publications. Her *The Stuarts: A Pindarique Ode*, published in 1707 on the occasion of the Act of Union, surveys the history of the British monarchy from the houses of York and Lancaster to James II. For Aubin, the latter is "James the Just," of "elevated soul" (lines 144, 155). Of William of Orange (William III, r. 1689–1702) she writes, less enthusiastically, "Something is due to thee I cannot leave / The Subject, and thy Reign in Silence pass" (lines 196–97). The poem also celebrates her own descent from one who served Charles II: probably her maternal grandfather Walter Charleton. The poem links her grandfather's decline in circumstances—his "Fortune's lost" (line 112)—with his support for the Royalist cause, though the reality may have been less clear-cut.[1] Perhaps Aubin saw herself as taking up from him the mantle of royal service. *The Extacy*, her panegyric to Queen Anne (r. 1702–14)—the last Stuart monarch—celebrates British victories at Ramillies, Blenheim,

---

1 Charleton claimed that he was excluded from the College of Physicians for over twenty years because of his political allegiances, but it may be that some of his publications were judged to be dangerously close to religious heresy. See Booth 21–24.

and Oudenarde during the War of the Spanish Succession (1701–13). Here, Aubin refers·to the monarch's "Godlike Birth" (line 216) and "Sacred Majesty" (line 59). Jacobite sympathies surface again later, in the fiction of the 1720s. The grandfather of the eponymous heroine in *The Life of Madam de Beaumount, A French Lady* (1721) is described as a faithful servant to King James II "tho a Protestant"—just like Aubin's own grandfather (20). In 1709 Aubin published a poem addressed to Whig hero the Duke of Marlborough (1650–1722) rather misleadingly entitled *The Wellcome*. The Duke is now returning to Britain without recent victories to boast of, as the poet does not hesitate to point out: "Wise heaven, has not pleas'd to Bless, / Thy Glorious Arms again with such Success" (lines 25–26, qtd. in Welham, *Delight* 248–55). *The Wellcome* often links Marlborough with the Queen— "Great *ANNA*'s Choice"—and reminds the reader that the hero of the poem assists the monarch with his counsel (line 45). It seems likely that Aubin's concern was more with the influence over Queen Anne of Marlborough and his wife Sarah (1660–1744) and rather less with military triumph. She was not alone: Jonathan Swift (1667–1745) also expressed uneasiness about the potentially pernicious effect of the duke's prestige and influence in the *Examiner* of December 1710 (188).

By the 1720s, when his wife was publishing fiction, Abraham Aubin was a half-pay officer, once again involved in the family business. Whatever money came from sales of his wife's novels no doubt augmented the family income, but whether they were essential to it is likely to remain unknown (Welham, *Delight* 116–17). What we can say is that from the beginning, Penelope Aubin's work gave her a platform from which to mount a campaign of reform, whether literary, moral, social, or political. She drew on a wide knowledge of literature in *The Noble Slaves* but changed her models to suit her own purpose.[1] She took elements of Daniel Defoe's *Robinson Crusoe* (1719; see Appendix C3, pp. 197–98) and the seduction narratives of Eliza Haywood and Delarivier Manley, though without the individualism of the former or the eroticism of the latter. Aubin's Teresa, like Crusoe, finds herself washed ashore and surviving on what an isolated island has to offer—albeit with the assistance both of a man who was enslaved by her father and of a helpful Japanese family. She is soon aiding others whom she discovers have been similarly

---

1 For an account of Aubin's rewriting of Delarivier Manley's "The Wife's Resentment" as the interpolated tale "Conjugal Duty Rewarded," see Welham, "Political Afterlife."

stranded: the author favours collective values. Like the heroines of amatory fiction, Aubin's women are the objects of male lust, but her female protagonists never show any signs of desire themselves and see off attempts at seduction or rape by managing to escape, by reforming their attackers, or by stabbing them. Casting women as the reformers of libidinous Arabic despots, Aubin draws on the Orientalist[1] plays of Manley, Mary Pix (1666–1709), and others (see Appendices B3–B4, pp. 179–91) and translates them to the world of fiction. William Warner points to Aubin's debt to the French heroic romances of Madeleine de Scudéry (1607–1701) and Gauthier de Costes, seigneur de la Calprenède (c. 1609–63), with their aristocratic protagonists, exalted heroines, and repeated abductions (184). Aubin reduces the romances' massive length and adapts them for the new middle-class reader. Her novels are also indebted to Robert Challe (1659–1721), an eighteenth-century French writer less well known in English, whose *Les Illustres Françaises* (1713) Aubin translated as *The Illustrious French Lovers* (1726), her longest published work (See Appendix D1, pp. 201–12). Challe takes up the heroic romance involving separated lovers but, as Aubin was later to do, makes the obstacles to their union the more mundane ones of social class and money. At the same time, Aubin tones down the rebelliousness and independence of Challe's women, as well as their passionate declarations of feeling (de Sola xxx–xxxiii). Aubin's tales of Oriental captivity, of which *The Noble Slaves* is one, can be placed in a tradition of such stories dating back to the putatively factual accounts of the seventeenth century (Snader 149–58; see also Starr 35–52; Bannet 53ff).[2] Unlike the authors of such stories, Aubin places women centre stage, even if her heroines, in Joe Snader's analysis, "fall short of the masterful colonialist aptitude" demonstrated by such

---

1 The term "Orientalist" is used here to describe works in which the action takes place in the Near East or North Africa and which deploy certain tropes and stereotypes. Bridget Orr summarizes these as "erroneous religion, despotism and the enslavement of women" (132). This is somewhat different from, though not entirely unrelated to, the presumption of Western superiority involved in "Orientalism" as defined by Edward Said in his seminal study of 1978. See also p. 21, n. 1.

2 In *Transatlantic Stories*, Bannet sees Aubin drawing on late-seventeenth and early-eighteenth-century American stories of women held captive by Indians, though the demotic register and the class of the narrators are far removed from Aubin's noble protagonists and the "polite" style (53ff).

figures as Robinson Crusoe or William Chetwood's eponymous hero Robert Boyle (1726). Snader rightly notes, however, that the plots provide women with opportunities for self-reliance and transgressive behaviour. Rather than demonstrating their superiority to foreigners, Aubin's heroines are likely to form alliances with Middle Eastern women—providing they have converted to Christianity.

Twelve of the characters in *The Noble Slaves* are captured by Barbary pirates, and the publication of the novel coincided with the release of almost three hundred captives from Morocco (see Appendices A1–2, pp. 159–67). The event was obviously pending when Aubin was writing *The Noble Slaves*, as she refers to it in the closing paragraphs of the novel. Negotiations between George I (r. 1714–27) and Muley Ismaïl (1646–1727), emperor of Morocco, resulted in a treaty being signed at the Spanish exclave of Ceuta in January 1721. Under the terms of the treaty, piracy was to cease, Moroccan ships were to trade freely with Britain, and the captives were to be returned home. In fact, piracy did not cease, and in 1729 another envoy was in Morocco negotiating the release of enslaved Britons (Colley 64). Although the captives in *The Noble Slaves* are French and Spanish, the frequent capture of vessels in the novel can be read as a veiled criticism of the Walpole administration's failure to protect British shipping. On a personal level, as we have seen, Aubin was well acquainted with the threat to shipping posed by pirates, given her involvement in the matter of the possible repatriation of British pirates from Madagascar. In 1720, her brother-in-law David's ship the *Prosperous* was boarded and taken by French pirates in the Caribbean, with the governor of Martinique claiming that the attackers were in fact Spanish privateers (see Appendix C1, pp. 193–95). Privateers differed from pirates in that the former had a licence or "letter of marque" from the sovereign authorizing the captain of the vessel to attack and capture enemy shipping in times of war. Piracy at sea was a real danger, even if merchants and traders might utilize sensational accounts of it to press for protection by the government (Lincoln 85–87). By 1718, piracy was making trade in the West Indies and along the North American coast almost impossible (89). Capture by Muslim corsairs (also authorized by their own rulers) and subsequent enslavement in North Africa was a real risk for European sailors and other travellers in the Mediterranean. Large numbers of ships and, primarily, men were taken during the sixteenth and seventeenth centuries, though in the absence of documentation, estimates of the numbers vary. Robert C. Davis calculates the average population of enslaved people in the Ottoman regencies of Tunis, Algiers, and Tripoli in any given year to have been around 35,000 and the total number of enslaved white European Christians between 1530 and 1780 over a million (Davis 108, 118). Historians view the defeat of Ottoman imperial forces besieging Vienna in 1683 and the subsequent Treaty of Karlowitz in 1700 as marking the decline of the Sublime Porte (to use the contemporary metaphor for the Empire), and the threat of capture by corsairs and subsequent enslavement was receding. It still existed, though: a report in the *London Evening Post* for May 1751 described the return of seventy-one British captives from Tangiers after four years of slavery.

The title of Aubin's novel foregrounds the issue of slavery, and in the eighteenth century the word *slavery* could be invoked—to us loosely and promiscuously—in a range of contexts. For eighteenth-century Britons, slavery existed when tyranny prevailed, and such "tyranny" might be that of Muslim despots over their supposedly abject populations; of husbands over their wives, as Mary Astell (1666–1731) famously saw it; of an absolutist monarch—such as Louis XIV of France (r. 1643–1715) or perhaps James II—over his subjects; of Roman Catholicism over its adherents; or of a corrupt British administration over the nation (see Appendices A6–10, pp. 171–76). As Srividhya Swaminatham and Adam R. Beach argue, many Britons might see the Atlantic slave trade as a necessary evil and the enslavement of white Europeans in the Mediterranean as an atrocity, whilst at the same time deploying the language of tyranny and slavery to attack the government (1; see Appendices A3–5, pp. 167–70). It would be pleasing to think that the foregrounding of slavery in *The Noble Slaves* represents a coded attack on the transatlantic slave trade, and Eve Tavor Bannet characterizes Aubin as an abolitionist *avant la lettre* (57). In *Charlotta Du Pont* (1723), Aubin's novel of the following year, there is a strongly worded rejection of chattel slavery. The eponymous heroine declares,

> The selling human Creatures is a Crime my Soul
> abhors; and Wealth so got ne'er thrives. Tho [Black
> Domingo] is black, yet the Almighty made him as well
> as us, and Christianity ne'er taught us cruelty: We
> ought to visit those Countrys to convert, not buy our
> Fellow-creatures, to enslave and use them as if we were
> Devils, or they not Men. (89)

However, ownership of enslaved people by Europeans or Christians in *The Noble Slaves* doesn't seem to trouble Aubin. Teresa is saddened by the death of Domingo, the man who has been enslaved by her father, but there isn't a hint of an objection to his enslavement. Eleonora's father, a Venetian, buys enslaved people. Tanganor, a Persian convert to Christianity who entertains Don Lopez and de Hautville in his home, owns three "well-drest Slaves" along with carpets, porcelain, quilts, paintings, and screens (p. 56).

Aubin's use of the language of slavery and tyranny in the Preface to *The Noble Slaves* has more to do with the contemporary English political scene than it does with Britain's own trade in enslaved people. Aubin begins thus:

> In our Nation, where the Subjects are born free, where
> Liberty and Property is so preserv'd to us by Laws, that no
> Prince can enslave us, the Notion of Slavery is a perfect
> Stranger. We cannot think without Horror, of the Miseries
> that attend those, who, in Countries where the Monarchs are
> absolute, and standing Armies awe the people, are made
> Slaves to others. (p. 37)

The claim that Britain was a uniquely free nation ruled by laws rather than an absolute monarch became a hackneyed source of self-congratulation after 1688 when James II was forced to leave the throne. That boast, most closely associated with the Whig party, could also be used to frame a warning about how that same liberty was in imminent danger of being lost. Liberty might be lost if absolutism or tyranny prevailed, and such tyranny might be that of an over-mighty monarch or, in the thinking of the time, of a corrupt executive wielding power in its own interests. The Walpole administration was attacked on precisely those grounds in the Opposition campaign fostered by Viscount Bolingbroke (1678–1751) in the political journal the *Craftsman* from 1726 onwards. Before the *Craftsman*, Whig journalists John Trenchard (1688/89–1723) and Thomas Gordon (d. 1750) warned of the twin dangers of tyranny and slavery in the essays now known as *Cato's Letters* that appeared in the *London Journal*, and subsequently the *British Journal*, between 1720 and 1723 (see Appendices A8–9, pp. 173–75, and B2, pp. 178–79). Cato was Trenchard and Gordon's collective pseudonym, taken from the Roman senator (Cato the Younger, 95–46 BCE) who committed suicide rather than accept a pardon from Julius Caesar (100–44

BCE). In Joseph Addison's highly successful play *Cato, A Tragedy* (1713), the eponymous hero was the heroic champion of liberty against the threat of Julius Caesar's tyranny.

The immediate context for *Cato's Letters* was the collapse of the South Sea Company, the directors of which had conspired to inflate the price of shares. Despite the political and religious differences between "Cato" (a radical Whig) and Aubin (an Anglican Tory), the prefaces to Aubin's novels owe much to *Cato's Letters*. Like the *Letters*, her early fiction is set against the recent frenzy of financial speculation and the subsequent crash. An aside in Aubin's Preface to *Count de Vinevil* alludes to the possible suicide of Postmaster-General James Craggs (1657–1721), one of the architects of the conversion of government debt into South Sea stock and a major shareholder in the company: "The age has convinced us that guilt is so dreadful a thing that some men have hastened their own ends, and done justice on themselves" (115). The Commons inquiry of 1721 found that Craggs held £30,000 worth of stock for which he had not paid and £50,000 worth on behalf of the joint head of the ministry, the earl of Sunderland (Handley). Cato calls for stock-jobbers—meaning dealers in stocks and shares—to be punished severely to "stop the progress of the contagion" and for the good of the state ("A Further Call" 1).[1] In February 1721 he explains "what Measures have been taken by corrupt Ministers ... to ruin and enslave the People" ("What Measures" 1). Such measures include maintaining a standing army—a point taken up by Aubin in her Preface to *The Noble Slaves*—squandering public money for selfish gain, promoting idleness and luxury, and preferring for office those who are devoid of virtue. For Trenchard and Gordon, men become enslaved whenever tyranny prevails: that is, they lose the capacity for autonomous and virtuous action. Knowingly or unknowingly, their behaviour is regulated by the will of another, who has his own self-interest at heart. Absolutism and corruption go together, and the East is where the worst excesses of despotism may be found. "Despotick power has defaced the Creation," as may be seen in Asia, where "The Grand Seignior [the Ottoman emperor] who ... is the viceregent of heaven, frustrates the bounty of heaven; and, being the father of his people, has almost butchered them all" (Cato, "Considerations" 1). In Turkey, similarly, "Nothing is to be

---

1 For ease of identification, titles for individual letters have been taken from *Cato's Letters; or, essays on liberty, civil and religious, and other important subjects. In four Volumes* (1733), collected and "corrected" by Thomas Gordon, though the text is from their first publication.

seen but the Terrors of Absolute Monarchy, and the abject Postures of crouching Slaves" (Cato, "The Natural Passion" 1). Also locating corruption in the East, Aubin conjures up the same picture of avarice and self-interest at the top of the political order as Trenchard and Gordon:

> *The Grand Signor knowing that Money is able to procure all earthly things, uses his Grandees like the Cat's Paw, to beggar his People, and then sacrifices them to appease the Populace's Fury, and fills his own Coffers with their Wealth.* (p. 38)

In 1721, it would not be hard for the reader to make the connection between avarice and corruption in the Ottoman Empire and the South Sea Bubble.

That political critique informs *The Noble Slaves* more broadly. Aubin depicts a social world that demands a moral corrective, which she supplies in the characters of, particularly, idealized women. Outweighing the framing narrative in terms of length and circumstantial detail are eleven interpolated tales told by characters who either seek help from the four chief protagonists or act as their saviours. These tales typically involve love matches thwarted by parental prohibition, women abducted and sometimes held captive by European men, and enslavement. The point of departure for most of these interpolated tales is arbitrary authority motivated by self-interest, which manifests itself as lust, ambition, avarice, or an obsession with rank. Deciding that Emilia is too poor and of too low a rank to marry his son, Hautville's father has her drugged, abducted, and shipped to Québec. Andrea, the Venetian narrator of another story, is not permitted to marry beneath his own rank, and so his father has his intended wife Eleonora abducted. Eleonora's brothers might also have plotted to place her in a monastery against her will so as to claim her fortune. Eleonora has a companion, Anna, whose father, a French nobleman, abducted her mother because his family would not consent to his marrying one below him in rank. That father kept the mother in near-captivity in a remote castle, refusing to marry her: there is not much to choose between confinement at the hands of an Oriental tyrant and confinement by a European aristocrat.[1] Chateau-Roial becomes a priest because

---

1 Adam R. Beach describes Aubin as a "feminist Orientalist," that is, a writer who, implicitly or explicitly, draws parallels between the confinement of women under Ottoman rule and their situation in the West (586).

he is the third son and cannot inherit the estate. Clarinda is forced into a monastery against her will so as not to place a financial burden on the estate of her father, the Count de Villeroy. In due course, Eleonora, Anna, Chateau-Roial, and Clarinda are all forced into slavery. If we follow the chain of causation, Aubin makes the same link between self-interest, arbitrary power, and slavery as Cato. Countering the prevalence of "interest," as the eighteenth century would define it, is the positive virtue of disinterest, embodied in part by Aubin's ubiquitous priests and hermits who live a life of retreat, frugality, and charitable acts. Disinterest is primarily embodied, however, by her virtuous women. Where Don Lopez and the Count de Hautville finally give in to the temptation to eat whilst held in captivity, Emilia and Teresa do not. Captive Christian women are plied with rich clothes, jewels, and promises of passionate love and elevated status but remain consistently unmoved. Her women are never tempted, not even by "one of the most beautiful and accomplish'd Men of his Nation" (pp. 67–68). Despite the amatory content, there is no female longing, nor voyeuristic scenes such as one finds in Manley or Haywood. Aubin's women would defend their chastity by acts of self-denial, Maria's tearing out of her own eyeballs being the most extreme example. Aubin makes selflessness a measure of male *and* female worth, but the onus falls on women to exemplify it.

In addressing the issue of self-interest, Aubin takes on one of the deepest and most troubling dilemmas of her time. Samuel Richardson would later encounter the same problem in *Pamela* (1740) when he devised rewards for his virtuous heroine. Richardson supplied the incentives of elevated rank, fine clothes, and social admiration to induce his first readers, whom he imagined to be women of the servant class, to follow Pamela's chaste example. She was not meant to be seen as self-serving, though Henry Fielding (1707–54), in *Shamela* (1742), portrayed her as exactly that. Aubin undoubtedly values self-denial. "He that would keep his Integrity, must dwell in a Cell," declares the Preface to *Madam de Beaumount* (vii), and Aubin's characters repeatedly retreat from the world to woods and caves. Self-sacrifice, taken to an extreme in Maria's tearing out of her own eyes, is a key measure of moral worth. It may be no accident that Teresa's ordeal begins with a trip in a pleasure boat. In a notable anticipation of the plot of Richardson's *Clarissa*, but with a reversal of gender, the eponymous hero of Aubin's last novel, *The Life and Adventures of the Young Count Albertus* (1728), is a chaste man who finds a "glorious end" in death as a Christian martyr (7). In the Augustinian and subsequently the Calvinist traditions, the essence of the religious and moral life is selflessness. Man must prefer God to himself, prefer God's will to his own. For John Calvin (1509–64), the sum of the Christian life is self-denial: "We are not our own; therefore let us forget ourselves as much as possible, and all that is about us" (685). Classical Stoicism also taught the containment of passion and desire of all kinds, and Aubin's editing of Thomas Gibbs's translation of Marin le Roy de Gomberville's *La Doctrine des moeurs tirée de la philosophie des stoïques* (1646) as *The Doctrine of Morality* in 1721 confirms her familiarity with stoic principles. When Bernard Mandeville (1670–1733) declared in "A Search into Society," an essay added to *The Fable of the Bees* (1714) in 1723, that "[t]he generality of Moralists and Philosophers have hitherto agreed that there could be no Virtue without Self-denial," he was articulating a traditional though rigorist view (329). The difference between Mandeville and most of his contemporaries was that he was prepared to accept both that men were corrupt and that such corruption was a necessary driver of national prosperity: private vices equalled public benefits. The debate about morality and human motivation had taken a decisive turn with Thomas Hobbes's *Leviathan* (1651), in which he portrayed human beings as driven only by self-interest. Rewards, then, must be offered as incentives for proper conduct, just as Richardson advertised in the subtitle to *Pamela*: "Virtue Rewarded." Lord Shaftesbury (1671–1713), Francis Hutcheson (1694–1746), and other moral philosophers of the time who would counter Hobbes work to construct an account of human nature that includes an obligation to moral behaviour. For such thinkers, it is the "natural affections" of friendship and sociability, to which man is naturally inclined, that are intrinsically valuable and bring true contentment. "Self-love and social," as Alexander Pope (1688–1744) put it in the closing couplet of the third Epistle of *An Essay on Man* (1733–34), were—conveniently and comfortably—"the same."

Yet the South Sea crisis demonstrated how thoroughly self-interest had penetrated and permeated the social order; and the crash was itself only the most dramatic revelation of the forces of capitalism that were now at work. The first two decades of the eighteenth century were characterized by growing unease about the "financial revolution," a revolution brought about by the need to finance King William's expensive continental wars. The need for credit—and the opportunity to make money from that need—

brought into being a National Debt, the Bank of England, a boom in joint-stock companies, the Stock Exchange, and a State Lottery. A suspicion arose that the war with France only continued so as to enrich or advance private individuals, the Duke of Marlborough among them. The disruptive forces of paper credit, speculation, and self-interest combined to disastrous effect to produce the crash in the autumn of 1720. At this point, a whole system of credit that had grown up as part and parcel of an expanding economy over the last fifty years fell apart (Carswell 191ff.).

A sense that everyone is corrupted by self-interest is pervasive in Aubin's fiction. Bribery is a frequent plot device. When, in *Count de Vinevil*, Count Longueville attempts to bribe a Muslim who has been enslaved to reveal the name of his wife's would-be seducer, he receives a rebuke aimed at the prevalence of greed in British society: "[N]ot all the wealth, the damning gold, that would procure a set of courtiers great enough to depose a Christian king or to create two new ones should seduce me to reveal his secret" (119). Yet in the end Aubin too caters to self-interest, if not for her heroines then for her female readers, and it is this contradiction that leads to the moral ambiguity identified by Mounsey. Aubin offers her readers the thrills of amatory fiction but wants them to imitate exemplars of chastity. Her women never aim to go on voyages to foreign lands, but Aubin satisfies what she must have believed to be her readers' desire for excitement and escapism by sending them there. Aubin's female characters show no sexual desire, but her readers might enjoy the fact that her heroines are the constant object of male admiration. As Aparna Gollapudi has argued, Aubin wants to make virtue exciting. By so doing, she was bound to cater to a desire for entertainment and pleasure. Aubin's heroines are always unwillingly separated from their husbands, but when they are they enjoy adventures and a kind of independence where they might live by their own wits: presumably Aubin believed that her female readers would welcome that possibility. She also shows them dressing as men and committing acts of violence and destruction. The otherwise passive Ardelisa, in *Count de Vinevil*, sets fire to the seraglio as she escapes. That implicit acknowledgement of women's urge to resist the gendered roles constructed for them sits awkwardly with the depiction of women as models of duty, just as there is a mismatch between Teresa's rejection of worldly temptations and Aubin's own cultivation of a public role.

Aubin must have been well aware of the extent to which her fiction catered to the reader's desire for thrills and transgression. At the same time, she wanted to be seen as respectable and took steps to guide an interpretation of her work and her own character as a novelist. It would take the publication of novels by Samuel Richardson and Henry Fielding for readers to begin to see fiction as both entertaining and morally worthy, and for a woman, an appearance in print routinely required an apology or a defence. Sarah Prescott sees Aubin's exemplary reputation as a textual construct created by the author herself, "a self-conscious but sophisticated ploy to be read but also respected" (101). Aubin's pious language and prefatorial persona, Prescott argues, were borrowed from that of the English translator of *The Doctrine of Morality*, while Aubin cannily implied her fiction's respectability by creating links between herself and those who were socially esteemed or genteelly born. The same work is dedicated to Mary Butler, Duchess of Ormond, who, according to Aubin, presented her "Memorial" (perhaps one of the Odes) to the late Queen Anne: a claim hard to disprove. *The Noble Slaves* is dedicated to Anne, Lady Coleraine (1699–1754), wife of Henry Hare, third baron Coleraine (1693–1749), and speaks of the friendship between the couple and Aubin's husband, Abraham. In 1726 Aubin dedicated *The Life and Adventures of the Lady Lucy* to the baron, while referring to her earlier address to his wife. Lord and Lady Coleraine had in fact been estranged since 1720, an anomaly leading Prescott to suggest that Aubin's representation of a connection between herself and the Coleraines is merely strategic. The strategy, if it was one, seems to have worked. Including *The Noble Slaves* in her *Collection*, Elizabeth Griffith thought that Aubin's acquaintance with Lord and Lady Coleraine and many other persons of distinction showed her to be "a decent and virtuous woman" (3: 47). Chris Mounsey characterizes Aubin as "duplicitous," pointing out that she confines to a brief footnote the fact that the Mrs. Rowe addressed in the Dedication to *Charlotta Du Pont* is *not* the esteemed and pious poet Elizabeth Singer Rowe (1674–1737) but rather the daughter of Dr. Barker, Dean of Exeter (61). No such dean has been found to have existed.

Penelope Aubin's fiction, then, was neither entirely pious nor merely sensational. Entering the market for books in the eighteenth century provided an opportunity for intervention in the public sphere, particularly for those who might not find one anywhere else, but it also demanded concessions to public taste and accepted social standards. In this respect, Aubin is no different from any other writer of the period, and *The Noble Slaves* finds Aubin negotiating the tensions that arise from the conflict between moral reform and participation in the marketplace. It also finds her engaging with the release of enslaved Britons from Morocco, as well as implicitly commenting on the protection of trade, the prevalence of corruption, national moral decline, arbitrary authority, and the situation of women. These concerns make her novels more than mere diversions. Aubin has long been seen as a precursor to Richardson, but her pioneering contribution to fiction as a vehicle for addressing the deepest moral and political concerns of her time is still undervalued (see Zach). Bringing her fiction back into print can only help to promote further investigation of both Aubin and the genre she helped to develop.

Penelope Aubin: A Brief Chronology

c. 1679   Penelope Aubin born, illegitimate daughter of Sir
           Richard Temple and his mistress Anne Charleton,
           daughter of royal physician William Charleton.
1696   Penelope Charleton marries Abraham Aubin,
           eldest son of a merchant family from Jersey,
           without parental consent.
1697   Penelope's father dies, leaving nothing to his
           daughter. She is in Jersey for the birth of her first
           child.
1699   Aubin family return to London. Second child
           born.
1702   Advises Thomas Fairfax, fifth Baron Fairfax of
           Cameron, and Richard Savage, fourth Earl Rivers,
           about a salvaging expedition in the Caribbean.
1703   Penelope and Abraham take a case against Pene-
           lope's mother in the court of chancery, claiming
           that she defrauded her daughter of money left to
           Penelope by her father.
c. 1706–12 Abraham serves as a lieutenant in the Dragoons
           during the War of the Spanish Succession.
1707   *The Stuarts: a Pindarique Ode* celebrates the Act of
           Union.
1708   *The Extasy: a Pindarique Ode to her Majesty the
           Queen* celebrates British victory at the Battle of
           Oudenarde and the repelling of the Pretender,
           James Francis Edward Stuart.
1709   *The Wellcome: a Poem to his Grace the Duke of Marl-
           borough* offers an unenthusiastic welcome to Marl-
           borough on his return to England. Aubin gives a
           deposition to the Board of Trade, declining to play
           a part in a scheme to repatriate British pirates from
           Madagascar.
1720   Brother-in-law David's ship the *Prosperous* captured
           by pirates in the West Indies.
1720   Inherits the estate of Thomas Mannington Gibbs, a
           young Oxford scholar.
1721   *The Strange Adventures of the Count de Vinevil and
           his Family*; *The Life of Madam de Beaumount*; *The
           Life and Amorous Adventures of Lucinda*; Thomas
           Mannington Gibbs's translation of Marin le Roy,

sieur de Gomberville's *La Doctrine des moeurs* ... is published as *Doctrine of Morality*, with an introduction by Aubin.

1722 *The Noble Slaves*. Anonymous publication of translations of Louise-Geneviève Gomez de Vasconcellos, dame Gillot de Beaucour's *Les Mémoires de la vie de Madame de Ravezan* as *The Adventures of the Prince of Clermont, and Madame de Ravezan*, and François Pétis de La Croix's *Histoire du Grand Genghizcan, premier empereur des anciens Mogols et Tartares* as *The History of Genghizcan the Great*.

1723 *The Life of Charlotta du Pont*.

1724 Performance of John Dryden's *The Spanish Fryar* on 2 January at the Theatre Royal in Lincoln's Inn Fields referred to as being for the benefit of Mrs. Aubin in *The London Stage*.

1726 *The Life and Adventures of the Lady Lucy*. Republication of *Doctrine of Morality* as *Moral Virtue Delineated*. Publishes her translation of Robert Challe's *Les Illustres Françaises* as *The Illustrious French Lovers*.

1728 *The Life and Adventures of the Young Count Albertus*.

1729 Translation of Marguerite de Lussan's *Histoire de la comtesse de Gondez* published as *The Life of the Countess de Gondez*.

1729–30 Establishes "The Lady's Oratory" at York Buildings, Villiers Street, London, in opposition to Dissenting minister John "Orator" Henley. Attacks the ministry of Sir Robert Walpole.

1730 *The Merry Masqueraders, or, The Humorous Cuckold* performed at the New Theatre in the Haymarket. Aubin delivers the epilogue.

1734 Antoine-François Prévost (Abbé Prévost) writes a hostile profile of Aubin in *Le Pour et le Contre*, characterizing her as the ugly and now-dead daughter of an impoverished émigré French officer.

1738 Aubin dies and is buried at the church of St. George the Martyr, Southwark, in London.

A Note on the Text

The copy-text of *The Noble Slaves* is the first edition of 1722. The novel was reprinted twice in Dublin in 1736. I have intervened in the text as little as possible, retaining capitalization of nouns, italicization of proper names, and apostrophes to indicate a missing 'e' in such words as "pleas'd" and "heal'd." Though odd at first sight to the reader unfamiliar with eighteenth-century punctuation, such conventions should not present an undue problem in terms of comprehension. I have changed the eighteenth-century long "s" to a modern "s." Dialogue originally rendered in italics has been retained. Where the dialogue is in roman, punctuation has been slightly altered in that a change of speaker is indicated by closing and opening inverted commas. Variable spellings such as "monastry" and "monastery" or "vertue" and "virtue" have also been retained. However, I have regularized the spelling of characters' names and titles to avoid confusion.

The same policy of reproducing original texts as closely as possible has been followed in terms of material included in the Appendices, where printed documents are all first editions. Decisions possibly made by later compilers or editors are thus avoided. An exception is the third edition of Mary Astell's *Some Reflections Upon Marriage* (Appendix A7), which is the first to contain the prefatory material cited.

All definitions of words are taken from the *Oxford English Dictionary*.

The Noble Slaves

J. Pin inv. & Sculp

THE
NOBLE SLAVES:
OR, THE
Lives and Adventures
OF
TWO LORDS and two LADIES,

who were shipwreck'd and cast upon a desolate Island near the *East-Indies*,[1] in the Year 1710. The Manner of their living there: The surprizing Discoveries they made, and strange Deliverance thence. How in their return to *Europe* they were taken by two *Algerine* Pirates near the Straits of *Gibraltar*. Of the Slavery they endured in *Barbary*;[2] and of their meeting there with several Persons of Quality, who were likewise Slaves. Of their escaping thence, and safe Arrival in their respective Countries, *Venice*,[3] *Spain*, and *France*, in the Year 1718. With many extraordinary Accidents that befel some of them afterwards.

Being a History full of most remarkable Events.

By Mrs. AUBIN.

LONDON:

Printed for *E. Bell, J. Darby, A. Bettesworth, F. Fayram, J. Pemberton, J. Hooke, C. Rivington, F. Clay, J. Batley, J. Batley,* and *E. Symon.* M.DCC.XXII

1 A term that can be used to comprehend what is now the Republic of Indonesia and the Malay archipelago or, more broadly, the southern half of the Indian subcontinent and all of maritime southeast Asia. It came into use in the seventeenth century as trade increased between Europe and Asia.

2 Barbary was the name given by Europeans to the coastal region of North Africa then comprising Morocco and the Ottoman regencies of Tripoli, Tunisia, and Algiers. Between 1530 and 1780 there were "almost certainly a million and quite possibly as many as a million and a quarter white, European Christians enslaved by the Muslims of the Barbary Coast" (Davis 118). Barbary corsairs raided as far north as Iceland and Norway. Captives were taken mainly from vessels in the Mediterranean but also from Mediterranean islands and coastal regions of Ireland, England, Spain, and Italy. See also Introduction, p. 18.

3 Venice was a sovereign state and a maritime republic from the thirteenth century until 1797, with territories along the eastern shore of the Adriatic as well as, at differing times, the islands of Crete and Cyprus and the Peloponnese peninsula.

TO THE
RIGHT HONOURABLE
THE
LADY COLERAIN.[1]

MADAM,

THE Friendship my Lord and you have been pleas'd to honour my Husband[2] withal, lays me under an Obligation of making some Returns, and must create in me a particular Veneration for You both. But there are many other Reasons why I should make choice of you, Madam, to beg your Protection for these *Noble Slaves* and my self, to skreen us from the ill-natured Croud of Criticks, who condemn without Judgment; and Atheists, who deride God's Providence, which this History was chiefly design'd to vindicate, and to excite Men to put their Trust in, at this time when they scarce know how to trust one another.

You, Madam, have Beauty to charm them all into Silence; a Look, a Smile will disarm their Malice, and a Frown awe the whole Sex. What Man dares to condemn what so fair a Lady approves? And tho our own Sex generally look with Envy on such Excellencies as you are Mistress of; yet the good Nature and Sweetness of your Disposition disarms their Spleen, and they must love, as well as admire you; and consequently favour every thing that you honour with your Esteem, or approve.

For these Reasons, Madam, I presume to dedicate this Book to you; and relying on your Goodness, hope you will pardon my Presumption when I tell you, that I do it with the ambitious Desire of being admitted into the number of those who have the Happiness to call themselves your Friends; of which none has a more profound Respect for my Lord and you, than

> *Your Ladyship's*
> *most sincere Friend*
> *and devoted Servant,*

Penelope Aubin.

---

1 Anne Hanger (1699–1754), only daughter of John Hanger, merchant and Director of the Bank of England, and his wife Mary Coles, who married Henry Hare, third Baron Coleraine (1693–1749) in January 2018 and became Lady Coleraine. By 1722 the couple had already been estranged for two years.

2 Penelope Aubin's husband was Abraham Aubin (d. 1740), the eldest son of a merchant family from the island of Jersey. The extent of his friendship with Baron and Lady Coleraine is unclear. He and Lord Coleraine belonged to the same Masonic Lodge, and Coleraine left Abraham ten guineas *(continued)*

mourning money and a fur cap in his will. Abraham's first will in 1728 was witnessed by Marmaduke Hart, Lord Coleraine's butler at Bruce Castle in Tottenham. A later will mentions the "close friendship" between Abraham and the baron's second wife, Rose Duplessis. A mutual friend of the Aubins and the Coleraines was Thomas Reason, who witnessed the will of Thomas Mannington Gibbs, which bequeathed the manuscript of *The Doctrine of Morality* to Penelope Aubin (Welham, *Delight* 20, 33).

THE
PREFACE
TO THE
READER.

IN our Nation, where the Subjects are born free, where Liberty and Property is so preserv'd to us by Laws, that no Prince can enslave us, the Notion of Slavery is a perfect Stranger. We cannot think without Horror, of the Miseries that attend those, who, in Countries where the Monarchs are absolute, and standing Armies[1] awe the people, are made Slaves to others. The Turks and Moors[2] have been ever famous for these Cruelties;[3] and therefore when we Christians fall into the Hands of Infidels,[4] or Mahometans,[5] we must expect to be treated as

---

1   In debates throughout the late-seventeenth and early-eighteenth centuries, Whigs often argued that a standing army maintained by the monarch was a potential instrument for the enforcement of absolute rule. Tories more typically objected to a standing army on account of the expense involved and because they would give priority to the navy as the protector and promoter of British interests.

2   Historically Moors were Muslims from Mauretania, a region of North Africa corresponding to parts of present-day Morocco and Algeria. They were believed to be Black or very dark-skinned, and Aubin uses the word interchangeably with "Blackmore."

3   The Western view of Eastern culture as especially cruel and barbaric may be traced back at least as far as the Crusades, though receiving particular emphasis in Italian humanists' reaction to the taking of Constantinople by the forces of the Ottoman Empire in 1453 (Bisaha 60–73). The first early-modern account of Turkey in English is Sir Richard Knolles's *Generall Historie of the Turkes* (1603), in which the barbarity and cruelty of Turkish emperors is a recurring theme. For seventeenth- and eighteenth-century Britons, an influential characterization of the Turkish government as corrupt and despotic and of Turks as lustful, sensual, ambitious, vengeful, and avaricious was that of Sir Paul Rycaut in *The Present State of the Ottoman Empire* (1668; see Appendix B1, pp. 177–78). The two works were published together between 1687 and 1700, along with other continuations and additions. A further significant influence is Antoine Galland's *Mille et une Nuits* (1704–17), subsequently published in English as *Arabian Nights' Entertainment* between 1705 and 1721. At least twenty editions followed. Staving off undeserved and arbitrary execution is the starting point for Scheherazade's stories and a recurring plot in the tales themselves.

4   From a Christian point of view, any adherent of a religion opposed to Christianity, especially Islam.

5   Signifying Muslims, based on an inaccurate European rendering of the name of the prophet Muhammad.

those heroick Persons, who are the Subject of the Book I here present to you. There the Monarch gives a loose to his Passions, and thinks it no Crime to keep as many Women for his Use, as his lustful Appetite excites him to like; and his Favourites, Ministers of State, and Governors, who always follow their Master's Example, imitate his way of living. This caused our beautiful Heroines to suffer such Trials: The Grand Signior knowing that Money is able to procure all earthly things, uses his Grandees like the Cat's Paw, to beggar his People, and then sacrifices them to appease the Populace's Fury, and fills his own Coffers with their Wealth. This is Turkish Policy, which makes the Prince great, and the People wretched, a Condition we are secur'd from ever falling into; our excellent Constitution will always keep us rich and free, and it must be our own Faults if we are enslav'd, or impoverish'd.

But to leave this unpleasant Subject, let us proceed to reflect on the great Deliverances of these noble Slaves: You will find that Chains could not hold them; Want, Sickness, Grief, nor the merciless Seas destroy them; because they trusted in God, and swerv'd not from their Duty.

Methinks now I see the Atheist grin, the modish Wit laugh out, and the old Letcher and the young Debauchee sneer, and throw by the Book; and all join to decry it: 'tis all a Fiction, a Cant they cry; Virtue's a Bugbear, Religion's a Cheat, tho at the same time they are jealous of their Wives, Mistresses, and Daughters, and ready to fight about Principles and Opinions.

Their Censures I despise, as much as I abhor their Crimes; the Good and the Virtuous I desire to please. My only Aim is to encourage Virtue, and expose Vice, imprint noble Principles in the ductile Souls of our Youth, and setting great Examples before their Eyes, excite them to imitate them. If I succeed in this, I have all I wish.

The charming Masquerades[1] being at an end, our Ears almost tir'd with Italian Harmony,[2] and our Pockets empty'd of Money, which

---

1 Advertisements for masquerades, or masked balls or assemblies, began to appear in London around 1711, with early masquerades being held by the French ambassador the duc d'Aumont (1667–1723) at Somerset House in 1713. Masquerades were organized and promoted by Swiss entrepreneur Johann Jakob Heidegger (1666–1749) from around 1715 until the 1730s. Crowds of seven hundred to a thousand people could gather at such weekly events, paying as much as a guinea and a half for a ticket. English opponents often saw the craze as a perverse and pernicious foreign intrusion (Castle).

2 Italian opera, or opera in the "Italian manner"—meaning that it might be translated into English or sung in English and Italian—was highly successful on the London stage in the first two decades of the eighteenth century. The form and its popularity were attacked from the

must prevent extravagant Gaming, unless our private Credit outlives the Publick;[1] *it is possible that we may be glad of new Books to amuse us, and pass away that time that must hang heavy on our Hands: And Books of Devotion being tedious, and out of Fashion, Novels and Stories will be welcome. Amongst these, I hope, this will be read, and gain a Place in your Esteem, especially with my own Sex, whose Favour I shall always be proud of: Nor have they a truer Friend, than their humble Servant,*

Penelope Aubin.

---

outset as a sign or cause of the degradation of national taste, as in an essay by John Dennis (1658–1734) titled "Essay on the Opera's after the Italian Manner which are about to be establish'd on the English stage: with some Reflections on the Damage which they may bring to the Publick" (1706).

1   "Publick Credit" signifies the ability of the national government to borrow money. The need to restore public credit led to the South Sea Company's refinancing of the National Debt in 1711 with the debt secured against projected profits, largely from the Atlantic slave trade. In late 1720 the Company's artificially and fraudulently inflated value sank disastrously, leading to another crisis of public credit.

THE
NOBLE SLAVES, &c.

CHAP. I.

A FRENCH West-India[1] Captain just return'd from the Coast of
Barbary, having brought thence some Ladies and Gentlemen, who
had been Captives in those Parts, the History of whose Adventures
there are most surprizing, I thought it well worth presenting to the
Publick. It contains such strange variety of Accidents and strange
Deliverances, that I am positive it cannot fail to divert the most
splenetick Reader, silence the Profane, and delight the Ingenious;
and must be welcome at a time when we have so much occasion
for something new, to make us forget our own Misfortunes. The
Providence of God, which Men so seldom confide in, is in this
History highly vindicated; his Power manifests itself in every
Passage: and if we are not better'd by the Examples of the virtuous
Teresa and the brave Don Lopez, 'tis our own Faults.

These Persons, who are the principal Subject of this Narrative,
were both Natives of Spain; the Lady Teresa's Father was Don
Sancho de Avilla, a Gentleman of Castile;[2] who, being a Widower,
took this young Lady, his only Child, then but ten Years of Age,
and went for Mexico,[3] where he resolved to reside the remainder
of his Days; having received some disgust at his Master the King
of Spain, who had refus'd him the Government of a Place in
Castile, which he had ask'd for.

He left Spain in the Year 1708, and arrived safe at Mexico with
all his Effects[4] and Family. There he soon increas'd his Fortune

---

1 From the seventeenth century onwards, France had significant colonies
   in the West Indies, a name given to Caribbean islands in the Antilles
   archipelago. French possessions included the islands of Grenada, Martinique, Guadeloupe, Saint-Barthélémy, and Saint-Christophe (now
   Saint Christopher or "Saint Kitts").
2 Now divided into the regions of Castilla-La Mancha and Castilla y
   Leòn, the kingdom of Castile was the centre of Spanish monarchical
   and imperial power in the seventeenth and eighteenth centuries. Such
   was the dominance and prestige of Castile that it was often identified
   with Spain itself.
3 Mexico, also known as "New Spain," became part of the Spanish
   empire in the sixteenth century. Spanish settlements extended beyond
   present-day Mexico and into what is now the US state of New Mexico
   as well as territories in modern Texas, Arizona, and California.
4 Property.

greatly, and the fair *Teresa* improv'd in Stature and Beauty, so that in two Years time she was admired by all the Men, and envied by all the Women. She was moderately fair, but her Eyes were black and shining, and inspired Love with every Glance. Her Mouth and Features were so sweet, so charming, that her Smiles still heal'd the Wounds her Eyes did give. Her Shape, her Air, her Voice, were all divine. Her Soul was noble, full of solid Sense and Honour. She was affable, pious, witty, chaste, and free from Pride. Her Father was so fond of her, he thought his Happiness consisted wholly in her Life and Welfare; priz'd her above his Wealth, and resolved to sacrifice all he had got, rather than not place her nobly in the World.

But alas! Heaven smiles at our Designs, and soon convinced him he could live without her. One Evening the fair *Teresa* being at a Country House of her Father's, at *Segura*,[1] going to take the Air in a Pleasure-Boat, with her Servants; a strong Wind rose, and blew them out to Sea: Three Days and Nights they remain'd, tossed to and fro, in the extremest Danger and Despair. At last the Boat over-set, and the merciless Waves swallowed that, and all her Attendants, except a *Blackmore* Slave, who leaping into the Sea, cry'd, *My dear Lady, throw yourself upon me, and I will bear you up till I die.* It was Dusk, and no Land appear'd: But as she held him round the Neck, he (swimming) cry'd, *Land, Land, hold fast, I tread on Land.* Then getting nearer to the Shore, he found his hopes answer'd; for they were cast on a desolate Island, where no Signs of any Inhabitants appear'd. Here the half dead *Teresa* fainted, and the poor *Black* laying her upon the Grass, sat down weeping by her, having nothing to give her, to comfort her or himself. She at length recover'd, and with that weak Voice she had left, return'd God thanks for her Safety.

At break of Day they saw an old *Indian*[2] Man come down towards them, drest in Beasts Skins, a Hat of Canes, and Sandals of Wood upon his feet: He went to a Tree, drag'd a Canoe of a strange Fashion, that stood against[3] it, down to the Sea; and was entring into it when he perceived *Teresa* and the *Moor.* He presently made up to them, and by strange Gestures exprest his Surprize, seeming to admire her Habit and Beauty; the *Black* who was skill'd in them, by Signs inform'd him of their Distress. The

---

1 Segura de la Frontera, a town founded by Hernán Cortés (c. 1485–1547) in southeastern Mexico in 1520, now known as Tepeaca.
2 The word "Indian" could denote any Indigenous people.
3 First edition: agaist

Indian who proved a *Japanese*, cast on Shore there, with his Wife and three Children, in the *Chinese* Language invited them to his Home. The *Moor* understood him, and informing his Lady, they went with him. They found his Wife and Children in a poor Cottage, or Hut; she was drest in Beasts Skins, and the Children were naked: The Hut was built of Boughs of Trees, and Hurdles made with Canes to fill the Spaces; the Roof was thatched with Plashes[1] and Leaves, yet so that the Rains could not enter: the *Indians* were humane, and treated her the best they were able, bringing out dry'd Fish, and Eggs, which the Woman roasted in the Embers of a Fire they had made to warm them. There was only one Room where they must all eat and lie; Rushes and dry'd Leaves, with no Coverlid but Beasts Skins, were their Beds; *Indian* Corn, dry'd in the Sun, their Bread; Water their Drink. This was a hard Trial for so young a Creature as the fair *Teresa*, who had been bred with such Delicacy and Indulgence: But her Virtues exceeded her Years and Strength; she eat thankfully what was set before her, was wholly resign'd to the Will of Heaven, and murmur'd not at Providence. Here she and the *Moor* continued eight Days. The poor *Indian* who was a Christian, converted with his Family by the Missionaries in *Japan*,[2] and shipwrecked here as he was going with Goods for the Merchants to *China*, with a small Bark[3] which he was then Owner of; he and the *Moor* went daily out to fish, hoping to get sight of some Ship, or Bark, that would carry them to *Japan*, or *Mexico*. Meantime the Lady not being able to converse with the poor *Indian* Woman, whose Language she was a Stranger to, walk'd out as far as her weak legs would carry her, to view the Island, which seem'd of no small Extent: Here she found Fruits of divers Kinds, pleasant and good, especially Grapes which, tho' wild, were of excellent Taste; these she eat and brought home; where pressing out the Juice, she mixt it with Water, making a pleasant Drink of it. This raised a Curiosity in the *Black* to range about the Island, hoping to discover something worth his Labour. He found Nests of young Birds, and Rice, Olives, Honey in the hollow Trees; and every Day brought home something acceptable, and of great use in their melancholy Condition. But Providence was determin'd to

---

1 Interwoven branches.
2 Christian missionary activity in Japan ceased long before Aubin's lifetime. The first missionaries, led by the Jesuit Francis Xavier (1506–52), arrived in Japan in 1549, but all missionaries were excluded from the country by an edict of 1614.
3 A small ship.

deprive *Teresa* of this Comfort also; for one Morning she walk'd out with *Domingo* (for so was her faithful Slave call'd) to divert her self with the sight of some pleasant Walks he had discovered in a woody Place about two Miles from the House; which being arrived at, they ventured into the thickest part of it: There *Domingo* espy'd a Tree with Fruit he had never seen before, not unlike a *European* Pear; he boldly ventured to gather, and taste it, tho *Teresa* warn'd him to forbear tasting it till they had shewn it to the *Indian*: He eat two of them, putting more in his Pocket; and in few Minutes after found himself sick, and began to vomit. They hasten'd to return home; but before they could reach half way, he fell down, and embracing his Lady's Knees, cry'd, 'Farewel my dear Mistress; may God, to the Knowledge of whom your dear Father brought me, keep you, and deliver you hence; comfort you when I am gone, and have Mercy upon the Soul of your poor Slave. Remember me, charming *Teresa*; my Soul ador'd you, but Christianity restrain'd me from asking what my amorous Soul languished to possess. I brought you to the Woods with Thoughts my Soul now sinks at. I was born free as you, and thought I might with Honour ask your Love, since Heaven had singled me out to save your Life, and live your only Companion and Defender; but God has thought fit to disappoint me. May no other rob you of that Treasure which I no longer can protect. Angels guard you. Give me one Kiss, and send my Soul to rest.' Here he grasp'd her Hand, and strove to rise, but fell back and expir'd. The fair *Teresa* remain'd so afflicted and surprized, that she was not able to stand; her tender Soul was so shock'd, she was even ready to follow him; the Generosity and Love he had shewn, the desolate Condition she was left in, distracted her: yet she could not but applaud the Goodness of God, who had so wonderfully prevented her Ruin; for tho he had a Soul fair as his Face was black, yet *Domingo*, her Father's Slave, was not fit to enter her Bed.

She was now left alone, no human Creature left that could understand her Language; very small hopes of ever being delivered from this dismal place, the poor *Indians* having lived here five Years already.

These sad Thoughts o'erwhelm'd her for some time; one while she turn'd her Eyes to the insensible *Domingo*, then to the distant Sea, and *Mexico*: At length she cast them up to Heaven, and cry'd, 'My God, pity my Youth and Innocence; Death would now be a Favour to me. What shall I do in this sad Place! How spend those wretched Hours thou hast allotted me to live! Who shall close my Eyes, or lay me decently in my Grave? But why do I reflect on that? Who shall improve by any good that I can do, whilst living, or teach me to sustain the Miseries of Life as I ought? Oh! thou who madest and canst not hate me, encrease my Faith and Patience; or free my Soul from this Extremity of Grief by Death. But, alas! do I instruct my God? do I point out to him the way to help me? am I fit to die, and not resign'd to him? Forgive me, gracious Heaven: I rest satisfied: This lonely Place shall henceforth be my *Patmos*:[1] Here free from Temptations that delude Mankind I'll live; the Woods shall be my Oratory: I'll only eat to live, count Things the most distasteful, wholesom and good, and live to die.' Here she attempted to rise, but was not able. She remain'd here some Hours. At last, the poor *Indian* Woman came to seek her, and after having exprest in her Language much concern for *Domingo*, led her home.

She continued thus ten Days, beginning to understand something of their Language: The *Indian* bury'd *Domingo*, and *Teresa* grew very sick, yet refrain'd not to walk daily to the Wood, where she offer'd up her Prayers to God.

One morning as she was at her Devotion, she was interrupted by the Voice of a Woman, who was making sad Lamentation in the *French* Tongue for the Death of some Person. *Teresa* rose from off her Knees, and following the sound of the Voice, came to the farther side of the Wood, where she perceived a dark Valley betwixt two small Hills, which were so covered with Trees as rendred the Valley very obscure; here sat a Woman with her Hair dishevell'd; her Habit rich, but altogether negligent, upon the Ground: upon a Scarlet Cloak lay a Man, whose Habit spoke him no common Person, a Death-like Paleness reign'd in his Face, and he appear'd as one just dead. The Woman wrung her Hands, tore her Hair, and shew'd all the Symptoms of a Person in Despair. *Teresa*, who spoke *French*, after some time addrest her self to her in this manner: 'Madam, behold here a Person, who is, perhaps, wretched as your self, yet not quite unable to help you; tell me your Grief; and if I cannot repair your Loss I may yet comfort you.' The Woman looking up, discover'd the most lovely Face imaginable. 'Speak not, *said she*, to me of Comfort; since the too charming *Hautville* is no more, I am inconsolable. See here a

---

1   A small Greek island in the Aegean Sea, where St. John the Divine is said to have received the visions in the Book of Revelation that are delivered to the "seven churches which are in Asia" (Rev. 1.4), meaning those of Asia Minor, now Turkey.

Man, who has left his Country, Fortune and Friends to follow me; and being cast on this cursed Shore by an unskilful Pilot, has perish'd at my Feet for want of Food. We have been here five sad Days in this inhospitable Place, where the Bruises he had received against the Cruel Sands upon his Breast, bringing me upon his Back to Shore, made him unable to go farther. I gathered Fruit and Honey; but alas! he wanted other Food, refus'd to eat enough to support Life, and is now departed, leaving me the most unhappy Wretch on Earth.' Here she renew'd her Transport of Sorrow, kist his pale Lips, and beat her Breast against the Ground; which *Teresa*, who wanted Strength to hold her, beheld with the utmost Compassion. At last the Gentleman fetch'd a deep Sigh, and opened his Eyes. 'Fond Woman, said *Teresa*, sit not thus to weep, but rise and follow me; the God which Grief makes you forget, sends you Help by me: Make haste, I'll give you Food and Wine, which tho but poor, will sustain Life.' At these Words *Teresa* ran back to the Hut as fast as her Weakness would permit, and made the *Indian* Woman follow her with Food to the Wood, where they found the Lady and Gentleman, both almost senseless; but pouring some of the Grape Juice down their Throats, which was strong, tho not purify'd like Wine, they revived, and having got a little Food into their Stomachs, made shift to rise, and walk a little Way, but could not reach the Hut till Evening. *Teresa* stay'd by them all the Day, o'erjoy'd that she had Company; and after having eat and drank a second time, the Gentleman repaid her Courtesy with this handsome Acknowledgment: 'Blest Angel, for such you have been to me, and my dear *Emilia*, how came you here? Such Beauty and such Youth, and Innocence as appears in your Face, might surely have secured you from the Miseries of Life. What cruel Accident brought you to this desert Isle?' Here *Teresa* recounted her Misfortunes, and in return, desired to know theirs, if his Strength would permit. The Count de *Hautville* readily consented to gratify her, and began the fair *Emilia*'s and his own History, in this Manner.

CHAP. II.

'Madam, we are natives of *France,* born both in one Province, *Poictou*[1] is our Country; I was the Son of the Marquess *de Ventadore,* a man whose Fortune and Quality render'd him vain, and me unhappy. This Lady was the Daughter of a Gentleman, who, tho not equal to my Father in Fortune, was as nobly descended. He was the younger Son of a General, and related to the Duke *de Vendome.*[2] *Emilia* was his only Child, whose Beauty and Vertues made her worthy a Prince's Bed. I saw, and loved her from her Infancy; our Affection was encreased by Years, and grew up with us. When I was fourteen, my Father carry'd me to *Paris,* show'd me the Court, and all the celebrated Beauties that shine there, where Art is used to improve each Charm, and Jewels and Habit join with Nature to subdue the Heart; but *Emilia* was possest of mine before. I view'd them all unmoved, was impatient to return to *Poictou;* and then my Father first began to mistrust my being pre-engaged to some Person there. He carry'd me back with him, and set a Watch upon my Actions. Soon after my return home *Emilia*'s Father died, and she was taken by an old Aunt to be educated. The Fortune left *Emilia* was about two thousand Pounds, the Estate was entail'd, and could not descend to a Daughter, so a Kinsman enjoys it. This Lady was a sordid, malicious old Maid, who pretended to Devotion and Sanctity, but was really a vile Hypocrite: She used her with great Severity, and gave my Father intelligence of my frequent Visits and Presents to *Emilia,* hoping to gain his Favour and a Reward, which she did not fail of. He urged me often to address my self to one Lady or other, and finding me firm to my first Choice, resolved to rid her out of my way; in order to which, he sends for a Captain who was going to the *French Canada*[3] for to trade, and offers him three hundred Crowns to carry her away with him. The Villain accepts the Offer, visits the Aunt, acquaints himself with *Emilia,* at last invites them to *Rochel,*[4] where his Ship

---

1 Poitou, bordering on the Bay of Biscay and south-east of Brittany, once a French province.

2 Louis-Joseph, duc de Vendôme (1654–1712), was a French army officer who led successful campaigns in Italy between 1702 and 1705.

3 "French Canada" refers to an area along the St. Lawrence River, stretching for some 250 miles, colonized by France during the sixteenth and seventeenth centuries. It includes what are now the cities of Québec and Montréal.

4 Now the city and port of La Rochelle on the Bay of Biscay in south-western France.

lay, to a Treat on board: She takes my Father's Coach, which she pretended to borrow, and with the innocent *Emilia* goes to the cursed Entertainment, where they gave her Wine with an Infusion of Opium, which soon bereft her of all Sense; then the hellish Fiend left her on board, and set out for *Paris*, where soon after my Father went. There they contrived a Story together to blind the World, pretending *Emilia* was retired into a Monastery near *Paris*; which when I heard, who was sufficiently alarm'd before with her Absence, I posted to *Paris*, searched every Place to find her, and quickly learn'd the fatal Truth: and now having vented my Passion, I consulted my Reason, and resolved to sooth my Father into giving me some Fortune, and then to follow her. Providence, who never fails to punish such enormous Crimes, in a short time gave me the Means of executing this Design. An Uncle of my deceas'd Mother died, and left me a handsome Estate, being a Batchelor, and my Godfather; I immediately sold it, secretly put the money into the *India* Company's[1] hands, taking Bills;[2] and one morning left a Letter for my Father on my Table, and attended with one Servant only went post for *Rochel*, where a Ship lay ready to sail with me to *Canada*, the Company having had an account of the other Ship's safe Arrival at *Quebeck*. The Letter contained words much to this purpose.

My Honoured Lord and Father,

*THAT you may not condemn me unjustly, or be surprized
at my leaving you and my Country so suddenly and
secretly, I leave this to inform you, that I am gone in search
of* Emilia, *whom I have promised to make my Wife, to
repair the inhuman Injury you have done that charming
Maid. If I never return, 'tis the Will of Heaven. Whether
ever I am blest with your Favour, and a Sight of you again,
or not, I shall never cease to honour, respect, and love you as
a Father, and to be your*

Most obedient Son and humble Servant,
Francis Edward, *Count* de Hautville.

---

1 Meaning the East India Company. In the seventeenth and eighteenth
   centuries, a number of nations, among them Britain, France, and the
   Netherlands, gave charters to their own East India Companies. Such
   companies were formed to promote trade with Southeast Asia, but they
   were also agents of European colonization.
2 Before paper currency became a reliable and commonly held form of
   exchange, bills of credit allowed a named person to draw money to a
   specified amount from the issuer's agents, here presumably the French
   East India Company or *La Compagnie française des indes orientales*.

I left *France* before those my Father sent after me could over-take me, and in six Weeks arrived at *Quebeck*, where I soon learn'd where the Villain Captain lodged, who had robb'd me of *Emilia*. I addrest my self to the Governor, and Merchants on whom my Bills were drawn, who all promised to assist me. I obtained an Order from the Governor to secure him, and search his Lodg-ings; but could hear nothing of her. He deny'd the Fact, pleaded Ignorance, so I was forced to let him go, and use my Sword to do my self Justice. I got what Money I could of the Merchants, dis-counting the Bills, secured a Ship to carry me off, and then one Evening dog'd him out of Town with my Servant. So soon as he was at the Fields, I came up to him; and demanded Satisfaction. We drew, fought, and it was my fortune to wound, and disarm him; he beg'd his Life, and confest that he had left *Emilia* at *Panama*,[1] designing so soon as he had dispatched his Affairs at *Quebeck*, to return thither and make her his Mistress, which he had in vain attempted when he had her at Sea; she having threatned him with Death if he offer'd to force her: But now being left in a Widow-Woman's care, where he had placed her, destitute of Money and Friends, he doubted not of her comply-ing with his Desires at his return to her, since she could not subsist in a strange Country without him. I was so provok'd at this, that I could scarce refrain killing him in the Place; however, I govern'd my self, my Servant and I led him to Town, and put him into a Surgeon's Hands: Then I went directly to the Gover-nor's, and acquainted him with what had past, desiring he would go and hear the Villain confess the Truth himself. He went with me, and now all the Place rung of him, so that had he lived he must never have return'd to *Quebeck* again: but in a few Days after I left it, he died of his Wounds; of which a Merchant sent me word to *Panama*, to which place I went with Horses which I hired, and there found the Widow's House, but not *Emilia*. The Woman inform'd me that some Days after the Captain left her, she heard of a *French* Captain's arrival, who was come to trade and bound to *New Mexico*,[2] and with him she was departed thence. I presently embark'd in a small Vessel I hired, and went

---

1 The isthmus of Panama was conquered and settled by Spain in the early sixteenth century and became a major link between Spain's Atlantic and Pacific trade.

2 Not to be confused with the present-day US state, though including much of it, *Nuevo México* was a kingdom of the Spanish empire from the late sixteenth century until 1821.

thither, and found her on board the honest Gentleman's Ship, who had treated her with extraordinary Civility, and design'd to carry her home to *France* with him. What Joy and Transport we both felt at this Meeting, you may imagine. I there marry'd my charming *Emilia*, and resolv'd to return with her home. The Captain was not long before he had dispatched his Affairs here, and then set sail for *Japan*, where he was obliged to deliver Goods; but we had not long past the Straits of *California*,[1] before a Hurricane rose, and our Pilot being unskilful, we ran foul of one of those Islands that lie near Cape *Orientes*;[2] there our Vessel struck, and split to pieces, every one shifted for their selves, my dear *Emilia* was my only Care. I threw my Cloak into the Boat, threw her and my self into it, and fortunately got clear of the Ship before she split, taking only the Captain with us, whom I call'd to me. We had but eight hands aboard of Sailors, and they doubtless all perished in the Sea. The poor Captain, Monsieur *De Bonfoy*, holding the Rudder to steer the Boat, was by a Wave washed over-board and drown'd. We were left to the Mercy of the Winds and Seas, but by Providence preserv'd; for the Boat oversetting, I took *Emilia* on my Back, and seeing my self near this Island, made towards it: but my Strength was not sufficient, had not God caused the Waves to cast me on this Shore. We were both so spent we lay almost senseless for some time: at last we made shift to creep to the Wood, being wet, cold, faint, and hungry; I being bruised, and my Limbs numm'd with lying on the Ground, could not rise, or walk farther; so my dear *Emilia* strove to supply my Wants and her own, and finding my Cloak on the Sands, brought and dry'd it, in which we wrap'd ourselves, and found much comfort: But when God sent you to our Relief, Nature was no longer able to support us, and we were near to dying for want of Food.'

Teresa embrac'd *Emilia*, saying, 'Now I repent not my own Misfortunes in being cast on this Place, since it has preserved you both from perishing; we will chearfully support the Inconveniences of it, till Heaven sends some Vessel to deliver us: come let us try to reach the homely Cottage that must shroud us from the cold Air, and revive you with Food and Firing.' They got to it, and found the poor *Indian* and his Wife ready to receive them: They made a Fire, boil'd them Eggs and Fish, gave them boil'd Rice;

---

1 The Gulf of California, separating what is now the Mexican state of Baja California from the Mexican mainland.

2 Cape Corrientes, a cape off the Pacific coast of west-central Mexico.

and tho they could not converse with, or understand their Language, exprest much Compassion for them. Here they lay this Night much comforted, and *Teresa* much o'erjoy'd that she had such Companions to converse with; conceiving strong Hopes of God's delivering her thence, who had so wonderfully provided Comforts for her in that dismal Place.

CHAP. III.

THE next Morning the poor *Indian* went a fishing; the number of his Guests being now increased, it was necessary to use more diligence than usual to get Food for them. The *Indian* Woman prepared all at home, whilst her Guests walk'd out in search of Fruits and Roots, of which they fail'd not to bring back some, especially Grapes, which were of great use to them. Thus they continued to live, tho very poorly, for some Days.

One Night the Wind blew hard, and it thunder'd as if Nature had fallen into Convulsions, and the World was unjointed. Towards Morning it clear'd up, and *Teresa, Emilia,* and the Count, walk'd out to view the Shore, desirous to see what havock that dreadful Night had made: They found on the Shore several Coffers, Boxes, Pieces of Timber, &c. which shewed some Vessel had been shipwreck'd there. By this time the *Indians* came to them, and the Count help'd them to bring up some of the Chests and Vessels, which they could reach, to Shore.

Mean time the Ladies walk'd on farther, and at some distance *Teresa* perceived a Man floating upon a Chest, which the Waves at length threw on the Shore: His Habit was *Spanish*, very rich; his Shape incomparable; his Hands were clinched on the Chest, and when she took hold on him, she thought him dead. *Emilia* and *Teresa* pitying him, strove to lift him up: But how great was *Teresa's* Surprize, when discovering his Face, she knew him to be the brave Don *Lopez!* a young Gentleman, only Son to the Governor of *Mexico*; a Youth of great Hopes, Quality and Fortune; who had ador'd her from the Moment he first saw her, and one who had made an Impression in her Heart, which she had carefully conceal'd, but could not efface. *My God*, she passionately cry'd, *can I see him perish thus without Regret? Must Don* Lopez *charm the undone* Teresa *no more, nor my Ears hear that pleasing Voice? Help me,* Emilia, *to save, if possible, the Man I esteem above the World.*

By this Time the Water pouring out of his Mouth, his Spirits recover'd, and with a deep Groan he gave Signs of Life. *Teresa* calling for help, the Count and *Indians* came up; they took the Stranger up, and carried him to the Hut; there they warm'd, chafed, and brought him to himself, some Quarts of Water having first been vomited up. And now the *Indian* having discover'd that a Vessel of Rack[1] was amongst the things they had sav'd of the

---

1   Arrack, a spirit typically made in the Indian subcontinent or in southeast Asia from the fermented sap of the cocoa palm or from rice and sugar.

Wreck, ran and fetch'd a Cup made of a Calabash,[1] full of it; which holding above two Quarts, serv'd to revive them all, and mixt with Grape Juice and Water, made excellent Drink for that Day.

And now Don *Lopez* lifting up his Eyes, saw the lovely *Teresa*, who was behind him, supporting his Head with a Concern that had made her forget the discovery she made of her tender Affection for him, to the Standers by. *Blest God!* he cry'd, *do I again see* Teresa? *Is Life restor'd with such a Blessing?* Here he fainted, at which she was so much surpriz'd, that she turn'd pale and swooned. They were in some time both recover'd; then he clasp'd her in his Arms, saying, 'Charming Maid, I have sought you every where, resolving to find you, or die in the Attempt. I no sooner heard of your Disaster, but I procured a Ship, having visited all the Coast of *Peru* and *Canada*. Missing you there, I determined to go to *Japan*, it being the nearest Coast to which you could be drove. I fear'd, indeed, that the cruel Waves had swallow'd you; but not being able to live at *Mexico* without you, I rather chose to range the World, and court Death amongst *Pagans*[2] and *Mahometans*. I design'd to visit the *Holy Land*, and retire to some Desart, and so spend my Days in Fasting, Prayers, and Contemplation: But indulgent Heaven kindly drove me here, and would not let me perish. Now I am happier than Eastern Kings. This Place is as Paradise, where *Teresa*'s Presence makes all things lovely. Say, my good Angel, did you wish me living when you thought me dead? Am I welcome?' *Teresa* much confused, conscious of the discovery she had made of her Passion for him, answer'd: 'Don *Lopez*, I have shewn too much Concern for you, not to explain the Sentiments I have for you: My Thoughts of you are too well discover'd by my Actions.' Here he bow'd, saying, 'I thank thee, gracious Heaven, my Vows are heard: If I return in safety with her to my home, I'll build a Church, and consecrate it to the Honour of our God.' The Count and *Emilia* join'd in congratulating these transported Lovers; and now store of Salt Meat, Bisket, Brandy, Wine, and Sugar, which was cast on shore, being secured, they prepared such a Dinner, as the poor *Indians* had not tasted of some Years.

Don *Lopez* remember'd to ask what was become of the Coffer he was brought to Shore upon, which was not once thought of before,

---

1 A gourd that can be used as a vessel for liquid.
2 Followers of a pantheistic religion. In the early-modern period, the term was used to characterize those beliefs or practices deemed to be savage, primitive, and unenlightened.

saying, *It had much Treasure in it.* 'When I found (said he) how great the Storm was, I caused it to be brought upon Deck. The Ship, tho small, being not loaded, and a good Sailer, held out a long time: At last the Lightning fired the Shrouds: We got the Boat out strait, and had but just time to throw that Chest and our selves into it, before the Ship was all on fire. We saw this Island, and made for it; but the Waves rose so high, the Boat overset near the Shore: We leaped into the Sea, and I threw my self across the Chest, the Wind driving to the Island. At last losing my Breath, I fainted, so the Water enter'd my Mouth, and God's Providence brought me ashore.' They went forthwith, and found the Chest where they left it; but the Tide flowing, had they staid much longer they had lost a great Treasure, for Don *Lopez* had put into it much Gold, Plate, Jewels, and Clothes, designing to return no more home.

And now nothing was wanting to make this Company happy, but a Ship to carry them and the poor *Indians* to *Mexico*; for they were resolved to take them and their Children with them, in Gratitude for the Assistance they had given them. Meantime, to pass away the tedious Hours, they walk'd daily out, and found beyond the Wood a ruinous Pagan Temple, in which were several strange Images, the chief of which represented a Man whose Head was adorned with the Rays of the Sun: It was rudely cut in black Marble, but the Rays were gilded finely. They concluded it to be the Work of some *Chinese* or *Persians*, who had inhabited that Place in antient times. It was a curious Building, and seem'd to be founded upon Vaults. Near this Place were several Pits and Altars where Sacrifices had been kill'd and offer'd. Beyond this Place was a high Hill over which the Ladies did not dare to venture; several times they return'd to this Temple, and still found something more of Antiquity to admire in it. One Morning the Count *de Hautville* and Don *Lopez* walk'd out very early to this Place, resolving to go over the Hill; and entering the ruin'd Temple, to rest before they pursued their walk, they considered it more attentively than ever; and Don *Lopez* observed a Door that went down behind the Altar on which the Image of the Sun was placed: He boldly pull'd it open, saying, *In the Name of God let us enter, and see what this Place contains.* They descended by some Stairs, and enter'd a large Room, where a Lamp was burning before a hideous Image, whose Face was bigger than a *Buphalo*; his Eyes were two Lights like Torches; his Mouth stood open; his Limbs were proportionably large, made of burnish'd Brass; on his Breast was a Lion's Head; his Feet were like a Camel's: He had a Bow and Arrow in his Hands, a Mantle of curious Feathers hung over his right Shoulder:

He stood upon a Crocodile of Stone, whose Jaws seem'd open to devour all that enter'd: Sculls and Jaw-bones, with Locks of clotted Hair, hung up against the Walls of this dreadful Vault, and Skeletons of Cats, Wolves, and Screech-owls: Several Grave-stones were in the Floor. As they enter'd the Bones began to rattle, the Image shook, the Crocodile's teeth gnasht, and distant Thunder seem'd to roar. The Christian Heroes, tho surprized, went not back, but falling on their Knees, besought God to assist and keep them. As they pray'd the Lightning flash'd from the Image, the Graves open'd, and Voices were heard in the *Chinese* Language, which they understood not. At last the Lion's Mouth open'd in the Image's Breast, and a Voice pronounced these Words in *French:* 'Christians, you have conquer'd. Ador'd by Pagan *Indians*, long have I been worshipped here, and human Sacrifices offer'd to this hideous Idol, by which I was honoured: But now my Power is taken from me; the God you serve has silenced me. Depart; thro this Room you'll find a Way leads under the great Hill, by antient *Persians* made: There are Christians will assist you to depart from this sad Place and Isle. Avoid the *Indian* Shore, and Men. It will be long e'er you will see your native Country, and Friends again. My fatal Hour is come, and I am henceforth dumb.' Here the Image fell in Pieces, the Graves shut, the Lamps in its Eyes went out; and by the Light of the Lamp before it they departed, full of Wonder, and past thro another Door which led to a long passage, at the end of which they found themselves on the other side the Hill, in an open Country; there they saw the open Sea, and on the Coast a small Stone Building, which coming nearer to, they found to be a House. At the Door of it stood a venerable Man in a *Persian* Dress: He observed them as one amaz'd; when they came near, he came to meet them, and speaking *Spanish*, ask'd whence they came, and who they were: Don *Lopez* inform'd him. He embrac'd him, saying, *Welcome Christians, in God's Name; enter, and refresh your selves.* They came in and found a House neat, and well furnish'd, with Carpets, Porcelane, Quilts, Painting, Screens, and such Furniture as the *Persians* of Distinction use; with three well-drest Slaves, who brought Wine, Sherbet,[1] and Fowl, and boil'd Rice. Being seated with much Ceremony, the *Persian* stay'd not to be intreated, but said, *Eat, Gentlemen, and I will tell you how I came to this Place, and why I dwell here.* They bowed, and respectfully kept silence, much desiring to know who he was, which he thus inform'd them of.

---

1 A cooling drink made of fruit juice and sweetened water.

CHAP. IV.

'I WAS born in *Persia*, my Father was a general in the Emperor's Service. I was made a Captain of his Guard at 20 Years of Age, much esteem'd by him, and in great Favour, and knew no greater Happiness than to be Great, or Religion but Mahometanism: I had a noble House and a Seraglio,[1] where five Women of great Beauty serv'd my Pleasures, and sweeten'd all those Hours that I dedicated to my Diversions. It happen'd that a *Turkish* Captain brought some Slaves to sell at *Ispahan*;[2] amongst which was a *Spanish* Girl, a Virgin of but 13 Years of Age, fair as Nature ever made: Her Complexion exceeded Art, her Eyes were dark blue, her Hair light brown, her Features soft and charming; she had an Air so innocent, so modest, so engaging, that she attracted the Eyes of all that past along: It was my Fortune to be going to the Palace that way: I saw her, and stopping to admire her Beauty, I presently ask'd the Price of that sweet Girl; the Captain ask'd me a hundred Crowns: I paid him down the Money, and sent one of my Slaves home with her. It is impossible to describe to you how uneasy I was to go home; my Impatience was so great, that I thought each Hour a Year whilst the Emperor detain'd me. He was going to ride in the *Almaidan*,[3] which would have obliged me to stay with him all Day; I therefore feign'd a sudden Indisposition, and beg'd leave to retire; he consented, and I flew to my charming Slave: The Eunuch that kept my Women had placed her in a Chamber to wait my Commands. I hastily ask'd for her; they told me Dinner waited: But I neglected eating, and entring the Chamber, found the charming *Maria*, for that was her Name, seated upon a Couch, pale as Death, her Head gently reclining on her lovely Hand, her Face all bathed in Tears. She rose at my coming up to her; I took her in my Arms with a Transport I had never known before, and bid the Eunuch bring in Wine and Meat, and I would eat here. He withdrew: I kist, embrac'd, and

---

1 A word of Italian derivation denoting the women's quarters in a Muslim household. For Europeans, the word was synonymous with *harem*, understood to mean a place where the wives or concubines of a polygamous man were kept.

2 Isfahan, a major city in Iran around 250 miles south of Tehran. Under the Safavid dynasty (1501–1736) it became one of the largest cities in the world, with a population of perhaps half a million inhabitants, acting as a significant cultural, commercial, and administrative centre.

3 Possibly Aubin's understanding of the Arabic word also transliterated as al meydān, the square or marketplace.

shew'd her all the most tender Marks of Esteem: she trembled, wept, look'd down, and sigh'd as if her Heart would break. Dinner brought in I courted her to eat and drink, but she refus'd. Unable to delay my Bliss, I took her by the Hand, led her into the Bed-Chamber; but then she fell upon her Knees, still silent, not answering one Word, and shew'd such Fear and Grief, that I was shock'd; my Blood cool'd, and I resolv'd to court her to my Arms, and stay till she would make me happy. I took her up, wip'd away her Tears, and ask'd her in *Spanish*, why she treated me so cruelly? having ask'd what Nation she was of, when I bought her. "You are, *said she*, an odious Mahometan, and I a Christian: I am your Slave, by Heaven's Permission; but my Soul is free, and can't consent to such a hateful Deed. Leave me or kill me; for I prefer Death to a disgraceful Life. Force me, and I'll hate you, loath you, ruine your Joys, and fly you with Scorn and Coldness: but spare my Virtue. Oh! spare my Shame, and I'll adore you, do any thing that you command." In short she melted my Soul; I treated her as if I had been her Slave, and used her so, that she promised if I would turn Christian, she would yield to be my Wife. In few Days the Emperor was inform'd what a beautiful Virgin I had purchased: He ask'd me gently, "*Tanganor*, may I not see the fair *Spanish* Girl you have at home? Pray bring her to me this Day: I have heard much of her." I remain'd silent, as one Thunderstruck for some time; at last recovering, "My mighty Lord, said I, she's not what Fame reports, but I will fetch her to you." I departed from Court that Moment so distracted, I knew not what Course to take; I acquainted *Maria* with what happen'd, who appear'd as disorder'd as I: I resolved not to part with her, yet dared not keep her: The Emperor was not to be trifled withal: If he were disobliged, Death and Ruin must follow. Whilst we were debating, my Eunuch enter'd the Room trembling; "My Lord, *said he*, the Emperor has sent *Bendarius* his chief Eunuch with a Guard to demand the fair Slave." E'er he had finish'd the Eunuch enter'd, and taking her by the Hand, who was all in tears, "Weep not, fair Virgin, *said he*, for such I hope you are; an Emperor's Bed courts your Acceptance; you are too fair for any Subject to possess." He gave her no time to reply, but took her away in a Sedan,[1] leaving me in the utmost Distraction and Despair.

I knew my Ruin was decreed, and was too well satisfy'd of *Maria*'s Virtue, to believe that she would yield to the Emperor, without such Reluctance as would inform him she loved me; and

---

1 A closed vehicle for one person, carried on poles by two bearers.

then my Death was certain: I therefore resolved to convey into some secret Place what Money, Jewels, and Plate I could; and disguising my self, retire to some Place where I might lie conceal'd. *Achmet*, my Eunuch, generously offer'd to attend, and conduct me to his Mother's House, which was far from *Ispahan*, near Mount *Taurus*.[1] I accepted willingly his Offer, and loading two Horses with what was most valuable, departed that Night, and travelling all Night and the next Day, got clear of all pursuit.

So soon as I was arriv'd at Mount *Taurus*, I black'd my Face and Hands, and changed my Dress for that of a Slave; bury'd my Treasure, and resolv'd to continue here till *Achmet* return'd to *Ispahan*, and learn'd what *Maria*'s Fate was; charging him to procure a sight of her, if possible, and to return and tell me; resolving if she had yielded, and was content, to cross the Mountain, and retire to the Desarts, and there spend my Days.

Achmet departed, and it was many Days before he return'd; during which you may imagine the anxious Thoughts that possest my Soul: but just God, how great was my Surprize when I saw him enter the House with *Maria* in his Hand! She had a Veil on, which I throwing up to salute her, saw that she was blind. "My Lord, *said she*, start not at the sight, my Eyes are sacrificed to Virtue, with the loss of them I have procured your Happiness; I would have done more, had Christianity permitted, and would have died, but I have cheaply bought my Repose with the Loss of one Sense." "Thou glorious Woman, *said I, clasping her in my Arms*, what Words can express my Wonder, and Affection? Thy Virtues shine more than thy lovely Eyes did, and shall procure thee an immortal Name." I led her into my homely Chamber, refresht her with Wine, and Food, and there she told me what had befallen her. "I was, *said she*, brought to a noble Apartment, which you, no doubt, have seen in the Palace: There the Eunuch brought two Female Slaves to me, with a Habit suiting a Queen, and departed. The Maids drest me, whilst my Soul was tortured with a thousand Apprehensions. I fancy'd my self preparing to be sacrificed, and almost wished I had not been a Christian. When they had deck'd me as they pleased, they withdrew; and soon after the Emperor came in, a Man whose Person and Mien was noble and agreeable. He gazed upon me some time, then took a

---

1   The Taurus mountains run parallel to the Mediterranean coast of present-day Turkey for around 350 miles. Even supposing that Achmet's mother's house was on the eastern edge of the mountain range, the distance to Isfahan would be close to a thousand miles.

Ring of great Price from his Finger, put it upon mine, and said in *Spanish*, 'Fair *Maria*, you are worthy a Monarch's Bed: Fame has done you wrong, and *Tanganor* was a Villain to his Prince and you. I'll make you Mistress of Queens, and shew you what a *Persian* Monarch can bestow on her he loves. Come to my Arms, and let your Soul welcome mine.' Here he embraced, and almost stifled me with Kisses; I gently strove to loose my self, and falling down at his Feet with Tears, beg'd to be heard: 'My mighty Lord, *said I*, look not upon me with Desire, I am unworthy you, I am a wretched Maid, torn from my Friends and Country, by a Villain, a Robber, and by his means now made a Slave; but I'm a Christian, and a Virgin, and e'er I'll yield to your desires will die. *Tanganor* is by promise my Husband, he has vow'd to be a Christian, and to marry me; Oh! let your Bounty give me back and make me happy, or resolve to see me die here at your feet: I will be only his, and never yield to gratify another.' 'Fond Maid, *said he*, I've heard too much, all that my Slaves possess is mine, and you are, and shall be so; your Vertue charms me more than your Eyes. Now I am resolved never to part with you: Force must I find procure me now what your Consent shall afterwards secure me of.' Here he took me in his Arms, and carry'd me to a rich Bed, on which he threw me. My Soul was shocked at this, and so surprized, I soon resolved what to do; 'My Eyes shall never see my Shame, *said I*, nor more inflame Mankind: These I offer up to Vertue, and they shall weep no more in ought but Blood.' At these Words I tore my Eyeballs out, and threw them at him. I saw no more, but heard him say, '*Ah cruel maid, what have you done? Tanganor*, you are happy: Had I been so fortunate to be beloved like you, I had been more than mortal. *Maria*, I would give all *Persia* to restore your Sight: By *Mahomet* you are more than Woman, and I will never presume to sue again for what you must deny. Tell me what I shall do to expiate my Crime.' 'Restore me to my Lord, I beg only that grace, *said I*, and I will pray for you with my last Breath.' He answer'd, 'I will resign you to my Rival; but 'tis hard. Blind as you are, you charm me, and to keep my Word I must not view your Face again; go, and take care I never see you, nor *Tanganor* more, lest I forget my Promise, and relapse.' Here he call'd *Bendarius*, kist my Hands, on which I felt his falling Tears, and left me. I was carry'd strait back to your House, where *Achmet* found me sick of a Fever, which recovering I came with him; and now am happy, if you keep your Faith with me." Thus *Maria* finish'd her sad Story; and after this I need not tell you I adored her, and there sought, and found a Christian

Monk who first baptized me, and then marry'd us. I then considered what Course it was best for us to steer; and resolved to retire with her into this Island on this side where the *Japanese* Vessels often call for fresh Water. I carry'd her through the great *Mogul's* Dominions[1] down to *Goa*,[2] and there we took Ship for this Island, where my Slaves which I brought with me repair'd and fitted up this House. Here I have now lived fifteen Years, and have three Children by my dear *Maria*, who keeps much in her Chamber, because of her being blind. Once a Year we receive Letters from my Friends, and Returns from my Estate of Fruits, Spices, Clothes, and what is wanting. The Emperor never enquired more after me, nor molested my House or Friends; my Brother manages, and lives upon my Estate. And thus, Gentlemen, I have related to you my unfortunate Life; and if I can assist you, command me. The Ship we expect soon, it shall carry you where you please.' They return'd him many thanks, and he desired them to bring the Ladies. 'I have, *said he*, a Priest, my Chaplain in the House, whom I brought from *Goa* with me, he shall supply your spiritual Wants, and my dear *Maria* shall with Joy entertain the Ladies. My House is large enough to receive you all, and it will be a great Happiness for us to be all together: I have often wonder'd there were no Inhabitants to be seen when I have walk'd over the Hill, but never thought it worth while to search farther.' Don *Lopez* and the Count *de Hautville* took leave, being impatient to inform *Teresa* and *Emilia* of the strange discoveries they had made, and promised to return to the noble *Tanganor's* the next Morning.

---

1 The successive heads of the Muslim dynasty founded by Zahīr-ud-Dīn Muḥammad Bābur (1483–1530) were frequently styled "the great [or grand] mogul." Between 1526 and 1724 the Mogul empire grew to include most of the Indian subcontinent and territories in modern Afghanistan.

2 An estuarine island on the Mandovi river, a port, and now a state on the southwestern coast of India. Goa was under Portuguese colonial rule from 1510 to 1961.

CHAP. V.

IT was Noon before Don *Lopez* and the Count reached the Cottage, where they found the Ladies, to whom they related all the surprizing Adventures they had met with. 'And now, my charming *Teresa*, (said Don *Lopez*) we may quit this dismal Place; Providence has directed us to a better, where we shall have Company and Entertainment suiting our Desires and Wants. And you, (said he to the poor *Indians*) our generous Hosts, shall be receiv'd, and if you like of it, entertain'd at ease, or return to your own Country in that Ship that will, I hope, carry you to *Japan*, and us to *Mexico*.' An universal Joy now spread it self thro this little Family; Dinner was got ready, and nothing spared of what Provisions they had got. The poor *Indian* got out his Canoe in the Evening, to put aboard it what Wine, Brandy and Salt Meat they had left. They lay down at Night to sleep, but Don *Lopez* slept not at all; his Soul was transported, having nothing in view but the Possession of his dear *Teresa*: He knew a Christian Priest was at *Tanganor*'s, and resolved to press her to make him happy. At break of Day they all rose, and set out for *Tanganor*'s; the poor *Indian* and her Children follow'd, loaden with the mean Furniture their Cottage afforded; which they could not consent to leave behind them. Don *Lopez* and the Count empty'd the rich Chest that belong'd to Don *Lopez*, and fearing to venture it in the Canoe, carry'd all the Plate, Money, and Clothes that were in it, with them, the Ladies assisting. In some Hours, resting often in the way, they arrived at *Tanganor*'s, who receiv'd them courteously, with Father *Augustine*, his Chaplain, a Man whose humble Appearance, and affable Behaviour spoke his Virtues; he embraced, and welcomed them with great Tenderness, and taking the Ladies by the hand, said, 'Come, my Children, I will lead you to a Lady, who tho blind, shall welcome you; and one whose Vertues you may be proud to imitate.' *Tanganor* conducting the Gentlemen, they all went to his Lady's Apartment, whom they found sitting in a Chair with her three Children seated on little Stools by her: Her Son who was then about eight Years old, was reading a holy Meditation for the Morning; whilst the two little Girls, *Maria* and *Leonora*, were at work. *Tanganor* inform'd her of the Ladies being there, whose Story he had told her the Night before. She rose to salute them, saying, 'Ladies, excuse me, if I pay respect to the younger first, since I cannot see you. My Soul rejoices at the arrival of such Company; tho' I cannot see the Light, yet I can relish the Charms of Conversation.' Here *Teresa* and *Emilia* embraced her, admiring her Beauty, which could not be altogether eclipsed by the black Ribbon that cover'd her Eye-lids; her Shape, her Features and Complexion, were incomparable. 'Madam, said *Teresa*, I wonder not that an Eastern Monarch adored you; you are still so lovely, that your Lord may justly account himself supremely happy in the possession of such a Wife. The want of Sight adds to your Charms, and causes us to love and admire you, even before we converse with you.' *Emilia* join'd in her Praises; and, in fine, the Lady put an end to the Discourse, by begging them to accept of a Breakfast with her, which was brought in. They past the Day with much Pleasure: In the Evening, Don *Lopez*, who had privately acquainted Father *Augustine* with his Design, taking *Teresa* by the Hand, led her aside into a Room, where he thus addrest himself to her: 'Charming *Teresa*, God has been pleased to preserve and bring us together, in a wonderful manner; I know that you are not insensible or ignorant of my Passion for you, nay I even hope that you love me; do not longer, charming Maid, defer to make me happy. Here is a Priest to join us; give to my Arms and Care, that Person that my Soul adores and loves above all earthly things. 'Tis I must guard and carry you to *Mexico* again. Tho you are very young, yet you are of Years to marry. Fate has decreed you mine, keep me no longer languishing; but crown my Hopes, and yield to Heaven's Will, who brought me safely to you.' Here he embraced her tenderly; she blush'd and answer'd, 'Don *Lopez*, you shall be happy. Tho with much confusion I consent to make you Master of *Teresa's* Heart and Hand, do as you please: If we must perish on the Sea, or wander in strange Lands, 'tis better we should be marry'd, and my Honour so secured, than to be still but Friends. I own your Merit, and confess I love you.' He claspt her in his Arms transported, led her to the Priest, who that joyful Night perform'd the Ceremony, making Don *Lopez* blest as Man could be. And now for some Days they past the time in Pleasure, *Tanganor* diverted them with Hunting, Fishing, and shew'd 'em many curious Caves, and Pagan Oratories which yet remain'd on the Island. At last the Ship arrived from *Japan* bringing much Goods, as rich *Persia* Silks, Cotton, Linen, Spices, Fruit, Sugar, Tea, Chocolate, Liquors, live Fowls of several kinds for breed, tame Beasts, and all things wanting. *Tanganor* with these treated and made Presents to his Guests of what they wanted: And the Ship being to return to *Japan*, he proposed to them what to do. They resolved to go for *Mexico* with the Ship, which being now unloaded, might easily go thither before it returned to *Japan*; so taking their

Leaves, the Count and Don *Lopez*, with their Wives, departed, leaving the poor *Indians*, who chose to live with *Tanganor*. The Wind sitting fair they soon arrived at *Mexico*, where they found the Governor, Don *Lopez*'s Father, gone for *Spain*, being recall'd, and Don *Sancho de Avilla*, *Teresa*'s Father, they found very sick; her Loss having thrown him into a deep Melancholy, and lingring Fever, of which he never perfectly recovered, but in less than a Year's time died, leaving a vast Estate to his Daughter *Teresa*. In short time after, the Governor being gone, his Son Don *Lopez* resolved to go home to *Spain*, in order to which he sold off all his Effects, and Lands, taking Bills on Merchants at *Barcelona*; and with *Teresa*, the Count *de Hautville*, and *Emilia* who desired to accompany him, designing to go to *France* from *Spain*, went on board a *Spanish* Ship with much Riches, and set sail for *Spain*. They had good Weather and a prosperous Voyage many days, but when they came near the Entrance of the Straits of *Gibraltar*, the Wind began to blow hard, and drove them on the Coast of *Barbary*. Here two Pirates of *Algiers* came up with them, and soon gave them to understand who they were, by firing at them, and summoning them to surrender; they made all the Defence they were able, but, alas! the Ship was heavy laden, their Hands and Guns few: howsoever, the Captain was very brave, and Don *Lopez* and the Count *de Hautville* assisting, they resisted the *Turks*, till such time as the grapling Irons having hold of the Vessel the cruel Infidels boarded it, and enter'd in such numbers as obliged the poor Christians to retire into the great Cabin, which the *Turks* broke into Sword in hand. The Captain was kill'd before upon the Deck, both the young Lords wounded, the Seamen mostly dead, or dying, so that none were left but the two helpless Ladies, and their wounded Husbands, whom they held bleeding in their Arms, and a poor Boy who stood weeping by. The poor affrighted Ladies fell on their Knees, imploring the Infidels pity: their Beauty pleaded more than all they could say in their favour. The *Turkish* Captains raised them from the ground, gazing on their charming Faces; and having given orders to their Men to plunder the Ship of what was most valuable, and bring her into *Algiers*, they order'd them and their Husbands to be brought on board one of their Ships, where *Achmet Barbarosa*[1] who com-

---

1 Aubin borrows the name "Barbarosa" from that given by Europeans to three brothers who carried out highly successful raids on Spanish and papal vessels in the early sixteenth century and were instrumental in wresting control of the North African coast from Spain.

manded the biggest received them, ordering the Lords Wounds to be drest by his Surgeon; and entertain'd the Ladies with much Civility, and seeming Compassion. *Teresa* was big with Child, and so disorder'd with the Fright, that Don *Lopez* was in the utmost Concern for her.

In few Hours they landed at *Algiers*, and were conducted to *Barbarosa*'s House together, and lodged in an Apartment, where he left them to go to the Governor of *Algiers*, to acquaint him with the rich Prize he had taken, and to offer him what share he pleased of the Slaves and Plunder. Our unfortunate Travellers thus left alone, Don *Lopez* was the first who broke the melancholy Silence, that till then reigned amongst them. 'Charming *Teresa*, said he, my Joy, my Love, my All, soon we shall be parted; all my Hopes of Happiness are ended; your Youth and Beauty now will cost my Life and your Repose; you will be ravished from me by some powerful Infidel, who will adore your Charms, and force you to his curst Embraces.' *Teresa*, drown'd in Tears, fell on his Neck, and could not speak. Then the Count, whom loss of Blood had render'd faint, and scarce able to speak, looked on *Emilia*; 'My Dear, said he, do you hear this unmov'd, what may your wretched Husband hope? Can you consent, and live another's?' 'No, my dear Lord, said she, you know me better; my Soul is prepared for all Events, and I will die rather than live a Vassal to a vile *Mahommetan*'s unlawful Lust.' 'And so will I, answer'd the reviving *Teresa*. Fear nothing, brave *Emilia*, we'll go together, trusting in that God who is able to preserve our Souls and Bodies. Slaves we are doubtless doom'd to be, but our Minds can't be confined; our Lives must not end with our own Hands, but may resist all sinful Acts till Life and Sense be lost.'

At these words a Servant enter'd the Room, a Renegado[1] *Spaniard*, wicked as Hell, and one who renouncing Christianity, had endear'd himself to the Governor of *Algiers*, and was by him made rich, and used by him for his beastly Pleasure:[2] he told the Ladies in *Spanish*, they must go with him to the Governor; 'and you, Gentlemen, said he, must prepare to go in a Litter[3] that will presently be here, to carry you to his Country Seat, where you

---

1 A person who has renounced their faith, especially a Christian who converts to Islam.

2 The association of sodomy and homosexuality with Islamic nations was widespread and long-lasting. As Nabil Matar points out, "Nearly every travel or captivity account includes references to Muslim sodomy" (112).

3 A bed or seat enclosed by curtains and carried by men or animals.

may recover your Health, and write to your Friends to send what Ransom shall be required for you.' At these Words, the brave Don *Lopez* rose, and clasping *Teresa* in his Arms, reply'd, 'Vile Slave, depart before these Hands stop your damned Voice, and rend you in pieces: I will die, Apostate Villain, before I will part with her; my Arms shall grasp her even in Death, and bless the Hand that kills us together.' The Count *de Hautville* stood before *Emilia*; they had no Swords or Arms of any kind to defend themselves. The Slave, as if amazed, departed the Room, shutting the Door fast after him, but soon return'd with a Band of Soldiers, who rushing in, seized the Ladies and Lords, giving them no time to speak to one another. They led, or rather drag'd, *Teresa* and *Emilia* through the Streets to the Governor's Palace, and there secured them; their Arms pinion'd, they tyed them to two Pillars in the Hall, and so retired to the Gate. Mean time the Lords were bound hand and foot, thrown into a Court, and drove to a Country-House of the Governor's, forty miles from the City; there they were carry'd into a spacious Room, and chain'd to the Floor by the Leg; a Mattress and Quilts lay there upon the Boards, on which they might lie down. Here they had Food and Wine brought them, for the *Turks* guessed by the vast Treasure they found in the Ship, and their Habit, that they were Persons of Quality, and therefore fear'd to lose their Ransoms[1] if they kill'd or starved them. They refused to eat two Days, but the third, Hunger compell'd them to it. Thus they remain'd some Days, in the most disconsolate Condition that ever Men were in; where we must leave them to enquire what became of *Teresa*, and *Emilia*.

The Renegado *Roderigo* giving an account to the Governor of what was past, and of the Ladies Arrival, he soon enter'd the Hall with Captain *Barbarosa*, to whom he had promised to give her he least liked; but he beheld them with Admiration, seem'd divided in himself, not knowing which to chuse. He was a Man of excellent Shape and Stature, his Mien great and majestick, his Vest and Tunick were made of Cloth of Gold, his Turbant glitter'd with Jewels, Diamonds, Rubies, and Emeralds, which seem'd to emulate each other; in fine, he was not much above thirty, and was one of the most beautiful and accomplish'd Men of his

---

1   Enslaving people for ransom was "highly profitable" (Davis 106). In Spain and France, the Trinitarian and Mercedarian orders developed expertise in redeeming Christian captives of Islamic powers, while in Protestant states the raising of ransom money was less well organized. England in particular "had a reputation in Barbary for being more miserly than other states in its response to its captives" (Colley 53).

Nation, which I mention out of Respect to those unfortunate Ladies, whose Vertues are to be the more admired in resisting the passionate Sollicitations of such a Man. *Teresa*'s Youth, and the charming Innocence that blooms in Virgins Faces at fourteen, which she had not lost by being a Wife wonderfully struck him; Grief added to her Charms, her downcast Eyes received new Fires when lifted up. He gazed upon her with such Transport, that had not the Captain who was inflamed with her Beauty reminded him of *Emilia*, he had fixt on *Teresa*; but turning to the other he was doubly wounded: Her riper Charms, with the heroick Soul that sparkled in her Eyes, a second time inflamed his Soul, and he could part with neither. '*Barbarosa*, said he, I must have both these lovely Women, name the Price, and make some other Choice, these must be mine.' The Captain murmur'd, but seeing he was obstinate, he dared not tempt his Fate, but told him they were at his Service. The Governor pleased, strait order'd him two hundred Pieces of Gold; so he departed horribly vexed, and meditating Revenge. Then the Governor order'd the Ladies to be unbound, and placed in two different Chambers, with Slaves to watch and attend them. Here the Trunks of rich Habits they had brought from *Mexico*, were, to their great Surprize, brought and presented to them; nothing being taken from them by the Governor's order.

Nothing was more dreadful to these Ladies than this Separation; they both refused to eat or drink, and by Night were so faint, that they were scarce able to stand. About ten a Clock in the Evening a Supper was brought into *Teresa*'s Chamber; and soon after the Governor enter'd, the Renegado waiting on him, retired to the door, which he shut, and stood without: The Governor seeing her look pale as Death, sitting unmoved, approached her with much Tenderness, fearing she had taken up some fatal Resolution to destroy her self: He kiss'd her Hands, kneeled at her Feet, and intreated her to rise and eat. He courted her with all the Eloquence Love can inspire, to which she gave no Answer but Sighs and Tears; at last she look'd upon him earnestly: 'Governor, said she, you plead in vain; I'm deaf to all Intreaties, and can never yield to gratify you. I am marry'd and with Child by a noble Husband, whom I am bound to love, and for whom I will preserve my Person, nor will I ever consent to your Desires; nor will I ever eat again, till you have freed me from this Place: Resolve therefore to see me die, or generously set me at Liberty. Do not attempt to force me, lest I do some dreadful Deed, and fill your Soul with endless Remorse.' Here she fell at his Feet, and let fall a shower of tears, then fainted. This touch'd his Soul, and made him relent; tho a *Mahometan*, he was generous, and compassionate. He took her in his Arms, pour'd Wine into her Mouth, and with much difficulty brought her to Life again. Then she renew'd her Complaints; to which he reply'd, 'Charming, matchless Woman, where Virtue, Beauty, Wit, and every Grace conspires to captivate my Soul! too happy he who calls you his. Fly not from me to Death; but give me leave to wait upon, and merit your Esteem, by all a Lover can perform. I'll never use base Force, but Prayers and Sighs shall thaw your Breast, and *Selim* will be your eternal Slave. To prove I'm so, this Night I'll leave you to Repose, and not presume to urge you farther.' He kist her Hand, and, opening a Door, withdrew into another Room. Then a Black-amore Maid enter'd, and folding down the Bed, made Signs to her to undress; which she fearing to do, tho in great want of Sleep, refused, and only lay down upon it. The Maid left a Candle burning, and withdrew, shutting the door after her. Soon after *Teresa* heard *Emilia*'s Voice in the next Room, with *Selim*; and hearkening, heard him say, 'Are you then cruel like *Teresa*? You are more experienced and more ripe for Joy: Come, come, trifle not with me; I'm resolved to possess you, and will not be deny'd.' She heard a Noise, and then *Emilia* said, 'Villain, I fear you not, I'll sacrifice you to preserve my Vertue; die Infidel, and tell your blas-phemous Prophet, when you come to Hell, a Christian spilt your Blood.' Then she heard a dismal Groan, and soon after *Emilia* enter'd the Chamber, with a look that spoke the Terrors of her Mind, and the strange Deed her Hands had done. She had *Selim*'s Habit on, and in her Hand a Woman-Slave, 'Disguise your self in this, *said she*, my dear *Teresa*, and follow me; with this I'll free us both or die.' Here she drew forth a bloody Dagger *Selim* wore. *Teresa* trembling put the Habit on, and follow'd her: They past thro the Chamber *Emilia* came out of, for *Teresa*'s Chamber-Door was lock'd, and there she saw *Selim* lying on the Bed, wel-tering in his Blood. They found another Door; opening which, they descended a pair of Back-stairs, and enter'd a Garden, in which the Renegado *Roderigo* was diverting himself with one of his Master's fair Slaves: He started, and came boldly up to them, doubtless suspecting something; but *Emilia* stabbing him, pre-vented any Noise; the Woman he was sporting with, having retired the Moment they appear'd. They forced open the Garden-gate, and not knowing where to go, hasted out of the Town, nor stop'd till they had reached the Fields. Here they wander'd, ready to die for want of Food and Rest. At last unable to go farther, they sat down under a Tree in a Wood, and consulted what to do; they supposed they should be pursued, and if taken, surely put to death. *Teresa*, whose Courage was not equal to *Emilia*'s, was almost ready to despair; and she seem'd so dispirited, that *Emilia* used all her Eloquence to comfort her. 'My dear Friend, *said she*, look up to Heav'n that never fails to succour the distrest: The God that this Day strengthen'd my feeble Arm to deliver us, will, I doubt not, send us Help. Death is the worst that can befall us, and that is only what we are born to suffer, and what no human Power can shield us from; nay, what we ought to meet with Joy, since we have an eternal State in view, that shall compensate for all the miseries we suffer here. Since no Guilt does wound our Consciences, we need not fear to die, or dread all our inhuman Enemies can inflict upon us. Come chear up, and strive to go yet farther from that hateful City, which we are fled from; perhaps some hospitable Cottage may receive and shelter us.' At these Words *Teresa* cast a dying look upon her. 'Alas, *said she*, my dear, my Faith is stronger than my Body, tho not so great as yours; I cannot rise, my trembling Limbs are now unable to bear my Weight; and if no help be sent us soon, then I must lay down the tedious burden of Life in this sad Place, and leave you.' Here she fainted. At this Instant *Emilia* heard a rustling amongst the Trees, and looking behind her, saw a young Man of about 20 Years of Age, whose handsome Face and Shape surprized her; he had on the Habit of a Slave; he came down from the Tree they were sitting under; he approached her with much Respect, and in *French*, which he had heard them converse in. He was by Birth a *Venetian*, as the sequel of this History will inform us, and addrest himself to her in this manner: 'Madam, be not surprized that I have overheard you: I am joyful to tell you, it is in my power to serve you. I am Servant to a Widow-Woman who lives not far from this Place, to whose Husband it was my good Fortune to be sold; she by my means has embraced the Christian Faith, tho we keep it a Secret: She gets her living, and mine, by making Turbants and Embroidery, which I carry home to our Customers, and the Shops. We live very comfortably, and I am certain if you will give me leave to conduct you to her, she will receive you kindly, for she is a Person of great Goodness.' *Emilia* gladly accepted his Offer, and they lifting up *Teresa*, who was scarce alive, led her along to the Widow's House, which was just behind the Wood. The Slave, whose Name was *Antonio*, gave his Mistress a brief account of their Condition: She embraced and welcomed them, bringing out Meat and Drink; with which being much refresh'd, they related to her the cause and manner of their Escape from the City; upon which she advised them to change their Clothes, since they would surely discover them: But when *Emilia* came to pull off her Turbant and Vest, she was amazed to see the rich Jewels it was adorn'd with: In the pocket of the Vest she found 100 Sultana's[1] of Gold, the Buttons were Diamonds. They blest God for this Treasure, which would enable them to live here, and procure them means to escape hence together. They immediately cut the Clothes in pieces, which served to make the Caps of the Turbants; and the Jewels they rip'd off, and hid in a Box in the Ground, resolving *Antonio* should dispose of a few of them at a time, as they had occasion, to the *Jews*,[2] many of whom the Widow-woman work'd for in Embroidery, particularly in rich Belts which they traded with to *Spain* and other Parts of *Europe*. The good Widow, whose Name was *Seraja*, brought them mean *Turkish* Habits, such as she wore, saying, 'Ladies, you must now conceal your Quality and Beauty with this homely dressing, and pass for young Maids whom I have bought to assist me in my work.' *Teresa*, who was much joy'd at this unexpected good fortune, reply'd, embracing her, 'I will assist you, *said she*, in working with all my Heart; we both know how to use our Needles.' A Bed was laid for them in *Seraja*'s Chamber after the *Turkish* manner, that is, a Carpet was spread upon the Floor, on which were laid a Quilt, Blankets, Sheets, and Coverlids: And now had they known what was become of their Lords, they had been tolerably easy. *Antonio* set out for the City the next Morning to learn what News he could, and return'd at Night with this Account: 'I am, *said he*, acquainted with a Christian Boy, who is Slave to the Governor: I walk'd two or three times before the House to watch his coming out; at last I saw him come sweating up the Street with a Surgeon; I wink'd upon him as he past by, he return'd the Sign and enter'd: I waited not long, before he came out again: "*Lorenzo*, said I, can't we drink a dish of Coffee together this Morning? I am obliged to wait for some Mony, one of my Mistress's Customers owes her, and therefore have an Hour to spare; which if you can, we will pass together." "Lord, *said he*, our House is all in Confusion; my Master bought two

---

1 Sultanines, or sultaneens, formerly Turkish gold coins.
2 Jewish settlements in North Africa date back at least as far as the Roman period, but the number of Jews living in the region increased greatly as they were expelled from Spain, Portugal, and Sicily during the early years of the Spanish Inquisition (1478–1834).

Christian Women yesterday, one of whom has this Night wounded him cruelly, and left him weltering in his Blood upon the Bed; our Renegado *Roderigo* they have likewise kill'd, as we suppose, for we found him dead in the Garden, and they are escaped. Hearing some dismal Groans in the Night, I enter'd the Room, and found my Master in this condition; so I raised my Fellow-Servants, and we have brought him back to Life, and the Surgeon has some hopes of his recovery. We inform'd him the Women were fled, but he commanded us to make no search after them. He praised their Virtue, and seem'd to pity them, saying, he wish'd their Happiness, and commended their Courage." I ask'd *Lorenzo* whom these Women belong'd to? He said, he did not know. So I suppose none but *Roderigo* knew any thing of your Lords.' Thus ended *Antonio*.

Here the Ladies remain'd undisturb'd seven Months, never stirring abroad but in the dusk of the Evenings, when they walk'd only into the Wood. Mean time *Antonio* often enquired of *Lorenzo* for News, but heard none. Several Ships sail'd for *Europe* in this time; but the Ladies resolved not to leave *Barbary*, till they heard of their Husbands. We shall therefore leave them at the Widow's, and proceed to give an Account of what befel the unfortunate Don *Lopez*, and the Count *de Hautville*.

CHAP. VI.

THE two Lords being chain'd, as has been before recited, had no hopes of getting their Liberty: They had writ, the one to *France*, the other to *Spain*, to their Friends, of whom they knew not who might be living: but alas! the Sum demanded was very great; and the time they must wait, before it was possible for them to receive any answer from either of those Places, so long, that there were little hopes of their living to receive it. But these Considerations were nothing grievous to them, in respect of those relating to *Emilia* and *Teresa*; their Ignorance of their Condition, and distracting Apprehensions of their Ruin, almost overcame their Reason and Christianity: They were both sick with Grief, and incapable of comforting one another. But Providence, that saw their Wrongs, at length provided a way for their Deliverance: A fair Virgin, who was a Slave to the Governor, waited on a Mistress of his, whom he having enjoy'd, slighted, and had sent to this his Country-House, where she had now been two Years: This Girl, who was then but twelve Years old, often came into the Chamber where these poor Gentlemen were confined, to bring them Tea and Coffee from her Lady; who, having had a sight of them, admired Don *Lopez*, and therefore ventured to do something to oblige him. This pretty Girl they ask'd some Questions of; as what Country she was of, what Religion. She told them, she was a *Venetian*, that her Mistress was the same; that they both were brought there by Misfortunes, but seem'd shy of saying more. One Evening she enter'd the Room, follow'd by a Lady, in a *Turkish* dress exceeding rich; she was about five and twenty, her Shape and Mein was enchanting; her Face so lovely, that it would have charm'd the most Insensible: A Cloud of Blushes overspread her Face, and her disorder was such for some Minutes, that she could not speak. The Count and Don *Lopez*, whose Weakness and Chains hinder'd them from rising to pay her the civilities due to her Sex, bow'd their Heads and kept Silence also, expecting her to tell the Business that brought her there. At last she spoke to them thus in *French*: 'Is it possible, that the cruel Governor can be so void of Humanity to treat you thus barbarously? Can he see such noble Persons as you appear to be, perish in Chains, and not relent?[1] Tho I risque my Life to do it, charming Strangers, I will free you. But,' continued she, addressing her self to Don *Lopez*, 'may I hope to find you grateful? Will you give her a Place in your

---

1 First edition: relent.

Heart, who gives you Life and Liberty? Will you preserve her Life, who is determin'd to save yours? With you I am resolved to live or die. Speak then, for time is precious, and deserve my Love, or Hate.' Don *Lopez* was too well skill'd in the fair Sex, not to perfectly understand this Lady's meaning; and since no other means but this was left to free them, wisely conceal'd his being preengaged. Nay, doubtless he was not altogether insensible of *Eleonora's* Charms, for so was the Lady named; he was a Man, and tho he was intirely devoted to *Teresa*, yet as Man he could oblige a hundred more: Life is sweet, and I hope my Reader will not condemn him for what his own Sex must applaud in justification of themselves: for what brave, handsome young Gentleman would refuse a beautiful Lady, who loved him, a Favour? He bowed with a look full of Love and Gratitude, saying, 'Liberty, which in it self is the greatest blessing Man can possess, join'd with so great a Good as your Favour, who would refuse? Your Charms would even render Confinement supportable, a Dungeon with such a Companion would be pleasant: Shew me the way to Freedom, and it shall be the study of my Life to make you happy: I will defend you to the last drop of my Blood.' At these Words he grasped her Knees and sigh'd. Poor *Eleonora* suffer'd her self to be deceived, and thought of nothing but being happy with the Man she loved. The Count *de Hautville* was amazed at Don *Lopez's* Proceedings; his Soul was constant and noble, and would have refused a Life offer'd on so hard Terms as the breach of his Faith to his lovely *Emilia*. But his Years were more than his Friend's, and his Temper more sedate. The sweet Girl *Anna* fetched Wine and Sweet-Meats to them. *Eleonora* sat down by them, eat, and suffer'd Don *Lopez* to kiss her Hands, and say a hundred tender things to her. They appointed Midnight for their Escape, when she promised to bring them Files to take off their Fetters, and Disguises to put on to prevent all Discovery. She had provided a Place for them to retire to also, near the Sea-side: She had, by this means when she was first a darling Mistress to the Governor, prevail'd with him to free a Slave whom she fancy'd; it was a young *Black* whom her Father had purchased when a Child, of a Captain, and given her, and being taken with her in the Ship she was taken in, by an *Algerine* Pirate, lived some time with him at the Governor's, his Name was *Attabala*. The Governor at her Request gave him a little House and Garden, which he used in the Summer to repair to for his Pleasure, to fish on the Sea-coast, and take the Evening Air on the Water with his Pleasure-boat. This Place he gave to *Attabala* to live in, and take care of; and it being now Winter, there was no fear of his going thither. In this Slave she could confide; to him she had declared her Design the Day before, when he came, as he often did, to see his dear Mistress, bringing her little Presents of Fish and Fruits, as grateful Acknowledgments of the Favour she had done him. From this Place it would be no difficult matter for them to escape to some Christian Ship or Port. Having stay'd with them two Hours, she retired; and then the Count enter'd into Talk with Don *Lopez* in this manner: 'My dear Friend, Heaven now seems to smile upon us, a gleam of Hope appears to comfort us; but tell me, was it well done to dissemble? Are you changed? Is your Wife forgot? and the sacred matrimonial Vows no longer valued? Excuse me if I blame you; let nothing make you buy our Liberty by a Crime; it is better to die here, than live with Heaven's Displeasure.' Don *Lopez* blushing, reply'd, 'Forgive my Weakness; I do not mean to proceed farther than an innocent Deceit, *Teresa* is always present with me: But had I refused this Lady's Offer rudely, we had, perhaps, been here detain'd and murder'd; and then *Teresa* and *Emilia* never can be rescued from the Villain that robb'd us of them. Be satisfy'd therefore, that I have acted prudently, and not design'd amiss.' The Count was then contented, and now the joyful Hour approach'd when Darkness and Sleep had lull'd the busy World to rest; *Eleonora* came with *Anna* loaden with Jewels, Gold, and Clothes; they quickly filed their Fetters off, and found the faithful *Attabala* at some distance from the House, with three Horses, swift *Barbaries*, that run fleet as the Wind; on two of these the Lords mounted, Don *Lopez* taking the Lady, and the Count the Girl behind him; the *Black* riding the other Horse led the Way, with which he was perfectly acquainted: In few Hours just at Day-break, they reached the House, and being safely lodged, began to taste the Pleasures of Liberty. Next day the Governor, who was recover'd, was inform'd by the Servants, that remain'd in the Country-house, of the Lords flight: but he had that night received an order from the Emperor to repair to *Fez*,[1] to take a Command in the Army, to which he was determin'd to send him. This took up all his Thoughts, so that he took little notice of their Escape; and, as they afterwards learn'd, he never return'd to *Algiers*, but dy'd in the Army of a Fever. And

---

1 Or Fes, a city in northern Morocco founded some 1,200 years ago under the Idrīsid dynasty. It was the site of an imperial palace and became a centre for commerce and learning in the mid-fourteenth century.

now Don *Lopez* had an opportunity to enquire who *Eleonora* was, and the fatal accident that brought her to this Place. He treated her with such Respect and Affection, that he could ask nothing of her, but what she was ready to grant. One Morning as the Count and *Anna*, whom *Eleonora* now treated as her Friend, letting her lie with her, as became a person who was indeed her Equal, were conversing together, Don *Lopez* intreated her to relate the Adventures of her Life. 'Yes, my Lord, *said she*, I will, provided *Anna*, and you Gentlemen, will do the same; for she would never let me know who she is, tho a *Venetian* as well as I.' *Anna* reply'd 'Madam,[1] whilst I was a Slave I was not willing to be known: Now I shall take Pleasure to entertain you with a Story full of strange Adventures.' Then *Eleonora* began in this manner.

_____

1 First edition: *reply'd Madam*

CHAP. VII.

'I was born at *Friuli*,[1] a place situate on the *Adriatick* Sea, in the *Venetian* Dominions; my Father was a wealthy Merchant, in the City of *Aquilegia*;[2] he had no Child but me by my Mother, who was his second Wife, and the Daughter of a noble *Venetian*. He had two Sons by a former Wife, who loved me not, because my Father seem'd to prefer me in his Affection before them; all his Ambition was to see me well disposed of during his Life. I was also very apprehensive that my Brothers, if he died before I was marry'd, would clap me up in a Convent, to get my Fortune, and be revenged upon me. The great Portion he offer'd with me, with that tolerable Person the World thought me, procured me many Admirers, as soon, or indeed before I was of an Age to marry. Amongst these, there was a Kinsman of my Mother, the eldest Son of a *Venetian* Senator, whom the Custom and Laws of that State will not permit to marry out of a noble Family,[3] became much enamour'd with me: His Name Signior *Andrea Zantonio*. He secretly courted me, my Mother and Father giving Encouragement; my Heart soon yielded, and I gave him the Preference above all others. I was now almost fourteen, and it was resolved that we should be privately marry'd at a Country-Seat of my Father's. These Proceedings could not be kept so secret, but that the Servants were some of them privy to them. Amongst my Lovers, there was a rich Captain of a Ship, who had cast his Eyes upon me in my Infancy, and was one of the first that entertain'd me with Discourses of Love; he was in Years, and I treated him with Ill-Nature, and indeed could not indure him: yet he persisted, till at length I used him so ill, that he concluded I had made choice of another, and made it his business to find out who

---

1 Friuli-Venezia Giulia, an area of north-eastern Italy now bounded by Slovenia to the east, Austria to the north, and the Veneto region to the west. Friuli came under Venetian rule in 1420.

2 Aquileia, now a small town sited about ten miles from the Adriatic in the Friuli-Venezia Giulia region. It was a centre for trade under Venetian rule.

3 The Venetian Republic was governed by a Great Council, of which membership was restricted to a formally defined class of wealthy governing families. Patrician status was normally inherited, with the exception being the admittance of women, who were required to make a formal application in writing, and through a male representative, to the *Avogaria di Commun* for permission to marry into the nobility (see Cowan, ch. 2).

was the fortunate Man: In order to which, he gain'd my Maid, who waited upon me, by Bribes to discover all to him. She inform'd him from time to time of Signior *Andrea Zantonio*'s courting me, and all that past. His Business obliged him to be often absent on Voyages to *Spain*, and elsewhere; and he arrived but the Day before my intended Wedding, of which being inform'd, he resolved to prevent it if possible. He therefore went to Signior *Andrea*'s Father, and acquainted him with the ill News, promising if he would assist him, he would prevent it; which he soon agreed to do, being much enraged at his Son. The Captain desired three or four Men to aid him, which he immediately procured him, sending four Ruffians disguised along with him; with these he lay in Ambuscade,[1] in the way which we were to pass to my Father's Country-house, where Signior *Andrea* was to come to us the next Morning, not thinking it proper to go with us. There were none in the Coach but my Father, Mother, and me; two Men-Servants rid before the Coach, and my poor *Black* was behind it: As we past by a Wood, the Captain and his Crew bolted out upon us, with Vizards upon their Faces, and Pistols in their Hands; they stop'd the Coach, and tore me out of it, whilst my Mother shrieked, my Father storm'd, and one of the Servants going to lay hold of me, was shot dead. They fled with me into the thickest Part of the Wood, where they bound and gagg'd me. The poor Black *Attabala*, who has now help'd to deliver you, being very nimble of foot, pursued me, and running after them, came up crying just as they were binding my Hands. They seized and bound him also; then they placed us before two of them on Horseback, and made for the Sea-side; where being soon arrived, we found a Boat ready, into which one of them enter'd, we were next lifted in by the Seamen that row'd it; and then the four Villains that assisted in taking us, cry'd, Farewel, and rode off. The Captain taking off his Vizard so soon as we were put from the Shore, discover'd to me the Author of my Misfortune. "Madam, *said he*, I have you see done a bold deed to manifest my Love, and secure you to my self; fear nothing more, you are now in the hands of a Man that adores you, and it is your own fault if you are not happy." I could not answer, being gagg'd; but the disorder of my Mind cannot be exprest. I saw myself in the hands of a Man whom I hated, and no way left to escape. I was ten times more sensible of the loss of him I loved, than I could have before imagin'd. My Soul shiver'd at the thoughts of what was to follow.

---

1 An ambush or surprise attack.

I could no more hope to see my Country and Friends, for thither it was not to be supposed this Villain would ever venture to bring me again, at least not in some Years. I was tortured with a thousand such dismal Apprehensions, when I saw the Ship which lay'd by to receive us. He took me up in his loath'd Arms, and with the Seamens Assistance, tho I struggled, put me on board. *Attabala* and I were presently unbound, and now I began to expostulate with *Alphonso*, for that was the Captain's Name. "What do you propose, *said I*, in taking me thus by force against my Inclination? do you vainly imagine to be happy with me, whilst I hate and detest you, and view you as the only cause of my being wretched? Never will I pardon or love you, unless you carry me back to my Father's. I will make you as miserable as my self, and never suffer you to rest while I am with you. I always disliked you, but now my Aversion is confirm'd, and I would prefer the most vile Wretch on Earth before you." "Rage on, *said he*, fond Girl, whilst I possess you, you shall be mine, and only Death can free you from me." Here he suddenly kissed and embraced me. "You shall, *said he*, this Night marry me, that I may have a lawful Title to you, and you have nothing to reproach me. I will not be a Ravisher, but having secured your Person, and your Honour, take what will then be my Due." "No, Villain, *I reply'd*, my Tongue shall never call you Husband; I would sooner suffer hot Pincers to rend it from the Root than speak those Words, or answer to such a Question." "Silence, *said he*, does give Consent, and I shall not want Witnesses to prove our Marriage." Here he went out of the Cabin, and left me in the extremest Grief and Despair. Poor *Attabala* comforted me the best he could, offering to risque his Life to kill him; but I regarded nothing he said to me.

It was now Night, and very dark; I heard the Winds blow, and a mighty Disorder and Noise upon the Deck, the Captain storm'd and call'd loudly to the Seamen in Terms I did not understand; he came twice down into the Cabin, kiss'd me, and said, "Madam, 'tis a rough Night, but fear nothing:" yet I read a Concern in his Face that spoke our Danger. I cannot say that I was much terrify'd with the Thoughts of Death, because at that Instant I was apprehensive of something worse. I recommended my self to God, and calmly expected the Event of his good Pleasure. Before day the Ship had lost her Masts, and most part of her Rigging; she was so shatter'd that nothing but getting to some Shore, or meeting with some Ship, cou'd save us. We were now drove in sight of *Barbary*, when a Ship coming up our Ship's-Crew haled her. She soon came near, and lay by, hoisting *French* colours. The Captain sent his Boat aboard, but to their Surprize they were all clap'd under Hatches, it proving a Pirate Ship of *Algiers*. The Captain wonder'd the Boat stay'd, but at last seeing the Ship bear up to us, he suspected the Truth. He would have made some Defence, but the Ship was disabled; so he hastily catched up his Sword, and mounting the Deck was there met by a crowd of the Pirates, who had boarded the Ship: he was soon dispatched, and his men all kill'd, or taken. I remain'd with poor *Attabala* in the Cabin all this while, and was so lost in thought, I was scarce apprehensive of my Danger: when the *Algerine* Captain enter'd the Cabin with his Men, they took me, and convey'd me into the Pirate Ship, rifled ours, and then set her adrift. They put me into the great Cabin with *Attabala*, and in few Hours we came to *Barbary*, landed at *Algiers*; and the next Morning *Ibrahim* the Captain presented me to the Governor. What my Thoughts were, and how I exprest my Sorrows under all these Misfortunes, would be too tedious to tell you: in fine, the Governor treated me kindly, pretended to love me passionately, and forced me to his Bed; after which he deny'd me nothing, purchased and freed *Attabala* at my Request; and for eight Years, tho he had many other new Mistresses, gave me the Preference, and loved me with the same Ardour as at first. He reproached me often that I brought him no Child, which Providence no doubt did not think fit to give us: at last a *French* Lady, of incomparable Beauty, was presented him, and she brought him a Son the first Year of their acquaintance. This caused him to grow cold to me, which I resenting, we quarrell'd; so he sent me away to the Place you found me in. There I mourn'd my Misfortunes with a Christian Sorrow, and never thought to see the World again. Here I and my dear *Anna* came together; she was purchased by him a Month before I left him, and I beg'd him of her to keep me Company. Thus I have given you a true Narrative of my Misfortunes; and now Don *Lopez*, if we reach a Christian Shore again, and you prove grateful, I may yet live to be happy.' 'Madam, *said he*, it shall be my study to make you so.' 'Fair Anna, *said the Count*, we will refer your story to the Afternoon, it being now Dinner-time; and I doubt not but we shall hear something as extraordinary as what Madam *Eleonora* has related to us.' They rose, and Don *Lopez* led *Eleonora* to the Table; they dined, and then return'd to her Chamber, which was a pleasant Room, having the prospect of the Sea. Here they sat down, whilst *Attabala* made their Coffee, and then they importuned *Anna* to keep her Word; which she with a Sigh consented to do, saying, 'My Story is little worth hearing, and were it not to oblige *Eleonora*, I would beg to be excused.'

CHAP. VIII.

'I AM the Daughter of an unfortunate Prince, who was once a Lieutenant-General in the *Venetian* Army. My Mother was a Lady of great Birth; but the Family being ruined, had no Fortune; my Grandfather, being one of those who headed the *Hugonot*[1] Party against his Sovereign *Lewis* the Fourteenth,[2] lost both his Life and Estate. My Mother, then an Infant, was bred up by a *Hugonot* Sister of my Grandfather, who spared no cost upon her Education, but could give her no Fortune proportionable to her Quality. She had Beauty, Wit, and was certainly a very charming Person. My Father, who was the eldest Son of one of the noblest Families in *France*, saw and loved her; he visited her in secret, often made her large Presents; and knowing his Father and Family would never consent to his marrying her, he resolved if possible to debauch her; but her Vertue made her resist him, tho she loved him: So that he was forced to have recourse to Stratagems to accomplish his Desires. He used to walk with her often in her Aunt's Garden alone, she thinking her self secure from all attempts there. He had procured a Key to the Garden-gate, pretending it was more convenient for him to come in that way, because it was most private; and therefore her Aunt gave him one she had used to carry in her Pocket, to let her Niece and her in when they thought fit. He sent three of his Servants in the Night, who going in, hid themselves in this Garden. His Page, who conducted them where he order'd, brought back the Key to him. In the Morning the Prince comes himself in a travelling Coach to the Garden-gate; there alighting, he enters the House, calls for my Mother, and pretends he was going in haste on a Journey on some extraordinary Business for the King. After some Talk with Madam her Aunt, he takes her into the Garden, to say some little tender things to her alone, as she supposed. As they were walking in a close Walk, his Servants disguised started out upon her, and stopping her Mouth, bore her to the Coach, into which he enter'd, drawing up the Canvasses; and the Coach driving swiftly,

---

1 French Protestant.
2 In 1695 Roman Catholic king Louis XIV (r. 1643–1715) revoked the Edict of Nantes, which had allowed Huguenots freedom of worship. A program of suppression and forced conversions to Catholicism followed. In the first two decades of the eighteenth century, the Camisards, Huguenots from the Cévennes region in southeastern France, formed a resistance movement, but Aubin may intend "party" in a more general sense here.

he carry'd her thirty Miles off to a remote old Castle which belong'd to his Father, but had not been inhabited by any thing but Servants a long time. When he enter'd, the Gardiner and his Wife, who had lived there to look after the Furniture and Gardens many Years, made haste to open the Rooms, and ask'd no Questions. Here he accomplisht his ungenerous Design, and here he kept my disconsolate Mother some Years: her Aunt conceal'd her Loss, and, as she thought, her own Dishonour, as much as was possible, concluding she was gone with him by her own Consent; she therefore pretended she was retired farther into the Country to some Relations: yet it reached the Ear of my Grandfather, who only laugh'd at it, calling it a piece of Gallantry in his Son to receive a Lady who fled to his Arms. He often prest my Father to marry, but his Affection to my Mother, and Conscience, which now began to awaken him, made him always decline it. The Lady her Aunt loved her so tenderly, that she soon after the loss of her, fell sick with Grief, and died. And now the War being broke out between the *Turks* and *Venetians*,[1] my Father resolving to marry my Mother, who was young with Child, and with her charming affable Behaviour and Tears, had entirely gain'd his Heart, he proposed to the Duke his Father to go to *Venice* a Volunteer, with an Equipage suiting his Quality, to make a Campaign or two. To which his Father readily agreed: All things were got ready, and my Mother, conceal'd in Men's Clothes, went with him. So soon as they arrived at *Venice*, the Doge[2] presented him with the Command of a Regiment of Horse. Here he acquainted a Bishop with the Engagements that were betwixt my Mother and him, together with the Reasons why it must be a Secret: The good Bishop marry'd them, and placed my Mother with a Widow Lady of great Quality and Worth, who was his own Relation. Here my Mother was brought to bed of me, and unfortunately died in Child-bed; so that my Father returning from the Army at the end of the Campaign, found my Mother just dead, and me at Nurse. His Grief was very great, and his Fondness of me so extreme, he beg'd the Bishop and Lady to take all the care imaginable of me. The next Campaign he was made a Lieutenant-General, and was kill'd, dying in the Bed of Honour,

---

1 There were three wars between the Turks (synonymous with the Ottoman Empire) and the Venetian Republic between 1645 and 1718, continuing a pattern of conflict dating back to the fourteenth century.
2 Title given to the holder of the highest civic office in the Venetian republic.

leaving me a helpless Orphan, whose greatest Happiness at that time was, that I was too young to be sensible of my Loss. My Father had deposited into the Lady's hands a great Sum of Mony, as a Provision for me in case of his Death. The generous *Angelina*, for that was her Name, bred me up with as much Care and Tenderness as if I had been her own Child. She had a lovely Youth, her only Son, who was seven Years older than me; for him she declared she design'd me, provided we loved one another: his Name was *Carolus Antonio Barbarini*: we lived together, and his Name was one of the first things she taught my Infant-Tongue to pronounce. At seven Years of Age I found how dear he was to me, and he being fourteen, began to feel the glowing Passion he had for me warm his Breast. I was caress'd and loved by all his Family, and had a Prospect of being one of the happiest Women in the World. The *Turks* gaining many unfortunate Victories over the *Venetians*,[1] I was not thought safe at home, but sent with some young Ladies of *Angelina*'s Family to a Monastery. There, with a world of others, I was taken Captive by the cruel Infidels, and carry'd to *Constantinople*,[2] where my tender Years preserved my Vertue. A Sea-Captain bought me, and carrying me to *Algiers*, made a present of me to the Governor, whom he used to supply with Mistresses, for which he was doubtless well rewarded. This is my unhappy story. I suppose the Governor reserv'd me for his Use, when I was older; but God has been pleased to deliver me out of his Hands, for which I bless his Name, and I hope to see *Venice* once again with his Assistance.' Here she finish'd, and *Eleonora* rising up, embrac'd her, sheding some tears. 'Are you then, *says she*, the charming Girl the noble *Angelina* bred up? Fair *Anna*, forgive my Ignorance that made me treat you as a Servant: My Mother was *Angelina*'s Sister; you are dear to me by the ties of Blood, and far my Better in your noble Father. May Providence restore you to my Kinsman, and bring us safe to *Venice* again.' Here the two Lords related part of their Adventures; Don *Lopez* concealing that part only that related to *Teresa*, whom he mention'd as his Sister: They related the manner of their being cast on the dismal Island, their Escape thence and unfortunate

---

1   In 1718 the Ottoman Turks regained the Peloponnese peninsula (then called Morea) from Venice.

2   Now Istanbul, a city straddling the Bosphorus Strait that separates the Black Sea from the Sea of Marmara to the east and the Aegean and Mediterranean seas to the west. It was under Ottoman rule from 1453 to 1922.

meeting with the *Algerian* Pirate, with the Ladies being ravish'd from them for the Governor. At last they declar'd they would not leave *Barbary* till they were found and rescued. *Attabala* undertook to go to the Governor's, and learn what was become of them, which he faithfully perform'd in few days after. He went to enquire after his Master's Health as usual, found none but Servants who inform'd him of the Lady's Escape thence, and how the Governor had been wounded by one of them, and that *Roderigo* was likewise kill'd; in fine, of all they knew, but where the Ladies were retired to, they could not tell. So *Attabala* return'd with this Account; upon which the Lords resolved to disguise themselves, and go together in search of them in all the Villages near the City, to one of which they supposed they must have fled for Shelter. They drest themselves in the habit of *Grecian* Merchants, which Habits *Attabala* bought for them at the City, and both speaking Greek, they doubted not to pass for such if question'd. Thus metamorphosed they went daily out, and ventured to enquire if any Ladies in *European* Dresses were arrived in that Town or Village which they past through. Thus they did in every Place they could think of; but finding all their search in vain, they began to imagine they were hid in some Wood or Cave, and therefore concluded to visit all lonely Woods and Places least frequented: This they did for several days also, but without Success. One evening as they were returning home, they past by a small Wood, into which it was difficult to find an Entrance: they stop'd, and having view'd it well, they perceived some Footsteps and beaten Ways over the Grass. They enter'd into the thickest part of it by this path, and there found a dismal sort of Hut made only with Boughs of Trees, and a piece of Sail-Cloth; under which, upon some Straw, lay a Woman, whose Face, tho very beautiful, exprest the greatest Want and Misery. She had a Canvas-Wastecoat and Petticoat on, was barefoot, had a silk Handkerchief tied about her Head, and a piece of Flannel wrapped about her Shoulders; she was young, fair, and finely limbed, but her Eyes were sunk: she was meagre, pale, sick, and so weak she could not rise. The Lords view'd her with such Compassion that they were ready to weep. 'In the name of God, *said the* Count de Hautville *in* French, what are you? and how came you to be left in this dismal Place?' 'I am not able, *said she*, to tell you; if you are Christians, give me something to eat or drink, for our Saviour's sake.' They had nothing with them, but *Attabala*, who went with them as a Guide, hasted to the next Village, and soon brought some Bread and Wine, with some of which they a little revived her. She drank a good Draught of the Wine, but had not Strength to chew or swallow the Bread. As they were assisting her, a Man came up, whose Face, Shape, and Mien engaged their Attention; He was dress'd in a Jacket and Drawers of Canvas, his red Cloth Cap upon his head with Fur, barefooted, and so pale and lean, that he appear'd the very Image of Death; in a ragged Handkerchief he held in his Hands, he had Nuts and wild sour Grapes with a few dirty Bones, such as seem'd to have been flung out into the Streets for Dogs. He retired back when he saw the Lords; at which the Woman called to him in a sort of Extasy: 'Come here, my dear Lord, God sends us Friends and Food.' He then bowing, approached them. Their Surprize was such, when they saw him nearer, they could not speak. His Feet bled, his Sinews and Nerves were all open, his Bones stared upon one another; in fine, he was the most miserable Object their Eyes ever saw. They put the Bottle of Wine and Bread into his Hands, at which a Flood of Tears pour'd from his Eyes; and going to lift the Bottle to his Mouth, he stagger'd and fell down; at which the Woman shrieked, and fell into strange Convulsions. Don *Lopez* who caught the Bottle when the Man fell, endeavour'd with his Friend's Assistance to get some Wine down his Throat; but his Teeth being set fast, it was very difficult. Mean time *Attabala* was employ'd to hold the Woman, who beat her Breast, gnash'd her Teeth, roll'd her Eyes, and appear'd to be in the Agonies of Death. In some time both recover'd a little, and *Don Lopez* order'd *Attabala* to run back to the Town and hire Horses to carry them to *Attabala's* House. This was soon done, and the Lords mounting, took the Man and Woman up before them, and so posted home: where being arrived, they put them into warm Beds, not being certain they were Man and Wife, *Attabala* having first washed their Feet. This with some burnt Wine, and Bread sop'd in it, threw them into a profound Sleep till the next Morning; when *Eleonora*, *Anna*, and the Lords visited them to enquire who they were, and how they did: They first enter'd the Man's Chamber, who no sooner saw them, but he raised himself up in the Bed, and lifting up his Hands broke out into these passionate Expressions: *To thee, first, my merciful Creator, I return my Thanks'; 'tis to thee I owe this great Deliverance, and all the good Things I have received in my whole Life. I bless thee for the Miseries I have suffer'd: 'tis most just, my God, that I should be punish'd with Cold, Hunger, and Thirst, who broke my Faith with Thee, and fled thy Altar for a sensual Satisfaction. 'Twas I seduced the virtuous* Clarinda, *from her bless'd Retirement, for which she suffers both in Mind and Body; but no more will I offend my God. Now pardon us, and as thou hast deliver'd us from Death, so grant Peace to our Souls.* Then bowing to the Lords, 'To you blest instruments of Heaven's bounty, *said he*, who have saved the Life of her whose Life is dearer to me than my own, you who sav'd both from certain Death, I return unfeigned Thanks, and will make all the grateful Returns my present Circumstances will permit.' They embraced, and congratulated him with much tenderness, and promised to return to him so soon as they had visited the Lady. To her they went, and found her waking. She was very faint, and the Ladies welcoming of her, desired she would drink Chocolate with them, and not spend her Spirits by talking; yet she utter'd many affectionate Thanks and Acknowl-edgments to God and them. The Breakfast was brought in, and soon after the Gentleman being risen and drest in a Shirt, a thing he had not on before, Wastecoat, Breeches, Cap, Night-gown, Stockings, and Slippers of one of the Lords, enter'd the Room, and appear'd like what he really was, a Man of Quality, of excel-lent Parts and Person. *Anna* had likewise supply'd the Lady with Shift and Night-Clothes; she appear'd to be about two and twenty, and the Gentleman upwards of thirty. Being refresh'd with eating, the Gentleman handsomly, without asking, address'd himself to the Company thus: 'Gentlemen and Ladies, *said he*, I am positive you are very desirous to know who this Lady and I are, and what strange Misfortunes reduced us to the deplorable Condition you found us in; I will therefore as briefly as I can satisfy your Curiosity, and you must excuse me, if I do not relate every Particular with that exactness it ought to be done in, since my Strength is but little at present.' They assured him they would rather deny themselves that Pleasure, than trouble him; and begg'd that he would proceed.

CHAP. IX.

'This Lady and I, *said he*, were both born in *France*, in the same Province; *Dauphiny*[1] gave us Birth. My Father (which it is necessary I should mention first, because I am but ten Years older than she, which occasion'd my Misfortune, in being destin'd to the Church,[2] before she was grown up to inspire my Soul with that fatal Passion that has undone us) was the King's Lieutenant for that Province, and Marquess of *Harcourt*. I was his third Son, and therefore design'd for the Church, in which I could not miss of Preferment, being descended of so great a Family; nor did I want the Qualifications requisite to render me capable of that noble Profession. I was not inclined to any Vice; nor, I thank God, wanted Sense to learn, and retain, all that was taught me. In fine, I was very dear to my Father, and much esteem'd by my Friends and Family. I past thro my Study, and was ordain'd a Secular Priest[3] at twenty. I was soon dignify'd with being made a Canon[4] of the royal Cathedral of *Cambray*.[5] My Brothers were greatly preferr'd in the Army, and we were all very great and very happy: but Providence did not think fit I should continue so. I got an Ague and Fever, which render'd me very weak; the Physicians advised me to the Country Air. Upon which I retired to a Village, where my Father had a little Summer Seat. In this Town was a Monastery of *Benedictine*[6] Nuns: this place I visited, having two young Ladies my Relations there. Here I saw the charming

---

1 Dauphiné, a former province of southeastern France, bordered by the Rhône valley to the west and Provence to the south. The region now comprises the *départements* of Isère, Hautes-Alpes, and Drôme.

2 Under the European tradition of primogeniture, only the eldest son could inherit the family estate. Younger sons commonly found employment in the army, the law, or the Church.

3 A priest not belonging to a religious order or living in a religious community though still taking a vow of celibacy.

4 A cleric with administrative duties in a cathedral.

5 A cathedral was constructed in the town of Cambrai, in northern France, during the twelfth and thirteenth centuries, and in the following five hundred years it became grander and more imposing. The cathedral was damaged in 1792 during the period of the French Revolution. Aubin may have used the term "royal" because of the cathedral's association with François de Salignac de la Mothe-Fénelon (1651–1715), royal tutor, author of *Les Aventures de Télémaque* (1699), and Archbishop of Cambrai from 1695 to 1715.

6 The Benedictines are a Roman Catholic monastic order dating back to the fourth or fifth century.

Clarinda, who was then about fifteen; she was Daughter to the Count *de Villeroy*, who having ten Children, four Sons, and six Daughters, sent three of his youngest Daughters to this Monastry, of which the Lady Abbess was his Sister. He gave a thousand Pounds Sterling with them, and all possible persuasions and means were used to persuade them to embrace this holy way of Living, as is customary in *France*, because great Fortunes and Families should not be impaired and ruined, by portioning many Children; therefore they commonly dedicate some of them to the Church, which prevents their impoverishing Estates, and too greatly increasing the Family. Thus they were enabled to give such great Portions with their eldest Daughter, and making Settlements on the second Sons, as may marry them into noble and rich Families suitable to their own. But tho this be an excellent piece of Policy, yet it often causes the Children to be very unhappy, and the Church crouded with those, whose Inclinations do not suit the Habits they wear, but tend to the World, and sigh after the Pleasures of it; nay, too often do, as I have done, forget the sacred Vows they have made, and follow the dictates of their Passions. *Clarinda* was fair as an Angel, witty, free, affable, and in all things so engaging, that I soon lost my Heart to her; I struggled with the growing Passion, sometimes resolved to see her Face no more, but Love overcame all my Resolutions, and I at last resolved to possess her, or die. I soon found means to reveal my Passion to her, and she in short time yielded to fly with me to any part of the World, for in *France* we could not stay. I had a great deal of Money by me, and now I thought only of amassing such a Sum, as might provide handsomly for us in *Holland* or *England*, to one of which Places we were determin'd to go: In order to this, I made bold with some very rich Jewels, which were laid up in a Reliquary, of which I kept the Keys; to prevent discovery I employ'd a Hugonot Jeweller to set false Stones in the room of the true, which I picked out before he saw them, pretending to him that I was desirous to repair and beautify those sacred Things; and that Time having reduced them to this condition, I could not bestow Diamonds and Rubies, but was willing to make them decent, at my own Expence: And indeed I thought there was but little use for Diamonds, to adorn dry Bones and Relicks, which we were not certain belong'd to those holy Persons whose they were pretended to be; and that the Money bestow'd on the Poor, would have been much better employ'd. Tho in me this was Sacrilege, and a great Crime, yet having given the Reins to my Passion, I ran headlong to Destruction. All things being ready, I provided a Boat to carry us down the River *Rhosne*[1] to *Arles*,[2] from whence I doubted not to get passage to *England*, in some Ship from *Marseilles* that was going home thro the *Straits*.[3] *Clarinda* fail'd not to be ready at the appointed Hour, which was Midnight. I brought a ladder of Ropes, which throwing over the Wall of the Garden, which was not very high she mounted, and turning it over on the other side descended. I received her with open Arms, and all the transport a Man may be supposed to feel, who has rigorously lived to his Duty, denied himself all the Pleasures of Sense, and gives a loose to his Desires. The sad Prisoner who has lived long confined in a dark loathsome Vault, feels not a greater Joy at the sight of Day and Liberty than I did then. I hasted with her to the Boat, into which I had already convey'd Habits for us both, with all things necessary. The Jewels I had hid about me in a Purse, and my Pockets were stuff'd with Gold, besides all I had put into the Trunk I had got aboard with our Clothes and Linen. As soon as we were come aboard, and alone in the Cabin, we drest both in Gentlemen's Habits, I threw our others into the River. And now 'tis needless to tell you that I enjoy'd the Maid I so much languished for, promising to marry her so soon as we were arrived in a place of Safety. When we came to *Marseilles*, which we soon did, we discharged the Bark, and went ashore with our things and lodged at an Inn. And now grown distractedly fond of *Clarinda*, I long'd to perform my Promise of marrying her; and in few days after, having purchased some Woman's Apparel for her, we step'd out one Morning early, and going to a Country-Village two Miles from *Marseilles*, were lawfully join'd by the Parish Priest: and now had I not been before engaged to live single, I had been one of the happiest Men on Earth. We waited not long before an *English* Ship arrived homeward bound. I agreed for our Passage; we went aboard, and soon after set Sail. And now my fears were all over, I fancy'd my self going to a Country where I should rather be applauded than condemn'd for what I had done, where I should be free in all respects; and tho I never had a thought to change my Religion,

---

1 The River Rhône, which rises in the Swiss Alps and flows through Lake Geneva and southeastern France to the Mediterranean.

2 A city and a once-significant port at the head of the delta where the French River Rhône divides into the Grand Rhône and the Petit Rhône and then enters the Mediterranean.

3 The Straits of Gibraltar, the narrow stretch of water separating Iberia from North Africa.

yet I fancy'd I should be extreme happy in a place where I should live free from all Constraint: but God, whom I had offended, soon convinced me of my Folly. An *Algerine* Pirat met us, and after a sharp dispute took the Ship, and made us all Prisoners, carrying us into *Tunis*, where he sold us for Slaves.[1] It was *Clarinda*'s Fortune and mine to be bought by a Merchant's Widow, who sent her Steward to Market to buy a Man and a Maid-Servant. When he brought us home the Lady view'd us, seem'd pleased with his choice of us. She ask'd me many Questions, as what Nation I was of, what I could do, who *Clarinda* was, and such like; to which I answer'd, that she was my Sister, that we were born in *France*; that I could write, cast Accompt,[2] play upon several sorts of Musick, but neither of us had been bred to work: I said my Sister could work finely at her Needle. She told me it was our own Faults if we lived uneasy, and that she would use us kindly. In short she liked my Person, and in few Days gave me to understand what she expected. She was old, and very disagreeable; yet having given the Reins to Passion, the fear of being parted from, or of *Clarinda*'s being ill used, made me resolve to oblige the lustful Hag, which I accordingly did. And now I was treated as Master of all, I sat at table with her, and *Clarinda* with us; I was deny'd nothing, but managed her Affairs and Fortune as I pleased. I had still left of my own the Purse of Jewels, which I had hung about my Neck with a String; and when the Pirats took us, they staid not to strip us of our Shirts, so they found not what was conceal'd next my Skin. This I always kept about me; but I wanted two things which are the greatest blessings of Life, Liberty, and a good Conscience. I continued to please *Admela* the Widow some time; but one fatal Evening she being walk'd into the Garden, I stole to *Clarinda*'s Room, where she was working, as I often did undiscover'd, and taking the privilege of a Husband to enjoy my vertuous Wife, was by a malicious Slave watched, and betray'd: he envied my good Fortune in being beloved by his Mistress. He was an *Irish* Man, a sort of People who never want a good opinion of themselves, and are generally successful with the Women. He thought he had now a good opportunity to ruin me, and insinuate himself into her Favour. He gave her an account of what he had seen; and when I came

---

1   The city of Tunis was the site of a major slave market from the seventeenth century until 1841. The trade was not only in Europeans but also in Africans from western and central Sudan (Montana 16–19).

2   Present an account of financial transactions.

into the Garden some time after, and gave her my Hand, she looked upon me with such Rage and Disorder in her Face, that I quickly apprehended what was to follow. I entertain'd her as usual with pleasant talk; we supp'd, and I went into her Chamber, when her Servants withdrew, as I was accustom'd to do; but when we were alone, she explain'd her self in this manner. *"Malherb,* said she, for under that Name I conceal'd my self, *Clarinda* is more than a Sister to you, and I have nurs'd a Viper in my Bosom,[1] that steals your Affection from me. You adore her, and doubtless care not for me. I thought to have provided nobly for her and you; but since she makes me wretched I will remove her from my Sight, and yours for ever." Here she wept. What different Passions rent my divided Soul at this dreadful Moment, words can't express. I stood for some Minutes immoveable as a Statue: at last I endeavour'd to pacify her, begging her not to credit what a Villain said, who conspired my Ruin, envying my good Fortune. At last I gain'd so far upon her, that she receiv'd me to her Arms; and then I made her promise to put the Villain away that abused us, which the next Morning she perform'd, ordering him to be sent to a Country-House she had near the Sea-side, twenty Miles distant, to look after the Gardens. He utter'd a hundred Curses and Imprecations against me; but they did not hurt me, or serve him. And now I was obliged to caress *Admela* in an extraordinary manner, and be more circumspect than ever with *Clarinda,* on whom she kept a watchful Eye. We continued thus for some time; but *Admela* observed the tender regard we had for each other so well, that she was convinced I had imposed upon her: and being very cunning, she took no notice to me; but taking *Clarinda* with her into the Garden one Morning, when I was gone out to receive some Money of the Merchants for her, she had her seized, and put bound into a Cart, where being cover'd over with some Sacks, she was drove to the Country-house, where the *Irish* Villain was, and there locked into a Chamber, where they chain'd her by the Leg, and only one old Hag, who had been *Admela's* Nurse, left with her. Here she remain'd a long time: At my return home, I miss'd her; and asking where she was, none answer'd; at last my Devil-mistress told me

---

1   The expression originates from the fables of Aesop, the ancient Greek fabulist and storyteller. In "The Farmer and the Viper," a farmer finds a snake half-dead from the cold of winter, puts it inside his coat, and warms it back to life. The viper bites him and kills him. The moral is that kindness is wasted on evil.

she was where I should never see her more. I raged and storm'd in vain; nay, I used Tears and Prayers, but Jealousy had render'd her Soul obdurate and inflexible; in fine, none would inform me what was become of her. From this hour I resolved to shun *Admela*'s lustful Arms and Bed; at last she threaten'd me with *Clarinda*'s Death if I treated her so ill. Thus I lived two whole Years in perpetual Torment, and Anxiety of Mind; my Health decay'd, and I was no longer the same Man. *Admela* griev'd, and being old, fell into a lingring Illness that at last ended her Days, but not my Sorrows. And now having got much Riches of the Widow's into my Power, I resolved to find out where *Clarinda* was, tho I spent it all; but all my Designs were vain. *Mustapha*, a *Mahometan* Captain that was Nephew to *Admela*'s Husband and his Heir, comes home, and seizing upon all, cast me into Prison where I lay three Months, and then was turn'd out to be used as a Slave, with a clog chain'd to my Leg, to prevent my escaping. I was forced to carry Burdens as a Porter about the City to earn a morsel of Bread. Whilst these things past, my dear *Clarinda* remain'd a Prisoner very sick; the *Irish* Villain, and old Woman lived rarely, and grew great Friends; they feasted and lay together, he meditating how to revenge himself upon me, and having always view'd *Clarinda* with desire, prevail'd on *Dimas*, the old Hag, to let him sometimes visit her. He always brought her something, as Fruit, Coffee or Wine, to revive her poor decay'd Spirits; and tho Grief had much alter'd her Face, yet her Beauty charm'd the Villain. One Day when *Dimas* was gone to *Tunis* for Money for their Salary, which *Admela* allow'd them, he thus address'd *Clarinda*: "Madam, *said he*, I am touched to the very Soul with a tender Sense of your Sufferings. I adore and love you equal with him you are parted from; grant me the Enjoyment of your Person, and I will free you. *Malherb* is dead, the revengeful *Admela* poison'd him three days after you were brought here. *Dimas* has orders to poison you, but I keep her from it. I am a *European* and a Christian; give your self to me, and I will procure a safe Passage for us to *Ireland*, where I will marry you." At these words she lift up her Eyes, and with a Flood of Tears reply'd; "Is my dear Husband dead then? Can I no more hope to see him? Then why do I live?" At these words she swooned. *Mackdonald*, for that was the Villain's Name, held her up in his Arms, till she recovering, pour'd forth the most passionate Expressions of Grief. He then departed, fearing to hear her Reproaches and Subtlety, considering, that after the first Efforts of her Passion was over, Reason would take place, and she would reflect upon the Misery of her present Condition, and the Impossibility of being freed from it by any other means but by him; and so concluded, she would at last comply and fly with him, which was the thing he design'd to compass, by this invented Story of my Death. *Dimas* returning, wonder'd to find her so afflicted, and ask'd her the reason of her Grief; but *Clarinda* fear'd to tell her, and discover what had past betwixt her and *Mackdonald*, and so gave her no Answer. And now Heaven kindly inspired her with a Thought, that this Story might not be true: "Why, *said she*, am I kept here if he is dead? *Admela* has no need to fear me if the Man we love is dead; if she would have taken my Life away, she might have done it long since: no, doubtless, this Villain tells me this to make me despair of any help but his. My God, *continued she*, who can bring Good out of Evil, direct me what to do." Thus she past the sleepless Night, and at last resolved to dissemble with *Mackdonald*, and if possible, get her Liberty without injuring her Vertue. The next time he came to her alone, when *Dimas*, who was jealous of him, was absent, she pretended to hearken to his Proposals, and told him, if he would contrive a way for them to escape, she would gladly go with him. He seem'd transported; and the next Night, whilst *Dimas* slept, whom he had given a large Portion of Opium to, in some Coffee they had drank together, he rises; and packing up what Money and Clothes he could get in the House, he came into *Clarinda*'s Chamber, filed off her Fetters, and they hasted to a neighbouring Wood, where they sat down, fearing to lose themselves, it being a very dark Night; resolving to stay till the Day-break; and then he proposed to go down to the Sea-side, in hopes to find some Ship's Boat to go to Sea in; if not, he had made an Acquaintance with a poor Fisherman, of whom he used to buy Fish, in whose Cottage he doubted not they might likely stay. And now the Villain began rudely to press her to yield to him. "*Mackdonald*, that you are a Villain, *said she*, I am sensible; I have used you to obtain my Liberty, I never design to gratify you; therefore desist, or expect to die by my Hand, or kill me, for I prefer Death a thousand times before a Life of Infamy. If my Husband still lives, I may be happy; if he be dead, I have no more business with the World, and shall gladly die: but this be assured of, I will resist to Death." *Mackdonald*'s Surprize was very great, yet he persisted in his wicked Design, and when he found Persuasions would not do, proceeded to use force, saying, "*Clarinda*, 'tis in vain you strive; the happy *Malherb* ruined me, and I will revenge my self by robbing him of you." At these Words, she caught a Bayonet from his side, which he had arm'd himself withal, and stabb'd him, before he suspected her Design. And now guess but the Terrors of her Mind, alone in a dismal Wood, she knew not where to go, a dying Man lying by her. She withdrew some little distance from the Place, and there falling upon her Knees beg'd of God to deliver her from the Miseries of Life by a speedy Death. At last day breaking, she looked round her, and rising walk'd thro the Wood in a Pathway which led to a Hill. This she ascended with much Pain, being very weak. In a shady Valley on the other side the Hill, she saw an antient Man of a venerable Aspect, his Beard reached to his Waste, his Habit was a coarse grey Cloth, very old, his Feet were bare; he had a little Pitcher in his Hand, and was going to fill it with Water at a small Spring that rose at the bottom of the Hill. She approached him trembling, and fell at his Feet, crossing her Breast. He lifted her up, saying in *French*, "God save you Woman, what would you have?" "A place to conceal my self, Father, *said she*; I am a Christian, fled from those that sought to ruin me; I am faint, sick, and friendless: oh, assist me in what you can: if not, I must perish, for I cannot go much farther." He led her down the Valley, and brought her to a poor Cottage, there he gave her some Bread and boil'd Roots, which was what he lived on; and here she recounted to him how she was with her Husband taken and made[1] Slaves, with the Cause of her Confinement at the Country-House; how she escaped thence, and had kill'd, as she supposed, the Villain that would have forced her. Then the old Man, she having finish'd her Story, began thus: "Daughter, I am a Man who have long since retired from the World; I am a Priest, born in *France*, I was Chaplain to an *India* Ship; and being desirous to see the World, chose that Way to travel, in hopes to be useful to the Ignorant. We were taken by the *Algerines*, as you have been, and I was seven years a Slave to a Merchant at *Fez*, where I learn'd to live hard; he at last freed me, and being well acquainted with the Place and People, I resolved to live here the remainder of my Days. I never eat Flesh, nor drank Wine, but content my self with Bread and Roots, to which you are welcome. I get my living by practising Physick[2] amongst these poor Barbarians,[3] and so have frequent opportunities of baptizing Infants,

---

1 First edition: make
2 First edition: Physsck
3 Barbarians can be, simply, natives of Barbary, a name given by Europeans to that part of North Africa corresponding to parts of present-day Morocco, Algeria, Tunisia, and Libya. Historically, however, *barbarian* was a pejorative term applied by various nations to denote foreigners

unperceived by them, and sometimes converting poor Souls to the Christian Faith. Sometimes I paint small Pictures of holy Persons, for which they give me Bread and Roots. Thus have I lived these forty Years, daily visiting the Sick in the adjacent Towns and Villages. And now Daughter, if you can content your self to work, I will procure you a Cottage and Business, for with me it would be indecent for you to stay. You say you have kill'd a Man, a thing you ought to mourn for all the Days of your Life. Alas! could you find no way to touch his Soul, but to cut him off in that dreadful moment when he was least prepared for his eternal State? Why did you not rather call earnestly to God to deliver you? Are you certain he is dead?" "No Father, *said she,* but I believe so." He rose hastily, saying, "Stay here and I will go, and see if God has mercifully spared him to repent." He run to a Cupboard, took out a bottle of Cordial, and with his Staff in his Hand departed, going as nimbly as if he had been young, tho he was so old and feeble. This sight fill'd her Soul with an unusual Strain of Devotion: "My God, *said she,* What a lively Devotion glow'd in the Face of that good Man! How vigorously he performs his Duty, and how careless have I been of mine? How have I distrusted God, how lamented for a mortal Man, and how little for his and my Sins? I will henceforth resolve courageously to support all Adversity. Why did I imbrue my Hands in Blood, and rashly ruin the Soul of him whose Hands gave me Liberty but some few Hours before. I should have strove, and reason'd with him; God would have strengthen'd me no doubt, and touched his Heart. Well might the *Psalmist* cry out to be deliver'd from the guilt of shedding innocent Blood."[1] Here she melted into Tears, and truly repented her Rashness. Not long after, as she sat pensive, the good Father *Clementine* return'd, for that was his Name, and with much Joy told her, *Mackdonald* was sitting under a Tree when he came, so weak with the Loss of Blood, he could not rise. "I view'd his Wound, *said he,* after giving him some Cordial; it is in his Thigh, deep, but not mortal. I mention'd nothing of you to him, but admonish'd him seriously to prepare for Death, not letting him know that I thought his Wound not dangerous. He view'd me earnestly, and at last said, *Are you a Christian Priest?* I assured him I was, he seem'd o'erjoy'd, made his Confession to me, expressing great Sorrow for his Sins. I went

who did not subscribe to their customs or faith. Barbarians are seen as rude, uncivilized, or savage.

1 Psalm 106.37–38: "Yea, they sacrificed their sons and their daughters unto devils, / And shed innocent blood."

to a poor Man's House, and we have got him thither. There I have left him in Bed; at Night I have promised to return: he says your Husband is living at *Tunis*." Poor *Clarinda* blest God and him for this good News; he conducted her to a Widow-woman's House where she was to live till News could be got of me; there she help'd to embroider Belts with this good Woman, who maintain'd her self with that Work. It was a great Way from *Tunis* to this place, and it was some time before somebody could be found to go thither with her, which the good *Clementine* could not do himself, because he could not leave his sick Patient. Poor *Mackdonald* died, before her departure, of a Fever, occasion'd by his great Loss of Blood, and was very penitent. The Clothes and Money he had were by the good Priest taken care of; who having paid the Country-man for Lodging and Diet for *Mackdonald*, gave the rest to *Clarinda*. She took leave of the generous Father with Tears, promising him to return to him soon with me; he said he would provide for us to live. The good Widow loved her much, and invited her to live there again: the Woman's Son went with her, they came safe to *Tunis*, lodg'd at a poor Woman's who was kin to the Widow. Here they learn'd the News of *Admela*'s Death, my Imprisonment, and poor Condition. *Clarinda* got the young Man to inquire me out; at last he found and brought me to her, but when she saw me in so miserable a Plight, a Clog chain'd to my Leg, my beggarly Habit and alter'd Face, no Words can express her Concern; yet our Souls leaped for Joy. We kiss'd, embraced, and wept; so moving was the scene, the poor Country-man and Woman of the House could not refrain from Tears. She told me what a Retreat was provided us; but I fear'd being pursued, and thought it was better for me to stay at *Tunis*. We took a Lodging in this Woman's House, she promising to procure Needle-work for *Clarinda*, to help maintain us. In few Days the honest Country-man went home, carrying a Letter from us to the good Father, full of our Acknowledgments. And thus we lived for ten Months, in which time *Clarinda* found her self with Child. We lived very poorly; and no hopes of Freedom appearing, at last I resolved, she importuning me, to file off my Fetters and steal away to the Widow's House, where she could lie in more conveniently, and with *Clementine* the pious Priest's Assistance, be better supply'd with Necessaries. We had little Money, no Guide, and travel'd on Foot mostly in the Night, fearing to be observed and question'd in the Day. We soon lost our way, and wandering about, came to the Wood where you found us. Here poor *Clarinda* fell into the Pains of Child-birth, and was deliver'd of a dead

Child, which was doubtless lost for want of help. I did all I was able to assist and comfort her, but she was now in so weak a Condition as render'd her unable to go from this dismal Place. All I could do was to wander in the neighbouring Villages to seek for Food to sustain our Lives. In this Condition God sent you to us; and now if he assists us to get safe to *France* again, *Clarinda* and I are determin'd to do penance for our past Sins, and if a Dispensation[1] cannot be granted, part for ever: I will return to serve my God at the Altar, and she to her peaceful Convent, to wash away our stains and oversights with Tears, to obtain a happy Death, and rise again to everlasting Peace and Glory.' Thus he ended his moving Relation, which drew Tears from every Eye. The Lords and Ladies caress'd them both in an extraordinary manner, and the Praises of the good Father *Clementine* were confirm'd by every Tongue. And now the Count *de Hautville* call'd for Wine to refresh the Gentleman, whose Name they now knew to be Monsieur *de Chateau-Roial*. Soon after, Dinner being ready, they repair'd to the Parlor, and the Ladies charm'd with *Clarinda*, strove to entertain her as well as they were able, and to recover her Health, she being very weak, and much indisposed. We must now take leave of them for some time, and return to *Emilia* and *Teresa*, whom we left at the Widow's.

---

1 In Roman Catholicism a dispensation may allow for exemption from existing canon law, in this case the requirement for celibacy.

CHAP. X.

TERESA was a Month after her arrival at *Seraja*'s deliver'd of a dead Son, and lay sometime sick; but recovering, and both the Ladies working with their Needles all Day, gain'd a great deal of Money, whilst *Antonio* went frequently abroad, to make inquiry after *Don Lopez*, and the Count *de Hautville*. At last going to the City with work, he met *Lorenzo*, who told him how the Lords were escap'd with a Lady and Girl from the Country-house; but he knew not whither, and that the Governor was gone for the Army, from which he had sent him two days before on Business. This was all *Antonio* could learn, and enough to fill the Ladies with new Hopes of seeing them again. Sometimes they imagin'd they were got to some Ship, and return'd home; yet it seem'd not very probable they would leave *Barbary* without having found them: then they concluded they lay somewhere conceal'd, and would not fail to inquire them out. This, with the Knowledge of the Governor's being gone for the Army, made them more vent'rous than before, and they walk'd out sometimes to the adjacent Towns, and often in the open Fields, in hopes of meeting their Husbands. But it so happened, that *Muley*[1] *Arab*, youngest Son to the Emperor of *Fez* and *Morocco*, who was used to hunt often near this Place, it now being Winter, riding by one Evening with few Attendants, saw these unfortunate Ladies, attended by *Antonio*, walking home to the Widow's. Their Beauty surprized him, tho their Habit was mean; he order'd one of his Slaves to follow them, which he did, and return'd to the Prince, who the next Morning sent one of his chief Favourites to the House. He talk'd with the Woman in the *Turkish* Language, asking her who these Women were. She told them they were poor Maids, Captives, whom she had bought to work with her in Embroidery. He presently demanded what Price she would part with them at, saying he would purchase them. At these Words the poor Woman was confounded. She reply'd trembling, 'I love them so dearly I cannot part with them.' 'Then, *said he*, You shall go along with them; my Master the Prince of *Fez* will provide nobly both for you and them; he will be here this Night.' He instantly departed, and left the Widow and Ladies, to whom she explain'd what the *Mahometan* had said, in the utmost distraction: Whither to fly they knew not, and to stay there was certain Ruin. They therefore resolved immediately to pack up their Mony, Clothes, and Jewels,

---

1 Also transliterated from the Arabic as Moulay or Mouley, meaning a prince of royal blood.

and be gone towards the Sea-side. Whilst they were doing this, *Antonio* enters the House quite out of Breath. He had been out that Morning with some Goods to a Merchant's near *Attabala*'s House, and returning, saw the two Lords and *Attabala* walking in a Field near it. He concluded it was them by the description *Emilia* and *Teresa* had given of them, and therefore hasted to bring the good News, having never rested in the way, tho it was ten Miles from the good Widow *Seraja*'s. 'Ladies, *said he*, I have fortunately found your Husbands; now we shall be happy, and only *Antonio* will remain wretched.' *Teresa* and *Emilia* transported, reply'd, 'Blest be our God who ever helps us when distress'd, let us go hence, with them we shall be secured; and tho you our good Angel have not yet inform'd us who you are, yet I doubt not but we, or our Husbands, may be instrumental to make you happy also.' Here they inform'd him of *Muley Arab*'s Message, and the Necessity of their removing thence: 'I will then, *said he*, return to the House where they are, and give your Lords notice of your coming: meantime delay not to haste to us, we will meet you on the way; but if you meet any Company on the Road, conceal your selves behind some Trees, or stay in the great Wood till we come to you.' *Teresa* put the Box of Jewels into *Antonio*'s Hands, saying, 'Take you these into your Care, and give them to our Lords to secure, before they come to us: we will follow your Directions, and be soon with you.' He drank something to refresh him, and departed; it was not long e'er they follow'd, making what haste they were able to get to the Place appointed; but alas, Fate has otherwise decreed. The Moorish Lord returning to his Prince, related to him the Disorder *Seraja* was in at his Proposal, and advised him to be quick in securing the Women. 'My Lord, *said he*, they are the fairest Creatures my Eyes ever saw, and, if I mistake not, Christians, and of noble Birth.' The Prince more inflamed with this Relation, gave Orders to some of his Attendants to follow him, and mounting a swift *Arabian* Horse, set out for the Widow's, *Ismale* the Moorish Lord leading the way. They found the House empty; and all things being left in disorder, shew'd the Inhabitants were fled in the utmost Haste and Confusion. The Prince raged, commanding his Vassals to divide themselves into Parties, and pursue them with all Diligence. The cunning *Ismale* advised him to make for the Sea-Coast; 'They are doubtless, *said he*, fled thither in hopes to get off in some Ship or Boat to some of the *European* Forts or Consuls, to *Tripoli*[1] or

---

1   There was a British consulate in Tripoli, then a major port of Tripolitania (territory now corresponding with northwestern Libya and southeastern Tunisia).

Cuta.[1] *Muley Arab* follow'd his Counsel, and soon overtook the unfortunate Travellers, who being loaded, unused to walk fast, and afraid of every Passenger they met, were not got half way to *Attabala*'s. The *Moors* seized upon them; and it was needless to ask who they were, for their charming Faces betray'd them. The Prince view'd them with Transport, descended from his Horse; and speaking to the affrighted Widow, who spoke his Language, bid her tell them, they should not fear, he was passionately in love with them, would make them great, they should live in his Palace, and smile in his Arms. To all which she answer'd not, but with low Cursies, and downcast Eyes: At last she too well explain'd his Meaning to the almost despairing Ladies, whose prospect of approaching Happiness render'd this cruel disappointment insupportable: nor was their Terror less that their Lords should come up to them at this fatal juncture, and be exposed to the cruel Infidel's Fury. This is the uncertain Condition of Man's Life, that we scarce know what to wish for, or to fear. These poor Ladies but a few Moments before impatiently long'd to see their dear Husbands, and now they dread their Presence worse than Death. Thus the Fruition of our Wishes is oft our Punishment; and we ought to desire nothing earnestly, but leave all to Providence. *Emilia, Teresa* and the Widow, were placed in the middle of the Band of *Moors*, and led by three of them, who quitted their Horses, to take care of these unfortunate Ladies. It was with much difficulty they got them to the next Village, where the Prince order'd they should stay to rest, till one of his Coaches came to carry them to his Summer-Palace, which was not many Miles distant. Here he enter'd the House of a Bassa,[2] who was much overjoy'd at this fortunate Opportunity of obliging his Prince. Here the Ladies and Widow were conducted to a Chamber, where two Eunuchs waiting on them, hinder'd their conversing together; for they dared not discover their Thoughts to each other, for fear of being understood, and betraying their Lords. They sat looking dejectedly, Tears and Sighs only exprest the State of their Minds: Wine, Sherbets, Sweet-meats, Cold-Meats, and the most delicious things that please the Taste were presented to them; but they respectfully refus'd to eat, or drink. *Muley Arab* was magnificently treated by the Bassa, and his

---

1 Ceuta, a heavily fortified port at the Mediterranean entrance to the Straits of Gibraltar, became a Spanish exclave in Morocco in the sixteenth century.

2 An earlier form of the Turkish title *pasha*, meaning a military commander or a provincial governor.

Coach being come, departed, the Bassa waiting on him, with many of his Slaves, to guard the Coach into which he was enter'd, with the two Ladies, out of respect to whom the rich Curtains of the Coach were drawn. *Seraja* was presented with a Horse to ride on, which a Slave leading, she went next the Coach; for the Prince used her very kindly, designing to make her assist him in gaining the Ladies Affections. And now he had an Opportunity of viewing the charming *Teresa* and *Emilia* at leisure: the first having lain in but some Months before, and been long sick, look'd pale and thin; but her Youth, and the innocent Sweetness that bloom'd in her Face, rivalled *Emilia's* majestick Charms, where the Heroine appear'd, and every Look drew Admiration and Respect. *Muley Arab* gaz'd, and burn'd; his Eyes sparkled with desire, and he languish'd to possess both: He was divided in his choice, yet gave *Teresa* the preference; he long'd to speak his Passion; and having learn'd the *Spanish* Tongue, addrest himself in that to them, asking, if either understood it. *Teresa* reply'd, 'I do my Lord.' He was transported that she understood him, and began to speak the most tender and passionate things to her that Love could dictate; for the *Moorish* Nobility, and indeed the whole Nation, are much inclin'd to Love, very amorous and gallant. At length casting down her lovely Eyes, with a modest Blush, a Look, where Vertue, Fear, and Resolution were all blended together, 'Prince, said she, being so greatly born, as you are, and so generous in your Deportment to us Strangers, I presume to implore your Pity, and promise my self Success, since you appear so human and princely in your Speech and Mien; we are both Christians of noble Birth, already dispos'd of to two Gentlemen, who were unfortunately brought to this Place by Pirats, and made Slaves. None ought to have the Honour of sleeping in your Arms but Virgins, whose Hearts and Persons have not been sully'd with anothers Embraces, or Love. We are already preengag'd, and can't oblige you without Horror and Dislike, or meet your Love with mutual Warmth and Satisfaction; nay, we must rather chuse to merit your utmost Displeasure and die, than yield to gratify your lawless Love.' While she spoke, the Prince listned as if he had heard some *Syren* sing, and grew more mad in Love. Her Wisdom charm'd him, every Look, each Motion fired his Blood, and he thought every Moment was an Hour till he reach'd home. He answer'd with a Bow, and said, 'If Man can make you happy, *Muley Arab* will: by *Mahomet* I swear, you shall command my very Soul, and I will make you blest as Woman can be.' This he spoke to make her easy, and in mysterious Words conceal'd his Meaning, which was never to part with her; nor did he think *Emilia* less worthy of his Favour, tho he did not love her equal with the other.

They at last arrived at his Palace, where he took *Teresa* by the Hand, the *Moorish* Lord *Ismale* leading *Emilia*. They were conducted to a noble Apartment on the top of the House, where the Prince took leave of them, leaving a Female Slave to attend them. *Teresa* beg'd him to permit *Seraja* to come to them, which he immediately granted. So saluting both with Passion, he retired, the reason of which was this: He had received from the Emperor his Father's Hands, six months before, a Wife, who was the Daughter of an *Arabian* Prince, who had assisted him in reducing a powerful Rebel and his Party, who had rebelled against him, and dethroned him, had not *Abdela* the brave *Arab* come to his assistance. This Lady was very handsome, and of a haughty disposition, very proud and revengeful; she loved him passionately, and was so jealous of all Women that he but seem'd to like, that she had poison'd several of those fair unfortunate Creatures she found in his Seraglio's, whom he had purchased or received as Presents. He therefore dreading she would serve these Ladies so, if he omitted to visit her immediately upon his return home, left them; and going to her Apartment, appear'd very pleasant and obliging, sat down to Dinner with her, a particular Favour in that Nation; and after Dinner proposed to her to return that Night to *Fez*, to the Royal Palace, because he should go forth very early the next Morning to hunt, and should disturb her, and design'd to return to *Fez* in the Evening: to this she willingly consented. And now he thought he had secured himself one happy Night, in which he purposed to enjoy the two loveliest Women in the World: but the Prayers and Tears of the virtuous *Teresa* and *Emilia* had reach'd Heaven; God who disappoints the wicked, and preserves in a wonderful manner those that fear and love him, had otherwise decreed. *Ximene* the haughty Princess was quickly inform'd by a Slave whom she favour'd, that the Prince had brought home two *European* Women, fair as Angels, in the pursuit of whom he had spent that Day; that his hunting was but a pretence to procure her Absence. In fine, this officious Woman told her all that could excite both her Curiosity and Revenge; which she was spur'd on to do by a secret Reason, which was, that she had been in her Youth vitiated by the Prince, and afterwards neglected: This made her distracted whenever she saw him fond of any other, and study to make him wretched, which she could no other way bring about but to continually incense *Ximene* against him, who always rewarded her for these cruel malicious Services. The Prince, who had been those unlucky Moments absent, whilst the treacherous *Dalinda* had whisper'd this fatal Secret to her Lady, return'd to give her his Hand to the Coach, which was then ready with her Attendants to set out for *Fez*, but found her much disorder'd: 'I am not well, said she, and I cannot go tonight.' At these words she pretended to faint, and fell down on her Bed. The Prince was sufficiently vext at this cross accident, but did not suspect his secret designs were betray'd to her. He seem'd much concern'd (as no doubt he was) kist, embraced, and used all possible means to please her. She seem'd to recover, said she would lie alone that Night; tho she had a secret Design, and not Sickness, made her chuse to do so. In some time he asked her to take the Air in the Gardens; but she refused, and chose to let him go alone, for that was what she wanted. He long'd to consult *Ismale*, having perceiv'd a change in *Ximene*'s Face and Humour, that made him fear somebody had told her of the Ladies. Whilst the Prince and his Favourite walked in the Garden, *Ximene* conjures the Slave to show her *Teresa* and *Emilia*: she leads her Lady to the Room; *Ximene* only past thro it, and returning to her Chamber, was so surprized at their Beauty, and fired with Jealousy, that she resolved to poison them that Night, and commanded *Dalinda* to make a *China* Bowl of delicate Sherbet mixt with a deadly Poison, which she always kept ready prepared for such wicked purposes. *Dalinda* fail'd not to execute her Mistress's Orders, and having mixt the deadly Potion, left the Bowl upon a Table in the next Room, designing to carry it up to the Ladies as a Present from the Prince, whilst *Ximene* detain'd him with her, which she resolved to do that Night, knowing the Ladies would not live till the next Morning after drinking the fatal Draught. No sooner had *Dalinda* left the Room, but the Prince returning from the Garden enters it, and being very dry, takes up the Bowl, concluding it was Sherbet made for the Princess; and going into her Chamber, drinks to her. She not imagining *Dalinda* had been so indiscrete to leave the poison'd Sherbet there, refused not to pledge him, taking a good draught of it. She seem'd very obliging to the Prince, to engage him to stay with her, asking him to drink Tea with her. They sat down together, and *Dalinda* being call'd for, soon mist the Bowl, and perceived the fatal Error, yet dared not speak. In less than an Hour the Prince and Princess began to fall into strange Convulsions; which *Dalinda* perceiving, and fearing to be tortured and put to death, for being the fatal cause of theirs, pack'd up what she could, as Jewels and Gold, and fled to the Woods, where she was seen to enter, but never came forth again, being (doubtless) that Night devour'd by the wild Beasts, of which *Barbary* is very full. A great Distraction reign'd in the Palace; the Physicians were call'd, and used all their Endeavours to save them, but in vain. *Dalinda* was believ'd the Author of this Mischief, but none could guess the reason why. Before five in the Morning *Muley Arab* and *Ximene* expired, she confessing what she design'd, and acknowledging God's Justice in her end. And now the Slaves and Favourites of the dead Prince walk'd like silent Ghosts, looking upon one another. A Messenger was sent to acquaint the Emperor with this dismal News of his Son's Death, whom he was very fond of: *Ismale* the *Moorish* Lord bare the fatal message, and soon return'd with a Troop of Soldiers, who by the Emperor's Order discharged such of the Attendants as he thought fit; took all the Women in his Seraglio, and conducted them in Coaches, being all veil'd, to an old Seraglio where the Wives and Concubines of the deceased Princes are kept, some all their Lives, and others are disposed of to the Favourites of the Emperor, or Prince who succeeds the Prince to whom they belong'd. To this dismal Place was *Teresa* and *Emilia* carry'd; yet they in their Hearts praised God for their Deliverance from *Muley Arab*, whose surprizing Death, and the manner of it, they looked on as an Earnest of God's Favour, and were the more encourag'd to confide in his merciful Providence. The good Widow was offer'd her Liberty to return to her home; but she chose to attend the Ladies: They had in this decay'd Palace the Liberty of walking in the Gardens, lying together, and hoped soon to find an Opportunity to escape, resolving to fly to *Attabala*'s, if it were possible to find the way: but alas, it was more than sixty Miles thence, and almost impossible for them to reach it without falling into new Misfortunes: the Widow advis'd them rather to make to the Sea-side, and endeavour to get a Passage to *Spain* or *France*, promising to go her self to *Attabala*'s, which she could do safely. This Counsel they approv'd of, and tho they were very unwilling to part with her, yet they at last consented to her going; she easily obtain'd leave of the Governess of the Seraglio, and chief Eunuch, and so left them, setting out for her own home, where she doubted not to find News of *Antonio*, and the Lords. And here we shall leave the Ladies for a time, and relate what happen'd to Don *Lopez*, the Count *de Hautville*, and the rest of *Attabala*'s Guests, since *Antonio* parted from the Ladies, and the good *Seraja*'s House.

CHAP. XI.

ANTONIO SOON REACHED *ATTABALA*'s HOUSE, AND FOUND THE
TWO LORDS, MONSIEUR *de Chateau-Roial, Clarinda, Eleonora,* and
Anna, at Dinner: He ask'd for *Attabala,* who coming to him, he
desired to know if two Gentlemen were not there, whose names
were Don *Lopez,* and Count *de Hautville.* 'I come, said he, from
their Ladies, *Emilia* and *Teresa,* who are now on the Road,
coming to them.' *Attabala* ran into the Parlor, and told this good
News: All the Company rose from the Table. *Antonio* was call'd
in; but what Words can express the Transport he and *Anna* were
in, when she knew him to be her Lover *Carolus Antonio Barbarini,* the generous *Angelina*'s Son, that noble *Venetian* Lady
who had bred her up? they flew to one anothers Arms. He gaz'd
upon her, wept for Joy, at length swooned upon her Bosom; Joy
so disorder'd his Soul, that every Faculty stood still, and his
Heart and Pulse forgot to move. Don *Lopez* held him up, and all
the Company stood looking on surpriz'd. At last awaking, as it
were from a long Sleep, he lifted his Eyes, and cry'd, '*Anna,* thou
dearest thing on Earth, behold the Man that has follow'd you to
this barbarous Place, and for your sake ventur'd to brave both
Death and Slavery: we'll part no more whilst we do live; I'll
perish by your Side, or carry you safe to *Venice* again. And now,
Gentlemen, said he, arm your selves, and set out this Moment to
meet your Wives; as we are on the way I'll tell you more: We must
not delay one Moment to go to them; here is a Box of Jewels of
great value which they gave me for you, and I will give to *Anna*'s
care till we return.' At these Words *Eleonora* casting her Eyes
upon Don *Lopez,* cry'd, 'Ah! faithless *Spaniard,* you then are
marry'd, and another claims your Heart; you have deceived me
cruelly.' He was too much in haste to answer more than in these
few Words, 'Forgive me, Madam, I dared not tell you truth, nor
did I know whether *Teresa* were still living; had she been dead,
the charming *Eleonora* had a juster Title to my Heart than any
Woman: yet you shall be happy, I will esteem, respect and love
you next *Teresa,* keep you still near me, and make your Interest
always mine.' They hasten'd him to depart, and the three Gentlemen, *Attabala,* and *Antonio* set out well arm'd, to meet the
Ladies. They came to the Wood, hollow'd, call'd, and ran to every
corner of it, but in vain: At last they went quite to *Seraja*'s
House, and finding all in disorder, concluded they were fallen
into *Muley Arab*'s hands; in which opinion they were confirmed
by the Report of some Passengers whom they inquired of.

Nothing could be more afflicted than the Count and Don *Lopez*; they were even inconsolable, and Monsieur *de Chateau-Roial* and *Antonio* had much ado to prevail with them to return home. They would have pursued the Moorish Prince, but *Antonio* told them the Attendants he had with him were so numerous, and well-arm'd, that it would be the Action of Madmen to attempt an Encounter with them. The Lords seem'd quite abandon'd to Grief, and returning home, appear'd so cast down, that at last the charming *Clarinda* spake to them in this manner: 'My Lords, are you Men and Christians? have you been both deliver'd from perishing in the merciless Seas by God's Providence, from a desolate island, where he supply'd you not only with Bread, but with Friends, and a Ship to carry you thence in safety, and land you at the Port you desired? Has he preserv'd your Lives from the Pirates Sword, and freed you miraculously from Chains and Slavery? preserv'd your Wives from the vicious Governor? and have you now forgot his Mercies, and doubt his Power? Is there one of us here who are not living Monuments of the Almighty's Goodness, and shall we despair? Suffer not then your Reason to be silenced by Passion; but call to Mind the great things God has already done for you, and put your Confidence in him, who will never leave nor forsake us, whilst we trust in and love him. He will give his Angels charge of the virtuous Women you so mourn for, and restore them safely to you if he thinks fit: if not, by your submission to his divine Pleasure, endeavour to obtain his Favour, an happy end in this World, and eternal Joy and Repose in the next, where your Wives will be restor'd to you; and all your Sufferings here converted into Joy and Glory.' Here she ended her admirable Discourse, and the Count *de Hautville* return'd her this Answer: 'Madam, your Advice is good, and I will endeavour to take it. Come my Friend, said he to Don *Lopez*, shake off your Weakness, and let us leave all to God; this Life is short, and full of disappointments, let us behave our selves like Men and Christians. He that made us and our Wives, will preserve them.' Here fair *Anna* interrupted them, saying, 'My Lords, look upon this young Gentleman and me, and learn to trust in Providence, I have not yet had time to ask him how he came here, nor by what Miracle conducted to this Place.' 'Charming *Anna*, said *Antonio*, I will with pleasure satisfy both you and the Company; but first my Advice is, that *Attabala* should go to *Seraja*'s House, and see if any Person be there, and leave word in the Village which she and the Ladies, if they escape, will probably go to, to inquire after me: and let *Attabala* leave word with *Johama Benduker*,[1] her dear Friend, that her Slave *Antonio* waits for her and her Friends at the Place they were coming to, when he left them. *Attabala* may likewise inquire after the Prince, and what else he can. In the mean time let us continue quiet; for should we remove hence before we hear from them, they would never be able to find us, nor can we be so safe elsewhere.' They all approved of this Advice, and *Attabala* went to *Seraja*'s that Afternoon. And now the Company sitting together, *Anna* fetching the Box of Jewels, gave them to the Lords, saying, 'Here is the rich Treasure given to my charge, which I deliver to you, to whom it belongs: Upon my word it would sell for a Sum great enough to provide for us all handsomely.' The Lords were amaz'd at the number and richness of the Diamonds, and *Antonio* told them how the Ladies came by them. Don *Lopez* said, 'Since Providence gave them us, they shall serve us all, and provide for all our Necessities: since God has made us Companions in Adversity, we will mutually strive to make one another happy.' Now *Anna* proposed the hearing *Antonio*'s Story since he and she parted, and he related it in the manner following.

'Gentlemen and Ladies, said he, my Name and Birth I find fair *Anna* has already inform'd you of, and how our Affections grew with our Years, and the Manner in which she was ravisht from me. I must then begin my Narrative from the most unfortunate Hour of my Life. The Day that we were parted, I was with my dear Mother *Angelina*, at our House in the City, to which we were retir'd for safety, when the dismal News was brought, that the *Turks* had landed and ravaged all the Coast, and enter'd the Monasteries, and carry'd away a great number of the Nuns and Inhabitants round about,[2] destroying and plundering the most sacred Places; and that *Anna* was amongst those the Infidels had carry'd away Captives. This News fill'd all the City with Grief, and nothing but Sighs and Lamentations were heard in the Streets, Ladies of the first Quality ran about distracted, tearing out their Hair, and wringing their Hands, for the loss of their

1 Possibly a conflation of the names of two characters in *Don Sebastian: King of Portugal* (staged 1689; printed 1690) by John Dryden (1631–1700). In the play, Benducar is chief minister to Muley-Moluch, Emperor of Barbary, and Johayma is "chief wife" to the Mufti Abdalla.

2 Knolles records a raid made by Tunisian and Algerian pirates on the southeastern Italian region of Puglia in 1638, in which they "[carried] away a great Booty, with Slaves, and amongst them several Nuns which they prostituted to their Lust" (38).

Daughters, and Death of their Sons, kill'd by the cruel Infidels: Every Family had lost one or more out of it, and every Tongue was imploy'd in aggravating the publick Calamity. But tho my Grief was not so clamorous, yet I believe none more severely felt the loss of those they lov'd, than when I heard *Anna* was gone, my Soul was shock'd, and all my Faculties fail'd me, I could neither eat nor sleep. In few Days I resolved to follow her, and rather chuse to die in Slavery, than live free, and without her. I conceal'd my desperate Design from my Mother, who was highly afflicted at *Anna*'s Loss and my Melancholy, and pretended I would go to travel only to *Rome*, *Spain* and *France*. She was very unwilling to let me go, telling me with tears, "My dear Child, said she, God has been pleased to take your noble Father from me, and my sweet *Anna*, whom next you I lov'd, you are all that are left me, in you are all my Hopes placed; do not leave me then alone." Touched to the Soul with her tender Expressions, I delay'd to go, and confin'd my self to her presence. But seeing me every Day decay and pine away, she resolv'd to send me abroad, in hopes to divert me; and commanded me to go. I yielded, and all things being prepared, as Habit, Horses, and two Servants, with Bills for Money at the Places I past thro,[1] I took leave of my dear Mother and Friends; and with her Blessing departed, promising to return soon. Now my Reason for going to *Spain* was, because had I gone from *Venice*, which was then at war with the *Turks*, I should have been liable to be taken, and made a Prisoner of war; but if I went from *Spain* or *France*, in a Vessel belonging to either of those Nations, I might be safe, and have the Protection of their Consuls at *Constantinople*, by whom I might procure *Anna*'s Freedom, paying her Ransom. And I resolved, tho she had been ravish'd by the *Turks*, and sold or presented to the Seraglio of some Villain, for that her Beauty would doubtless occasion her to be, yet I would take her to my Arms, with as much Joy and Affection, as if she had ever been mine: Yet this her tender Years made me hope to prevent. In fine, I posted thro *Italy*, and arriving at *Barcelona* in *Spain*, I sent back my Servants with a Letter to my Mother of my true Intention, got a Letter to the *Spanish* Consul at *Constantinople*, from a great *Spanish* Merchant, to whom I declared my Design, and who had Money in his Hands for my use remitted to him from *Venice*; and with his Assistance got Passage in a *Spanish* Ship, with the Fleet arrived safe at *Constantinople*, and was well receiv'd by the *Spanish* Consul, who soon got me Information

---

1 First edition: pastthro

that *Anna* was bought by a *Barbary* Captain, who was bound to *Algiers*, to which he used to carry Slaves, and rich Goods. I presently resolv'd to go thither, from which he endeavour'd to dissuade me all he was able, but in vain. I left some Money in his Hands, and the next Ship that was going to *Algiers*, I went on Board as a Passenger, paying for my Passage before-hand; but the villanous *Mahometan*, so soon as he came into the Port, chain'd and sold me at the common Market for a Slave. I was bought by an old *Jewish* Merchant; and in one Year, keeping his Accounts, for he put me to no Drudgery or servile Employment, became his chief Favourite. I endeavour'd all I was able to learn News of *Anna*, but could get none. And now another Misfortune befel me; my Master's Wife, a handsome *Portugueze* Woman, whom he had marry'd, and extreamly doated upon, cast an amorous Eye upon me, and gave me several Invitations to be great with her: but I constantly avoided her, and seem'd to be ignorant of her meaning: This so highly provok'd her, that one Day, when I was alone in the Counting-House, and my Master abroad, she came in, and shutting the Door, said, "*Antonio*, must I be forced to tell you I love you to Distraction? Are you blind to your own Interest, and determin'd to refuse me? Am I not fair, and cannot I reward you? See here." At these Words she threw down a great Purse full of Gold: "Take this, said she, and take to your Arms a Woman who loves, and can make you happy." At these Words she clasp'd me round the Neck, and almost stifled me with Kisses; I put her gently from me, in great Confusion. At this Moment my Master enter'd the Room; some officious Slave who sought my Ruin, had observ'd my Mistress and me, and given him Intimation of her love to me; and he had thus contriv'd to surpize us, having only pretended to go forth, and staid conceal'd in the House: She swooned, I stood confounded, tho guiltless: He took me by the Hair, beat and kickt me unmercifully, and swore he would poison her, and sell me the next Day. He had so bruised me I could scarce crawl to a Hole under the Stairs, and there I laid me down, expecting to rise no more. I too late repented my rashness in leaving *Venice*; yet would have died contented, had I but once seen my dear *Anna* safe and free. In the Evening of this unpleasant Day, the good *Tomaso*, *Seraja*'s Husband, came to the House with embroider'd Caps and Belts, as usual; he staid in an outer Room, and as Providence decreed, espy'd me in this sad Condition, my Face was bloody, and my Clothes all torn: he seem'd much surpriz'd, having always seen me well drest, and caress'd by my Master; he ask'd me what was the Matter; I told him the Truth: he said, he would willingly buy me. I had catch'd up the Purse of Gold when my Master enter'd the Counting-house, I put some of it into his Hand to purchase me, when my Master call'd him into the Counting-house, to pay for the Embroidery: He ask'd him for me, to give me some thing, as he pretended, and sometimes used to do, when my Master paid him; my Master exclaim'd against me: The good *Tomaso* persuaded him that his Wife and I might be innocent, at least that I was very young, and might be seduced. In short, he asked to buy me, and my *Jew* Master, glad to be rid of me, sold me for a Trifle. With him I went, and he hired a Horse for me to get home to his House, where I was maintain'd, and look'd after as if I had been their own Child. In short time the good Man died, and since that I have converted *Seraja* to the Christian Faith, and assisted her in all I was able; and getting acquainted with great many Bassa's, and Merchants Servants, still desirous to find my dear *Anna*, I continually inquir'd for her, and never could learn any thing but this: *Lorenza* the Governor's Christian Slave told me, his Master had bought a Girl, much resembling her I describ'd; but he had sent her into the Country, and I could not see her. This kept my Hopes alive, but till this fortunate Morning I was never assur'd of my Happiness; but now I regret nothing I have suffer'd, and trust in God we shall be happy together, and return in safety to our dear Mother, whom I long to see again.'

All the Company admired the strange Adventures these two young Lovers had met with, and they all resolv'd to go away together from *Barbary*, the first Opportunity after *Teresa* and *Emilia* were found; for now such an intire Friendship was contracted betwixt these unfortunate Persons, that not one of them would consent to abandon the rest, till all could be happy together. Villany and base Designs often unite men for a time, but end generally in their Ruin, and Hatred to one another; but when Religion, and virtuous noble Designs are the Basis of Mens Friendships, they are lasting and successful.

CHAP. XII.

ATTABALA return'd home at Night, and related what he had learn'd of *Muley Arab*'s carrying away the Ladies; he had left the Message with *Johama Benduker*. And now they were oblig'd to remain in suspence for some Days, in which the Lords past their time very unpleasantly; and *Eleonora* secretly rejoiced that her Rival was more wretched then her self: She now behaved her self with much Reservedness to Don *Lopez*, who treated her with great Respect and Tenderness.

At last *Seraja* arrived, and gave them an Account of the Ladies wonderful Deliverance, by the tragick end of the Prince and Princess; as likewise of their being removed to the old Seraglio, from whence she said it would be no hard matter for them to escape. This News transported the Lords, and fill'd them with new Hopes of Happiness: They entertain'd *Seraja* with the Story of *Antonio*'s good Fortune, at which she much rejoiced. They made her promise to go with them to *Venice*, and to live with *Anna*, who call'd her Mother, and caress'd her extreamly for being so kind to her Lover. *Seraja* lay there that Night, and the next Morning they consulted what to do. They at last resolv'd, that the two Lords should accompany *Seraja* back, that she should go into the Seraglio, and acquaint the Ladies where they staid to receive them, they designing to lie at some Village near: So putting on their *Grecian* Disguise, like Merchants, they set[1] out with her, having bought a Horse for her to ride upon, which *Antonio* got at the Village where he and *Seraja* had liv'd. They took some Money sufficient for the Journey, and left the Company, with many good Wishes attending them. Monsieur *de Chateau-Roial* and *Antonio* would have gone with them, but it was fear'd it would render them suspected to be seen travelling so many together. It was but threescore Miles they had to go, and in two Days time they reach'd the nearest Town to the Seraglio. Here *Seraja* advis'd them to stay, and lodge, till she return'd to them from the Ladies: they did so. Entring the Town they went to an Inn, pretending they came to buy Goods, and took a Lodging. *Seraja* enter'd the Seraglio, but was told the Ladies were not there, but gone. She enquir'd whither: They told her *Ismale* the *Moorish* Lord had beg'd them of the King, and fetch'd them thence the Night before. The Governess said, '*Seraja*, they are fortunate, he is a generous Lord, and will use them nobly; here

1 First edition: sat

are many young Virgins in this Place would rejoice to be so prefer'd.' The Widow hid her Concern as much as possible, and took leave, returning to the expecting Lords with this sad news, which they took heavily, and return'd to *Attabala*'s House, more sorrowful than ever.

And now it is necessary we should inquire what befel these unfortunate Ladies, whose unhappy Beauties occasion'd them such great Misfortunes. *Ismale* having been charm'd with their Persons when he saw them at *Seraja*'s, study'd how to obtain them, and ask'd the Emperor for them. He readily bestow'd them upon this Favourite, who made haste to fetch them from the Seraglio, fearing their being seen by some Person more favour'd, and greater than himself, who might prove a troublesome Rival. When he came there, and told his Business, you may imagine how surpriz'd the Ladies were; but he expecting such Treatment, immediately put them into a close Coach, and carry'd them to his Palace, where he lock'd them into a Chamber, which was in the upper Floor of the House, out of which a Door open'd upon a lovely Terrass Walk made on the Top of the House, to take the Evening Air upon. Here the two wretched Ladies walk'd awhile ruminating on their sad Condition, and considering what to do. At last *Emilia*, whose presence of Mind was always extraordinary, and was at this time doubtless inspir'd by Providence, looking down into the Garden below, said thus: 'My dear Friend, shall we fear to tempt Death, by venturing some way or other down this Place, into the Garden, whence God may find us some means to escape; or shall we stay here and meet our Ruin?' *Teresa* thought a Moment, and then running into the Chamber, look'd about to see if she could find any Cord or String to help them: It was just the close of the Day; they found no Strings but took the Window-curtains, and Sheets, ty'd them fast together; and fastning one end to the Rails on the House top, *Emilia* slid down first as low as she could, which was some Yards from the Ground, which she ventur'd to leap down; *Teresa* follow'd, and both escaped without much Hurt. Recovering their Legs, they ran down the Garden, and finding a Door open, went out, not knowing where to go. They wander'd thro some Fields, and at last coming to a Wood, sought a Place to hide themselves till Morning, resolving at break of Day to be gone farther off. Here they sat trembling, full of dreadful Apprehensions of being taken again, or devour'd of wild Beasts. They knew not what part of the Country they were now in, nor how far from honest *Seraja*'s House, where they had so long liv'd secure: At last they resolv'd, if possible, to climb up into some low Tree, which with some Difficulty they did, and sat there in much fear. Mean time *Ismale*, who had been engag'd by some Company that waited to speak with him at his coming home, which occasion'd him to leave *Emilia* and *Teresa* so soon, having in some time got quit of his Visitors, went up to the Chamber, ordering Supper to be brought thither, designing to enjoy himself in their Company all that Night: But when he found the Room in such disorder, and the Ladies gone, his Surprize can't be exprest: He soon discover'd how they had escaped, and calling for his Servants bid them light Flambeaus, and search the Gardens and Fields adjacent, and if possible bring them back. The amaz'd Slaves ran up and down the Fields, and some of them entring the Wood searched here and there, but saw them not. What concern the poor Ladies were in is easily guest. At last the Servants return'd home; *Ismale* fretted and raged, but in vain, and then went to sleep in an old Mistress's Arms, at which the Servants rejoiced, and went to rest.

The Ladies past the Night in Prayer, and so soon as Day broke, came down from the Tree almost faint, and hasted over a high Hill, from whence they saw a lovely River at some distance: They hasted to it, and in a Boat that lay there to ferry Passengers over, past safely to the other side; and asking where they were, the poor Man told them the River they had past over was call'd *Omirary*,[1] a River that parts the Kingdoms of *Fez* and *Morocco*;[2] that they were not far from Mount *Atlas*, which if they past over, they would come into *Numidia*,[3] a Country inhabited by *Mahometans* and *Pagans*, govern'd by no King, but ruled by some chief Men, Heads of Tribes, chosen by the rest. 'They are a People, said he, inclin'd to thieving, *Turks* and *Pagans* in Religion, dwelling in Tents, living chiefly on Dates, feeding their Goats with the Stones, which make them very fat, and yield good store of Milk; a Country but ill inhabited.' The Ladies thank'd the poor Man, and went on towards the Mountains, not knowing which way to go, ready to faint for want of Food and Rest. They had no Money, their Habits were fine, such as are given in the Seraglio's to the Women of Condition; the Day was far spent, they had no

---

1 The River Oum el-Rbia, which rises in the Middle Atlas mountain range to the northwest of the Sahara desert and flows west to the Atlantic Ocean.
2 Morocco was traditionally divided into the "kingdoms" of Fez to the north, central Morocco, Sus to the south, and Tafilalet to the east.
3 An ancient kingdom and later a Roman province in an area of North Africa roughly corresponding to present-day Algeria.

Food. At last they came to the foot of a great Ridge of Mountains; there, unable to go farther, they sat down: *Teresa*, who was of the weakest Constitution, laid her Head on *Emilia*'s Bosom, and sighing, said, 'Surely now, my dear Friend, my unfortunate Life draws to a Period; if God sends us no help soon, we must perish here: Our Husbands know not where to find us, nor are we able to go to them. For my part, I have only this satisfaction, that having done my duty to God, and my dear Lord, I have no reason to fear Death. You, my dear Friend, will, I hope, not only survive me; but, by some Providence preserved, live to be happy with your Lord. Tell Don *Lopez* I died only his, virtuous and chaste as when he took me to his Arms, and hope to see him with Joy in the other World.' *Emilia* wept over her, and strove to comfort her.

Now Night drew on, and Darkness render'd the Place more dreadful. About Midnight *Emilia* saw a Light at some distance, in a House, as she thought; and looking stedfastly, she saw a Man kneeling at the Door, with a Candle in one Hand, and a Book in the other, as if at Prayer: She shew'd him to *Teresa*. 'My Dear (said she) let us try to get to that Place, perhaps he is some Christian; but if not, we must venture: to stay here is certain death, and therefore 'tis better to ask help of Infidels.' *Teresa* attempted to rise, but could not stand, the cold and fasting had so debilitated her Limbs, they were useless. *Emilia* was unwilling to leave her, but at last was forced to it: She hasted to the Place, and approaching near, saw a Man of middle Age, tall, well shaped, and would have been very handsome, had not Abstinence, Sickness and Hardships alter'd his Face: He had a coarse Frize[1] Coat, like a *Turkish* Dervise[2] or Hermit, a Fur Cap, short Boots like an *Arabian*. He was so intent at his Devotions, he saw her not, tho now very near him: She listen'd, and hearing him pray in the *Latin* Tongue, was encourag'd to speak to him. She threw her self on her Knees before him, saying, 'Generous Christian, help two unfortunate Women, almost dead with Want and Travelling, fled from a vile *Mahometan*'s House who would have ruin'd us: My Companion lies yonder on the cold Ground; give us Shelter in your House, and a little Food or Drink, to save our Lives.' The Hermit being risen, view'd her with Amazement: 'Lovely Creature, said he, you may command my Life; who would refuse to receive such a Guest? Let us haste to your Companion, and fear

---

1 A coarse woollen cloth.
2 A member of a Muslim religious order (specifically Sufi), living a life of austerity and poverty.

not to live with a Man, in whom you shall find a Protector and Friend.' He fetch'd a Lanthorn, and putting a Candle into it, went with her, carrying a Bottle of Rum in his Hand. *Emilia's* care for *Teresa* was such, that she staid not to drink; but forgetting her own weakness, ran to her, whom they found almost senseless. *Emilia* gave her some of the Cordial, and with their help she was got into the House.

And now the Hermit shutting the Door, hasted to kindle up a Fire of Leaves and Sticks, setting before them Bread, Meat, and Wine; of which having eat a little, they began to revive, and the Hermit, who waited on them with much seeming Pleasure and Respect, appearing very courtly in all things, said, 'Ladies, you are highly welcome to a Man who has liv'd many Years in a manner sequestred from the World. I believe we are of one Faith, and Equals in Birth; my homely Cell begins to look pleasant with such Company: May I ask who you are, and beg to know your Misfortune, that I may be the better enabled to serve you.' The Ladies had by this time observ'd the Room, and Man: The House was very poor and mean, containing below two Rooms, and (as they supposed) no more above: The Furniture was suitable; but the Master of the place appear'd to be noble, and of great Birth and Education. *Emilia* answer'd him, 'Sir, I think it is but reasonable that we should first know who you are, and your Adventures, since our want of Strength, and disorder of Mind and Bodies, may well excuse us from so tedious a Task, as the Relation of ours.' He bow'd, saying, 'Madam, forgive my Curiosity, which made me forget my Duty, and be too bold in asking so great a Favour, as to know you. Rest is fittest for you; my poor Bed and Chamber waits to receive you. Here is the Key, I shall not presume to wait on you to the Door; this Place will serve me to wait your Commands in to morrow morning, when I will freely, and with Pleasure, tell you all the Adventures of my Life past.' The Ladies were charm'd with his Behaviour; he presented a Candle and the Key to them, and would not admit their staying below any longer. They went up Stairs, and found a Bed and Chamber, neat as those in Palaces; there were some Chairs, a Carpet on the Floor, with Quilts, Sheets, and Coverlids neat and good; in a Closet were many Watches, and Tools of all sorts belonging to the Art of Watch-making: many Pictures of fine Painting without Frames, adorn'd the Walls of the Chamber. They shut the Door, undrest, and having return'd Thanks to God for this signal Mercy, went to Bed, and slept sweetly. At break of

Day they waken'd and rose; the Hermit heard them, and prepar'd a Fire: they came down, and he receiv'd them with a chearful Countenance; he was preparing Coffee for their Breakfast: and now they desir'd to hear his Story, which he thus related.

CHAP. XIII.

'I AM by Birth a *Venetian*, my Father was a noble Man, and I was his eldest Son; my Name is *Andrea Zantonio Borgornio*. I was related to a Lady, who having marry'd a wealthy Merchant, had one Daughter, with whom I fell passionately in Love; but the Custom of my Country forbidding me to marry with any Woman whose Father was inferior to my own in Quality, I resolved to marry her in secret. The Day was appointed when I was to meet her at a Country-house of her Father's to espouse her; but the Evening before, she being in her Father's Coach with her Mother and Father, attended by three Servants, was forcibly taken out of it, and carry'd away with a black Boy who follow'd her. The Ravisher was a Captain of a Ship, who was an old Man, very rich, and had loved her from her Infancy. She was then about fourteen; he carry'd her aboard his vessel, set sail with her, and was taken by an *Algerine* Pirat who carry'd her to *Algiers*, as I have since been inform'd; but how she was disposed of, I could never yet learn. It is almost eleven Years since we parted. Her Father sent a Messenger to inform me of our Misfortune the same Night she was taken away. We soon discover'd by what means we lost her, and I that minute resolved to hire a vessel to follow the Villain's Ship. Her Mother being my Father's Relation, flew to him for Redress, but his Behaviour soon inform'd me that he was consenting to the hateful Deed: He treated her very coldly; and when I importuned him to procure an order from the Senate to arrest the Villain and his Ship, offering to go my self to execute it, he look'd upon me, and said ironically, "I don't doubt your Readiness to follow him; you are too much concern'd about what ought not to concern you at all, mind your Duty; your Kinswoman is fitter to be his Wife than yours, speak no more to me about her." I understood him perfectly, and was so enraged, that I almost forgot he was my Father. I went out of the Room from him immediately, took a great Sum of Money with me, and attended only with one Servant, went directly to the Port, where I hired a light Brigantine[1] and went after her. I guest he was gone for *Spain* or *France*. In few hours we met a Ship bound for *Venice*, who told us he met Capt. *Alphonso*'s Ship; they saluted one another, *Alphonso* came aboard him, drank a Bottle of Wine, and said he was bound for *Spain*, taking some Sweetmeats and Wine this Captain had brought from *Leghorn*.[2]

---

1 A small vessel equipped both for sailing and rowing.
2 Livorno, a city and port on the western coast of Tuscany, in Italy.

This made us steer our course that way. A great Storm rose that Night, and shipwreck'd us upon this Coast. I know not what is become of the Captain and his Men, but I was saved on a piece of the Rudder, and cast on the Coast of *Barbary* near *Tunis*. Here I was taken up almost dead by a Peasant, who was very kind to me. So soon as I could walk abroad, I began to enquire where I was, what the Manners and Customs of the Country were. But I was soon taken notice of, and sent for by the *Turkish* Governor of *Tunis*, who examining me, took a fancy to me, and said if I would live with him, he would use me kindly; if not, I should be sold to somebody else. It was my best way I thought to accept of his Offer, by which I might have an Opportunity to get off for *Spain*. He employ'd me in the managing many of his Affairs, sending me with Letters and Presents, to several Ministers of State and Friends: he was very gentle, and familiar to me, and, in fine, clothed and kept me so, that I began to apprehend he had an ill Design upon me, and liked me for a use the *Mahometans* often keep young Men for. As I suspected, it proved; one Evening he call'd for me into his Closet, and gave me a rich Vest, Turbant, and an intire *Turkish* Dress of Sattin embroider'd with Silver, with Linen suitable. He bid me take it and go and dress me, for I must cease to be a Christian and a Servant, and live at ease. Then he kist me eagerly; I turn'd pale, bow'd, took the Clothes, and went out trembling, determining in my self to fly thence whatever was the Consequence. Whilst I dwelt with this Bassa *Solyman*, for that was his Name, he had a Renegado Slave, by birth a *Hollander*, who indeed had not more Religion than Honesty or Conscience. This Man's Name was *Cornelius Vandunk*, he was a Watchmaker by Profession, and having, as he own'd to me, been extravagant, and run in Debt, he fled his own Country, and went with a Merchant to *Constantinople*, to work there with him. His unconstant Temper made him uneasy there, so he wanted to be gone elsewhere, and went aboard a *French* Merchant Ship, which was taken by an *Algerine* Pirate. There he was sold to a *Jew* Merchant who used him ill; coming to *Tunis*, he resolved to free himself by renouncing Christianity. He did so, by which he ingratiated himself with the Bassa *Solyman*, and became a Favourite, working for him in curious Work: He was certainly a great Artist at his Trade, and of him I learn'd so much, as to be able to put a Watch together, and mend one tolerably; I took much delight in it; and painting in Water-Colours I was also a tolerable Master of. Being now resolved upon quitting my Service, I was considering how I could provide Bread for my self, and enjoy my Religion, the thing

I valued far above my Life. I thought now if I had a good Sum of Money with me, I might escape to some Place far distant from *Tunis*, and retire to an obscure Place where I might work and sell what I did make, till I could hear something of *Eleonora*, for that was my adored Mistress's Name; and having learn'd from a Merchant that arrived from *Algiers*, who came to bring a rich Present to *Solyman*, that *Alphonso*'s Ship had been taken and plunder'd, and the Crew and Passengers brought in and disposed of there, I was determin'd to stay in *Barbary*, till I got farther News of her. I had some Money by me, but not sufficient for such an Undertaking. I was now perfectly acquainted with the Customs of the Country, and under the religious Disguise I have now on, I knew I could pass undiscover'd and live safe. I at last resolved to take some Jewels of *Solyman*'s, which I had by his Order laid up in a Cabinet: This I did, and at Midnight departed, having provided my self of an excellent *Arabian* Horse out of his Stable. I stay'd just without the Town till Break of Day, when I set Spurs to my Horse, and rid towards *Algiers*, where in short time I arrived safe. I went to a Merchant's House, with whom my Master was acquainted, knowing he could not send after me so far, not knowing which way I went, at least till I had dispatched my Affairs; and I design'd to stay here no longer than till I had sold the Jewels, and made a full Enquiry after *Eleonora*. With the Assistance of this Merchant, the Jewels were sold in three Day's time; a *Jew* gave me five thousand Crowns for them. I was inform'd the *Algerine* Pirat had presented a Lady that was in *Alphonso*'s Ship to some *Turkish* Governor, but it was not known who; and that the Captain was dead. At last despairing to find her, and fearing to be discover'd and taken, I left *Algiers*, and went thro *Fez*, which being too populous I quitted, and retired to this lonely Place, having worn this holy Disguise seven Years, which I have lived in this Place. I bought this poor Cottage of a Merchant for whom I work, I pass for a religious Man, a Hermit; the People reverence me as I pass. I mend Watches for several Merchants in the adjacent Towns and Cities. I sell my little Pictures likewise to *Europeans*, and live comfortably, bringing home what I want. I receive no visits but at my Door. I am call'd *Ismael* the Holy Hermit.[1] I give what Alms I am able to the Poor; sometimes clothe the Naked, and secretly assist Christians who are in distress. I have made my self a Rule to live by; I dedicate every third Hour to

---

1   After the biblical Ishmael, son of Abraham and Hagar, who is sent out into the wilderness with his mother (Gen. 21.14–20).

Devotion in the Day, and rise once in the Night to Prayer, and am now so reconcil'd to this retired kind of Life, that I am indifferent whether I ever return to *Venice* or not, unless I could be so happy as to have *Eleonora* with me, or be assur'd she were dead; and then I would mourn her here, and die in this Place.'

Here he ended his Relation; *Emilia* said, 'What was the *Black*'s Name who belong'd to the fair *Eleonora*?' He answer'd, *Attabala*. 'Then, *said she*, I shall tell you Wonders; blest be our God who has brought us together.' She then began the Relation of their Adventures, and in conclusion told him of the Lords being at *Attabala*'s House, which she had learn'd from *Antonio*, 'but whether the Lady is there or not, *said she*, I cannot tell.' The Hermit, for so we must call him till he leaves his Cottage and Habit, was fill'd with Admiration at the things he heard: and they mutually acknowledged God's Goodness in preserving them all in such an extraordinary manner. And now they were very chearful, and fell to considering what was best to be done. They were above a hundred Miles distant from *Attabala*'s House; and the Hermit knew not whom to trust to send thither: At last he proposed that they should stay there whilst he went, tho it was dangerous for him to go so far. The Ladies were very unwilling to be left behind, but it was altogether unfit for them to go. The Hermit said he would buy a good *Arabian* Horse to ride on, and be soon back; to which at last they consented. He gave them Money, show'd them where he kept it hid, and counsell'd them to put on such Habits as he wore. He went and bought them such, with Food and all things necessary; and in five days time, having put all his Affairs in order, pretending to his Customers some extraordinary Business at *Algiers*, departed, having first taken leave of the fair Hermits with much Tenderness and many Blessings; they praying fervently for his safe Return. And here we must leave them till we have learn'd what is become of the Lords and the rest of *Attabala*'s Guests.

CHAP. XIV.

THE Lords being now at home in *Attabala*'s House with *Antonio*, and the charming *Anna*, who wanted nothing but a safe Passage to *Venice* to be completely happy, as likewise the fair *Clarinda* and her Lord Monsieur *de Chateau-Roial*, who were passionately fond of each other, yet determin'd to part, if they could not obtain a Dispensation for them to live together lawfully; and the fair *Eleonora*, who liked Don *Lopez* so well, that she thought no more of her first Lover, Signior *Andrea Zantonio Borgornio*: All the Company began to importune Don *Lopez* and the Count to think of returning to their Homes: 'Consider, *said they*, the dangerous Consequences that attend our staying here longer; if any one of us is discover'd, it will be the ruin of the rest.' The good *Seraja* likewise pleaded for their going: 'My Lords, *said she*, *Ismale* knows my House, you are sensible; and should he have the least Intimation of your being here or any Strangers, he would doubtless have you all taken, and examin'd. You must submit to the Will of Heaven; if God pleases he can send your Wives to you into *Spain* or *France*; but I am sorry to tell you, 'tis very unlikely, for being now in *Ismale*'s Hands, he will probably keep them too safe; Force cannot fetch them thence, you are in a strange Country, and have none to assist you. It is now the Season of the Year for Ships to come, and go to *Europe*: let *Attabala* look out for a Ship to carry you hence to *Venice*, or any part of *Europe*, from whence you may go to your several Countrys, and stay not here to be made Slaves, and the poor Ladies who have escaped hither torn from you again.' In fine, all Arguments were used to persuade them to go thence; but none was so prevailing as the generous Regard they had for their Friends, who could now be happy if they were not detain'd there by their respect for them. The Lords begg'd them to go and leave them to Providence, offering to divide all the Money and Jewels amongst them, and desiring to be left with none, but a Servant of *Attabala*'s, and in his House; but *Eleonora* opposed that strenuously, and all the rest refused to hear of leaving them alone. But now an Accident happen'd that in few Days obliged them to come to a Resolution: The incensed *Ismale*, mad to be thus disappointed, and resolving in his Mind that *Seraja* was the only Friend the Ladies had, and that it was most probable they[1] would fly to her, resolves to go to her House with his Slaves, and force her to discover where they were. He accordingly comes to the House, enquires for her, but could learn

---

1 First edition: the

nothing. He levels the House with the Ground and departs, threatning to return again, and search all the adjacent Towns and Villages. He likewise offer'd a great Reward to any Person that should find and discover her or the young Women, or her Slave *Antonio*. No sooner was he departed than *Johama Benduker*, *Seraja*'s Friend, runs to *Attabala*'s, and warns them to be gone: 'If you are discover'd, *said she*, as you certainly will, because of the Reward *Ismale* offers, you are ruined.' This News both surprized and pleased Don *Lopez*, and the Count; they were transported that the Ladies had escaped *Ismale*'s hands, yet fear'd to stay his coming: At last, *Seraja* persuaded them to leave *Johama* the Care of the Ladies, if they came; 'For, *said she*, the Slave here left, and she will conceal, and get them off if they come, with less Trouble than you can, who will be watched and question'd.' *Attabala* hasted to the Sea-side, and going off in the honest Fisherman's Boat, went aboard a *Spanish* Ship which lay there, and agreed with the Captain to carry them to *Venice*. Returning home, *Attabala* hasten'd them to get off; they packed up all, leaving with *Attabala*'s Servant Money for *Teresa* and *Emilia* to get home; *Johama* promising to take care of them. But when the Count and Don *Lopez* enter'd the Boat, their Concern appear'd; they both turn'd pale, and the big Drops roll'd down their Cheeks: 'My God, *said* Don *Lopez*, pity me, and preserve *Teresa*, whom I am now forced to leave behind me: ye Angels, guard her, and conduct her to me safe.' The Count only lifted up his Hands and Eyes, and sigh'd deeply. Thus come on board, they were by the *Spanish* Captain well received. They rewarded the Fisherman, and he departed. And now Joy fill'd every Face, but the two Lords, and they were extreme sad. The Ship lay that Night at an Anchor, and the Wind being contrary, they were obliged to wait its turning. This doubtless Providence order'd; for towards the close of the Day *Attabala*'s Servant comes in the Fisher-Boat with the Hermit, who entering the great Cabin with him, saw *Eleonora*, whom he immediately ran to, catching her in his Arms with such Transport, that she had not time to discover who he was; but his Voice soon inform'd her, it was Signior *Andrea Zantonio*. She seem'd equally glad, and if she was not so transported, yet she was doubtless pleased to see the Man she had once loved so well. After some passionate Expressions to her, he turn'd to the Company, saying, 'I know not which of these Gentlemen are the fortunate Husbands of the vertuous *Emilia* and *Teresa*, for to them my Business is.' The Lords soon inform'd him; he told them how he had saved and left the Ladies safe at his House at the Foot of Mount *Atlas*. The Lords embraced him, and made him welcome, with repeated Acknowledgments for his generous Treatment of their Wives, whom they were impatient to see. *Eleonora* also was curious to know his Adventures after they were parted, which he related to her and the Company. Then she presented *Anna* and *Antonio* to him, telling him who they were. He embraced them tenderly, glad to find some of his own Nation there, *Antonio* being his Kinsman. They now deliberated what to do; *Venice* being the nearest Place, they resolved to call there first. *Antonio* and *Anna*, *Eleonora* and Signior *Andrea Zantonio* our Hermit, fear'd not to be welcome to his Father, if he was yet living, after so long an Absence. He had always resolved to marry *Eleonora*, who now told him, with much Confusion, what had past between her and the Governor, which force excused; so that his Passion being sincere as ever, he took her to his Arms with as much Joy as if she had been a Virgin, and the Chaplain of the Ship perform'd the Ceremony that Evening; which gave *Antonio* an opportunity of pressing the charming *Anna* to make him likewise happy. Her Youth and Innocence made her hard to be persuaded to yield; but all the Company joining, she gave him her Hand, which he received with Transport; and the next Morning the whole Company meeting in the great Cabin, resolved what to do farther. The two Lords determin'd to go with the Hermit to *Emilia* and *Teresa*; the rest of the Company were to stay aboard; and it being unsafe for the Ship to be there long, they agreed it should weigh Anchor, and put out to Sea for two or three Days, and then return and stay at an Anchor till they came back with the Ladies, which could not be sooner than five or six Days, because they could not travel so fast with them. The Hermit taking leave of his Bride, who look'd with Confusion upon Don *Lopez*, and was concern'd both for him and her new Husband, not being able to quite stifle the Passion she had conceived for that charming *Spaniard*, parted with them with much Uneasiness. The Lords took a tender Farewel of the whole Company, and so departed, going ashore in the Ship's Boat. They stay'd that Night at *Attabala*'s House, where none remain'd but the faithful *Abra*, a *Turkish* Boy *Attabala* had bred up and made a Christian of in secret, to whom he had given his House and Effects. The next Morning he went and hired Horses for the two Lords, on which they set out for the Hermit's House; and travelling thither, we must leave them, and give an account of what befel the Ladies in the Hermit's Absence.

CHAP. XV.

THE second Night after the Hermit's Departure, *Teresa* and *Emilia*, having recommended themselves to God, went to Bed, and composed themselves to rest. About Midnight they were waked with dismal Groans and Lamentations, which seem'd to proceed from some Person near the House. They listen'd awhile, and heard a Woman's Voice, who express'd her Grief in these Words, in the *French* Tongue: 'My God, where shall I find shelter? Who shall assist me in this barbarous Place? When shall my Sorrows end? Why is my wretched Life prolong'd? and to what end dost thou preserve me yet on this side the Grave, to suffer farther Miseries? Has not thy Vengeance yet o'ertaken him that ruined me? and can thy Justice suffer me, who am innocent, to be thus miserable? Must I live still to be the Slave of cruel lustful Infidels? Oh, show me some hospitable Cave or Cavern in the Rocks to hide my self, and die at Peace in.' Here she sigh'd, her Voice seem'd to decay, and Groans succeeded. *Teresa* and *Emilia*, whose Hearts melted at these moving Sounds, were both fearful to propose what both desired to do, which was to open the Door, and take the Stranger in. They were alone, and in a lonely Place, unable to resist whatever Violence were offer'd. It might be some Imposture. At length, Compassion forced *Emilia*, whose Courage was extraordinary, as she had before manifested, to speak thus to *Teresa*: 'Shall we deny that Charity to another, which we were saved by in this Place? Shall we not relieve a Christian and one of our own Sex in Distress?' *Teresa* answer'd, 'Do what you please.' *Emilia* went to the Window, and call'd, but none answer'd. Then she struck a Light, and they went down Stairs, and opening the Door saw at a little distance from it, a Woman fallen down upon her Face. They dragg'd her into the House, and fastening the Door, set her in a Chair, and pour'd some Cordial down her Throat, upon which she revived. She was richly drest in an *Arabian* Habit of Silk embroider'd, her Hair was hanging loose, very fair, and in great quantity. She had a small Wound in her left Breast, a Necklace of brilliant Diamonds about her Neck, Earrings of great value, and her Face and Person delicately handsome. She appear'd to be about five and twenty, and extremely frighted. At last having recover'd her Reason, she looked round her, and then perceiving the charming *Emilia* and *Teresa* in their odd Hermits Dress to be Women speaking words of Comfort, and very earnest to help her, she broke out into these passionate Words, 'Am I with Christians? Are Angels provided to take care of the unhappy *Charlot?* Has my God heard me at last? and brought me to a place, where Vertue and Charity reside? And am I freed from impious Infidels?' Here she kiss'd *Emilia*'s Hands, who was putting Balsam[1] to her Wound. And now the Ladies asked her who she was, and her Misfortunes that brought her there. She willingly inform'd them: 'I will recount to you, *said she*, a Story full of Wonders, so moving and so strange, that you will be fill'd with Admiration.' They made a Fire, and having given her Wine and Meat sat down by her, she desiring them to put out the light for Reasons she would tell them.

'I am, *said she*, a native of *France*, born in *Paris*. My Father was a celebrated Painter. He had by my Mother, who was the Daughter of a *French* Colonel, a Woman of great Beauty and Fortune, no Child but me. Our House was frequented by a great many of the Nobility, who came to have their Pictures drawn, or see my Father's curious Paintings, he having a Collection of the choicest Pictures, both antient and modern, of any Painter in *Paris*. He was very rich, and design'd me a great Fortune. I was tolerably handsom, and this caused me to be extremely courted, both for a Mistress and a Wife; but my Father's Ambition was so great, and he thought so well of me, that he refused to give me to several good Tradesmen and Merchants, hoping to match me to some great Officer or Count: In fine, a young Nobleman coming to have his Picture drawn by my Father, saw and loved me, courted and visited me often in private, fearing his Father's Displeasure, who was of great Quality. I was so foolish to imagine his Designs were honourable; and being charm'd with his agreeable Person, Behaviour, and bewitching Conversation, grew insensibly to love him passionately. He too well perceiv'd my Weakness, and made his Advantage of it. He made me many Presents of Value, caress'd my Father and Mother highly; so that they entertain'd and gave him all the Liberty imaginable with me, suspecting nothing of his base Design, which was to ruin me, which he thus effected: He had gain'd my Maid to be his Creature, she fill'd my Ears with his Praises daily, and encreased my Distemper. One Day when my Father and Mother were invited to dine abroad with some grave Company, where it was not proper for me to go, my Lover who had information of their being absent, comes in a

---

1 An aromatic and resinous substance used in medical preparations, though more generally any substance with healing or soothing properties.

Hackney-Coach,[1] and after some amorous Discourses, as gallant and pleasant as usual, asks me to go abroad with him, taking *Phillis* my Maid with me. "We will go to a Friend's of mine, *said he,* whom I can trust, and be merry." I was proud that he would show me to his Friends, and thought my self very safe, having *Phillis* with me; nay, I thought him so noble and sincere, that I had not the least distrust of him. I drest my self richly, and went into the Coach with him, leaving my Parents and Home, which I fear I shall never see again; he carry'd me ten miles from *Paris,* there we alighted at a House, hired for his fatal purpose, as I was too soon sensible; I saw none but two Servants, a Man and Maid, who received him as their Master. The House stood in a Garden, and no House within call. Here he gave me Wine, and a Dinner, which was ready prepared. I began to be much surprized, and apprehensive of what follow'd. He told me after Dinner he was tired, and must lie down upon the Bed: In fine, I trembled, and saw too late I was betray'd. And to dwell no longer on the dismal Subject, here he forced me to Bed, and tho I used Prayers, Tears, and resisted all I was able, he at length overcame me, swearing he would marry me. Here he stay'd all Night, and left me the next morning in the Hands of my Betrayer, *Phillis,* and his two Servants, who watched me as a Prisoner. I knew not where to go; I loved the Villain that had undone me, was ashamed to be seen, and was so well watched, that if I would have gone thence I could not. He came frequently, kept me nobly, and used me tenderly. My poor Father and Mother too well guest their Misfortune, and mourn'd for me in secret. My Lover went no more to visit them. My Father attempted to speak with him, but the Servants used him rudely. The Neighbours laugh'd and ridiculed him, because he had disoblig'd many of them, whose Sons and Brothers had been refus'd when they adrest me: In fine, he fell sick, and in less than two months died, leaving my Mother a rich but disconsolate Widow. I was kept no longer so very strictly, being big with Child, and my Father dead. I was permitted to visit my poor Mother, to whom I related my Misfortune; we wept together, but could find no Remedy. I was kept thus five Years, in which I never appear'd abroad, but with a Masque. I had three Children. My dear Mother often came to me privately, and past some days with me, my two Sons died at Nurse, my Girl grew,

---

1 A four-wheeled coach for hire, typically drawn by two horses with seating for six passengers.

and my Betrayer was very fond of me and the Children. I still flatter'd myself he would at last marry me, but his Father, who had took little notice of his keeping a Mistress, thought it was time for him to marry, and give an Heir to his Family; he proposed a young Lady of Quality and Fortune suitable; and having now glutted himself with me, my Lover made no difficulty to oblige his Father and himself with a new Dish. He marry'd the Lady, who was handsom and a Virgin; he grew fond of her, and slighted me. I never saw him, but I reproached him with my Wrongs, so that he not only continued to slight me and came seldom to see me, but used me so unkindly that we never met but we quarrel'd. This, with the Torments of his Conscience, doubtless made him resolve on being rid of me. He comes to me in his own Coach as usual, for now he made no secret of our Converse, which made him not very easy with his Lady; he appears very sad, and treats me with unusual Tenderness, sups, and goes to bed with me, and there with all the Marks of Affection and Penitence, says thus to me: "My dear *Charlot*, I have wrong'd you cruelly, my Conscience is wounded, I have not had a Moment's Quiet since I marry'd, and now I am resolved to make you Reparation; I am yours, and not hers whom I sinfully marry'd. I am determined to leave her, and have provided a Ship to carry and Money to maintain us in *England*, whither I mean to fly with you and my dear Child." You may imagine, loving him as I did, how easily I was persuaded to credit him: In fine, I agreed to all he proposed with Joy, and a few days after he came, took me, and would have had the Child but my Mother would not be persuaded to part with it: he carried me to *Calais*, where we went aboard a Merchant Ship. I had carry'd only my Clothes and Maid, and he pretending he had remitted his Money to *England*, brought only two large Portmantuas[1] on board. He led me into the Cabin, where we supp'd, and lay all Night. He left me dressing in the Morning to go talk with the Captain, I suspecting nothing. In some time I sent *Phillis* to call him to breakfast, and she staying long, I call'd, but no body came: At last I look'd out, and saw the Ship under sail. The Captain came, I ask'd for my Lord and Maid; he told me they were gone on shore in the Boat. I wrung my Hands, and wept; he told me it was all in vain, he had Orders for what he did. In short I fell sick with Grief, kept my Bed, and was brought to *Tripoli* before I knew where I was. Here I was

---

1 Another form of "portmanteaux," meaning cases for carrying clothes.

brought to Shore, carry'd to a House, rob'd of my Clothes and Jewels. The Portmantuas brought aboard by my villanous Lord, were empty, as I satisfied my self before: In this Place I was sold to an *Arabian* Captain, or Chief of a Tribe. He carry'd me with him, and what became of the Christian Dog that sold me, I know not. *Abenbucer* the brave *Arab* used me kindly, lov'd, and prefer'd me before all his Women; but, alas! what Joy could I take in this dismal course of Life? A thousand times I've wished to die. I was carried up and down with the rest of his Women, in a cover'd Waggon, when we mov'd our Habitations, which we did twice in the sad year. I liv'd with him three Days since we came near this Mountain. A Brother of *Abenbucer*'s, great as himself in Power, of a Humour different, resolute and revengeful, some time since saw and liked me, and studied how to take me from his Brother. Yesterday *Abenbucer* being gone with his Band to forage, *Abdelan* comes with his Band of Soldiers to the Tent, and takes me away: just as he was going off, *Abenbucer* comes by, in short I screem'd, a bloody Dispute ensued, in which I was the Victim to their Rage, being drag'd by the Hair from one side to the other; here I receiv'd my Wound: at last seeing the two Brothers sharply engag'd, I ran from them, and escap'd over the Mountain, where I wander'd the rest of the Day, fearing to be pursued, till Darkness, loss of Blood and Weakness oblig'd me to stop; at last my Senses fail'd, and had not God sent you to assist me, I had perhaps perish'd on the cold Ground.'

The Ladies admired, and wept at the sad Story; and then lighting a Candle, got her to bed, where they spent the remainder of the Night in Discourse, telling her part of their Adventures. Towards Morning they slept, and rising later found *Charlot* so ill she could not rise; and now she exprest her Fears to them: 'Ladies, (said she) I fear it will not be long before the incensed Brothers, at least he that survives, will come in search of me over the Mountains; 'tis my Advice therefore, that we remove to some Town of Strength for some Days, lest you are discover'd and ruin'd by protecting me. Your Beauty, which far excels mine, will perhaps cause them to bear you hence with me; you are very unsafe here.' This alarm'd the poor Ladies, who finding but too much probability in what she said, were now afraid to remain here; *Emilia* therefore goes to a neighbouring Village, where the Hermit was known, says they were his Kinsmen whom he had left in the House, and desires a Lodging, and some Lad of Integrity to stay in the House for some Days till *Ismael* their Kinsman return'd, because they had been frighten'd with a Band of Robbers, who were roving on this side the Mountain; which was not very frequent, they not often venturing to come on that side. The honest *Moors* reverencing their Habit, offer'd them a House to live in till the good *Ismael* came home. *Emilia* gave the Poor of the Place a large Alms, which highly encreased their Respect for her: And so she return'd with a Lad with her, the Son of one of the principal Men of the Village. She had before she went, pack'd up their Money, and drest the sick Lady in an old Habit of the Hermit's, packing up her rich Habit and Jewels in a Bundle. They led her betwixt them, and left nothing of much value behind them, ordering the Lad to bring the Hermit, and whoever came with him, to them. The Boy did not fear the Robbers, when nothing was left in the House worth their taking: but the fourth Night of his stay the poor Lad was murder'd by some Robbers, who enter'd the House in the Night, and plunder'd it, and fearing Discovery, kill'd him in the Bed as he slept; which some Days after was discover'd by the Thieves being taken, one of whom being put to death, confest this Fact, with many others.

The next Morning after the Boy was kill'd, the Hermit and the Lords arrived, and entring the House, were entertain'd with this dismal Spectacle: The Door was open, the House plunder'd, and the strange Lad lying dead, the Hermit concluded the Ladies were murder'd; and now the Lords Grief cannot be exprest. The Hermit found all the Money gone, and believing it to no purpose to stay there longer, persuaded the Lords to go back: 'My Friends (said he) it is in vain to stay here and mourn, 'tis Heaven's Pleasure: If the Ship sails without you, you will perhaps perish here also. The virtuous Ladies are, no doubt, happy and at rest; God has permitted it to be so, and we as Mortals must submit: If we stay here one Night, it may be our Fate to be murder'd also, or carry'd by the Robbers into Slavery.' They yielded to his Advice, and return'd in great Affliction to *Attabala*'s House; and the Ship coming again to an Anchor, they went aboard, and set sail for *Venice*, leaving word with *Johama*, if the Ladies were ever heard of, to send them word, and to assist them, if they came, to get to them; resolving to stay some time at *Venice* before Don *Lopez* and the Count went to *Spain*, where the latter resolved to stay with Don *Lopez* the rest of his days, both determining never to marry again: *Clarinda* and the Count *de Chateau-Roial* having agreed likewise to go with them to *Spain*, and to stay there till Interest could be made for them by their Friends in *France* for a Dispensation from *Rome*, for him and *Clarinda* to be Man and Wife, by discharging him of his Vows; he fearing to be punish'd if he return'd home without Permission, and a Pardon for the Crimes he had committed. They all past their time very agreeably in the Ship, except the two Lords, who sincerely mourn'd the loss of their Ladies; and the Ship arrived safe at *Venice* the Tenth of *March*, 1715.

CHAP. XVI.

THE Ladies waited some Days, in expectation of hearing by the Lad of the Hermit's Arrival: at last the Father of the Boy went to the House, and return'd with the melancholy News of his Son's Death, and the House being plunder'd; and having inquired of some poor Goat-herds who were upon the Mountain, they inform'd him, that they had seen three Men, two of whom appear'd *Grecians*, and the old Hermit, alight at the Cottage Door and go in; but they stay'd not long, but mounted their Horses, and turn'd back by the Way they came. From this Account the Ladies concluded, that they finding the House rifled, a strange Lad dead, and no body to inform them what was become of them, departed, imagining them dead, or fled thence: they therefore resolved to set out immediately for *Algiers*, and go to *Attabala*'s House, where they supposed their Lords would wait, in hopes to hear of them, at least till they were better inform'd what was become of them. They took their Money, Clothes, and Jewels; and having given some Alms to the Village, and a Present to the Man whose Son was kill'd in their Service, departed the Town in a cover'd Waggon they hired to carry them, it being the most easy and private way for them to travel, leaving a good Name behind them. The poor Villagers having conceiv'd a high Opinion of their Sanctity, accompany'd them on the Road a great way, praying for the good Dervises welfare, as they call'd them; and in four Days time they got safe to *Johama*'s House, where they first stop'd to alight, for they lay in the Waggon all the three Nights on the Road, and went not into any House, only walk'd sometimes in the lonely Places they past thro, to stretch their Limbs. Here they discharged the Waggon, taking their things out, and sent it back: and here *Johama* inform'd them of their Lords being gone for *Venice*, and advis'd them to go early the next Morning to *Attabala*'s House, which she thought more safe than hers. The poor Woman entertain'd them kindly, and they rejoiced at the good *Seraja*'s being gone to *Venice*, hoping to find her well and happy there. *Johama* entertain'd them with the Adventures their Lords had met with, and the fortunate meeting of the Hermit and *Eleonora*, at which they were much pleased. This night they rested sweetly, being in great want of Sleep: The next Morning early they went to *Attabala*'s, there *Abra* made them very welcome; they were oblig'd to stay here till an Opportunity of a Ship could be found to carry them to *Venice*. And now poor *Charlot*, whose Wound was not perfectly cur'd, fell very sick; the disorder of this long Journey threw her into a Fever, of which she was so dangerously ill, that her Life was despair'd of: *Emilia* and *Teresa* us'd all their Endeavours to save her. Whilst she lay in this Condition, *Emilia* walk'd frequently down to the Sea-side with *Johama*, who came and stay'd with them, to wait upon, and keep them Company, till they got off; and as they were musing one Evening on the Shore, they saw a Man lying upon the Sand, who appear'd so miserable that it mov'd their Compassion and Wonder together. They drew near to him, he was young, but his Face was so pale, and disfigur'd with Dirt and Want, that it appear'd frightful; his Hands were so lean that the Bones and Nerves were visible, the Skin being shrivel'd and wither'd, his Clothes were miserably torn and ragged; he had no Shirt on, only a poor Coat and Breeches, with Shoes and Stockings suitable; he had three Wounds in his Stomach and Breast, which appear'd not to be fresh, but foul and rankled, and not cover'd with any Plasters: *Emilia* was so touched with this dreadful Object, that she wept. The Man look'd stedfastly upon her, she being in her Hermit's Dress, and that made him silent, believing her a *Turk*. At last he said in *French*, 'Why do you stand staring upon me, am I not a Man? What do you see to wonder at? If you compassionate my miserable Condition, relieve me, or kill me, for I am weary of living.' *Emilia* answer'd, 'Are you a Native of *France*, and a Christian?' 'I am, (said he) one, who being cast on this barbarous Shore, am reduced to this misery.' 'Follow us, (said she) and we will relieve you.' He look'd eagerly upon her, and scrambling up, made shift to crawl to the House after them: Being enter'd the Door, she desir'd *Johama* to give him Wine and Meat, which he devour'd with great greediness; and a few minutes after fell into strange Convulsions; they gave him some Cordial-water, and *Abra* ran and brought a Quilt, Coverlid, Sheets and Boulster; and on a Carpet spread and made a Bed: The Lady withdrawing, *Johama* and he washed his Face and Hands, put him on a Shirt, and lay'd him in Bed: Then they put Balsam to his Wounds. He seem'd almost insensible of all they did to him; but Nature which struggled hard to digest what he had eat, at last threw him into a Sweat, and then he fell into a Slumber; upon which they retir'd, leaving him to rest. *Emilia* going up to *Charlot*'s Chamber, who was now on the mending hand, related to her and *Teresa*, the strange Adventure she had met with, which drew Tears from their Eyes also. The Stranger slept all Night, as they supposed, for *Abra* who lay in the next Room, heard nothing of him, only sometimes a deep Sigh, or Groan. About eight in the Morning *Emilia* sent *Johama* to ask how he did: when she enter'd the Room, she was surpriz'd at the change of his Countenance, and concluded he was a Person of Quality, and very handsome when in Health: he made the most grateful Acknowledgments imaginable, begging to know who the charitable Person was, to whom he ow'd his Life. She answer'd, that she was commanded by that Person to ask his Name and Quality, if it were not improper, that they might know how to treat him. 'Alas! (said he) the Gentleman's Curiosity will not be much more satisfied, when I tell you that I am the Son of a Marshal of *France*, and that my Name is *Victor Amando*, Count of *Frejus*; born to a plentiful Fortune, and by one unfortunate Action ruin'd. I was going to *Rome* in a Ship from *Marseilles*, and by a Storm cast on this Shore: Here I have been robb'd in a Wood, wounded and left for dead; and not knowing where to go, or who to apply to, being unable to go far, I wander'd about the Wood for these ten Days past, eating nothing but wild Fruits and Nuts, which threw me into a Bloody Flux.[1] I at last crept to the Sea-side, and there sat down, unable to go farther, having no other Design, but to lie there and die, which God prevented by your generous Master's Hands.' At these Words *Abra* enter'd the Room with a *Grecian* Habit for him which Don *Lopez* had left behind, and waited to dress him: At which *Johama* retir'd, and went to her Ladies with an Account of what he had told her: But who can express the Surprize poor *Charlot* was in when she heard the Stranger's Name, and knew him to be her faithless Lord, who had ruin'd, and basely sent her here? 'My God, said she, how wondrous are thy Ways, and how miraculous thy Power? Has thy Justice then found him out, and brought him here to suffer? I thank thee my God.' Being very weak she fainted; the Ladies were much amaz'd at her Words, and soon guest who the Stranger was: They reviv'd *Charlot* with Cordials, and beg'd her to compose her self, lest her Fever should return with this great Disorder of Mind, and consider with them, whether it would be proper for her to see him now, or stay till they had sounded his Inclinations, and learn'd whether he were single, and inclin'd to repair the Injury he had done her, by an honourable Marriage. She thought that best: so *Emilia* and *Teresa* went into the Parlor, and sent for him to breakfast; they were both in their Hermits Dress, as Men. When the Count *de Frejus* enter'd the Room, they gave him a good Morning with great Gravity; he return'd the Complement:

---

1 An abnormal flow of blood, or excrement, from the bowels or other organs.

they treated him now with Ceremony: He much admir'd at the Beauty of these young Men, and soon perceiv'd by their Voices and Mein that they were Women disguis'd. At last *Emilia* enter'd into a serious Discourse with him, in this manner: 'My Lord, I am no Stranger to you, nor the Actions of your Life; nor am I sur-priz'd at the Misfortunes that you have met with, which I hope the Almighty will sanctify to you, and turn to your Advantage. Where is the unhappy *Charlot* and her Child? Oh! my Lord, how could you expect Prosperity to attend you, till you had expiated by Repentance the cruel Injury you did that lovely Maid?' At these Words the Count was even thunder-struck, to hear a Stranger in *Barbary* reproach him for a Crime he thought a Secret to the greatest part of his own Acquaintance. He at last lifted up his Eyes, the big Drops rolling down his Face. 'My God, (said he) I own thy Justice.' And falling at the Ladies Feet, 'Bright Angels (said he) for such doubtless you are, who pry into the Hearts of Men, and know our secret Actions, pray for me to the Almighty: I have sin'd so greatly that an Age of Penance cannot expiate my Crimes. Oh! teach me what to do to appease Heaven.' The Ladies rais'd him, saying, 'Rise, Sir, we are frail Mortals like your self, and living Monuments of the Divine Mercy, preserv'd in this inhospitable Land by Miracles. But tell us, were *Charlot* living yet, would you repair her Injuries?' 'Witness (said he) that God in whom we trust, he who has seen my Tears, and heard my Prayers, that I would marry her that Hour I were blest with her dear Presence; nay I would chuse to beg with her, and suffer every Ill, nay Death it self, rather than wrong her any more, or marry with a Queen: Long have I mourn'd my Sin, nor can I e'er deserve so great a Blessing, as to see her Face again.' 'Are you then single? (said *Teresa*) is your Lady dead? and may we credit what you say?' 'Oh! what a Wretch am I (said he) that cannot be believ'd.' Here *Charlot*, who had listen'd, enter'd the Room. 'I would believe you, my Lord, (said she) but have so suffer'd for my Credulity already, that I hardly dare trust you.' He fell at her Feet transported, all he said was confused, he embraced her Knees, gaz'd on her Face, and at length fainted falling down on his Face. Her Tenderness for him reviv'd; she strove to raise him, but thro Weakness and Surprize swooned, falling by him. This Sight was extreamly moving: The Ladies calling, the Servants enter'd, and took them up; in some time they recover'd, were laid together on the Bed the Count had lain on. And now looking tenderly upon her, he said, 'Charming, much injur'd *Charlot*, can you forgive me? I am now single, our dear Child is well, and is my Heir; God has cast me on this Shore to bring me to my self and you; this happy Place has brought me Peace of Conscience. Do you but pardon me; and consent to marry me, I'll bring you home to *France* with Triumph, with God's leave.' She gave him her Hand. 'Tell me (said she) what has befallen you since the fatal Day you left me.' 'I will,' said he. The Ladies being seated, he thus began.

CHAP. XVII.

'THE unhappy Day (said he) when I basely left you, a Day I ever must repent of, I went safe ashore with the treacherous *Phillis*, whom God has already punish'd, having struck her soon after with Madness, in which she died insensible, and I fear unrepenting. I return'd to *Paris* to my fine Wife, and thought my self happy, vainly fancying I had secur'd my Peace for the future. Your Mother inveigh'd against me, saying, I had trepan'd[1] you: but I dissembled with her, pretending you had by Misfortune fallen over-board, and was drown'd to my inexpressible Grief which I was forc'd to stifle for fear of my Father, and my Wife's Reproaches. This *Phillis* justify'd to be true; and my great Fondness of our Child, and the large Presents I made your Mother, prevail'd with her to credit this Story; so I remain'd quiet from all Clamours but my Conscience, which hourly reproach'd me: I had no rest, my Soul was on the Rack; I grew surly and morose to all the World; my Wife grew to hate me, and we liv'd miserably. A thousand times I wish'd for you again: At last I discover'd that she did me justice, in dishonouring my Bed with one of my Pages: I exposed her to the World; we parted, and in a short time after she died in Childbed of a Child, which I did not believe mine: And that dying with her, put an end to all Disputes. And now being little esteem'd by my Friends, and conscious to my self of my Wickedness and Shame, I left *France* in that cursed Vessel which brought you here, being forc'd to be civil and keep a Correspondence with the Villain who commanded it. We were bound to *Italy*, where I design'd to see *Rome*, and pay my Devotions at all the holy Places there. I ask'd him when he came in sight of this Coast, if he thought it was possible to find you, resolving to purchase your Freedom with all I was worth; but he soon told me it was in vain to attempt it: Soon after this Discourse a Tempest arose that tore our Ship in pieces, and cast me on this Shore; the Captain perish'd in my sight. I was half dead when I reach'd the Shore; and was scarce able to walk: I saw a small Coffer on the Sands, and taking hold of it, I made shift to drag it into the Wood: Considering I was in a strange Place, I thought it must contain something that would be useful to me, having neither Clothes, Food, nor Money. I sat down, and rested that Night, having nothing to eat to refresh me. At break of Day I found my Limbs stiff, and a great Faintness all over my Body; I broke open the

---

1 Entrapped or lured.

Coffer, and found Money, Clothes, and many rich things in it, by which I judg'd it belong'd to the Villain Captain. As I was looking into it, three *Moors* appear'd who coming up to me, one struck me over the Head with a Sabre, which stun'd me quite; they gave me three Stabs in the Stomach and Breast with a Knife; and emptying the Chest, fled, leaving me for dead. It was long before I came to my self; but when I did, you may guess my Condition: I bled much, I sought for some Dust to stench the Blood, and that perform'd it; but being unable to walk far, and not knowing where to go, I remain'd there destitute of Food and Help. Here I examin'd my self as I ought, prepar'd to die, and, I hope, made my Peace with God, whose Mercy has been signally manifested in my Deliverance, and our wonderful meeting.'

The Ladies admir'd, and blest God for their good Fortune, and his Conversion; and wish'd nothing more than to see them marry'd, which they could not accomplish till a Christian Ship arriv'd, which was in less than a Month's time; when a *French* Ship came to them, sent from *Venice*, to inquire after them; which no sooner arrived, but *Abra* went aboard in the Fisher-boat: Monsieur *Robinet* the Captain welcom'd him. When the Ship was ready to depart, he gave notice, and they came aboard, bringing their Money, Clothes, and Jewels; and taking leave, with much Affection, of the good *Johama*, whom *Emilia* and *Teresa* offer'd to take with them, but *Abra* and she had agreed to marry, so she chose to stay in *Barbary*. The Captain entertain'd them nobly, as became the Generosity and good Breeding of a *Frenchman*, and a Christian. They related to him all their Adventures, excepting the Occasion of *Charlot*'s Misfortunes, which they conceal'd in respect to the Count *de Frejus*. And here he and *Charlot* were marry'd by the Chaplin, a good *Carmelite*,[1] who made them an excellent Discourse upon the Subject of the Deliverances they had all met with in that barbarous Place, from whence God had now been pleased to free them. They were bound for *Venice*, where they expected to find their Lords.

It will now be proper that I should inform you what Reception the Lords and the rest of our Travellers met with at *Venice*. *Antonio* and his fair Bride invited all the Company, at their landing, to go home with them to his Mother, the noble *Angelina*'s. At their Arrival, the Servants seeing their Lord and the beautiful *Anna*, were so transported, they scarce knew what they

---

1 Member of an order of friars founded in the twelfth century with a tradition of austerity.

did: They wept for Joy, and so great a Noise was made in the House, that *Angelina*, who had been long sick in her Chamber, imagin'd the House was on fire, and crept out to the Stairs-head, to see what was the matter: But when she saw her Son and *Anna* coming up to her, she was scarce able to express her Joy. They threw themselves at her Feet; she blest and raised them, clasping them in her Arms and weeping on their Bosoms. They inform'd her, that they had brought other Persons of Worth and Quality with them, whom they would recommend to her Favour. She composed her self a little, and her Son led her down, where she receiv'd them with Demonstrations of Respect: But when she saw her Niece and Signior *Andrea Zantonio*, she was amazed: 'Just Heavens (said she) Kinsman! who thought to have seen you together?' 'God hath decreed it so, Madam, (said he;) and therefore Seas and Barbarians could not prevent it.' *Angelina* call'd for Supper, saluting *Clarinda*, welcoming the Lords, the Count *de Chateau-Roial*, and the good *Seraja* at Supper, which was splendid, as the Company and Occasion merited. Great part of the Company's Adventures were related, and *Angelina* informed Signior *Andrea*, that his Father was dead, very much afflicted for his Son's Loss: 'But my Brother and Sister, Niece, (said she to *Eleonora*) are well, and to morrow we will go and see them.' Beds were made for all the Company, and no Excuse would pass but the Lords, *Clarinda*, and her Lord, must all stay there while they continued at *Venice*. The next Day the whole City rang of this strange Story, and all the Noblemen and Ladies, who were Friends or related to *Angelina*, crouded hither to see, and welcome *Antonio* and his charming Lady to *Venice*. A Messenger was dispatch'd early in the Morning to *Eleonora*'s Father's, who by Noon arrived at *Angelina*'s, with her Mother. Poor *Attabala* was likewise much caress'd for his faithful Service to his Lady. In fine, a Month was past in nothing but Feasts, Balls, and Entertainments, to welcome these noble *Venetians* home; in all which the *Spanish* and *French* Lords shared. Yet Don *Lopez* and the Count *de Hautville* were deeply melancholy: They had related the Story of their Misfortunes, and *Emilia*'s and *Teresa*'s Loss; and a *French* Ship lying in the Harbour, *Angelina* proposed to them to send for the Captain, and agree with him to cast Anchor and call at *Attabala*'s House, to which they should direct him, and make enquiry after these unfortunate Ladies. They did so; and this was the Ship that *Abra* went aboard of at his coming to an Anchor. And in this Vessel they came safe to *Venice*, but not before the Lords had left it; for Don *Lopez* desirous to see his Father and native Country again, having little hopes of *Teresa*'s being found, or escaping if alive; growing uneasy at the multitude of Company he was obliged to be engaged in every Day, and wanting to be alone with his Friend, whose melancholy Humour suited best with him at that time; he therefore proposed to the Count *de Hautville* to go thence soon: However, they were detain'd two Months longer; in which time Monsieur *de Chateau-Roial* fell sick of a Fever. And tho all possible means were used to save him, yet all prov'd ineffectual, and the Physicians gave him over. He behaved himself in this the last Scene of Life so like a Christian and a Hero, that it charmed all that attended him. At last the pangs of Death being on him, he took a solemn leave of every one there present, but particularly of the two Lords who had preserved him and *Clarinda* from perishing. He at last having received the last Sacraments, concluded all with taking leave of the disconsolate *Clarinda*, who had not for many Days gone into a Bed, or left his Bed-side: He grasped her Hand, and fixing his dying Eyes upon her, said, 'My dear *Clarinda*, the Hour is now come when we must be parted, tho not for a long time; God does not think fit to continue us longer together. I have unfortunately occasion'd you many Misfortunes, we have known little Satisfaction in the Enjoyment of one another; now human Passions will cease to fire my Soul, and my Reason will govern. Believe me, sensual Pleasures are bitter in Reflection, and in Death afford no Consolation; I hope my Peace is made above. I am glad to leave the World, and can advise you but two things: The first is, To be contented with our Separation, submit to God, and acquiesce in all things he decrees: nor murmur at Misfortunes, which are the holy Fires that must purge our Souls of Vice, and make us fit for Glory. And next, I beg that you will quit the World, and in a Convent spend the remainder of your Life, where you may be no more in danger of being again unhappy. Nor give that lovely Person to another, who may involve you in worldly Cares. Alas! my Dear, Life is well spent in learning how to die; live so that we may meet again to part no more.' 'Yes, my dear Lord (said she) I will obey you, and never venture into the World again.' Here his Agonies encreasing, his Confessor began the Prayers, and in few Hours he departed. *Clarinda*, after he was handsomely inter'd in the *Benedictine*'s Church near the Altar, was invited into the Convent of Nuns adjoining; to which she went, attended by *Angelina*, *Antonio*, *Anna*, *Eleonora*, Signior *Andrea*, the two Lords, *Seraja*, and all *Angelina*'s Relations and Friends, who lov'd her much, and left her there to enjoy uninterupted Peace, where no worldly Cares can enter to disturb her.

After this *Seraja* chusing to stay at *Angelina*'s, the Lords took leave, and went for *Spain* in a *Spanish* Vessel. They arrived safe at *Barcelona*, from whence they went to *Madrid*; and there at his Seat near that City found Don *Lopez*'s Father, Don *Manuel de Mendoza*, who was astonished to see him. He and the Count *de Hautville* entertain'd him with a faithful Account of all the strange Adventures they had met with, which fill'd him, and all his Friends to whom their Story was related, with Admiration. But no part of their History was more wonder'd at than that of *Tanganor* and *Maria*; the heroick Action she did, in pulling out her Eyes to save her Virtue, charm'd all that heard it related.

And now Don *Lopez* was worse fatigued than ever, being oblig'd to receive Visits from all his, till then, unknown Relations, and all the *Spanish* Nobility that heard of him; so that he had scarce an Hour to himself, or to give to his Friend alone. At last he retir'd to a Seat of his Father's in the Country, where he past a few Days to the Satisfaction of his Mind, but the Prejudice of his Body; for here he and the Count talk'd, and thought of nothing but *Emilia* and *Teresa*, and that Melancholy, which Company and Noise before diverted, seiz'd their Spirits; so that in few Days they both grew alter'd, forgot to eat or sleep as Nature requir'd; and nothing but leaving the World, and retiring to a Convent was thought of.

One Morning about ten a clock, a Coach stop'd at the Gate, with an elderly Lady in it, who much desir'd to speak with Don *Lopez*. The Servants brought her in, and Don *Lopez* being inform'd of her being there, readily came to her, hoping to hear something of the Ladies, but it prov'd otherwise: 'My Lord (said she) I have heard with Amazement your Adventures, and your noble *Venetian* Friends; it is the Subject of all Peoples Discourse in this Province: But there is one Story in particular, in which I am nearly concern'd, which relates to a Lady whose Name was *Maria*, lost from her Country, and me her afflicted Mother long since. I beg to hear from your own Mouth what I have heard from others, that being inform'd of each particular Circumstance, I may be able to judge whether the Lady you have seen be my dear Child or not.' Don *Lopez* sitting down by her, related all the Story of *Tanganor*, and his Lady, and then beg'd to know how this excellent Lady came into the Hands of the *Turks*. The Lady was much transported, being now positive that it was her Daughter he had seen, wiping away the Tears, which Joy had fill'd her Eyes withal, proceeded to satisfy his Request in this manner: 'My Lord, my

Husband, Don *Fernado Valada*, was a Merchant at *Barcelona*; it had pleased God to give us a very handsome Fortune, but it was many Years before he blest us with a Child, which was the only thing we wanted in the World, to make us compleatly happy. At last I proved with Child, and was deliver'd of this lovely Girl, which we bred up with the utmost Care and Tenderness. When she was turn'd of twelve years old, my Husband having a Ship very richly laden return'd from *Goa*, which lay at Anchor in the Road, invited a great many of his Relations and Friends on board, to give them a Treat: I was at that time unfortunately indispos'd, and therefore sent my Daughter with her Father to supply my Place. It was *Autumn*, and late at Night before the Company broke up: The Pinnace[1] carrying part of them ashore, and returning to fetch my Husband, *Maria*, and the rest, it grew dark, the Wind rose, and my Husband was afraid to let her venture to go so late, and apprehending a Storm, thought it best to stay aboard till Morning: but alas! the Storm encreased, and about two a Clock the Ship was drove to Sea, having lost her Anchors, and running before the Wind, was drove on the Coast of *Barbary*: there the Ship was beset with three *Algerine* Pirates, and after a sharp Fight, in which my dear Husband was kill'd, the Ship was taken and carry'd into *Algiers*. A *Turkish* Captain, who was come there to purchase fair Slaves for his villanous Masters to make sale of, bought my dear Child; but where he carry'd, or how dispos'd of her, I could never be inform'd till now. What I tell you, I got information of by Means of a Fryar, who was Chaplain to my Husband's Ship, and being a very sickly Man, and unfit for Slavery, the Pirate Captain dismist him, and put him on board a *French* Ship they made Prize of, in their way to *Algiers*; and having plunder'd it, put on board it all the wounded and disabled Persons, and some Provisions, and bid them go home. But alas! they were unable to manage the Ship, and had not God sent an *English* Ship, who met them at Sea, they had perish'd: The *English* Captain putting some Hands aboard, brought the Ship to *Barcelona*, to which Place he was bound. Thus, my Lord, (said she) I have inform'd you of what you desir'd to know; and now I beg only one Favour more of you, which is to direct me to how I may send to my dear *Maria*, whose Virtues have now made her ten times dearer to me than she was by the Ties of Nature.' Don *Lopez* told her the only way was to send by some *East-India* Ship, as he would direct. After many Thanks she took leave, and having

---

1 A small light vessel used to attend on a larger ship.

a Brother who was a Captain of a Merchant Ship,[1] got him to go to that Island, and had the Satisfaction of having a Message from *Maria*'s own Mouth, with a Letter from *Tanganor*, promising to come to *Spain* the next Year, so soon as he had got another return from *Persia*. In the mean time he sent her his eldest Daughter, the lovely *Leonora*, whom she receiv'd with the greatest Joy imaginable. This was a Year after she was with Don *Lopez*, whom we shall now leave at his Country Seat, and return to enquire after the Ladies.

---

1 Aubin's brother-in-law David Aubin was captain of the *Prosperous*, a merchant vessel captured by French pirates off Martinique in 1720.

THREE Months after Don *Lopez*, and the Count *de Hautville*'s Departure from *Venice*, the charming *Emilia* and *Teresa* arriv'd, with the Count *de Frejus*, and his Lady the now happy *Charlot*, and were by Monsieur *Robinet* conducted to *Angelina*'s House; where they were receiv'd with great Joy and Civility: And here they put on Habits suiting their Sex and Quality, and were obliged to stay some Days both to refresh themselves, and in compliance with the Importunities of their Friends, Signior *Antonio Borgonio* and the engaging *Anna*, and Signior *Andrea* and *Eleonora* his Lady, who mutually strove to divert and treat them; rivaling each other in the Magnificence of their Feasts and Balls: and all their Relations visited and invited them to Entertainments; so that a Month was past before they could handsomely take leave. They forgot not to pay a Visit to *Clarinda*, whom they dearly lov'd and honour'd, lamenting Monsieur *de Chateau-Roial*'s Death, whom they much pity'd whilst living; fearing no Dispensation would be granted to him to live with *Clarinda*. And now Monsieur *Robinet*, who obligingly stay'd for them, prepar'd for their Departure, taking aboard Wine and fresh Provisions of all Kinds, to accommodate them in the way. And now taking leave, tho with some Uneasiness, being much prest to stay longer, they went on board, accompany'd by all their generous Friends, who waited on them to the Ship. The good *Seraja*, who was overjoy'd at their Arrival, gladly went with them, being amaz'd and charm'd with the Treatment, and fine things she met with, and saw in *Europe*. Abundance of fine Presents were made to *Emilia* and *Teresa* by the *Venetian* Ladies, of rich *Venetian* Brocades and some Jewels, to be the Monitors to remind them of their absent Friends; rich Wines, Lace, perfum'd Gloves, Sweetmeats, and all sorts of things useful and ornamental. Nor did *Emilia* and *Teresa* omit to make such Returns as became them to do, promising the noble *Angelina* and *Anna* never to neglect an Opportunity of writing to them, and to keep their Friendship alive with frequent Converse of Letters. And thus embracing one another they parted, and the Ship setting sail, arrived at *Barcelona*. The Captain took a Lodging for the three Ladies and the Count *de Frejus* at their Landing, and then making inquiry for Signior *Manuel de Mendoza*, Don *Lopez*'s Father, was soon inform'd where he was; and going the next Morning to his Seat, which he rid to in few Hours, he inform'd that noble Lord who was arriv'd in his Ship. He receiv'd the News with much Joy, and curious to see his Daughter in Law and *Emilia*, of whom he had heard so much; as likewise desirous to bring the Lady, and good News to his Son himself; he order'd his Coach and six to be got ready against the next Morning; when he set out with the Captain for *Barcelona*, where he found the expecting *Emilia* and *Teresa*, whom he tenderly embrac'd, and welcom'd the Count *de Frejus* and his Lady, admiring the Ladies Youth and Beauty, especially *Teresa*'s, which he had expected to see much changed. He carry'd them to his Seat the next Day, having entertain'd them at a Relation's House the Day of his Arrival at *Barcelona*, and the Night of his stay there: Then he paid Captain *Robinet* nobly, making him promise to call on him at his next Return from *France*. He treated his Daughter and Company in such a manner at his Seat, that even amaz'd them; and then set out for the Country Seat, where those they most long'd to see were. When the Coach came near the Gate, he beg'd the Ladies to abide in it, till he went in and prepar'd his Son, and the Count to see them; 'lest (said he) the Surprize of seeing you on a sudden may hurt them.' They consented. 'Ladies (said he) I assure you your Husbands are much changed for the worse, that is, they are pale, lean, and dispirited, but you will be the best Cordial to revive them.' He quitted the Coach, and attended with two Servants only, enter'd the Gate, and asking for his Son, was inform'd the Count and he were in the Gardens. Thither he went, and found them sitting together in a deep Discourse: They started at his coming up to them, like Men lost in Thought. 'Gentlemen (said he) why do you pass Life thus in Solitude, unactive, and lost to the World? Son, I blush to think the loss of a Woman (tho a Wife) should rob you of your Reason, make you forget your Duty to your Prince and Country. Come, wake, shake off this Lethargy, rouse at the Call of Glory and Honour, and let your Ancestors Souls no longer mourn, to see you waste your Youth in pining for a Woman, which should be imploy'd in doing Deeds worthy your Birth, and to perpetuate your Name.' 'Alas! my honour'd Lord (said he) you cannot comprehend what I have lost: Consider the amazing Proofs *Teresa* gave me of her Virtue, and the sad Condition I have left her in. See here, my Friend, a Man brave as the World can shew, he droops like me, for such another Woman. Why should we be censur'd if we leave the World, and live retir'd? Are not our Convents fill'd with such, and don't they merit our Esteem?'[1] 'My Son (reply'd the old Lord) they leave the World by choice, you only

---

1 First edition: Esteem.

because you are disgusted; suppose your Wives are dead, must you rebel and murmur against Providence?' 'Ha! (said the Count *de Hautville* starting) Dead! what are you going to prepare us for? if they are so, tell us at once, our Resolutions are already made, a Cloister shall secure us from all future Mischief; we will not make a second Choice. Let Glory and the idle Ambition that deludes Mankind tempt them to venture in a Crowd, and end Life in a Tumult; we will study how to die, and wait our Maker's Pleasure, till he rids us of a tedious Life, and calls us to eternal Rest.' Here the cold Sweat trickled down his Face, and the old Lord admiring their Constancy and Affection, took him by the Hand, and said, 'Come Friends, revive, God has heard you; I have some good News to tell you; I have heard from your Wives, they are not far off, follow me.' Here turning about, he went to the Gate, they following in such disorder that they scarce knew what they did: But when they saw the Ladies, they forgot all Ceremony, and rushing into the Coach, regardless of *Charlot* the Stranger, they fell on their Knees before their Wives, embracing them, who were so transported the Tears flowed from their Eyes, and they mutually blest God, and said so many passionate things, that the old Lord, *Charlot*, and the Count *de Frejus* wept. In some time they began to remember who waited, and Don *Lopez* recovering himself, beg'd Pardon of his Father. 'My Son (said he) it is a laudable Error; you have a Wife worthy the Affection you bear her, she merits all your care, and God has blest me beyond my Desert in such Children.' The Ladies alighting, enter'd the House. And now a universal Joy spread it self thro all the Family, and ten Days were past in nothing but Balls and Entertainments.

They departed thence for *Madrid*, where Fame had spread the News of their Adventures before their Arrival; and there they saw the Splendor of their glorious Monarch King *Philip*'s Court,[1] where the *French* Gallantry has taken place of the *Spanish* Gravity, and Wisdom and good Manners seem to walk hand in hand; where solid Sense and Generosity, Greatness and Goodness, appear united; where Men are Statesmen and Courtiers together.

---

1 The court of Philip V of Spain (r. 1700–46), formerly Philippe, duc d'Anjou, grandson of Louis XIV and member of the House of Bourbon. He inherited the Spanish monarchy through his great-uncle Charles II of Spain. The prospect of the unification of French and Spanish thrones under a Bourbon monarch provoked the War of the Spanish Succession (1702–13).

For six Months they past the time agreeably, and then the Count *de Hautville* having receiv'd News from *France*, that his Father was dead long since, and the Title and Estate his due; tho his supposed Death had consign'd it to another, who was ready to resign it to him with Pleasure; communicated this News to the Company: But *Teresa* and *Emilia* knew not how to think of parting, they were both with child. At last it was resolved the Count *de Hautville*, now Marquis *de Ventadore*, should go to *France*, settle his Affairs, and return to them; *Teresa* begging *Emilia* might lie in with her.

The Count *de Frejus* and the Marquis, with *Charlot*, who long'd to see her Mother and Child, went together to *France* over the *Alps*, *Emilia* making her Lord promise never more to go upon the faithless Seas. They arrived safe in *France*, where they were greatly welcomed, and *Charlot*'s lovely Daughter received by her Parents with great Transport.

The Marquis *de Ventadore* quickly return'd to *Spain*, and was not long after blest with a Son, which *Emilia* brought him on the 10th of *August*, 1719. and the charming *Teresa* made her transported Lord Father to a Son and Daughter on the 13th of *September* the same Year: The two Lords stood Godfathers to each others Sons, and Don *Lopez*'s Father and *Emilia* to *Teresa*'s Daughter, who bare *Teresa*'s Name; and Don *Lopez* in performance of his Vow, built a Church, and dedicated it to St. *Teresa*.[1]

And now one would suppose, that having past seven Years in an almost continued Scene of Misfortunes, and thus fortunately arrived in their native Country, the happy Don *Lopez* and his charming Wife might expect to pass the remainder of their Days in Peace. 'Tis true, the fair *Teresa* was but Nineteen, and that fatal Beauty that had occasioned her so much Sorrow, was rather improved than diminished: But her known Virtue would have awed any bold Admirer from one daring to disclose his Flame, and secured her from all attempts of Love, one would have imagined. But alas! it was otherwise decreed: A young Nobleman of *Spain*, Son of a Duke, and Favourite of his young Prince, the Prince of *Asturias*,[2] whom he was bred up with, Nephew to Don *Manuel* Father of Don *Lopez*, coming frequently to visit him and *Teresa*, who was now up again, and seem'd to rise like the glorious Sun to

---

1 St. Teresa of Ávila, or Teresa of Jesus (1515–82), an ascetic Spanish nun who initiated a reform of the Carmelite Order, restoring traditions of poverty, austerity, and contemplation.
2 Title given to the heir to the Spanish throne.

bless the World, with new Charms in her Face and Fire in her Eyes, Content adding Smiles to her natural Sweetness; the unfortunate Don *Fernando de Medina* gazed away his Liberty, and grew so mad in Love, that he forgot all Ties of Blood, Honour, and Christianity; and resolved to possess her, or die in the Attempt. He knew her Virtue render'd all means but Force impracticable, despairing to gain her any other way; and therefore subtly contriv'd how to effect it, without her being aware of it, or her Husband able to find out where she was, who had stolen her. In order to this, he hires four desperate *Catalonian*[1] gentlemen, Sons of Fortune, who had been imploy'd before in such, or as bad Undertakings: These he promised a great Reward to. One of these hir'd a House next a Wood, about five Miles from *Fernando*'s Country-seat, and placed in it two old Hags, proper for such a wicked Design. Here they made a Chamber strong as a Prison, furnish'd it with a Bed, and all necessary things. Thus prepared he goes to his Kinsman's, invites him and the Marquis to a Hunting-match, with the Ladies. They willingly consented to go, and the next Morning went to his House, where after being magnificently treated, they went into the Field; and the Ladies loving the Sport, excellently mounted, pursued the frighted Stag, till the heat of Day made them retire to this fatal Wood, where Don *Fernando* had prepared a Treat for them. Here they din'd in a Tent pitch'd for that purpose: and then he proposed to the Lords, to leave the Ladies there to repose, whilst they hunted another Deer, and so return to conduct them home in the Evening. Two Servants were left to attend the Ladies. About an Hour after their Lords were gone, the four Villains who lay in Ambush, with Vizards on their Faces, and Pistols in their Hands, rushed into the Tent, and seizing upon *Teresa*, carry'd her away before the Servants, who were fallen asleep on the Grass behind the Tent, awaked with the Alarm of *Emilia*'s Crys. *Fernando* kept the Lords some Hours, and then returning to the Tent, they found *Emilia* almost distracted with Grief, and the Servants standing there mute as Statues: The cunning *Fernando* shew'd a mighty Concern for his Kinsman's Misfortune. Don *Lopez* raved, and storm'd like a Man in despair, but all in vain. They searched all the Wood, and passing by the lonely House, saw one of the old Hags, who stood at the Door on purpose. The Lords enquir'd of her, if she had seen any Man with a Lady pass by that Way: She told them, Yes; about two

---

1 From Catalonia (also Cataluña, or Catalunya), an historic region of modern northeastern Spain that came into conflict with Castile in the seventeenth century.

Hours before she saw four Men ride by, with a Lady bound Hand and Foot before one of them, and supposing them Thieves, shut the Door. 'They turn'd to that Road' (said she) shewing a contrary Way, to that they had really taken: *Emilia* and the Lords went on that Road the Woman directed, but to no purpose. At last Night approaching, they went home. Don *Lopez* was inconsolable, and the dissembling *Fernando*, who inwardly triumphed at the good Success of his cursed Plot, stay'd with him all Night. Next Morning he took leave, pretending he would make it his Endeavour to find *Teresa*, and bring the Villains to Justice: but alas! he burn'd to possess her, and flew with the utmost Speed to the Place, where he knew she was. And now I must inform my Reader, that the Villains did not carry her directly to the House by the Wood; but rid twenty Miles farther thro unfrequented Places, having put her, bound Hand and Foot, into a Horse-litter, which they had placed just beyond the House. Here they stop'd till it was dark; then lighting Torches they had brought in the Litter, they return'd by the same Ways to the House, and left her in the horrid Room where the old Hags attended to watch her. Here they laid her bound upon the Bed, ungagg'd her, and strove to pacify her, but in vain: She wept and lamented her Misfortune, in Terms so moving it would have melted the Hearts of *Barbarians*: but these vile relentless Women, derided her, asking, what she fear'd from a Man who passionately loved her. Thus poor *Teresa* past the remainder of the sleepless Night and Morning, taking no Sustenance, but refusing to eat or drink, they fear'd to unbind her. About Noon the base *Fernando* arrived so disguised, it was almost impossible to know him; he put a Vizard upon his Face before he enter'd the Chamber, then shutting the Door, he came to the Bed-side, and used all his Rhetorick to persuade her to yield fairly to him. Then he proceeded to Threats, yet she remain'd inflexible, used Prayers and Tears to dissuade him from so horrid a Crime: 'Heaven (said she) will find you out, and pour its Vengeance on your Head; my Lord will discover you, or some Thunder-bolt dispatch you, and bring your Soul to the dreadful Tribunal, where your Sentence will be given.' He seem'd deaf to all she said, rudely kissing and embracing her. At last summoning all her Reason, she changed her Behaviour: 'Well then (said she) since Love makes you deaf to all Entreaties to dissuade you from this dreadful Deed, unbind me, give me something to drink, and let me find some Humanity in the Treatment you give[1] me; if

---

1 First edition: gve

I must be yours, shew that you love me.' *Fernando* transported at her seeming so consenting, readily call'd for Wine, unbound her Hands and Feet. Having first lock'd the Door, she drank, and watching an Opportunity, threw a Glass of Wine in his Eyes, then flew to the Door, broke the Lock, and attempting to run down Stairs, her Foot slipt, and she fell down, and unfortunately broke her right Leg short at the Instep, so that she could not rise. By this Time he had recover'd himself, and hearing her groan, ran down Stairs, where he found the old Hags standing as amaz'd. He took her up in his Arms, carry'd her up to the Bed, and seeing the Blood running on the Floor, soon discover'd what had happen'd; she swooned, and the Shin-bone was shiver'd, so that it had cut thro the Skin and Sinews, and appear'd. This Sight dash'd his amorous Fires, and awaken'd his Care to preserve her. He ran down, took his Horse, and went to a Village for a Surgeon; who came, and was doubtless surpriz'd to see so fine a Woman in such a dismal Place. But *Fernando* had told him, it was his Wife, who was lunatick, and had broke loose, and endeavour'd to escape, and so came by this sad Accident; pretending himself to be a Gentleman who belong'd to the Court, and could not keep her in his own Apartment there. The Surgeon drest her, not regarding her Complaints; and *Fernando*, who was oblig'd to unmask, lest the Surgeon should suspect something, took care to hide his Face from *Teresa*. No sooner was the Surgeon gone, but he put on his Vizard, and approaching the Bed-side, said many kind and tender things, to which she gave no Answer: Excessive Pain, and the Fright, with the Fatigues of the foregoing Night, having made her almost unable to complain. At last he left her, it being necessary for him to appear in sight, to prevent his being suspected of the Villany he was guilty of. One of the old Hags watch'd by her that Night, and in the Morning when the honest Surgeon return'd, he found her light-headed, with a strong Fever which had seized her, in which she talk'd of Don *Lopez*, *Emilia*, her Child, and of being stole. This made him begin to suspect something. She remaining dangerously ill for some Days, in which time *Fernando* came often to see her, he was much concern'd, and took care to let nothing be wanting but a Physician, whom he durst not send for, for fear of discovery. In this time great Inquiry being made after *Teresa*, the Surgeon heard of it, and immediately took horse, and went to the Lords, informing them of what he knew. Don *Lopez* and the Marquis desir'd much to know who the Villain was, but that the Surgeon was ignorant of. They took Horse immediately, attended by five Servants well-arm'd, and conducted by the Surgeon, went to the House; it being Midnight before they reach'd it, the Door was made fast, a Horse being ty'd near it, and a Light in the Chamber: They consulted what to do, fearing if they knock'd, it might alarm the old Hags, and the Ravisher, who might by some back Door or Window escape; so they concluded to wait till he came down to take horse. They did so, and towards day-break one of the old Hags open'd the Door. The Lords, who were dismounted, and stood ready, rushed in, and running up Stairs, found *Fernando* in the Room masked. Don *Lopez* stay'd not a Moment to deliberate, but shot him thro the Head: he fell dead at his Feet, not uttering one Word.

Thus he perished in a moment, unprepared for Death, and got a just Reward for his Villany. *Teresa*, who was almost dying, and delirious, looked up, and knew her Lord; she strove to rise to reach him, but fell back: He laid his Cheek to hers, and strove to stifle his tumultuous Joy, and hush her to Repose. The Hags were seized, and some of the Servants dispatch'd for a Horse-litter, in which *Teresa* was carry'd home to her Lord's, and the vile Women sent to Prison. *Fernando*'s Body being known, was sent home: and tho Don *Lopez* had receiv'd so great an Injury, yet he fear'd a Trial, or private Injury, from *Fernando*'s Family, Revenge being very natural to the *Spaniards*; he therefore absconded, resolving to retire to *France* with the Marquis *de Ventadore*. And now able Physicians being sent for, in some Days *Teresa* got rid of her Fever, and began to recover: At last she got up again, but went lame, and never expects to do otherwise while she lives: She rewarded the honest Surgeon nobly.

Don *Lopez* got safe to *France* first, and the Marquis, with the Ladies, Children and Servants, follow'd; Don *Lopez*'s Father having taken care to make a noble Provision for his Son to live in *France*. They travell'd gently, and arriv'd safely at *Poictou*, where they are all happily seated together.

AND now it is fit that we make some Reflections for our own Improvement, on the wonderful Providence of God, in the Preservation and signal Deliverances of these excellent Persons in this Narrative.

A great number of Christian Slaves are at this time expected to return to *Europe*,[1] redeem'd from the Hands of those cruel Infidels, amongst whom our noble Slaves suffer'd so much, and

---

1 The *London Journal* for 9 December 1721 reported that enslaved Britons freed from captivity in Morocco had paraded to St Paul's Cathedral in London on the previous Monday (see Appendix A1, pp. 159–60).

lived so long; and no doubt but amongst these, if we enquire, we shall find some whose Misfortunes, if not their Virtues, equal these Lords and Ladies. It is in Adversity that Men are known: He is only worthy the Name of a Christian who can despise Death, and support even Slavery and Chains with Patience; whom neither Tortures or Interest can shake, or make renounce his God and Faith. How frequent is it for us, who boast so much of Religion, to sacrifice our Consciences to Interest? How impatient are Men for small Injuries or Disappointments?

The Gentlemen in this Story well deserve our Imitation; the Ladies, I fear, will scarce find any here who will pull out their Eyes, break their Legs, starve, and chuse to die, to preserve their Virtues. The Heathens, indeed, shew'd many Examples of such heroick Females; but since the first Ages of Christianity, we have had very few: The Nuns of *Glastenbury*, who parted with their Noses and Lips to preserve their Chastity,[1] are, I think, the last the *English* Nation can boast of. 'Tis well in this Age if the fair Sex stand the Trial of soft Persuasions; a little Force will generally do to gain the proudest Maid. But I forget that to give good Advice, and not to censure, is at present my Business; I shall therefore sum up all in few words.

Since Religion is no Jest, Death and a future State certain; let us strive to improve the noble Sentiments such Histories as these will inspire in us; avoid the loose Writings which debauch the Mind; and since our Heroes and Heroines have done nothing here but what is possible, let us resolve to act like them, make Virtue the Rule of all our Actions, and eternal Happiness our only Aim.

FINIS.

---

1 Aubin is referring to the story of the nuns of Coldingham Priory in the Scottish county of Berwickshire, who, according to the Benedictine monk Matthew Paris, cut open their lips and noses to resist the possibility of rape by Viking raiders. Aubin's error was corrected in one of the Dublin reprints in 1736.

Appendix A: Slavery

1. From *London Journal*, no. CXXIV (9 December 1721), p. 5

[In 1720 Commodore Charles Stewart (1681–1741) was dispatched to negotiate a peace treaty with the emperor of Morocco, Mulay Ismaïl (1646–1727). The treaty was signed at Ceuta in January 1721. Under the terms of the treaty, piracy was to be prohibited, some 296 enslaved Britons were to be released, and Moroccan ships were to trade freely with Britain. Detailed information about the ships taken by Moroccan corsairs, a list of the captives, and an account claiming to describe the conditions they endured appeared in *A Description of the Nature of Slavery among the Moors, and the Cruel Sufferings of those that fall into it* (1721) (see Appendix A2 below).]

On Monday last the English captives that have been redeemed by the late Treaty made with the King of Fez and Morocco, to the Number of above Two Hundred and Sixty Persons, marched in their Moorish Habits in good Order through a great Part of this City to the Cathedral of St. Paul's, to return Thanks to Almighty God for their Redemption from Captivity; on which Occasion the Reverend Mr. William Berryman, Chaplain to the Lord Bishop of London, who was also present there, preach'd a suitable Sermon from Psal. 102.v. 19, 20, 21. Afterwards they went up to St. James's to return Thanks to his Majesty,[1] for interposing in their Behalf; but by Reason of the vast Multitudes of People that crowded to see them, they were forc'd to divide themselves into several Companies, and to take different Ways thither. Upon their Arrival they were let into the Garden behind the Palace, where his Majesty and their Royal Highnesses view'd them. We hear that his Majesty hath order'd Five and fifty Hundred Pounds for their Relief, and his Royal Highness[2] Two Hundred Pounds and that above One Hundred Pound was collected for them at St. Paul's; and 'tis believed that a much greater Sum would have been gather'd, if many charitable Gentlemen

---

1 George I (1660–1727), Elector of Hanover, and King of Great Britain and Ireland from 1714 until his death.
2 George (1683–1760), son of George I, then Prince of Wales and later George II on the death of his father in 1727.

and Citizens could have found Access through the prodigious Crowd: However, it is still hoped that such well disposed Persons will send in their respective Contributions.

2. **From Anonymous,** *A Description of the Nature of Slavery among the Moors, and the Cruel Sufferings of those that Fall into it; With the Manner of their being brought and sold like Beasts at Publick Markets; and several Curious Incidents now in use with the Barbarians, from the King to the meanest Peasant. To which is added, An Account of Capt. STUART's[1] Negociations for the Redemption of the* **English** *Captives, as also the Success thereof; with an exact LIST of the Persons that were redeem'd, the Number of those that turn'd* **Moors,** *or dy'd during the Treaty, and their Passage Home, and the Names and Ladings of the respective Ships taken by the* **Sallee Rovers,** *from* **October 5, 1714, to** **July 14, 1721.** **Written by one of the said redeem'd captives (1721), pp. 1–11**

[This anonymous narrative purports to be a genuine account of the experiences of one sailor taken captive by Barbary pirates and subsequently sold into slavery. He is released thanks to the treaty negotiated by Charles Stewart (see p. 156, n. 1). The circumstantial detail bolsters the claim to historical veracity, but the supposed sexual adventures of the sailor whilst enslaved undermine its plausibility. Some elements of the account anticipate and may have influenced the plot of William Chetwood's *The Voyages and Adventures of Captain Robert Boyle* (1726). Like Boyle, the narrator of the tale is taken by Barbary pirates, works as a gardener for his master, and catches sight of a beautiful woman who is also held captive.]

Having an Opportunity of shipping myself from the Island of *Minorca*, whereon I had suffer'd Shipwreck in my Voyage to the *Levant*,[2] for *Lisbon* (whence I proceeded on that unhappy Voyage) I went on Board the good ship *Experiment*, *Adam Rigdon*, Commander, bound for that Port, in order from thence to get Passage for *England*. We set sail in the Month of *April*, (the 20th Day)

---

1 Capt. Stuart is Commodore Charles Stewart (see headnote to Appendix A1, above). Modern historical records use the latter spelling.

2 The eastern part of the Mediterranean, with its islands and adjoining countries.

1720, with 16 Hands, besides the Master of the Vessel before-
nam'd, and six Guns; but, through the Means of bad Weather, did
not make the Streights[1] Mouth, so as to come in Sight of it, till
the 6th of *May* following, at five in the Morning, when we also
espy'd a Ship, built Sloopwise,[2] bearing towards us, with all her
Sails aloft. Our Master instantly perceiv'd her Design, and since
from the Advantage of her Swiftness, and the Manner of her
Working, so as to get ground of us by vast Odds, it would be
impossible for us to get protection in the Road of *Gibraltar*, sum-
mon'd his whole little Crew together, to tell us the Danger we
were in; and exhorted us, since we had a Sallee Rover[3] to deal
with, who would carry us all into the worst of Slavery, to sell our
Liberties, that were as precious as our Lives, as dear as possible.
The Company agreed to defend the Ship to a Man; and after rec-
ommending ourselves to God, got into a Posture of receiving our
Enemy, that bore down upon us with all imaginable Resolution,
with Intention to board us without firing a Gun: But we made the
Sallee Man (for such he was now discover'd from his Colours) to
repent his Rashness, by bringing our whole Artillery to fire on the
Starboard Side, which he made his Onset upon, and causing him
to lie by a while in a Posture of refitting. But alas! the great Disproportion between us, as to the Number of Men and Guns,
made all Manner of Success, from our weak Endeavours, to be
dispair'd of; insomuch, that after we had kill'd 15 *Moors*, without
the Loss of one Man on our Side, we found ourselves oblig'd to
strike,[4] and admit the Rover to board us.

The Captain thereof, *Ibrahim Coggia*, no sooner had our Commander, who was wounded, brought before him, but enrag'd at
his Obstinacy, in daring to engage with such a superior Force as
his was, of 28 Guns, and 120 Men, to bare 6 Guns and 17 Men,
that he caus'd him instantly to be put in Irons, and threaten'd him
with Death, as soon as he should be brought on Shore. I too, with
the Mate of the Ship, and four more of the Men, were taken into
the Sallee Man, ten of whose Hands were put on board our
Vessel, in order to carry her into *Tetuan*,[5] with the Prisoners, and

---

1 The Straits of Gibraltar.
2 Built like a sloop, that is, either a small, one-masted vessel or a relatively
   small ship-of-war, carrying guns on the upper deck only.
3 The name given by the West to those pirates or corsairs operating out of
   the port of Salé, on the Atlantic coastline of Morocco.
4 In nautical terms, to take down sails or a mast as a gesture of surrender.
5 Tétouan, one of the major ports of Morocco, a few miles south of the
   Straits of Gibraltar.

Cargo, which consisted of several rich Goods, besides the Equipage of one of the Colonels of the two Regiments in Garrison at *Port-Mahon*,[1] that was to have been shipp'd on Board the *Newcastle* Man of War,[2] then lying in *Lisbon* River, on its Return to *England*.

It will be needless to recount the barbarous Treatment we met with, on Board this cruel, insolent Infidel; Chains were the least of our Misfortunes; even a Complaint was what drew upon us an immediate Bastinado;[3] *Christian Dogs* were the best Names we were to go by; and if they gave us a little Rice, or some of their Sherbet, it was done with such Scorn and Contempt, as if we were not worthy of their very Offals; so that we had nothing to do but to apply to God for Relief, all visible Hopes of it (from human Assistance, unless we should be retaken by one of our Cruisers,[4] whereof several were abroad at that Juncture) being vanish'd. But it was appointed otherwise by that Providence of God, which, by the Means of Afflictions, makes Trial of our Patience, in order to bring us nearer to himself, and to manifest his Goodness to us, in the very Display of his Judgments; for though we were in Sight of two or three Ships of War of our own Nation, the *Crescent* (for so was the Rover call'd) was too swift a Sailor, and got a-Head of them all; and so, after the *Moors* had pick'd up two *Spanish* Sattees[5] more, laden with Goods and Provisions for *Ceuta*, they, with the Prizes, put into *Tetuan*, whereof *Muley Zeidan*, one of *Muley Ismael*, the King of *Morocco*'s Sons, was Alcaid,[6] or Governor.

This Prince, or Zeriff,[7] the Moment he was appriz'd of our Arrival, caus'd all the Slaves on Board the *Experiment*, the *Crescent*,

---

1 In Spanish, Mahón, a port and now capital city of the island of Menorca. The island became a British possession under the terms of the Treaty of Utrecht in 1713, and a Royal Navy dockyard was established in the harbour in Mahón in 1715.
2 A vessel equipped for warfare, or a commissioned warship belonging to the recognized navy of a country.
3 A blow with a stick or cane, especially on the soles of the feet.
4 Warships commissioned to cruise for the protection of commerce or pursuit of an enemy.
5 Sattee, or settee, a decked vessel with a long, sharply pointed prow and two or three masts, in use in the Mediterranean.
6 Probably from the Arabic *al cadi*, meaning the civil judge.
7 From the Arabic *sharif*, in Morocco meaning the ruler of a district but primarily designating one claiming to be a descendant of Mohammed through his daughter Fatima.

and the *Sattees*, to be brought before him; and no sooner was given to understand what Resistance we had made before our Surrender, but stamp'd, and cry'd out *Alla, Alla, my God, my God*, and caus'd each of us to be punish'd with 100 Bastinadoes on the Soles of our Feet. This Cruelty was succeeded by our being put into a Dungeon in an old Castle, wherein we were used with the utmost Inhumanity, till the King's Pleasure was known concerning us; which was, that we, the *English*, should be conducted to *Mequinez*,[1] the Capital City wherein he makes his Residence, there to be dispos'd of to the best Bidders, at the common Market. But first, we were to be brought in Triumph to Court, there to be survey'd as before; and, as the Humour took that Prince, to be used accordingly, either bastinado'd, or put to the Torture: But as Fortune would have it, who, amidst her very Persecutions, often Times shews some sort of Indulgence, one of his Favourite Sultana's, an *English* Woman, that, by Means of insupportable Cruelties, was forc'd to embrace *Mahometanism*, was that very Day brought to Bed of a Son: In Joy for which, he, after making Choice of two young Men, one *James Richards* and *Henry Negus*, who were very handsome Lads, of about 17 Years of Age, for his own brutish Lusts, caus'd a certain Distribution of mouldy Rice, brackish Sherbet, and dry'd musty Fish, to be given us, and then left us to our respective Fates at the next Day's Market, which is always in a large open Space, that extends itself before the Royal Palace ... [W]e, with others, amounting to the Number of 130 Prisoners of divers Countries, were led into the above-mention'd Area, or spacious Apperture, before the Alcassava,[2] or Imperial Palace, like so many Horses, or Heads of Cattle; where, stripp'd naked as we were born, we were to stand, with every Part of our Bodies open, to the View of such as come thither to be made Purchasers.

You are to judge what killing Reflections a Sight like this caus'd in Men, that were entitled, by their Birth in a free Country, to all the Sweets and Privileges of Liberty; and what Anxiety and Trouble we must labour under, to see ourselves handled in all Parts of our Arms and Legs, Backs and Breasts, nay, even in our very Privities, at the Discretion of opprobrious and relentless Infidels. *You Dog you*, said the *Talbe*,[3] or Doctor of

---

1   Meknès, one of four imperial cities in Morocco. It became the Moroccan capital under Moulay Ismaïl.
2   The casbah, meaning a castle or fortress, especially in a North African town.
3   Possibly a misunderstanding of the Arabic *tālib*, meaning a student of Islamic law, or a seeker or enquirer.

the *Law*, that pitch'd on[1] me for a Penniworth,[2] and fit for his Turn, *What Age are you of?* By a Runegade *Englishman*, his Interpreter; I told him that I was in my thirty second Year. That Question was back'd by another concerning my Trade; which had for Answer, *That I had, From my Infancy, been bred to the Sea.* Hereupon, *Villain*, said he, *but what Employment can you be most serviceable to me in? Can you bake Bread, till the Ground, or do Gardiner's Work; for in either of these Capacities you may be of use to me?* When, at the Instigation of my Countryman, his Interpreter, who told me, that he was one of the best Patrons I could have, and that being in religious Orders, he was less savage than the *Moorish* Laity, I gave him for a Reply, *That being a Gardiner's Son, I had some Insight into that Occupation before I went to Sea; and did not doubt to give him entire Satisfaction.* With that, forty two *Spanish* Ducats were paid down upon the Nail for me; and I was conducted home by the Renegado, who was Steward to the *Talbe*'s Family, and, by Virtue of that Post, was Overseer of the other Servants, subordinate to him. After I was made to eat and to drink, (a Civility seldom in Use with such Apostates, as abjure *Christ* for that vilest of Impostors, *Mahomet*) I was turn'd into the Garden, to the Business my Task-Master assign'd me; and Day after Day did hard Service enough, without seeing any other in the House, than my Patron, the *Talbe*, and his Steward; the first of whom, in Times of Rest, was always solliciting me to embrace the Doctrine of his Prophet: But God was pleas'd so far to bless me with his restraining Grace, that I no Way gave into his wicked Motion.

I continu'd in this Station for some Weeks, during which Time, I pleas'd well enough, as to the Discharge of my Duty, though I frequently bore the Bastinado for my Non-compliance with the other Article, concerning Religion; for these Biggots, especially the Doctors of this pretended Church, make no Scruple of attempting to bring about that Perversion by Force and Violence, which they cannot accomplish by Reason and Argument; when, at last, Fortune seem'd tir'd with my Afflictions, and administer'd some Comfort to them unexpectedly, after this Manner.

My old Patron, whose advanc'd Age had no Ways impair'd the Fierceness of his Lusts, whatsoever it had done by the Strength of his Limbs, had (in Pursuance of *Mahomet*'s Leave, who sets no Limits to the Number of Wives and Concubines)[3] a Seraglio of

---

1 Chose.
2 A small amount, or a bargain.
3 A misconception. Muslim jurists agree that Qu'rān 3:4 allows for men to have up to four wives, but only if they are all treated equitably. If this is not possible, then a man should marry only one woman.

his own, adjoining to his House: Near unto this was a fair Apartment, with several distinct Baths in it, set apart for the Ladies Use; each of which had a Door that open'd into the Garden, through which they used to take the Diversions thereof, at stated Seasons, when the Walks were empty, and they could do it unseen and in private. Close by these bathing Rooms was I, when, weary'd with my Day's Work, I sate me down upon a Grass Plat, expecting when my Deputy-Patron would let me out, (for I was always lock'd into the Garden 'till the stated Hour came round for my Admission) and bury'd in the deepest Meditations on my wretched Condition, when I heard the sweetest Voice that ever ravish'd an Ear, accompany'd with the Musick of a Lute, deal forth such agreeable Sounds, as even while they seem'd to bemoan the Person's Misfortunes from whom they came, and to add Increase to her Sorrows, altogether dissipated mine. Though the Language she sung in was unknown to me, yet the Manner of her Air, and the Cadence of her Notes, made me conclude, she was little pleas'd with the Confinement she was under; and would make no Scruple of a mutual Intercourse with something more entertaining, than what she was at that Time in Possession of; I therefore took the Opportunity of singing after my Way, which, it seems, was acceptable enough; for immediately I perceiv'd the Door to open, and the fairest young Lady to shew herself through it, and instantly to shut it again, and retire out of Sight.

'Tis not difficult to imagine what a Surprize I was under at this Sort of Interview: The Lady's Angelick Form, the Suddenness of her Departure, and the Manner of her exposing herself to my View with so inviting an Aspect, induc'd me to think that her Curiosity might be the Means of some lucky Events that might follow. But while I was in this fairy Land of Hopes, amusing myself with the Consequences of so strange an Adventure, my Goaler came into the Garden to take a Survey of my Work, and afterwards lock me up in my Hut of a Prison, there to refresh myself with my wonted Mess, and take my Rest after the Fatigues of the Day, wherein I had labour'd enough to stand in Need of it.

But my Thoughts were turn'd a quite different Way: The Vision I had seen was still present to my Eye, and drove away Sleep from the Lids of it: The Night was spent in Conjectures; and I had too much Youth, and Flesh and Blood on my Side, not to be wholly taken up with the delightful Ideas of so adorable an Object; insomuch, that I wish'd for Day, and to be at my usual Employment, how laborious soever it was, that I might be nearer to the fair and pleasing Cause of all my Disorders and Inquietudes. Day came at last, and the usual Discharge of my Duty; when I was happily set to work in diging Beds for Carnations, Tulips, and other Flowers, that were to be transplanted from the furthermost End of the Garden, to that Side of it, where stood the Bagnio[1] before spoken of. I look'd upon this as a lucky Appointment, and form'd to myself Hopes thereby of another Sight of my lovely Charmer; and for that End, while I was at Work, I tun'd my Pipes again in the *Portuguese* Tongue, which, by often making Voyages to and from *Lisbon*, I understood tolerably well; nor was I deceiv'd in my Expectation; for the Door open'd again, and the same Vision appear'd as before; but with an Addition of Richness of Dress and Beauty. She had a Turbant on her Head, set round at the Bottom with Clasps of Diamonds, and in the Middle stood a Jewel, from whence arose a *Heron*'s Feather: In a Word, nothing could be more commanding of Respect and Attention than her Looks, and her Garb; and I stood, like a Statue, Motionless, and as if fix'd to the Earth, whereon my Spade fell out of my Hand. She beckon'd to me; in a Word she spoke to me in the *Portuguese* Language, to come near her: I did so accordingly, when she said, *Stranger, we both run the Risque of Death, if seen, or overheard; but this being a Day of Devotion, set apart for the* Talbees *of the* Law, *among whom Achmet Benhadi is one, for visiting the Churches or Moschs, we have an Opportunity of discoursing together for some Time.* I told her that it would be too great an Honour. With that she smil'd, and shutting the Door after me, carry'd me into an inner Marble Apartment, where was an Alcove, and plenty of Sweetmeats, and rich Drams, wherewith I was extremely comforted. *You may think me forward and bold,* said she, Englishman; *but 'tis the Custom of this Country not to be long in telling their Mind. To be as breif as possible, I have taken a Liking to your Person; and if you are not indifferent to mine, it's at your Disposal; and since it's impossible to escape from the Servitude we are under, (for I account my Bondage, in being taken for a Wife by the old Curmudgeon I am wedded to, worse than yours) we have nothing to do, but to make it as easy as it can be to us, by frequent Opportunities of this Kind.* I, by this Time, had taken Courage, and was not behind Hand in affectionate Returns; but as Time was precious, especially on my Side, I made Use of it to the best Advantage I could, which gave me entire Possession of the lovliest Creature under the Sun: She seem'd equally pleas'd with me; but knowing the Necessity of my speedy Departure, dismiss'd

---

1   Here, a bathing house.

me to my wonted Task; to which I went with great Regret and Unwillingness, from a much more diverting Employment.

We had several meetings of this Kind; and not a Festival escap'd us, but we took the Opportunity thereof for mutual Endearments; when, at last, I understood, not from her own Mouth, but from a Note I saw her hastily throw out at the Door, that my dear *Moraima* (for so the Solacer of all my Afflictions was call'd) was eternally lost to my Embraces, and Hopes, in being demanded of my Patron *Benhadi* by King *Muley Ismael*; and that she was going to be bury'd alive in the Alcassava, after nine Days Purification; for that impious Tyrant touches none but Virgins, unless Women so used, after Coition[1] with other Men. No Words, but her own, can express the Tenderness she gave me in Writing upon this sad Occasion, and the Sorrows she lay under, in being depriv'd of the Continuance of our Conversation: Nor was I to be comforted, under a Misfortune that I foresaw would involve me in inextricable Miseries: For my Cares, that used to be alleviated by delightful Intervals in her Company, were now redoubled, through my Despair of never seeing her more; and my Patron *Benhadi*, Chagrin'd by the Loss of his beloved Wife, grew so enrag'd, that finding himself unable to vent his Passion at him (the King) that caus'd it, he made those about him suffer by it. I, for my Part, after receiving a hundred Stripes[2] Day after Day, for a whole Week, not only had my Diet chang'd from bad to worse, but my Work; and, instead of being employ'd in the Gardens, was order'd to draw a Cart, (in Concert with a Mule, then made my Fellow-Labourer) laden with Brick, Sand, Lime &c. towards repairing of a Mosque, whereof my *Talbe* was Chief Priest. In this insupportable Condition was I found, when the wise Negociations of Captain *Stuart*, with the Alcaid *Hamet ben Hamet*, at *Tetuan*, brought about mine, and the rest of my Captive Brethren's, Redemption.

3. From Daniel Defoe, *A Review of the State of the English Nation*, no. 127 (28 January 1710), pp. 505–06

[Daniel Defoe (d. 1731), Dissenter, writer, and trader, was one of the most prolific authors of the eighteenth century and an innovator both in journalism and in fiction. As many of his works were published anonymously or pseudonymously, the extent of the Defoe canon will probably never be known. The extracts

---

1 Sexual intercourse.
2 Strokes or lashes with a whip.

below demonstrate something of the inconsistency of his attitudes toward slavery: when writing about the promotion of British trade, he supports it, but when attacking middle-class hypocrisy in his satire *The Reformation of Manners* (1702), he condemns it. He is capable of sympathizing with the enslaved people captured by pirates in *Captain Singleton* (1720) but writes from the point of view of the pirates who make money by selling them.]

[W]ho can help talking a little of Trade, when they see Petitions[1] thronging into the *House* of *Commons*, so incongruous in themselves, so inconsistent with common Justice, and indeed with common Sense in Trade, that to me it seems, as if some Men had a Mind to see, whether the *House* knew when they were affronted.

To see Petitions to the *House*, of contradicting Natures, and some of self-contradicting Terms; Here they petition against Monopolies to destroy Trade, there they petition for Monopolies to preserve Trade; *Here* some petition for Power to prevent Fraud in Commerce, *there* to prevent Trade it self, on pretence of preventing Frauds in that Trade—And *there* men petition to have the Power of Fraud taken out of every Man's Hand but their own.

I could perhaps give you a great many Instances of these Things, and make you merry with the ridiculous Conduct on both sides—But I'll content my self to begin only with the Petitions from sundry Places, for laying open, *Anglicé*, destroying the Trade to *Africa*, and a most preposterous, not to say foolish, Petition of some People, for supplying the Colonies with *Negroes*, by laying open the Trade to *Africa*....

I think, both Sides agreed last Session, that the Trade to *Africa* was to be preserv'd, that it was essential to our Colonies to preserve them, and supply them with *Negroe* Slaves, that it was essential to the Nation to keep it out of the Hands of the *French*— Then it was agreed, that this Trade could not be preserv'd without maintaining the Forts and Factories[2] on the Coast of *Africa*: And the main Question should have been, Whether these could be preserv'd without an exclusive Company or no.

---

1 Between 1708 and 1712, petitions from independent slave traders challenged the Royal African Company's monopoly of the Atlantic slave trade, a monopoly granted in 1672.
2 Trading posts or warehouses.

4. From [Daniel Defoe,] *Reformation of Manners, A Satyr* (1702), lines 297–330

Satyr, the Arts and Mysteries forbear,
Too black for thee [to] write, or us to hear:
No Man, but he that is as vile as they,
Can all the Tricks and Cheats of Trade survey.
Some in Clandestine Companies combine,
Erect new Stocks to Trade beyond the Line:[1]
With Air and empty Names beguile the Town,
And raise new Credits first, then cry 'em down:
Divide the *empty nothing* into Shares,
To set the Town together by the Ears.
The Sham Projectors and the Brokers join,
And both the Cully[2] Merchant undermine;
First he must be drawn in, and then betray'd,
And then demolish the Machine they made:
So conjuring Chymists, who with a Charm and Spell,
Some wondrous Liquid wondrously exhale;
But when the gaping Mob their Money pay,
The Charm's dissolv'd, the Vapour flies away:
The wond'ring Bubbles[3] stand amaz'd to see
Their Money Mountebank'd to *Mercury*.[4]
Some fit out Ships, and double Fraights ensure,
And burn the Ships to make the Voyage secure;
Promiscuous Plunders thro' the World commit,
And *with the Money* buy their safe Retreat.
Others seek out to *Africk*'s Torrid Zone,
And search the burning Shores of *Serralone*;[5]
There in unsufferable Heats *they fry*,
And run vast Risques to see the Gold, *and die:*
The harmless Natives basely they trepan,
And barter Baubles for the *Souls of Men*:
The Wretches they to Christian Climes bring o'er,
To serve worse Heathens than they did before.

---

1   South of the Equator.
2   A dupe.
3   Those who have been tricked.
4   In Greek myth, the messenger of the gods but also the protector of
    thieves.
5   Sierra Leone, a country on the southwest coast of West Africa.

The Cruelties they suffer there are such,
Amboyna's nothing, they've out-done the *Dutch*.[1]

5. From [Daniel Defoe,] *The Life, Adventures, and Pyra-cies, of the Famous Captain Singleton* (1720), pp. 204–13

Immediately our men entred the Ship, where we found a large Ship with upwards of 600 Negroes, Men and Women, Boys and Girls, and not one Christian, or white Man, on board.

I was struck with Horror at the Sight, for immediately I con-cluded, as was partly the Case, that these black Devils had got loose, had murthered all the white Men, and thrown them into the Sea; and I had no sooner told my Mind to the Men, but the Thought of it so enraged them, that I had much to do to keep my Men from cutting them all in Pieces. But *William*, with many Per-swasions prevailed upon them, by telling of them, that it was nothing but what, if they were in the Negroes Condition, they would do, if they could; and that the Negroes had really the highest Injustice done them, to be sold for Slaves without their Consent; and that the Law of Nature dictated it to them; and that they ought not to kill them, and that it would be wilful Murder to do it.

This prevailed with them, and cooled their first Heat; so they only knock'd down twenty or thirty of them, and the rest run all down between Decks, to their first Places, believing, as we fancy'd, that we were their first Masters come again....

Having taken this Ship, our next Difficulty was, what to do with the Negroes. The *Portugueze* in the *Brasils* would have bought them all of us, and been glad of the Purchase, if we had not shew'd our selves Enemies there, and had been known for Pyrates; but as it was, we durst not go on Shore any where there-abouts, or treat with any of the Planters, because we should raise the whole Country upon us; and if there were any such things as Men of War in any of their Ports, we should be assured to be attack'd by them, and by all the Force they had by Land or Sea.

Nor could we think of any better Success, if we went North-ward to our own Plantations. One while we determined to carry them all away to the *Buenos Ayres*, and sell them to the *Spaniards*; but they were really too many for them to make Use of ...

---

1   In 1623, officials of the Dutch East India Company on the island of Ambon in the Indonesian archipelago tortured and beheaded twenty or twenty-one men, ten of them employees of the English East India Company.

6. From Anonymous, *An Essay in Defence of the Female Sex* (1696), pp. 20–22

[Authorship of *An Essay in Defence of the Female Sex* has been ascribed to Mary Astell (1666–1731), but it seems likely that the author was in fact Judith Drake (fl. 1696–1723), medical practitioner, writer, and editor of her husband James Drake's posthumous *Anthropologia Nova, or, a New System of Anatomy* (1707). James Drake (1667–1707) was a fellow of the Royal Society and of the Royal College of Physicians. In 1723 Judith Drake was summoned to appear before the latter by Sir Hans Sloane (1660–1753) to defend herself against a charge of "medical malpractice." An informant had told the Society that she had been dispensing medicines to women and children.]

[N]othing makes one Party slavishly depress another, but their fear that they may at one time or another become Strong or Couragious enough to make themselves equal to, if not superiour to their Masters. This is our Case; for Men being sensible as well of the Abilities of Mind in our Sex, as of the strength of Body in their own, began to grow Jealous, that we, who in the Infancy of the World were their Equals and Partners in Dominion, might in process of Time, by Subtlety and Stratagem, become their Superiours; and therefore began in good Time to make use of Force (the Origine of Power) to compell us to a Subjection, Nature never meant; and made use of Natures liberality to them to take the benefit of her kindness from us. From that time they have endeavour'd to train us up altogether to Ease and Ignorance; as Conquerors use to do to those, they reduce by Force, that so they may disarm 'em, both of their Courage and Wit; and consequently make them tamely give up their Liberty, and abjectly submit their Necks to a slavish Yoke. As the World grew more Populous, and Mens Necessities whetted their Inventions, so it increas'd their Jealousie, and sharpen'd their Tyranny over us, till by degrees, it came to that Height of Severity, I may say Cruelty, it is now at in all the Eastern parts of the World, where the Women, like our Negroes in our Western Plantations, are born slaves, and live Prisoners all their Lives.

7. From Mary Astell, Preface to *Some Reflections Upon Marriage*, 3rd ed. (1706)

[Mary Astell is now probably best known as a promoter of women's education in *A Serious Proposal to the Ladies* (1694), in which she argued for the creation of all-female academies, or secular convents, where women might pursue an intellectual life while retiring from the world. *Some Reflections Upon Marriage*, first published in 1700, takes as its starting point the death of Hortense Mancini, duchess of Mazarin (1646–99), who led a scandalous life after fleeing an unhappy marriage. Astell is critical of Mancini's conduct, but much of *Reflections* is concerned with the miseries of women's married lives. Despite the bitter irony of Astell's attack on the tyranny of men over women, she was a royalist and supporter of absolutism. The following widely quoted passage takes aim at John Locke's (1632–1704) conception of government by contract, a contract that nevertheless leaves women's subordination to men firmly in place.]

[I]f Absolute Sovereignty be not necessary in a State, how comes it to be so in a Family? or if in a Family why not in a State; since no Reason can be alledg'd for the one that will not hold more strongly for the other? If the Authority of the Husband so far as it extends, is sacred and inalienable, why not of the Prince? The Domestic Sovereign is without Dispute Elected, and the Stipulations and Contract are mutual, is it not then partial in Men to the last degree, to contend for, and practise that arbitrary Dominion in their Families, which they abhor and exclaim against in the State? For if Arbitrary Power is evil in it self, and an improper Method of Governing Rational and Free Agents, it ought not to be Practis'd any where; Nor is it less, but rather more mischievous in Families than in Kingdoms, by how much 100000 Tyrants are worse than one. What tho' a Husband can't deprive a Wife of Life without being responsible to the Law, he may however do what is much more grievous to a generous Mind, render Life miserable, for which she has no Redress, scarce Pity which is afforded to every other Complainant. It being thought a Wife's Duty to suffer every thing without Complaint. If *all Men are born free*, how is it that all Women are born Slaves? as they must be if the being subjected to the *inconstant, uncertain, unknown, arbitrary Will of Men*, be the *perfect Condition of Slavery*? and if the Essence of Freedom consists, as our Masters say it does, in having a *standing Rule to live by*? And why is Slavery so much condemn'd and strove against in one Case, and so highly applauded, and held so necessary and so sacred in another?

8. From "Cato," *London Journal*, no. CXXX (20 January 1722), pp. 1–2

[Between 1720 and 1723, John Trenchard (1688/89–1723), landowner and member of parliament for Taunton from 1722–23, and Thomas Gordon (d. 1750), a Scottish classical scholar and pamphleteer, published letters in the *London Journal* and later the *British Journal* under the pseudonym Cato, after Marcus Porcius Cato (95–46 BCE), who committed suicide rather than accept a pardon from Julius Caesar (100–44 BCE). The imminent danger of tyranny and the potential loss of British liberty—construed as "slavery"—are constant themes in the letters. Cato associates tyranny and slavery with arbitrary power, corruption, the maintenance of a standing army, and any religion considered irrational. The letters were subsequently collected and reprinted many times as *Cato's Letters*.]

True and impartial Liberty is ... the Right of every Man, to pursue the natural, reasonable and religious Dictates of his own Mind; to think what he will, and act as he thinks, provided he acts not to the Prejudice of another; to spend his own Money himself, and lay out the Produce of his Labour his own Way; and to labour for his own Pleasure and Profit, and not for others who are idle, and would live and riot by pillaging and oppressing him, and those that are like him.

So that Civil Government is only a partial Restraint put by the Laws of Agreement and Society upon natural and absolute Liberty, which might otherwise grow licentious: And Tyranny is an unlimited Restraint put upon natural Liberty, by the Will of one or a few. Magistracy amongst a free People is the Exercise of Power for the sake of the People; and Tyrants abuse the People, for the sake of Power. Free Government is the protecting the People in their Liberties by stated Rules; Tyranny is a brutish Struggle for unlimited Liberty to one or a few, who would rob all others of their Liberty, and act by no Rule but lawless Lust....

Where Liberty is lost, Life grows precarious, always miserable and often intolerable. Liberty is to live upon one's own Terms; Slavery is to live at the meer Mercy of another; and a Life of Slavery is to those who can bear it, a continual State of Uncertainty and Wretchedness, often an Apprehension of Violence, and often the lingring Dread of a violent Death: But by others, when no other Remedy is to be had, Death is reckon'd a good one.... Slavery, while it continues, being a perpetual Awe upon the

Spirits, depresses them, and sinks natural Courage; and Want and Fear, the Concomitants of Bondage, always produce Despondency and Baseness: Nor will men in Bonds ever fight bravely, but to be free. And indeed, what else should they fight for; since every Victory they gain for a Tyrant, makes them poorer and fewer; and increasing his Pride, increases his Cruelty, and their own Misery and Chains?

Those, who from Terror and Delusion, the frequent Causes and certain Effects of Servitude, come to think their Governours greater than Men, as they find them worse; will be as apt to think themselves less: And when the Head and the Heart are thus both gone, the Hands will signify little; they who are us'd like Beasts, will be apt to degenerate into Beasts. But those, on the contrary, who by the Freedom of their Government and Education, are taught and accustom'd to think freely of Men and Things, find, by comparing one Man with another, that all Men are naturally alike; and that their Governours, as they have the same Face, Constitution, and Shape with themselves, and are subject to the same Sickness, Accidents and Death with the meanest of their People; so they possess the same Passions and Faculties of the Mind which their Subjects possess, and not better. They therefore scorn to degrade and prostrate themselves, to adore those of their own Species, however cover'd with Titles and disguis'd by Power: They consider them as their own Creatures; and as far as they surmount themselves, the Work of their own Hands, and only the chief Servants of the State, who have no more Power to do Evil than one of themselves, and are void of every Privilege and Superiority, but to serve them and their State. They know it is a Contradiction in Religion and Reason, for any Man to have a Right to do Evil; and that not to resist any Man's Wickedness, is to encourage it; and that they have the least Reason to bear Evil and Oppression from their Governours, who of all Men are the most oblig'd to do them good. They therefore detest Slavery, and despise or pity Slaves; and adoring Liberty alone, as they who see its Beauty and feel its Advantages always will, 'tis no wonder they are brave for it.

9. From "Cato," *A Discourse of Standing Armies; Shewing the Folly, Uselesness, and Danger of Standing Armies in Great Britain* (1722), pp. 19–25

There are but two Ways in Nature to enslave a People, and continue that Slavery over them; the first is Superstition, and the last is Force: By the one, we are perswaded that it is our Duty to be undone; and the other undoes us whether we will or no. I take it, that we are pretty much out of Danger of the first, at present; and, I think, we cannot be too much upon our guard against the other; for tho' we have nothing to fear from the best Prince in the World, yet we have every thing to fear from those who would give him a Power inconsistent with Liberty, and with a Constitution which has lasted almost a Thousand Years without such a Power, which will never be ask'd with an Intention to make no Use of it....

'Tis certain, that all Parts of *Europe* which are enslaved, have been enslaved by Armies, and 'tis absolutely impossible, that any Nation which keeps them amongst themselves, can long preserve their Liberties; nor can any Nation perfectly lose their Liberties, who are without such Guests ...

10. **From William Stephens, *A Second Deliverance from Popery and Slavery. As it was set forth in a Sermon in the Parish Church of Sutton in Surrey, Sept. 19. 1714. Being the First Sunday after His Majesty's Landing* (1714), pp. 5–6**

[William Stephens (1649/50–1718) was a Church of England clergyman of strong Whig principles. His equation of popery and slavery in the sermon extracted below is a commonplace of eighteenth-century English Protestantism. Here he celebrates the coronation of George I on 1 August 1714 and the failure of the Jacobites.]

[W]e have frequent Reason to say with *David, Blessed be the Lord, who daily loadeth us with benefits: even the God of our Salvation* (Psalm 68:19). And what a particular Reason have the People of *England* this Day to bless the heavenly Majesty, who has brought Light out of Darkness, Order out of Confusion, by putting a Stop to the wicked Designs of those Sons of *Belial*,[1] who were nursing up a barbarous, bloody, civil, ceremonial War, on purpose to introduce a base ignoble Phantom of Majesty, to support the eldest Son of *Antichrist*, in his treble Capacity of Tyranny over Soul, Body and Property? What Reason have we this Day to rejoice that God has *scattered the people who delight in War?* (Psalm 68:39). What great Reason have we at this Day to rejoice with his Sacred Majesty, the true Defender of our Holy Faith, in the

---

1   The spirit of evil personified, or another name for the Devil.

Words of the Royal Psalmist, and in the same Spirit with which *David* indited that Psalm, *viz. The King shall joy in they strength, O Lord: in thy Salvation how greatly shall he rejoice! Thou hast given him his hearts desire, and hast not witholden the request of his lips. For thou preventest him with the blessings of goodness: thou settest a crown of pure gold on his head* (Psalm 21:1, 2, 3). But that Particular in which the Glory of King *David* did chiefly consist, is mention'd in the 5th Verse, *viz.* because God in Mercy both to himself and his People, bestowed this Glory and Majesty upon him. *His glory is great in thy salvation: honour and majesty hast thou laid upon him* (v. 5). And this is the Cause of our present joy, that when Snares were laid for us, and Terrors compassed us round about; when the palpable Darkness of Popery, with its concomitant Slavery hovered over our heads; then how joyful is it to say with *David, Blessed be the Lord, who has not given us over as a prey to their teeth....* (Psalm 124: 6, 7, 8).

Appendix B: Orientalism

1. From Sir Paul Rycaut, *The History of the Present State of the Ottoman Empire. Containing the Maxims of Turkish Politie, the most Material Points of the Mahometan Religion, their Sects and Heresies, their Convents and Religious Votaries. Their Military Discipline, with an Exact Computation of the Forces both by Land and Sea* (1666), p. 2

[Sir Paul Rycaut (1629–1700), a diplomat and author of Huguenot extraction, was chancellor of the Levant Company's trading station at Constantinople (Istanbul) from 1661, then British consul at Smyrna (Izmir) from 1667 to 1678, and finally Chief Secretary to the Lord Lieutenant in Ireland from 1685 to 1687. *The History of the Present State of the Ottoman Empire* (1666) was a hugely influential account, reprinted and translated into French, Italian, German, Polish, and Russian. Rycaut's *History of the Turkish Empire from the Year 1623 to the Year 1677* (1680), an account of Ottoman rule picking up where Richard Knolles's *General Historie* had concluded, provided Mary Pix with the plot for her play *Ibrahim, the Thirteenth Emperour of the Turks* (1696; see Appendix B4).]

[W]hen I have considered seriously the contexture of the *Turkish* Government, the absoluteness of an Emperour without reason, without virtue, whose speeches may be irrational, and yet must be laws; whose actions irregular, and yet examples; whose sentence and judgement, if in matters of the Imperial concernment, are most commonly corrupt, and yet decrees irresistible: When I consider what little rewards there are for vertue, and no punishment for profitable and thriving vice; how men are raised at once by adulation, chance, and the sole favour of the Prince, without any title of noble bloud, or the motives of previous deserts, or former testimonies and experience of parts or abilities, to the weightiest, the richest, and most honourable charges of the Empire; when I consider how short their continuance is in them, how with one frown of their Prince they are cut off; with what greediness above all people in the world, they thirst and hast to be rich, and yet know their treasure is but their snare; what they labour for is but as slaves for their great Patron and Master, and what will inevitably effect their ruine and destruction, though they have all the arguments of faithfulness, virtue, and moral honesty (which are rare in a *Turk*) to be their advocates and plead for them. When I consider many other things of like nature ... one might admire the long continuance of this great and vast Empire, and attribute the stability thereof without change within its self, and the increase of Dominions and constant progress of its arms, rather to some super-natural cause, then to the ordinary maximes of State, or wisdom of the Governours, as if the Divine will of the all-knowing Creator, had chosen for the good of his Church, and chastisement of the sins and vices of Christians, to raise and support this potent people....

But that which cements all breaches, and cures all those wounds in this body politick, is the quickness and severity of their justice, which not considering much the strict division and parts of *distributive* and *commutative*, makes almost every crime equal, and punishes it with the last and extreamest chastisement, which is death; I mean those which have relation to the Government, and are of common and publick interest. Without this remedy, which I lay down as a principal preventer of the greatest disorders, this mighty body would burst with the poyson of its own ill humors, and soon divide it self into several Signories, as the ambition and power of the Governours most remote from the Imperial seat administred them hopes and security of becoming absolute.

2. From "Cato," *London Journal*, no. XC (15 April 1721), p. 1

Despotick power has defaced the Creation, and laid the World waste. In the finest Countries in *Asia*, formerly full of People, you are now forced to travel by the Compass: There are no Roads, Houses, nor Inhabitants. The Sun is left to scorch up the Grass and Fruits which he had rais'd; or the Rain to rot them: The Gifts of God are left to perish; there being none of his Creatures, neither Man nor Beast, left to use and consume them. The *Grand Signior*, who ... is the Viceregent of Heaven, frustrates the Bounty of Heaven, and being the Father of his People, has almost butcher'd them all. Those few (comparatively few, very few) who have yet surviv'd the miserable Fate of their Brethren, and are reserv'd for Sacrifices to his Cruelty, as Occasion offers, and his Lust prompts him, live the starv-

ing and wretched Property of ravenous and bloody *Bashaws;*
whose Duty to their Master, as well as their own Avarice,
obliges them to keep the People, over whom they preside, poor
and miserable....

[N]either *Bashaws*, nor Armies, could keep that People [the
Turks] in such abject Slavery, if their Priests and Doctors had not
made Passive Obedience a Principle of their Religion. The holy
Name of God is prophaned, and his Authority belied, to bind
down Wretchedness upon his Creatures, and to secure the Tyrant
that does it. The most consummate of all Wickedness, and the
highest of all Evils, are sanctified by the Teachers of Religion, and
made by them a Part of it. Yes, Turkish Slavery is confirm'd, and
Turkish Tyranny defended, by Religion!

3. From Delarivier Manley, *Almyna: or, The Arabian Vow. A Tragedy* (1707; first performed 1706), act V, scene ii

[Delarivier Manley (c. 1663/70–1724) found fame (or notoriety)
as a writer with the publication of *The New Atalantis* (1709), a
roman-à-clef offering tales of seduction and betrayal by Whig
grandees of the early eighteenth century. *Almyna: Or, The Arabian
Vow*, her second Orientalist play, takes for its plot the framing
device from *The Arabian Nights' Entertainments*, as Antoine
Galland's *Mille et Une Nuits* (1704–17), a French translation of a
Syrian manuscript, was known in English. In *Arabian Nights*,
Sultan Schahriar, convinced of women's adulterous nature, vows
to murder every morning the virgin he has wedded the previous
day so that she can never dishonour him. Scheherezade, the
vizier's daughter, volunteers to marry Schahriar, and every night
her unfinished tales induce him to keep her alive so that he can
hear the conclusions. After the thousand and one nights of the
original title, he has fallen in love with her and lets her live.
Manley's Caliph Almanazor makes the same vow as Schahriar,
believing that he is doing nothing wrong because women have no
souls—a common eighteenth-century European misconception
about Islamic beliefs. Almyna volunteers to marry the Sultan
believing that she might reform him. The following dialogue
begins after the vizier expresses how he is "darted thro' and thro'
with woe" at the prospect of losing his daughter.]

Alm. My Lord, I beg you not to melt me thus.
Your tears are far more dreadfuller than Death;
Consider what I dye for, and the Cause.

My Gracious Lord, the Sultan has assur'd
My Life shall be the last; think but on that.
How glorious, and dear to Fame it makes me;
Am I not Ransom for so many Lives?
Was I not born to an exalted End?
I kneel with thanks to the Almighty Pow'rs,
Am proud, and pleas'd, that I'm become so useful!
What must I comfort you, is Death then nothing,
Am I to Combat in your Tears more pains,
Than that destroyer brings, or is not all,
My Constancy of use to face him,
That you anticipate it here.
   Viz. O Daughter! Daughter! Sure my heart will break....

Alm. Farewel! These Mournings make our Fate so dreadful.
I'le dye (to lose the torment of Reflection)
Before my Sister brings new Sorrows to me.
Where are the Mutes? Prepare your Bow-strings,
When I veil my Face, perform your Office.
What in a moment, shall I be? How chang'd?
What must I lose, my Husband, and his Love:
My tender Father, and his Care! My Sister too!
It wonnot bear to be reflected on.
Thus lowly then, I humbly do resign *[kneels*
All-seeing gracious Heav'n, dart mercy on me.
Pardon the Errors of Humanity!
And let thy failing Creature taste forgiveness.
Oh! holy Prophet! take me to thy care,
And be my loss of Life, the last of our
Great Emperor's wilful Crimes.
Comfort my Father, for his Daughter's loss.
And take *Almyna*'s Soul to thy protection.

As the Mutes are going to strangle her, the Sultan *speaks from
above.*

Sult. Mutes, on your Lives forbear, till I descend.
Alm. What Mercy does the op'ning Heav'ns foreshew?
It was my Husband's Voice, am I still living?
Or crost to those blest happy Plains, where Angels
Do in Mercy speak, like my *Almanazor*?
Do I once more, receive my Lord so near?

[*The* Sultan *enters, and runs to embrace her.*

Sult. Live, immortal as they Merit makes thee,
Thou can'st not think, how much at heart I'm pain'd,
At but imagining thy death, *Almyna*:
Tho' it was ne're design'd but as a Tryal,
How far thy bravery of Soul cou'd reach.
Quite vanquish'd, by thy heroic Deeds
We gain in losing of so false a Cause.
Henceforth be it not once imagin'd
That Women have not Souls, divine as we.
Who doubts, let 'em look here, for Confutation,
And reverence with us *Almyna*'s Vertue.
(*Omnes.*) Long live the fair *Sultana.*
Alm. Accept, my gracious Lord, the Life you give.
Thus let me at your Feet bestow my Thanks.
Bestow my self in Gratitude and Love.
To rescue me from hov'ring Death, just at
The fatal Instant, to give me Life and Pow'r.
To give me Love, to give me my *Almanazor*,
Is an extravagance of Gift, so vast a Joy,
That the Excess is as dangerous to Life
As Death it self, does almost rob me of it.
Sult. Look up, my fainting Dear, I am all thine:
For ever thine we're thus to part no more.

4. From Mary Pix, *Ibrahim, the Thirteenth Emperour of the Turks: A Tragedy* (1696), acts 3 and 5

[Mary Pix (1666–1709) was the named author of seven plays on the London stage between 1696 and 1706 and possibly five more anonymous productions. *Ibrahim, the Thirteenth Emperour of the Turks* was one of two plays by Pix performed in 1696, the other being *The Spanish Wives*, a comedy. In a Preface to *Ibrahim*, she acknowledges that she derived the story from her reading of Sir Paul Rycaut's continuation of Richard Knolles's *A General Historie of the Turks*, though remembering Ibrahim, wrongly, as the thirteenth rather than the twelfth emperor. Rycaut's account tells how Shechir Para, the sultan's discarded mistress, seeks out new women for the sultan in the public baths and comes upon the mufti's daughter. Father and daughter both resist Ibrahim's summons, but he abducts and rapes the girl. The mufti appeals for justice to a councillor and the general of the janissaries, the janissaries being the sultan's guard and an élite corps originally formed from non-Muslim children taken as tribute. They decide that the sultan is a tyrant and must be deposed. An insurrection follows: Ibrahim is imprisoned and then executed by strangulation, and his place is taken by his son. Rycaut has nothing to say about the fate of the mufti's unnamed daughter. Pix retained Rycaut's characterization of Ibrahim as one consumed by lust and sensuality but altered some other aspects of the story. In *Ibrahim* Shechir Para—Shekir Para in Pix's version—has been rejected by Amurat, general of the emperor's forces. Amurat is engaged to Morena, the mufti's daughter. Seeking revenge, Shekir Para tells Ibrahim about Morena, whom he abducts and rapes, as in Rycaut's account. In Pix's play, Amurat leads a rebellion, Ibrahim is killed, and power passes to his son. Morena takes poison and dies, and Amurat stabs himself. The play was a success, being revived three times in 1702, 1704, and 1715.]

From Act III

Ibr. As Heaven hath given me a Despotick
And unbounded Power: so shall my Pleasures be.
But oh! the Earth's too little; and its Pleasures
Too few! I cannot keep my mind
In a continued Frame of Joy; tho' the Slaves
That serve me, vie with the Stars for number!
Nay, tho' you, my Charming Mistress,
Whose very conceptions, like your Wit, Divine,
And like your Beauty pleasing: tho' you, I say,
Set your Invention at the Wrack, for my Diversion;
Yet still, to day's like yesterday: to morrow like to day.
And tho' my Paths lie all thro' Paradise:
Yet being still the self-same Road, I grow uneasie.
Shek. Alas! Dread Sir! we've been mistaken;
In vain we've searched *Persia,* and
Armenia, and Ransack'd *Greece* in vain;
Whilst within your own Royal Gates
Of this *Seraglio* lives a *Helene,* whose
Lovely Face strikes Envy dumb.
Late I saw her at the Baths;
But Heavens, such a Creature
My astonish'd Eyes ne're view'd before.
A Skin, clear as the upper Region,
Where Thickening Clouds can never mount:

And strow'd with Blushes, like the glorious space
Of Summer's setting Suns.
Her large Black Eyes shot Rays intermingl'd
With becoming Pride, and taking Sweetness.   [*The* Sultan
   Rises hastily.
Ibr. —Here in our Pallace—impossible
—Of what Name? what Quality?—
Shek. Morena, only Daughter to the *Mufti*—But
For what cause conceal'd I am ignorant.
...
Ibr. By Heaven! I'll see her, see her this very moment;
And if she answers your Description,
She's mine; first with Prayers, and Mildness
We'll proceed; but if the surly Fool denies
He soon shall find that Prayers are
Needless, when Power is infinite....

The Scene changes to the Mufti's *Apartment:*
He sits Reading.
A Servant Enters hastily.

Serv. Oh! Sir—I saw the *Sultan* pass the Long Gallery
That parts the Old *Seraglio* from the New;
And bend his steps directly hither—He's 'een at my Heels!
Muft. What can this visit mean?
But I am arm'd with Innocence
And therefore know no fear.

Enter Ibrahim, Sheker Para, Achmet [chief of the eunuchs], *and
several Attendants.*

Muft. Sacred Sir! I am amazed——
At these unwonted Honours; and if I fail
In the expressions of my Joy; let my
Confusion plead my excuse....
Let me kiss your Sacred Robe.
In thankfulness.—Oh! mighty *Sultan,*
Who daigns thus to oblige his Vassals.
Ibr. Mufti—I hear thou hast a Daughter—
Why dost thou start, Old Man?—
If Fame be believed thou need'st not shame
To own the Beautious Maid——
Send for her hither, for I will see her.

Muft. Oh! Pardon me Emperour, the Girl is most unfit
For you to see, Bred up in Cells, and Grotto's:
Tho' so near a Court, wholly unacquainted with its Glories.
Heaven not Blessing me with a Male, I have try'd
To mend the Sex; and she, instead of (coining looks)
And learning little Arts to please, hath Read
Philosophy, History, those rough Studies:
And will appear like a neglected Villager
To those bright Beauties that attend the happy Port.[1]
Ibr. Ha! Is this our entertainment—to be deny'd
What we desire! go some of you and fetch the Maid.

Exeunt two Eunuchs.

Muft. Tho' you are Lord of all, and may without controul
Command, yet Emperor, Remember,
My Daughter is no Slave, and our holy Law
Forbids that you should force the free,
Therefore if the unhappy Girl shou'd please,
And then refuse the offered Greatness; our Prophets Curse
Falls heavy, if you proceed to Violation.

Enter Morena *Veil'd.*

Muft. Kneel Daughter, to the Commander of the World.
Ibr. Take off her Veil—by Heavens—
A charming Creature!
Raise thee from the Earth, and lift thy eyes to Glory,
A Crown will well become that Brow; Destiny
Hath mark'd thee for Command—I see
Prevailing modesty is in her eyes;
The shining springs are full of tears;—
I'll urge no farther now; but leave my
Shekir Para, to prepare her for the Excelling Honours
I design her; *Mufti,* come you with me, and let us
Farther consult of this Important business.

Exeunt the Sultan, Mufti *and Eunuchs: except* Achmet.

---

1 Meaning the Sublime Porte, the court or palace of the Ottoman
  emperor at Istanbul.

Shek. Hail! Happy Maid! whom *Fate* has blest;
Whose Illustrious Eyes have caught
The Monarch of the Earth, *Ibrahim!*
Companion to the Sun, and Brother to the Stars!
His Sacred presence strikes an universal aw;
And next to the Immortals he is worship here.
What a long Train of glory is opening to your view,
Mounting on shining Thrones your beauties Merit!
Whilst thousand ready slaves stand watching
The Motions of your eyes, and e're you form
Your breath into command, 'tis done.
Mor. Cease Madam, you use your Eloquence in vain,
Menaces, Prayers, and Promises are lost on me.
Already I have Slaves, who wait on my desires,
And fulfil whatever I command: more is but superfluous;
No Crown I covet, but that which honour gives;
And my Ambition terminates in the contented paths
Of virtue. All your Efforts to alter me,
Like waves against a Rack, will dash themselves,
But stir not my Foundation.
Shek. Why do ye view me with that haughty
Regardless Air, as if I were your Enemy?
When I so long to be your Friend.
Mor. Oh! mistake me not,—If my looks
Carry a disdain, 'tis on the Crowns you offer;
Not on you. Alas! you only can be my Friend;
And divert the Emperour from the pursuit
Of this short lived passion; you do not know
The secret pleasing cause that will, I am sure,
Inspire me rather to dye than yield.
Shek. (aside) Too well I know it!
—If I cou'd assist, tho' your desires are strange,
Yet, you have something so ingaging,
If I cou'd, I say, I wou'd.
Mor. Oh! 'tis greatly in your power—
Tell the *Sultan* you have discovered,
As you easily may a thousand Imperfections
That I am sickly, peevish, ill Bred, and
Of a hateful disposition.—
Shek. I cannot so deny your Excellencies;
But I will do my best, that you shall hear of this no more.
Mor. And now, fair *Oratrix*,
Who plead'st too well for such a cause;
Apply thy Rhetorick to *Ibrahim*;

And defend *Morena*'s Life and Honour.

Shek. Rest secur'd, I am wholly yours,
Retire fair Innocence, for I see
This surprize has discomposed ye.
The Lively Red forsakes the charming Circle
Of your cheeks, and fainting paleness takes its place:
Retire, and let this Rancontre[1] never trouble you repose. *Exit*
   Morena.
Poor easy Fool*!* blush *Amurat*
At thy ill choice*!*—take me
For her Friend*!* yes to her destruction
I'll prove a constant onè.
Achmet!

Ach. Madam.

Shek. I go to seek the *Sultan,* chuse some
Of the Eunuchs you command, and fetch
Morena to him, if you meet resistance,
Bring her by force: I saw *Ibrahim*
Fasten his Eyes upon her, and I know
The present will be welcome, now if delay
The roving desires of that unstedfast Prince
May fix elsewhere, and my designs be lost;
Make haste, her Father is not yet returned,
And you may do it with much ease.

Ach. It shall be done e're you have time to think the consequence. *Exit.*

Shek. Revenge*!* How quick and lively are thy Joys?
Love is a sweetness, that but tasted cloys;
Love must be fondled with a gentle hand
Revenge is God like all, and shows command. *Exit....*

From Act V

Enter Morena *Drest in White*

Mor. Drest in these Robes of Innocence,
Fain wou'd I believe my Virgin Purity remains;
But oh! Memory the wretched'st Plague,
Still goads me with the hated Image of my wrong.
My Soul grows weary of its polluted Cage,

---

1   French *rencontre,* or meeting.

And longs to wing the upper Air, where
Uncorrupted Pureness dwells.

Enter Zayda [Morena's *Chief Slave*].

Come near, my *Zayda*, why dost thou
Tremble so? Oh! hadst thou known
The Horrours, thy poor Mistriss has,
Thou woud'st have less to fear!
Zayd. Who can express the Terrours of this dismal Night!
The mad *Janizaries* up, and raging for Revenge,
Put private Broils upon the publick score,
Murder and Rapine, with Fury uncontroll'd
Rang though the City, and make the Devastation
Horrible, the mangled *Visier* they have
Piece-meal torn; nor has their Vengeance
Stopt here: The Life of the Empire, the Man
We worship like a God, for whom
We still were taught to pray; even
The mighty *Ibrahim* is no more!
Mor. Is *Ibrahim* dead?—Oh *Amurat*!
I fear thou hast gone too far; and lest
Our Prophet, shou'd punish thy Disloyalty:
I will, of my self, an Offering make!
Morena, the unhappy cause of all these Woes;
Morena the Atonement—
Go to my Closet; bring from thence
The Golden Bowl—This News
Has much disorder'd me—
There is in that a soveraign Cordial!   [*Exit* Zayda
Look down ye *Roman* Ladies
Whose tracks of Virtue I with care,
Have followed—Behold! A
Turkish Maid—who to the last,
Your great Example imitates:
Scorns to survive when Honour's lost.

Enter Zayda *with the Bowl*.

I know my avenging Friends will instantly
Be here gay in their Purple Ruins, thinking to glad
My Soul with the fatal story; but like a sad Wretch,
Whose loss is irreparable, I must never aim

At comfort more! Deeply I'll taste this precious Juice,
And seek that sound long sleep, where sorrow,
Tormenting care those restless Anxieties
That keep in Dreams the mind awake, approach no more!
    [*Drinks the Poyson.*

Enter Amurat.

Amur. Hail my belov'd and charming fair!
Oh! I have bin, where Blood and Desolation Reign'd,
Where horror in a thousand shapes appeared:
But 'tis past: And I am arrived at the desired Land
Of Peace—Thou the Dove-like Emblem, whose
Long'd for sight Calms the rough Tempests
Of my Soul, and tunes my Heart to Joy!
Mor. That thou hadst stay'd some moments longer.
Amur. Why! My lov'd dear one!
Mor. I shame to cast my eyes towards thine
Wherewith such pleasure I was wont to steal
A glance, my Revenge is now compleat;
I know it, and am yet alive—
Lucretia[1] dy'd before!
Amur. Inhuman fair!
Death in the Person of my Friend![2]
Hath toucht my heart too near;
And now, to crown my misery
Cruelly you talk of yours!

Enter the Mufti, Mustapha [Aga of the Janizaries] *and several others*

Muft. The wrongs that Tyrrannick *Ibrahim*
Had heap'd on the *Sultana* Queens
Causes 'em joyntly to rejoyce;
They call you their preserver,   [*To* Amurat.
And send by me the Empire's Seal
With the Title of Prime *Visier.*

---

1 Lucretia, wife of Tarquinius Collatinus, was raped by Sextus Tarquinius.
   Her suicide because of her dishonour was the catalyst for the expulsion
   of the Tarquins by Lucius Iunius Brutus and thereby the founding of a
   Roman republic in the sixth century BCE.
2 Amurat's friend Solyman.

Begging you wou'd protect the Infant
King, whom you have so justly Rais'd.
Amur. All Honours, Titles, Glories, at the Feet
Of my Adored I lay, if she will bless me
With the sweets of Love, I am, what
They please, else nothing.
Mor. Can the great *Amurat* submit so low,
To talk of Fruition when 'tis past,
Or to his Arms receive pollution?
Amur. Name it no more! The Royal Blood
Of the offender hath cleansed and washed out
Thy Honours Stains, and white as thy
Robes, thy Innocence appears.
Shall I forsake the Christal Fountain,
Because a Rough-hewn Satyr there
Has quench his Thirst? No! The
Spring, thy Virgin Mind was pure!
Mor. Talk on, methinks I taste of Heaven
To hear thee! Let thy kind Breath
Proceed: Waft me from one Paradice
To another!
Amur. Distraction seize me! Either
My sight deceives me; or my Love
Looks exceeding pale; she Staggers too!
Help! Help! Remorseless Powers drive not
The Wretch you form'd to the Blasphemous
Sins Dispair may utter!
Muft. My Daughter! what has thou done!
Zayd. O my unhappy Mistriss!
I fear that fatal Cordial!
Amur. Inveterate Stars! Now ye've stretcht
Your power to the last degree, and
Ye can curse no more!
Oh! *Morena!* more savage—
Than our Lord! For ever thou
Hast Robb'd my Life of Joy, depriv'd
My Eyes of Happiness; which, till
They close, must gaze on Thee!
What hath my Love deserv'd for such
A punishment? *Morena!* Unkind!
Cruel! unkind!
Mor. My Father! draw near; forgive this
First last act of Disobedience!

You taught me, Sir, that Life no longer
Was a good, then a clear Frame attended it;
My Dishonour Rings through the Universe—
Pardon my quitting it!—
Now *Amurat!* To thee—Here I will
Lean a Moment, where I thought to Raign
A whole contented Age—I fear the Cordial
Will prove too strong*!* Antidote the Poison,
And let me live*!*
Amur. Thou shalt live! Since this Barbarous
Climate has wrong'd such worth;
I'll Raise another Empire large as this,
And fix thee there!—
Mor. Fix me in thy heart! More dear to me
Than gaudiest Thrones*!* Be that
The sacred Urn, where thy *Morena* rests;
Nor ever let the Face of newer brighter
Beauty drive her thence!—
Oh! Farewel!—   [*Dies.*
Amur. Oh! speak! speak once again!—
Open those rosy Doors! Dart from
The fairest Eyes that ever blest the World,
One Ray though 'tis a dying one*!*—
Oh*!* 'Tis impossible*!* Is there
A Dungeon, Galley,[1] Bedlam,[2] can
Produce ought so miserable as *Amurat!*
Muft. Dead, my lov'd Daughter!—
Angry Prophet*!* when will thy vengeance cease!
Amur. Oh! never let it! now let
Earthquakes shake the Basis of this Foundation,
And whirlwinds drive us like dust about*!*
Muft. Have Patience, Son*!* Honour was
The Mistress of thy Youth*!* Fair
Morena hath form'd the bright idea
To the Life, Copy her, and court only Glory.
Now let the great Business of the Empire

---

1 A low, flat-built, sea-going vessel, propelled by sails and oars, in
   common use in the Mediterranean in the early-modern period. Rowers
   were mostly slaves or condemned criminals.
2 Specifically, Bedlam refers to the Hospital of St. Mary of Bethlehem,
   founded in 1247 as an asylum for the reception and treatment of the
   mentally ill in Bishopsgate, London. The term Bedlam became synonymous with a "madhouse" or "lunatic" asylum.

Divert thy Sorrow?—
Amur. Ye say I am Visier, Guardian to the
Infant King; with Power unlimitted
Command a World, almost as large as
Alexander's[1]—Oh! *Morena*! once my
Living Mistress, now my dead Saint,
My Ever Worshipt Dear: I do remember
What I promised: no Crowns, Lawrels, nor
The greatest height Ambition raises
Shou'd ever mount me above thy Slave—
Thus—thus I keep my word—   [*Stabs himself.*
Slighting all offers here I prostrate ly;
No life so happy, as with thee to die!

---

1 Alexander the Great (356–323 BCE), king of Macedonia, ruled over a
   huge empire extending east from present-day Greece to the Indian
   Punjab and south to Egypt.

Appendix C: Piracy

1. From David Aubin, Letter to Abraham and Henry Aubin (3 June 1720), The National Archives, SP 78/168. Secretary of State, State Papers, France

[David Aubin was an elder brother of Penelope Aubin's husband Abraham, two of fourteen children of a successful merchant family from Jersey. Here he writes to brothers Abraham and Henry about the attack on his ship, the *Prosperous*, by French pirates in 1720. Later David lived in Barbados, where his daughter Mary married into the Minvielles, a prominent slave-trading family. Another brother Philip (or Philippe) Aubin captained or was aboard ships involved in the Atlantic slave trade. In 1722 he was aboard the *Ferrers* when mutinous slaves revolted and killed the captain. Once home on Barbados after the capture of his ship, David wrote to Abraham asking him to take up his case and complain about the treatment he had received at the hands of the French on Martinique.]

Barbados 3rd June 1720
To Abraham and Henery Aubin
Princes Street, Lothbury, London

I cannot but acquaint you with my last misfortune, being at anchor, with my Brigantine Prosperous, in Company with three French Sloops under the Island of Dominico,[1] on Sunday the 24 of Aprill last, I Persieved a large Sloop to leeward of us with French Collours plying to Windward, having inquired of som French Gentlemen which come on board of my Brigg Weather they knew the Saide Sloop, they assured me that she belonged to Guadaloup[2] and was going to Martinico,[3] the Saide Sloop having past within half Gunshot of us was gon near half a League to

---

1 The island of Dominica in the Lesser Antilles archipelago, colonized by the French for much of the eighteenth century.
2 Guadeloupe, a group of islands north of Dominica within the Lesser Antilles archipelago, annexed by France in 1674 and still an overseas *département*.
3 The island of Martinique in the Lesser Antilles archipelago, about 75 miles south of Guadeloupe. It became a French overseas territory in 1674 and is still an overseas *département*.

Windward, When on a sudden she tacked and bore down up^{on} me I ordered a Gun to be fired a Thuart her fore foot to oblige her to send her boat in, or to beare away from us, but she taking no Notice, I fired an Other Gun at her but she being com near us she fired her Chace Gun[1] loaded with Great Shot and Pathridge[2] and cried Vive le Roy, then fired a Volly of Great Guns and small Arms into us, I Returned all the great Guns I could, but before we could load them againe the Sloop Boarded us with her Bowspest[3] over our Stern and entered upwards of 50 of their Men, Which obliged us to Retire under the Quarterdeck (having only Eight men left with me, for two of my Men stole away in the French Boat at ye begining of ye Engagement,) there we Defended our Selves for near two Hours, but my Quarterdeck being at last cut to Peeses in Many Places and the Grenados and Powder flasks being thrown down amongst us, my Poeple cryed for Quarters[4] and the Stearidge Doors being openned the Enemy came in Furiously with their lances and Cutlasses and fell a cutting me and my Poeple in a most Barbarous Manner and I should have had no Quarters if one of the Privateers Men which did know me had not Resqu'd me from the hands of those Villains, we Were all Stripped and Beaten most unmersifully and besides two Musquet Balls which I Receaved in the Middle of the Action through rough my Right thygh, I was cutt in 3 places of my head after we had surrendered, I had one man kild and most of my Men wounded wth Cutlasses;[5] We kild 13 of the Privateers or rather the Pirates Men and wounded about 18 or 20 More of which several are since Dead, the Sloop is called the Unick comanded by one Joseph Pillie she mounts 6 Great Guns and about 20 Swivell Ditto,[6] and had between 80 & 90 men When she attacked me, most of them French Men, and she had French Collours out all the Time of the action. Two Days after we were taken we was carried to Fort S^t. Pieres at Martinico[7] & as soon as I was landed I made my Complaint to Monsieur De Pas de

---

1 A gun mounted in a port either at the bow or stern of a ship.
2 Partridge-shot, here similar to case-shot, meaning a mass of small projectiles packed together in a canister for firing from a cannon.
3 Bowsprit.
4 Escape, or mercy.
5 A short sword, with a wide, flat, slightly curved blade.
6 Smaller guns mounted on swivels so as to turn horizontally in any direction.
7 Fort Saint-Pierre de la Martinique, a French military fort constructed in 1635 and demolished in 1837.

Feuquires General of Martinico[1] of the Barbarous Usage and Cruell treatment I had Receaved from the Poeple of his Nation & Government, for most of ye French Men were of Martinico, but my Petition and the several letters I wrote to him and the Intendant (Monsieur Benard) to Desire Justice Were of none effect, they insisting that the Privateer had a Spanish Commission[2] but yet would not permit me to have a Sight of it, and refused to take Mine and my Poeples Depositions, and Refused also the Security I Tendered in Case of Damages, but gave leave to the Privateers Captain to sell and Dispose of my Vessell and Cargo to Whom he thought fitt in Martinico, without any further Process, and When I offerest to Protest against this Generall & Intendante for so unjust Proceedings I was Denied the doing of it by all the Notarists. I Desire you would make this my Case Publick that the World may see, the unjust Proceedings of som of the West Indies Governours.

2. Penelope Aubin, Deposition of Penelope Aubin to the Board of Trade (20 January 1709), The National Archives, Colonial Office 323/6, fol. 225

[In the late seventeenth and early eighteenth centuries the island of Madagascar became a refuge for hundreds of European pirates. In England, a conviction grew that British pirates on the island had amassed huge treasures. John Breholt (fl. 1697–1711), shipmaster and adventurer who had himself been charged with piracy and imprisoned in Lisbon, tried for several years to gain support for a project whereby the pirates would be granted an amnesty in return for a share of their supposed wealth. Such wealth, it was argued, would help to defray the huge National Debt that had built up as a result of the Williamite wars. The idea received support from Daniel Defoe in the *Review* of October 1707. Among those involved in Breholt's scheme were shipwright Peter Dearlove, a business partner; Charles Egerton (1654–1717), a Whig MP; George Douglas, thirteenth earl of Morton (1662–1738); Sir John Bennett, attorney and MP; William Wallis, MP; and Paul Jodrell, clerk of the House of Commons. In 1709 the privy council instructed the Board of Trade to investigate the scheme, and a number of witnesses came forward with testimony

---

1 Isaac de Pas, Marquis de Feuquières, Governor-General of Martinique, 1717–27.
2 In 1720 Britain was at war with Spain, hence the French claim that the vessel had a Spanish commission.

that damaged John Breholt. One of those witnesses was Penelope Aubin. The project was abandoned.]

Penelope Aubin wife of Captain Abraham Aubin maketh Oath, That she this depon^t: some years since being concerned with the Rt. Hono^{ble}: Thomas Lord Fairfax about an Affair of a Wreck which one Peter Dearlove pretended to discover to his Lordship, on which Occasion this Depon$^{t.}$ came to have some Knowledge of, & Discourse with the said Dearlove, who (as she was afterwards informed) had been acquainted with the pirats of Madagascar; she this Depon$^{t.}$ about ten or twelve months since, to the best of her remembrance as to the time, was desired by an Acquaintance to meet the Hono^{ble}: Charles Egerton Esqre. & one Capt: John Breholt & others,. upon a Design then on foot for fetching the pirats from Madagascar, but she refused to meet the said Breholt & and only consented to meet the said M^r. Egerton, which accordingly she did in about a Week after; And she saith that at such (first) meeting, the said M^r. Egerton did of his own accord tell this depon^t: that the Lord Morton & he the said M^r. Egerton & divers other Gentlemen whom he then named (of whom S^r. John Bennett M^r.Wallis & M^r: Jodrell were some) were engaged in an Affair of fetching home the pirats from Madagascar, & that Captain Breholt was one of the Trustees therein, & was to go Commander in the Expedition, And that they had three Ships provided for that purpose; And she asking him whether they had obtained a pardon, or upon what Grounds they were going to fetch the pirats home, he answered it was upon a new & secure Method never before thought of, but made no direct Answer at that time as to the pardon, but said that all those engaged would be great Gainers thereby (or to that Effect) for that they designed a Trading Voyage; But their principall design seemed to this Depon^t: to be the fetching home the pirats; And what he desired of this Depon^t. was to be assisting to them in such their Design, by bringing a person to them who would find out for them the Wives or Relations of some of the principall Pirats, And in particular the wife of Captain Avery,[1] whom he

---

1 Henry Avery (bap. 1659–c. 1696), also known as Henry Every or John Avery, was one of the most successful English pirates. He led a mutiny in 1694 and in 1695 seized a ship belonging to the Mughal emperor carrying large quantities of gold and silver. His exploits inspired ballads, a chapbook, and *The Successful Pyrate* (1712), a play by London dramatist Charles Johnson (1679–1748). In 1695 he stopped at the island of Madagascar for provisions but was not part of the pirates' colony there.

said he thought might be very useful to them; And he offered this said Depon^t: a Share in such their Undertaking. And she further saith, That meeting the said M^r. Egerton some time after on the said Affair, he brought M^r. Wallis to her & they conferred upon the same, & M^r. Wallis likewise acknowledged such their Design of fetching home the pirats; After which she had several Meetings with the said M^r. Egerton upon the said Affair, at which she acquainted him with the very ill Opinion she had of the said Breholt, & his Unfitness to be entrusted in the Expedition, & advised the said M^r. Egerton to quitt the Affair, which Advice he seemed to this Depon^t. to approve of; & thereupon she this Depon^t. declined all farther Meetings & quitted the same.

3. From [Daniel Defoe,] *The Life and Strange Surprizing Adventures of Robinson Crusoe, of York, Mariner* (1719), pp. 19–20

I was now set up for a *Guiney* Trader;[1] and my Friend, to my great Misfortune, dying soon after his Arrival, I resolved to go the same Voyage again, and I embark'd in the same Vessel with one who was his Mate in the former Voyage, and had now got the Command of the Ship. This was the unhappiest Voyage that ever Man made; for tho' I did not carry quite 100*l.* of my new gain'd Wealth, so that I had 200 left, and which I lodg'd with my Friend's Widow, who was very just to me, yet I fell into terrible Misfortunes in this Voyage; and the first was this, *viz.* Our Ship making her Course towards the *Canary* Islands, or rather between those Islands and the *African* Shore, was surprised in the Grey of the Morning, by a *Turkish* Rover of *Sallee*, who gave Chase to us with all the Sail she could make. We crowded also as much Canvass as our Yards would spread, or our Masts carry, to have got clear; but finding the Pirate gain'd upon us, and would certainly come up with us in a few Hours, we prepar'd to fight; our Ship having 12 Guns, and the Rogue 18.... [T]o cut short this melancholly Part of our Story, our Ship being disabled, and three of our Men kill'd, and eight wounded, we were oblig'd to yield, and were carry'd all prisoners into *Sallee*, a Port belonging to the Moors.

The Usage I had there was not so dreadful as at first I apprehended, nor was I carried up the Country to the Emperor's

---

1 One who trades with Guinea, on the West coast of Africa; often a slave trader, though here Crusoe has made money by selling gold dust.

Court, as the rest of our Men were, but was kept by the Captain of the Rover, as his proper Prize, and made his Slave, being young and nimble, and fit for his Business. At this surprising Change of my Circumstances from a Merchant to a miserable Slave, I was perfectly overwhelmed; and now I look'd back upon my Father's prophetick Discourse to me, that I should be miserable, and have none to relieve me, which I thought was now so effectually brought to pass, that it could not be worse; that now the Hand of Heaven had overtaken me, and I was undone without Redemption. But alas! this was but a Taste of the Misery I was to go thro', as will appear in the Sequel of this Story.

As my new Patron or Master had taken me Home to his House, so I was in hopes that he would take me with him when he went to Sea again, believing that it would some time or other be his Fate to be taken by a *Spanish* or *Portugal* Man of War; and then I should be set at Liberty.

4. **From [Captain Charles Johnson,]** *A General History of the Robberies and Murders of the most notorious Pyrates, and also their Policies, Discipline and Government, from their first Rise and Settlement in the Island of Providence, in 1717, to the present Year 1724* **(1724), pp. 238–39**

["Captain Charles Johnson" is probably a pseudonym, and the author is not to be confused with the London playwright (see p. 196, n. 1). In 1971, J.R. Moore included *A General History* in the Defoe canon, and Manuel Schonhorn's 1972 edition has Defoe as the author, but P.N. Furbank and W.R. Owens have cast doubt on this attribution. The *History* was published at a time of widespread concern about the impact of piracy on British trade. Merchants brought pressure to bear on George I and his government to do more to protect commerce (Lincoln 99ff.). The Introduction to the *General History* includes a Royal Proclamation of 1717, which offered pirates the chance of a general pardon, as well as an account of pirates based at New Providence in the Bahamas who initially accepted the offer and then returned to their old activities. Vivid accounts of the sensational exploits of numerous British and Irish pirates follow, along with records of trials and executions. The following passage is excerpted from the history of Captain Bartholomew Roberts and his crew after their arrival in Newfoundland.]

Roberts mann'd the *Bristol* Galley he took in the Harbour, and mounted 16 Guns on Board her, and cruising out upon the Banks, he met with nine or ten Sail of *French* Ships, all which he destroy'd except one of 26 Guns, which they seized, and carried off for their own Use. This Ship they christ'ned the *Fortune*, and leaving the *Bristol* Galley to the *French* Men, they sailed away in Company with the Sloop, on another Cruise, and took several Prizes, *viz.* the *Richard* of *Biddiford, Jonathan Whitfield* Master; the *Willing Mind* of *Pool*; the *Expectation* of *Topham*; and the *Samuel*, Captain *Cary* of *London*; out of these Ships they encreased their Company, by entring all the Men they could well spare, in their own Service. The *Samuel* was a rich Ship, and had several Passengers on Board, who were used very roughly, in order to make them discover their Money, threat'ning them every Moment with Death, if they did not resign every Thing up to them. They tore up the Hatches and entered the Holds like a parcel of Furies, and with Axes and Cutlasses, cut and broke open all the Bales, Cases and Boxes they could lay their Hands on; and when any Goods came upon Deck, that they did not like to carry aboard, instead of tossing them into the Hold again, threw them overboard into the Sea; all this was done with incessant cursing and swearing, more like Fiends than Men. They carried them with them, Sails, Guns, Powder, Cordage,[1] and 8 or 9000*l*. worth of the choicest Goods, and told Captain *Cary, That they should accept of no Act of Grace; that the K*[ing] *and P*[arliamen]*t might be damned with their Acts of G*[race] *for them; neither would they go to* Hope-Point,[2] *to be hang'd up a Sun drying, as* Kidd's *and* Braddish's *Company*[3] *were; but that if they should ever be overpower'd, they would set Fire to the Powder, with a Pistol, and go all merrily to Hell together.*

After they had brought all the Booty aboard, a Consultation was held whether they should sink or burn the Ship, but whilst they were debating the Matter, they spy'd a Sail, and so left the *Samuel*, to give her Chace ...

---

1   Ropes in the rigging of a ship.
2   A point on the Thames estuary near Gravesend, in Kent.
3   Referring to William Kidd (c. 1645–1701), pirate and privateer, and Joseph Bradish (d. 1701), a Massachusetts pirate. Both were hanged at Execution Dock on the Thames at Wapping.

Appendix D: Romance and Translation

1. From Penelope Aubin, *The Illustrious French Lovers*, 2 vols. (1726)

[Five of Penelope Aubin's published works are translations from the French, with *The Illustrious French Lovers* being the longest. It is both a translation and adaptation of Robert Challe's *Les Illustres Françaises* (1713), a collection of stories told by the male members of a group of friends, either about themselves or an acquaintance, to the company. *Les Illustres Françaises* was a publishing success, with many editions between 1713 and 1780, as well as translations into German and Dutch. The stories revolve around love, separation, constancy, and the constraints imposed by either parents or social class, themes that find many parallels in Aubin's own framing and interpolated tales in *The Noble Slaves*.]

a. From "Monsieur de Terney's and Madam de Bernay's History," vol. 1, pp. 115–25

'My Friend [Monsieur de Bernay] fell in love with a very fine Woman, and made me his Confident; but I was yet a Stranger to that Passion, and often rallied him for passing the Nights in talking of his Mistress. I was at this Time about Twenty-seven Years old; He had an elder Sister who was marry'd, and two younger who were Pensioners[1] in a Convent some Leagues from *Paris*. He one day ask'd me to go with him and Madam *de Ornex*, his marry'd Sister, to see them. I gladly accepted the Offer, having never seen these Ladies; I had often heard him speak of the eldest with great Affection; but when I saw her I was charm'd; She was dress'd in black, being in Mourning for her Mother, but I thought her an Angel, and griev'd that she was to be sequester'd from the World; for that I found they were both design'd for Nuns. Her Air and sprightly Look told me that she disapprov'd her Father's Choice, and was much fitter for the World. I took the liberty to speak my Thoughts aloud; "My Friend, *said I to* de Bernay, your Sisters are too charming to be ravish'd from our Sight; none but the Deform'd or Foolish should be cloister'd;

---

1 In France and other European countries, women paying for lodging in a religious institution.

Ladies who have such Wit and Beauty should be left at liberty, to increase the World; 'tis a Sin to hinder such from marrying." *Clementine* modestly answer'd with a Blush, That, on the contrary, it were an Injury to Heaven, to offer only those to it whom the World rejected; and that no Face or Mind could be too good to be a Votary to Piety. "'Tis not to God, *said I briskly*, Madam, that you make this Sacrifice; but to your Father's Humour, and to aggrandize your Brother and Sister; and had you been born the eldest of either Sex, the Convent would never have had the Honour of holding you; and, if I can read your Face, 'tis their Vows, not your own, that you offer up to Heaven": Madam *de Ornex* redden'd, and we broke off the Discourse. Returning home she quarrell'd with me for giving her Sisters such ill Advice; but I turn'd the raillery, saying, It was the Priest's Duty to cry up the heavenly Blessing and Excellency of a single Life, and a young Soldier's to preach Matrimony and to propagate Mankind; and that I would do so at every Convent I came to. But finding her grow serious, I said I would go no more to see the charming *Clementine*, and did all I could to remove all Suspicions out of her Head, of my future Designs, but I did not succeed; for Monsieur *de Bernay* told me some Days after, that she had alarm'd his Father about me; and that he blamed him for his Cruelty to his Sisters, and would do all he could to help me to free her I loved: "My Sister, madam *de Ornex*, *said he*, is already marry'd against her Inclination to a Man she does not love, he is a perfect Brute, she is sickly, and is continually tormented betwixt my Father and him: My Father is the most obstinate Man living, and will not give my younger Sisters a Groat[1] if they displease him, so that I see no Possibility of your succeeding." I told him I valued not a Fortune, I had enough of my own to make us happy, and begg'd his Assistance to gain her Consent for me. He readily granted my Request, and we secretly went to visit *Clementine:* I courted her, but she answer'd me as one resolved to leave the World. I repeated my Visits, and told her I would free her, if she would consent, from Grates and Walls, and a tyrannick Parent; but received no other Answer but such as made me almost to despair. I went alone to see her, and she bid me return the next Morning to take a Letter she design'd to send her Brother: I did so, and receiving her's, slipp'd another into her Hand, in which I begg'd her to explain herself some way or

---

1 An old English coin of low value, synonymous with a very small sum of money.

other, and let me know if she was compell'd to act as she did, which I suspected. When we read her Letter, we were convinc'd that I was in the right, and that she was watch'd, and had a Nun who stood in hearing whilst we talk'd; and now I was resolv'd to free her at all Hazards. Her Brother fear'd to act any thing in this Affair that might come to his Father's Ear, and could only assist me by getting Intelligence from her. When I return'd to the Convent to see her, I was refus'd, and school'd by the Abbess and two or three old Nuns in such a manner, that I curs'd them all, Bell, Book, and Candle,[1] and almost frighted them out of their Wits, so that they imagin'd me possess'd, and threw such a quantity of Holy Water upon me thro' the Grates, that having given them a Volley of Curses and Threats, I departed half drown'd like a pump'd[2] Pickpocket. They soon sent her Father and Sister a complete Account of my Proceedings, telling him I was a very handsome Gentleman, had a bewitching Tongue and Person; that she was grown careless of her Devotions, disobedient to the Superiors, and appear'd much disorder'd in her Mind, since I had visited there. And now I could no more get sight of her; but her Brother sent one of his Lacquey's, in whom he could confide, with two Letters; in the one he writ, That he was amaz'd at her impudence in permitting my Visits, and at the Complaints made of her by the Abbess; that he hoped she would be wiser for the future, or else he should no more be so indulgent to her as he had been; In fine, he said every thing that could oblige his Father and the Convent, with Design to have her show it them, to gain their good Opinion of him. And in the other Letter, which the Lad gave her privately, we told her our Design, bid her trust the Bearer with any Letter or Message for us. We succeeded, and I had much less Difficulty to gain her than if she had been at liberty; for Confinement in a Cloister makes a Woman so uneasy, that she gladly accepts an Offer from a Lover, and is as ready to run into his Arms as he is to receive her, unless her Mind suits that Place, and Choice has made her quit the World; The Veil hides her Blushing, and the Pen performs what the Tongue faulters to declare when at liberty; I received a Letter from her in these Terms....

---

1 The expression refers to the implements used in the rite of excommunication in the Christian Church of the Middle Ages, a spiritual exclusion imposed on those guilty of an exceptionally grievous sin.
2 Put under a stream of water from a pump, for punishment.

I AM much at a loss to know how I ought to answer you, lest I should say more than is fit for a Virgin, and not express the tender Sentiments I have of your Sufferings: I fear to give you a final Denial, lest I should never have the Means again of seeing you and the World, nor do I wish for one without the other; yet by condescending to your Desires I fear to lose your Esteem, and to render my self unworthy of your Affection; Mankind are but too ready, I am daily told, to scorn an easy Conquest; and you have never been confined to lonely Walls and Cells, where peevish old Maids watch over the blooming Virgins whose cruel Parents doom them to a Cloister, and do dwell debarr'd of all Delights. I know you pity me, but how well you love me I can't discover; unskill'd in all the subtle Arts of your deluding Sex I fancy you sincere. Why did you come to break my Peace, and give me a Disgust for this sweet solitary Life, which now appears a Hell: My Terrors of the World are vanish'd, and I fondly fancy that with you I could live happy, tho' exposed to all the various Troubles that attend a marry'd State. I confide in my Brother, and since you are his Choice, what he directs me I will do. My hand trembles, a Shower of Tears obscure my Sight, Blushes o'respread my Face and I am so disorder'd I can scarce say, that you may hope all things that Honour will permit from

CLEMENTINE.

I was transported at the receipt of this Letter. Monsieur *de Bernay* laugh'd: "Well, *said he*, my Sister at eighteen, is as expert in love Affairs, as if she had lived in the World: I find she will not be a Nun; but what must we do?" "Be you but true to me, *said I*, and I fear not your Father's Anger no more than a blast of Air: I will marry her in spight of all Opposition, do you but stand by me." He swore he would, provided I would keep the Secret; and offer'd to assist me, even in stealing her out of the Convent, on Condition that I design'd nothing but what was honourable: And from that Hour we became as Brothers and faithful Friends, for he was already engaged to a Lady in *Paris*, and I to my charming *Clementine*: But, alas! we both received Orders to be gone to the Army. *January* was past, and tho' it was early in the Season to take the Field, our glorious Monarch had enured his Troops to bear hard Marches, and the Toils of War, and we must immediately repair to our Commands, yet not without another sight of *Clementine*. We went strait to the Convent, and were refus'd

Entrance; he was permitted to go into a Room to her, in presence of the Sisters; but I was lock'd out. I was almost distracted, but forced to conceal it and keep silence. He testify'd his Dissatisfaction to me when we return'd to *Paris*; but I resolv'd to see her, let it cost what it would, and did thus effect it. I had a *Valet de Chambre* whose Name was *Gauthier* ... he could paint[1] finely, he was faithful, and I trusted him; we rack'd our Brains for some Invention to procure me a sight of her; and at last agreed that I should put on such a Disguise as render'd it impossible for any body to know me. *Bernay* was to send his Sister some Books she had ask'd for: I put on one of his Servant's Livery Coats, and my *Valet de Chambre* painted my Face with a certain Composition, which so changed my Features and Complexion, that I could not know my own Face in the Glass. I went to see her Brother, thus disguised, with a Letter from my self, desiring an Answer by the Bearer, having put on one of my own Servant's Liveries. He knew all my Domesticks, and ask'd me, seeing I was a Stranger, how long I had lived with Monsieur *de Terney?* I could not forbear laughing, and so my Voice discover'd me. He admired my Invention, and having himself an Amour with a marry'd Lady in *Paris*, whose Husband was very jealous, and who had made some Discovery of their Intrigue a little before, he made use of the same Stratagem that very Day to see her, and often afterwards.... And now fearing no discovery, I set out for the Convent with Letters from Monsieur *de Bernay* to both his Sisters; in that to *Clementine* I had inclosed one from my self, to inform her that I was the Bearer. She appear'd much alter'd, and so pensive and pale, that I could scarce hide my Concern; but her Sister appear'd as gay and sprightly as if she was design'd for the World, and look'd much fitter to make one in a Ball at Court, than to mutter *Ave Maria*'s in a Convent; and I was, in the End, the fortunate Instrument of freeing her, as well as my Wife.... I staid not long; but was order'd to return for an Answer to the Letters in the Afternoon, and then I receiv'd such a one as highly satisfy'd me. *Clementine* talk'd to me in Terms her Sister did not comprehend the meaning of; but Love had taught us to understand every Motion and Look of one another. I read her Letter so soon as I was out of sight of the Convent; it was full of the most charming Assurances of her being sensible of my Pains, and ready to share my Fortunes; and yet there was the most moving Reproaches on my leaving her: She concluded, that if I proved false, and return'd not soon to

---

1 Apply cosmetics.

free her, she would renounce the World, and never hearken to any more Proposals of Love. *Bernay* and I set out the next Morning for the Army; we went together to *Fribourg*,[1] but there we parted: The Mareschal *de Turenne*[2] took me with him to *Strasbourg*,[3] and he was sent away with a Detachment commanded by Monsieur *de Duras*. I shall not trouble you with the relation of this Campaign, which was one of the most glorious, this great Man ever made, whom we have so lately lost, and never can cease to lament: We repulsed the *Germans*, and pursued them; and when I thought I was near rejoining my dear Friend *de Bernay*, who was gone before, I learn'd the dismal News that he was kill'd three Days before my arrival, in a Skirmish near *Ostembourg*.[4] This Loss so much afflicted me, that it would but renew my Grief to continue the Subject. But I receiv'd News from *Paris* of a quite different nature: *Clementine* writ me word that Madam *d'Ornex*, her eldest Sister, was dead; and that her Father had taken her home from the Convent. I regretted this Lady (tho' my Enemy); her cruel Father and brutal Husband had broke her heart, and I hoped that Monsieur *de Bernay* would be touch'd with her Death, and not constrain *Clementine* and his youngest Daughter to marry against their Inclinations, since they were all he had left, and now sole Heiresses of his great Fortune. I was transported to know that *Clementine* was no longer lock'd up from me, and had great reason to hope that she would now be mine with his Consent, and with this flattering View I hasted back to *Paris*, and found her at her Father's House, who was very sick, but not with Remorse of Conscience; but the Fatigue he had undergone to get part of his Daughter's Fortune out of *d'Ornex*'s Hands, as had been agreed in case she died without Issue, for his Son-in-law and he were Men of the same Temper, and strove with equal Fury to cheat one another ... [H]e recover'd after keeping his bed four Months; during which I saw *Clementine* every Day without his knowledge, for he had forbid her either to see or speak to me the Moment he heard of my return to *Paris*; having been inform'd, as you know, what had pass'd at the Convent. I know not what occa-

---

1 Freiburg im Bresslau, a city on the German side of what is now the border between northeastern France and Germany.

2 Henri de la Tour d'Auvergne, vicomte de Turenne (1611–75), military commander during the reign of Louis XIV.

3 A city in northeastern France on the border with Germany, seized by Louis XIV in 1681 and then the site of a French garrison.

4 Offenburg, a city on the Rhine in southwestern Germany near the modern border with France.

sion'd his Aversion to me, unless it was that he knew we loved one another; and had *Clementine* hated me, I am positive he would have consented to our Marriage; but this I was then a Stranger to; therefore I went to pay him a Visit on his Recovery, and was very ill received; yet that I attributed to his having been sick, and fancy'd he was only fretful, and unfit as yet for Conversation: I saw his Daughter also with him, who to gain his favour waited on and condescended to the meanest Offices to oblige him, not only as his Child, but as a Servant. His Behaviour enraged me to the last degree; even in my presence he threw a Glass of Wine in her Face which she brought him, and he had called for. I staid not long, but quitted the Chamber, unable to restrain my Passion at this Sight, and waited below in the Parlour till she came to me, and here, being alone, we spake our Thoughts freely to each other. I said all Love could suggest to comfort her; she wept, and own'd she thought herself the most unhappy Creature breathing. We agreed on means to see one another every Day; all the Servants were ready to assist us, for none approved his brutish Conduct to their young Lady: There was not a Day past in which I did not see her, and learn some new Extravagance of him; yet she always retain'd the Respect due to a Father, for him. She grew at last so weary of his Usage, that she would gladly have return'd to her Convent had not I oppos'd it. At length I prevail'd with her to promise to marry me, without his Consent, if I could not obtain it ...'

b. From "The Constant Lovers: Monsieur de Jussy's and Madam de Fenoüil's History," vol. 1, pp. 151–62

'[B]efore I enter on Monsieur *de Jussy*'s History [*said* des Frans], which he himself related to me 'tis necessary that I inform you how our Acquaintance began: Two Years ago I met with him in *Portugal,* there our Friendship commenced, and we have never been asunder since till two Days ago, which are past since his Marriage. At our landing at *Rochel* he took a Certificate of the Day and Hour of his arrival in *France* from the Governour of the Place; from thence all the way to *Paris* we lay at what Places he thought fit, and staid for Letters, which he receiv'd at the Places we inn'd at, one every Night all the way on the Road till we came to near *Paris:* The Reasons of all this I was then a Stranger to, and my Curiosity was great to know the meaning of this mysterious Conduct of his; but I forebore to ask him any Questions, not thinking it proper to dive farther into my Friend's Secrets than he thought fit; but the Day before he enter'd *Paris* he acquainted me with all, and fully satisfy'd my Curiosity ... "Since we are now, *said he*, almost at our Journey's End, before we part it is but reasonable, as a return for the Honour you have done me in keeping me company these two Years past, that I acquaint you with the secret Reasons for which I then left my native Country, and let you into the Occurrences of my life past, and then you will no more wonder at the Precaution I have now taken at my return, in taking Certificates and waiting for Letters on the Way: Know then that all the Happiness of my Life has depended on the Constancy and Fidelity of a Woman, a Wife I mean. I have observ'd in all the Conversations you and I have had together, that you have a very ill Opinion of the Fair Sex, and hope now to convince you, that there are Women who even out-do us in Resolution and Constancy, and who will bravely suffer the utmost Extremity, rather than yield to break their Faith when given.

I was born in *Paris*, the Son of an eminent City-Attorney; but he having many Children, when he and my Mother died, the Fortune they left divided among us, was not sufficient to provide for and support us, equal to the Port we had hitherto carried: My Brothers and I took to the Law, as being the genteelest Employ: I study'd with great Application, and had pretty good Success, so that without Vanity I believe I should have been eminent in that Profession had I pursued it; but Love threw such Obstacles in my way, as oblig'd me to quit both that and my Country. My Person and Humour you are perfectly acquainted withal, the World was so kind as to think them not disagreeable; but Heaven gave me a Voice little inferior to any in the World, and I attain'd such Skill in Musick as was answerable to it: This was the means that introduc'd me to Monsieur *de Ivonne*'s Acquaintance, and gave me Access to his House.

This Gentleman had several Children, and among the rest a Son of my own age, with whom I was intimately acquainted: They had a great Estate, and my Family was far inferior to theirs. Monsieur *de Ivonne* was Guardian to a young Lady who was his Niece, an Heiress, who had a vast Fortune, and lived in the House: Monsieur *de Ivonne* managed all her Estate, and bred her up in the same manner as he did his own Children, except in Habit and Retinue, in which she excell'd his Daughter. This Lady being the Heroine of all my Adventures, 'tis necessary that I give you the Description of her Person at the time I first saw her, which is above eight Years since; she is now but twenty-five, yet there is no question but she is much alter'd.

Mademoiselle *Fenoüil* was tall and well-shaped, graceful and easy; she was as fair as *Venus*, her Hair and Eyes were black as Jet, but her Eyes were so bright, so sweet, so killing, that no Heart could resist their Glances; her Face was oval, and every Feature soft, and charming *Cupids* sat in the Dimples of her Cheeks; her Frowns darted Despair into her Lover's Breast, but her Smiles fired and chear'd their Souls: In fine, she was the most lovely among Womankind. This is her Picture, and you need no other Excuse to justify my loving her, since I have told you what she was. And that her inside was as lovely as her Person: Her Soul was noble, sincere, generous, and firm, an Enemy to flattery and hypocrisy, disinterested, brave, capable of the boldest Undertakings, and as resolute in the executing what she resolved ... She was just seventeen when I first saw her and had the Honour to be introduced to her Acquaintance: Her Cousin one day told her, he had a Friend that sung as well as any Man living, she desired him to get me to visit there that she might hear me sing; he gave me an Invitation to hear her, and it being natural for People who love the same Art and Science to desire to see one another, I readily accepted the Offer and went home with him that very Evening; there the charming Maid received me kindly, and made no difficulty to let me hear her heavenly Voice; she sung so finely that I even blush'd to sing after her and grew doubtful of my own Performance, yet I dared not to refuse, but did my best; and she applauded and seem'd pleased, and bid me come again; nay desired that I would improve our Acquaintance, and bring her all the new Songs I cou'd get to teach her, that we might sing together. Ravish'd with the pleasing Proposition, I fail'd not to obey; and there was not a Day pass'd in which I did not visit her on this Pretext.

We made an Opera-House of Monsieur *de Ivonne*'s, nothing but Musick and Singing was to be heard, and all the Opera Songs were there perform'd with such Skill and Voices that the Neighbourhood rung of us. Thus we pass'd four whole Months, whilst Love insensibly stole into both our Souls, and I was made her Slave before I was aware....

My Friends had found a very good match for me, a young Gentlewoman no elder than Mademoiselle *Fenoüil*, very handsome, well-bred, and rich; the little likelihood there was of my succeeding with her I loved, made me incline to hearken to this Proposal, and really the Lady deserved a better Husband, and was a better Match than I could ever hope for.... Mademoiselle *Fenoüil* ... was inform'd of all, and got a Sight of Mademoiselle

Grandet, who was the Person design'd for me; her Beauty alarm'd her and she forgot all Considerations, when she heard that the Marriage-Articles were ready for signing. I had been two Days absent from her, and the third, which was the Day fix'd for signing the Writings, I received this Note from her early in the Morning, containing these words:

> *Don't be too hasty in marrying; you will in the End repent of it: There is a Person in the World a Match for you much preferable to that now proposed to you. Let me see you immediately I wait your coming.*

I went, hoping to be back time enough to meet my Friends, as agreed: I found her alone in her Chamber very pensive, her Eyes swollen with crying: "I come, Madam, *said I*, to receive your Commands, and to know what Fate you design me, and who the Person is you propose for a Wife to me." She blush'd at this Question: "Before I tell you, Sir, *said she*, it is fit I should know if you really love the Lady that you are going to marry? and whether it be Inclination or Interest that guides your Choice?" "It is not Love I assure you, Madam, *said I*, for should I follow my Inclinations, I should never marry Mademoiselle *Grandet*; I confess she is a very charming Woman, but, alas! my Heart was pre-engaged before I saw her, and I passionately love another, whose high Birth, Merit, and Fortune, are so far above what I can pretend to, that my Reason enjoins me to be for ever silent, and abandon my self to Despair; and since I can never hope to possess what my Soul adores, I resolved to throw my self into the Arms of another, in hopes that Absence may cure my sick Soul of a vain Passion, and restore my Quiet ..."

"For whom do you thus suffer?" *said she with much Earnestness and Disorder.* "Under the Circumstances I now am in, *said I*, charming Tormentor, it is impossible for me to dissemble; (*then falling at her Feet*) my Eyes and every Action, and the Confusion I am in when I approach you, must needs have long since inform'd you, that 'tis you who have captivated my Soul, and inspired me with a Passion to which I was a Stranger till I was blest with a Sight of you: Yes, Madam, *said I embracing her Knees*, 'tis you I adore; nor have I failed in the Respect I owe you, since my Tongue never presum'd, till now, to tell you that I love; nay, I would have died silent, had not your Commands obliged me to declare the Secret."

"It is an heroic Resolution you have taken up, *said she smiling*; you love me, and yet consent to marry another, and for no other Reason but because you love me." "Yes, *answer'd I*, my Despair puts me on this desperate Expedient, and forces me to throw my self into the Arms of another, since I never can possess you." "And why do you thus despair?" *said she*. "Oh Heavens! *said I*, Madam, what Grounds have I to hope? the vast Disproportion of our Circumstances, your Merit, and my own Unworthiness, have set me so far below you, that it were a crime for me to wish that you should ever be so lost as to be mine." "If you love me as you profess to do, *said she*, why should you fear to hope? Love is a Leveller, and equals Kings and Swains; Who forbids Hope to the aspiring Lover? since no Obstacles remain but difference of Family and Fortune, those are at my dispose; my Fortune, when I come of Age, is mine to give; and if I make you my Husband, you will then be my Superior; by Birth we are Equals, since you are a Gentleman; And since Madam *Grandet*, whose Family, tho' not so rich, is nobler than mine, thinks you worthy of her Choice, I have no reason to refuse you: And now, to put you out of pain, I give you my Hand and Faith, to make you Master of my Person and Fortune so soon as I am of age, to do it: My Nobility is owing only to the great Employments my Father was possess'd of at his Death, you may hereafter purchase such since I can furnish you the Means to do it: My Uncle is my Guardian, to manage my Fortune during my Minority, but has no right to dispose of my Person;[1] it is not long ere I shall be at liberty to receive my own Revenues,[2] and dispose of my self. And now tell me, is not the Offer I make you, more advantageous, than that your Friends have procured you? and had not you better take what you love, than her you care not for"; "How blest am I, *said he*, to hear you make this generous Proposal, and yet must acknowledge that I am unworthy of you, and that 'tis pity you should condescend to make so mean a Choice; tho' I have all the grateful Sentiments of the Obligation, and a Passion for you so sincere and ardent, that it may supply the Want of Titles and a Fortune." "'Tis enough, *said she*, I ask nothing but your Heart." "Alas! Madam, *said he*, I tremble at the Thoughts of what Persecutions you will suffer; All

---

1 It was customary for parental consent to be obtained for marriage but not, strictly speaking, that of a guardian.

2 In eighteenth-century France, the age of majority for a woman was twenty-five. As Mademoiselle Fenoüil is an orphan and an only child, she would have control over her own inheritance at that age.

your Family will oppose my Happiness; nay, 'tis possible, time and their Persuasions may make you banish me and make some worthier Choice, and leave me the most wretched of all Mankind." "Trust me, *said she*, I am arm'd for all Events; time will pacify my Family, and when they find me resolute, they will cease to importune me; and they cannot force me from you: Besides, you may engage me to be true, and rid your self of all your Fears; 'tis in your Power to put it out of mine to change." At these words she blush'd and turn'd away, saying, "go break off the Treaty with Madam *Grandet* this Hour, and in a manner so publick that I may be secured from all Fears of your ever being reconciled, and whatever Injury you sustain by it, be assur'd I will make you ample Amends; make haste, the Hour is near when you must meet your Friends: See not my Face again till you have executed my Commands; but on your Life expose me not, nor declare the Reason of your acting thus, 'tis enough that you satisfy my Desires, and the world must not be inform'd of the Secret, it is your Interest to leave me no Cause of future Jealousy." "I go, *said he*, Madam, to break off this Match in so publick a manner, that you shall be convinced how ardently I love you; nor shall the Fear of angering all my Family and Friends, whom I am certain will be highly incensed, or the ill Consequences, that may arrive to me from the Indignation and keen Resentments of the Lady whom I must affront on no just Pretence, deter me; I will expose my self with pleasure to every thing Man can fear, to convince you all things else beside your Love and Hate are indifferent to me, and that I cannot live without the first, or wish to survive the last one moment; and this Night, either by Letter or from my own Mouth, you shall have an exact Account of my Proceedure." "Go, *said she*, and let me have that Satisfaction as soon as possible." "I obey'd, *said he*, and left her ...""

Works Cited

State Papers

Aubin, David. Letter to Abraham and Henry Aubin. 3 June 1720. Secretaries of State: State Papers Foreign, France. Folio 17. SP 78/168/6. The National Archives, Kew, London.

Aubin, Penelope. Deposition of Penelope Aubin. 20 Jan. 1709. Colonial Office 323/6, Folder 225. The National Archives, Kew, London.

Primary Sources

Astell, Mary. *Some Reflections upon Marriage*. 3rd ed., London, 1706.

Aubin, Penelope. *The Doctrine of Morality*. London, 1721.

———. *The Extasy: A Pindarick Ode to Her Majesty the Queen*. London, 1708.

———. *The Illustrious French Lovers*. London, 1727.

———. *The Life and Adventures of the Young Count Albertus*. London, 1728.

———. *The Life of Charlotta Du Pont, an English Lady*. London, 1723.

———. *The Life of Madam de Beaumount, a French Lady*. London, 1721.

———. *The Life of Madam de Beaumont* and *The Life of Charlotta Du Pont*. Edited by David A. Brewer, Broadview, 2023.

———. *The Noble Slaves: or, the Lives and Adventures of Two Lords and Two Ladies*. London, 1722.

———. *The Strange Adventures of the Count de Vinevil and His Family*. Popular Fiction by Women 1660–1730: An Anthology, edited by Paula R. Backscheider and John J. Richetti, Oxford UP, 1996, pp. 114–51.

———. *The Stuarts: A Pindarique Ode. Humbly Dedicated to Her Majesty of Great Britain*. London, 1707.

———. *The Wellcome: A Poem to His Grace the Duke of Marlborough*. London, 1709.

Calvin, John. *Institutes of the Christian Religion. The First English Version of the 1541 French Edition*. Translated by Elsie Anne McKee, Wm. B. Eerdmans, 2009.

"Cato". "Considerations on the Destructive Spirit of Arbitrary Power," *London Journal*, no. XC, 15 April 1721, p. 1.

———. *A Discourse of Standing Armies; Shewing the Folly, Uselesness, and Danger of Standing Armies in Great Britain*. London, 1722.

———. "A Further Call for Vengeance against the South-Sea Plunderers." *London Journal*, no. LXXI, 26 November–3 December 1720, p. 1.

———. "The Natural Passion of Men for Superiority," *London Journal*, no. CX, 2 September 1721, p. 1.

———. "What Measures Are Actually Taken by Wicked and Desperate Ministers to Ruin and Enslave Their Country," *London Journal*, no. LXXXII, 18 February 1721, p. 1.

Catalogus Bibliothecae Harleianæ: or, A Catalogue of the Remaining Part of the Library of the late Earl of Oxford and Mortimer. 5 vols., London, 1745.

Defoe, Daniel. *A General History of the Pyrates*. Edited by Manuel Schonhorn, Dent, 1972.

[———]. *The Life, Adventures, and Pyracies, of the Famous Captain Singleton*. London, 1720.

[———]. *The Life and Strange Surprizing Adventures of Robinson Crusoe, of York, Mariner*. London, 1719.

[———]. *Reformation of Manners. A Satyr*. s.l., 1702.

———. *A Review of the State of the English Nation*. London, 1710.

A Description of the Nature of Slavery among the Moors, and the Cruel Sufferings of Those that Fall into it.... London, 1721.

An Essay in Defence of the Female Sex. London, 1696.

Furbank, P.N., and W.R. Owens. *Defoe De-Attributions: A Critique of J.R. Moore's Checklist*. Hambledon Press, 1994.

Griffith, Elizabeth. *A Collection of Novels, Selected and Revised by Mrs. Griffith*. 3 vols., London, 1777.

["Johnson, Captain Charles"]. *A General History of the Robberies and Murders of the most notorious Pyrates, and also their Policies, Discipline and Government, from their first Rise and Settlement in the Island of Providence, in 1717, to the present Year 1724*. London, 1724.

Knolles, Richard. *The Generall Historie of the Turkes*. London, 1603.

Mandeville, Bernard. *The Fable of the Bees: or, Private Vice, Publick Benefits*. Edited by Phillip Harth, Penguin, 1989.

Manley, Delarivier. *Almyna: or, The Arabian Vow. A Tragedy*. London, 1707.

Pix, Mary. *Ibrahim, the Thirteenth Emperour of the Turks: A Tragedy*. London, 1696.

Reeve, Clara. *The Progress of Romance Through Times, Countries and Manners*. 2 vols., Colchester, 1785.

Rycaut, Paul. *The History of the Present State of the Ottoman Empire. Containing the Maxims of Turkish Politie, the most Material Points of the Mahometan Religion, their Sects and Heresies, their Convents and Religious Votaries. Their Military Discipline, with an Exact Computation of the Forces both by Land and Sea*. London, 1667.

Stephens, William. *A Second Deliverance from Popery and Slavery. As it was set forth in a Sermon in the Parish Church of Sutton in Surrey, Sept. 19. 1714. Being the First Sunday after His Majesty's Landing*. London, 1714.

["Stonecastle, Henry"]. *The Universal Spectator*. 2 vols., London, 1736.

Swift, Jonathan. *The Works of the Reverend Dr. Jonathan Swift, Dean of St. Patrick's, Dublin, in Twenty Volumes*. Vol. 5, Dublin, 1772.

Secondary Sources

Baer, Joel. "Penelope Aubin and the Pirates of Madagascar: Biographical Notes and Documents." *Eighteenth-Century Women: Studies in Their Lives, Work, and Culture*, vol. 1, edited by Linda V. Troost, AMS Press, 2001, pp. 49–62.

Bannet, Eve Tavor. *Transatlantic Stories and the History of Reading 1720–1810: Migrant Fictions*. Cambridge UP, 2011.

Beach, Adam R. "Aubin's *The Noble Slaves*, Montagu's Spanish Lady and English Feminist Writing about Sexual Slavery in the Ottoman World." *Eighteenth-Century Fiction*, vol. 29, no. 4, 2017, pp. 583–606.

Bisaha, Nancy. *Creating East and West: Renaissance Humanists and the Ottoman Turks*. U of Pennsylvania P, 2004.

Booth, Emily. *'A Subtle and Mysterious Machine': The Medical World of Walter Charleton (1619–1707)*. Springer, 2005.

Cahill, Samara Anne. *Intelligent Souls? Feminist Orientalism in Eighteenth-Century English Literature*. Bucknell UP, 2019.

Carswell, John. *The South Sea Bubble*. Cresset Press, 1961.

Castle, Terry. "Eros and Liberty at the English Masquerade, 1710–90." *Eighteenth-Century Studies*, vol. 17, no. 2, 1983–84, pp. 156–76.

Colley, Linda. *Captives: Britain, Empire, and the World, 1600–1850*. 2002. Pimlico, 2003.

Cowan, Alexander. *Marriage, Manners and Mobility in Early Modern Venice*. Ashgate, 2007.

Davis, Robert C. "Counting European Slaves on the Barbary Coast." *Past & Present*, vol. 172, 2001, pp. 87–124.

Eltis, David, and David Richardson, editors. *Extending the Frontiers: Essays on the New Transatlantic Slave Trade Database.* Yale UP, 2008.

Gollapudi, Aparna. "Virtuous Voyages in Penelope Aubin's Fiction." *SEL 1500–1900*, vol. 45, no. 3, 2005, pp. 669–90.

Handley, Stuart. "James Craggs the Elder." *ODNB* Online, 2004, https://doiorg.uea.idm.oclc.org/10.1093/ref:odnb/6567.

Lincoln, Margarette. *British Pirates and Society, 1680–1730*. Routledge, 2014.

Matar, Nabil. *Turks, Moors, and Englishmen in the Age of Discovery.* Columbia UP, 1999.

McBurney, W.H. "Mrs. Penelope Aubin and the Early Eighteenth-Century English Novel." *Huntington Library Quarterly*, vol. 20, no. 3, 1957, pp. 245–67.

Montana, Ismael Musah. *The Abolition of Slavery in Ottoman Tunisia.* UP of Florida, 2013.

Moore, J.R. *A Checklist of the Writings of Daniel Defoe.* Indiana UP, 1960.

Mounsey, Chris. " … bring her naked from her Bed, that I may ravish her before the Dotard's face, and then send his Soul to Hell': Penelope Aubin, Impious Pietist, Humourist or Purveyor of Juvenile Fantasy?" *British Journal for Eighteenth-Century Studies*, vol. 26, 2003, pp. 55–75.

Orr, Bridget. *Empire on the English Stage, 1660–1714.* Cambridge UP, 2001.

Prescott, Sarah. "Penelope Aubin and *The Doctrine of Morality*: A Reassessment of the Pious Woman Novelist." *Women's Writing*, vol. 1, no. 1, 1994, pp. 99–112.

Richetti, John J. *Popular Fiction before Richardson: Narrative Patterns 1700–1739.* Clarendon Press, 1969.

Said, Edward. *Orientalism.* Pantheon Books, 1978.

Snader, Joe. *Caught Between Worlds: British Captivity Narratives in Fact and Fiction.* UP of Kentucky, 2000.

Sola, Anne de. Introduction. *A Critical Edition of Penelope Aubin's Translation of Robert Challe's* Les Illustres Françaises (The Illustrious French Lovers), edited by Anne de Sola, E. Mellen Press, 2000, pp. xix–xxxix.

Starr, G.A. "Escape from Barbary: A Seventeenth-Century Genre." *Huntington Library Quarterly*, vol. 29, no. 1, 1965, pp. 35–52.

Swaminatham, Srividhya, and Adam R. Beach, editors. *Invoking*

Slavery in the Eighteenth-Century British Imagination. Ashgate, 2013.

Warner, William. *Licensing Entertainment, The Elevation of Novel Reading in Britain, 1684–1750*. U of California P, 1998.

Welham, Debbie. *Delight and Instruction: Women's Political Engagement in the Works of Penelope Aubin*. 2009. University of Winchester, Doctoral dissertation.

——. "The Particular Case of Penelope Aubin." *Journal for Eighteenth-Century Studies*, vol. 31, no. 1, 2008, pp. 63–76.

——. "The Political Afterlife of Resentment in Penelope Aubin's *The Life and Amorous Adventures of Lucinda* (1721)." *Women's Writing*, vol. 20, no. 1, 2013, pp. 49–63.

Zach, Wolfgang. "Mrs. Aubin and Richardson's Earliest Literary Manifesto (1739)." *English Studies*, vol. 62, no. 3, 1981, pp. 271–85.

From the Publisher

A name never says it all, but the word "Broadview" expresses a good
deal of the philosophy behind our company. We are open to a broad
range of academic approaches and political viewpoints. We pay
attention to the broad impact book publishing and book printing has in
the wider world; for some years now we have used 100% recycled
paper for most titles. Our publishing program is internationally oriented
and broad-ranging. Our individual titles often appeal to a broad
readership too; many are of interest as much to general readers as to
academics and students.

Founded in 1985, Broadview remains a fully independent company
owned by its shareholders—not an imprint or subsidiary of a larger
multinational.

To order our books or obtain up-to-date information, please visit
broadviewpress.com.

broadview press
www.broadviewpress.com